ISBN: 9798335683364

Cover design by: Erelis Design
Printed in the United States of America

AUTHOR NEWSLETTER

Sign up to the Dan Stone author newsletter and receive a FREE novella of short stories featuring characters from the Jack Kane series.

The newsletter will keep you updated on new book releases and offers. No spam, just a monthly update on Dan Stone books.

Sign up to the newsletter at https://mailchi.mp/danstoneauthor/sgno14d1hi for your FREE ebook

Or visit the Dan Stone website at https: https://danstoneauthor.com

THE PROMETHEUS CODE

Book 4 in the Jack Kane series

Dan Stone

For my family.

THE PROMETHEUS CODE

Book 4 in the Jack Kane series

By Dan Stone

CHAPTER ONE

Damp fog hung low and heavy, like a blanket of darkness cloaking the boulevards and arrondissements of Paris. Pallid yellow light coughed from a flickering streetlight, joining the neon signs of late-night cafés reflected in puddles to create a stale hologram-like glow across the cobbles. The air was thick with the stink of rain, mixed with the warm smell of roasting coffee and the faint, lingering reek of diesel. A handful of indistinct figures hurried home in the early hours of the morning, scurrying through the almost deserted narrow streets of St Ouen, a district famous for its sprawling flea market and labyrinthine alleyways.

Jack Kane moved silently through the wet, cobbled streets. He kept to the shadows, hands tucked into the pockets of his navy overcoat, tailored shoes splashing in the shimmering puddles. The icy damp air seeped beneath his jacket to kiss his neck with chill, and his shoulder ached in the cold as it always did; the legacy of an old bullet wound treated hastily in the field. That scar was one of many, littering his body like an old treasure map. Each one told a different story of painful memory. A Chinook helicopter crash had left a still-livid burn scar scorched across his chest. Knife wound scars on his arms, belly and back, bullet wounds on his thigh and hip, and a hook-shaped shrapnel scar on the rear of his left shoulder. Each jagged line of raised flesh had taken something from him, a part of Kane's soul chipped away by the chisel of pain to leave something harder, colder, stronger.

Kane hunted his prey, moving with a heightened sense of awareness, hearing each drop of water leaking from overburdened guttering, car engines humming two streets away, a couple arguing in an apartment across the road. He paused in the shadow of a closed-down music shop, shoes mulching dozens of faded, discarded flyers left beside the door, colours running into rainwater down the grey stone step.

Kane stared across the road into a murky alley where two rats scuttled beneath an overflowing dumpster. That was the address. Jill Faraday was there. It had been two weeks since Jill's mother, Frances, had made the call to request help, and since Kane had pursued the ruthless trafficking gang from London to Paris.

"That's the place," said Frank Craven's gruff voice in Kane's earpiece. "Remember, it's got three floors and there could be ten of the bastards in there."

"Only ten?" Kane replied, unable to hide the sarcasm in his voice.

"They'll be asleep now. Hopefully. Go in nice and quiet, get the girl and I'll meet you outside in five minutes." The noise of crunching and swallowing garbled Craven's words, followed by a slurp so loud Kane almost ripped the receiver out of his ear.

"What are you eating?"

"Finishing that cheese and pesto baguette from earlier, and just bought an espresso to keep me awake. I'm knackered. Wouldn't want to fall asleep and leave you all alone with ten Albanians chasing you through Paris, would I?"

"When you've finished your midnight snack, we might continue with the operation?"

"Keep your knickers on, Jack. I'll do my bit. You can go in and do yours. Try not to kill anyone if you can."

Kane ignored the comment and emerged from the gloom. He wore a black Hugo Boss suit beneath his overcoat with a CAC French Army knife tucked into the rear waistband of his trousers. Kane had bought the knife from the flea market that afternoon whilst he and Craven watched the gang's safe house. He'd rather have had a gun as he walked into a house full of armed and highly dangerous gang members, but the knife would have to do. Kane and Craven had flown into Paris the day before using fresh passports under fake names and hired a car using a credit card matching the name on Craven's passport. Airport security was far too tight these days to risk attempting to bring a weapon into France, so Kane came to Paris armed only with an address where to find the Albanians and Craven's less than razor-sharp wit.

A moped whined around the corner as he crossed the uneven cobbled street. Kane let it pass. Frances Faraday's sobbing voice leaked from Kane's subconscious into the forefront of his mind and he ground his teeth, allowing the anger to wash through him. He was here for justice because that was his calling. Kane and Craven responded to calls from those who needed them most, from people in trouble who could not find help from the authorities. Kane and Craven helped those in dire situations where bureaucracy and red tape stopped the police from doing what must be done. Craven and Kane were a solution for the desperate, for those fallen prey to the wolves of the world. Kane was their avenger, a former SAS soldier and MI6 agent with a talent for death and violence.

The alleyway reeked of rotting garlic and old meat, mixed with the damp stink of wet dog. Kane waited behind the dumpster and watched the doorway, an old art déco-type lintel above a heavy oak door once painted blue, but now chipped and cracked like the doorway to a Dickensian workhouse. The Albanians had snatched Jill Faraday in London. She was a nineteen-year-old art student moonlighting as a dancer in a seedy bar to pay for her rent and subsidise her busy London social life. The gang took her after work one night. Kane had seen the CCTV footage of four men in leather jackets and blue jeans bundling her into the back of a red Volkswagen Passat. Then she was gone. The police couldn't find her. They had linked in with the National Crime Agency and then Interpol, but it all took too long. An old copper came to Jill's mother. A man who wanted to help, and knew Jill had a matter of days before the Albanians whisked the young blonde across the Channel, into Europe and then East and gone forever. He gave Frances Faraday Frank Craven's number. A secret number known to a few trusted friends, and to those Craven and Kane had helped before.

The gang, known as the *Vëllezërit e Gjakut,* meaning Blood Brothers, had established a reign of terror across Europe. Originating from the rugged mountains of northern Albania, they had carved out a niche in the underworld with their ruthless efficiency in human trafficking. Their network was extensive, reaching from the Balkans to the heart of Western Europe. They became known for their swift retribution and ability to vanish without a trace. Tonight, Kane was going to test their reputation.

Kane's heart pounded as he approached the door, his every instinct sharpening, readying himself for the reckoning to come. Craven hoped to get Jill out with no violence. They had cased the safe house, and believed there to be three or four girls held inside waiting to be transferred along the French and German highways east, ever east until they disappeared in the mountains beyond Turkey into Albania. From there, the gang would sell the girls to the highest bidder in the Middle East or Asia. Three or four girls lost forever. Kane could not let that go unpunished. How many other girls had the gang taken, how many families destroyed, and lives ruined? Kane would get Jill out, but there must be a punishment. There must be violence.

The faded blue door loomed up before him, and Kane gave it a gentle push. Locked. He pulled the screwdriver and hairpins he'd bought at the flea market earlier from his coat pocket and carefully picked the lock. The old lock mechanism clicked, and the door creaked slightly ajar. Kane stepped inside into a hall lit by a single bulb hanging from a high ceiling above faded, grimy hallway tiles. The air was stale and musty. Strong tobacco smoke hung about the ceiling. A television blared in a room along the corridor, French commentary playing over Ligue 1 football highlights. Kane reached behind him and grabbed the CAC knife. He unfolded the 8.5cm blade and flexed his fingers around the khaki composite grip.

Jill would be upstairs somewhere, but Kane couldn't leave any Albanians waiting for him on the ground floor. If she screamed, or he encountered adversaries up there, he didn't want to have men waiting for him as he tried to exit the building with Jill Faraday clinging to him for dear life. Kane stepped slowly across the tiles, knife in hand, commentator hollering at a goal scored by Paris St Germain's Kylian Mbappé against rivals Lyon. Kane glanced into the room. A bearded man wearing what looked like a red and white Fair Isle Christmas jumper and jeans slumped on a holey armchair smoking a roll-up cigarette. He sniffed and coughed, and itched his mop of salt and pepper, greasy hair. Kane rushed him. He charged into the room and in three long strides; he was there. The Albanian turned, a look of surprise stretching his saggy, mottled face as he tried to rise. His belly wobbled beneath the jumper and Kane smashed his palm into the man's nose to drive his head back, and with the other hand, opened his throat with the knife's wicked blade.

The Albanian jerked and shook, and Kane left him to die. A man slept on a stained mattress in the next room and died with a knife blade stabbed into the back of his skull before he knew Kane was even there. Kane swept the kitchen and downstairs toilet and found no more enemies. Downstairs clear, he climbed the stairs. Old timbers creaked beneath his shoes and, halfway up, a barked voice stopped him dead. Too far to run back down the stairs, and not high enough to rush to the first-floor landing. A figure appeared above him, hair ruffled and eyes bleary from sleep.

"Shit!" Kane hissed. The man held a Beretta 92 pistol in his right hand. His hooded eyes met Kane's and his mouth opened to reveal a maw of brown, stumpy teeth. He cried out a warning and Kane charged at him. He thundered up eight steps as the barrel of the gun came up, pointing at his face, about to spit a 9mm parabellum bullet and open Kane's head like an over-ripe watermelon. Kane leapt forward as the gun boomed. He brought the knife down into the Albanian's foot, piercing a dirty white Adidas training shoe and the foot beyond, as a bullet slapped into the plastered wall behind him. The Albanian yelped in pain and Kane wrenched the gun from his grip, yanking on thumb and wrist until bones crunched. Kane tossed the screaming man down the stairs and checked the weapon. The Beretta could hold fifteen rounds in its magazine. This one had seven remaining.

A door burst open and a bulky man in a wife-beater vest stretched over his hairy belly fired a wild shot from a pistol and Kane shot him in the chest. He fell heavily, belly jiggling in his death throes, and Kane moved across the landing, gun raised, moving with cat-like litheness across the landing.

"Jill?" Kane called. "Jill Faraday? I've come to get you out."

No reply but shouting in Albanian from along the corridor.

"Jill Faraday?" Kane shouted again.

"Help me!" pleaded an English woman's voice, strained around a scream.

Kane moved towards the voice and kicked open a tall door which had once been white but was now faded to a sickly yellow. A shot rang out, bullet thumping into the door with the sound of chopping wood. A bow-legged man in brown Y-front underwear shouted at Kane and fired again, but shot over Kane's head. It is hard to kill a man, to shoot straight when death stands before you. Kane had seen it before, men armed with weapons they barely knew how to use and had rarely fired. The man closed his eyes as he fired, almost turning away from the shot. Kane shot him in the face and spattered the peeling wallpaper with hot blood.

A girl wept, curled up on a mattress beneath a filthy blanket.

"Jill?" Kane asked, and she nodded. Her blonde hair hung greasy about her long face. She was naked and Kane threw the fusty blanket about her bare shoulders and helped Jill to her feet. "It's all right now. I'll bring you home to your mother."

Kane poked his head quickly around the doorframe and a shot rang out, followed by angry cursing in Albanian. Kane waited, feinted to come out of the door and then ducked back in. Another shot. He knelt and swung around the doorframe and shot a man once in the stomach.

"Let's go," he commanded, looking Jill straight in her frightened blue eyes. "Stay close to me."

Kane pulled her behind him, striding along the landing and down the stairs. He could feel their eyes on him, Albanian gangsters hiding in the gloom, guarding their captured women and too afraid to fight the man who had turned their safe house into bloody ruin. Distinctive French police sirens wailed beyond the house. There was no time to free the other girls or to kill the rest of the gang members. Leaving the girls at the mercy of the Albanians curdled Kane's guts, and he hoped the police would arrive soon enough to save them from their fate.

Kane reached the ground floor hallway with Jill Faraday clinging to his back. Her sobs wracked her body and pulsed through Kane's overcoat. The Albanian he had stabbed on the stairs lay in the hallway, clutching his broken wrist as deep crimson pulsed from his foot. He snarled at Kane and hawked a gobbet of thick phlegm at Jill. Kane shot him in the mouth and once in the chest, and threw the gun on top of his corpse. He yanked the front door open and ushered Jill along the night-black alley. Her bare feet slapped on the wet cobbles and she sobbed with unrestrained horror combined with relieved joy as Kane helped her hurry towards the neon-lit street. A white Renault Austral SUV screeched to a halt before them and the back door swung open.

"Bloody get in before the Paris armed response unit gets here," Craven bellowed through the open driver's side window. "A quiet rescue. In and out, we said. Quietly, we said. It's not the gunfight at the fucking O.K. Corral, Jack."

Kane helped Jill into the back seat and sat beside her. Craven raced away as the sirens drew closer. Jill Faraday rested her head on Kane's shoulder and Paris whipped by in a blur.

CHAPTER TWO

Kyle Lavine held himself in the eight-angle pose, muscles quivering, sweat dripping from his brow to run down his clean-shaven face. His quad muscles tightened to keep his legs straight, feet hooked together to help keep his balance. Each of his ten fingers showed white at the knuckles, veins on the backs of his hands prominent as his fingers dug into the yoga mat. His elbows pointed at perfect right angles and Kyle kept his gaze forward, breathing controlled, focused and at peace with the universe, if not himself. How could a man like Kyle Lavine ever truly be at peace? The faces of dead men haunted him, and too much blood spilt over questionable causes rotted his soul from the inside out.

That blood and those corpses paid well. Kyle dealt in death. It was his speciality, his gift from a god as cruel as the humans he had created. He glanced at the monochrome clock beside the long bi-fold patio doors and released himself from the pose. Kyle stood and stretched his lithe muscles, reached for a soft white towel, and wiped the sweat from his body. He drank a protein shake and stared out the Alps, stretching away from his window like a painting of astonishing beauty. Blood paid handsomely indeed.

Kyle paced across the wooden floor of his mountaintop home, the slats cold and hard beneath the soles of his feet. Light flooded in from the powder-blue sky, and green valleys stretched away to jagged cliffs and rugged mountainsides. Kyle sat in his office chair, leather creaking as his yoga pants eased into the cushioned seat. He was forty years old, but as fit and strong as he had been when he'd left the US Delta Force a decade ago. Kyle leaned back in his chair and flicked open his MacBook, ensuring the laptop was connected to his secure server, IP address masked and bouncing around a dozen locations to out-fox anybody attempting to track his location. In his business, it paid to be cautious.

Kyle's ice-blue eyes focussed on the screen, and it flickered to life, revealing the crisp professional image of a serious-faced Asian man in an immaculate suit.

"Good evening, Mr Mentzer," the lawyer said, using one of Kyle's aliases, his tone clipped and businesslike, with a hint of British in his Singaporean accent. The lawyer's office of polished wood and glass glowed with artificial light, whilst behind him Singapore's magnificent skyline twinkled through the windows.

"Evening," Kyle replied, noting the difference in time zone.

"I know you are a serious man, Mr Mentzer, so I will cut to the chase, as they say." The lawyer adjusted his glasses and leaned forward, peering into the camera. "I represent the interests of an Asian government, and my client has a sensitive task requiring your rather unique set of skills. There is a certain individual, well-known amongst the computer-hacking community, who has come into possession of a highly dangerous computer virus known as the Prometheus Code. A virus with the power to destabilise European financial systems completely at the click of a button."

Kyle shifted in his chair, interest piqued. Rumours of devices or viruses with the power to take down legacy banking structures abounded in the world of intelligence and he had heard whispers of just such a tool with the unparalleled ability to cause total chaos and turn the world order on its head. "Go on."

"The virus is on an encrypted external hard drive, currently in the possession of a hacker we believe can be found in the United Kingdom. Our client would like you to locate the hacker, eliminate him, and retrieve the virus."

Kyle nodded slowly, processing the risk and reward of so dangerous a mission. "You are aware of my fee?"

"We are, and it will not be a problem. We will pay half to you on acceptance of the job, issued in Dogecoin, and the rest upon completion. But there is a layer of complexity which falls outside of your usual area of expertise."

"That changes the fee structure."

"We are aware of that, and propose to double your existing terms."

"Must be a whole pile of nasty, then." Kyle's Southern drawl poured over the words, an accent he normally kept hidden behind an unplaceable standardised American accent. He calmed himself, touching the tips of each finger to his thumbs.

The lawyer smiled, with a thin calculating expression shifting the features of his face. "To make the virus viable, my client would also like you to recover an EMP device from a European corporation."

"EMPs don't exist. We are getting into the land of make-believe now, if you don't mind me saying."

"A company has developed a prototype non-nuclear electromagnetic pulse device strong enough to take out power in a city the size of London, with no explosion. You will find and retrieve that prototype."

"The virus needs the EMP to work?"

"Just so, Mr Mentzer."

"Where is the hacker?"

"In the UK's north east. He had been operating out of a secure location using a dizzying array of technology to mask his location. But we shall share the coordinates we have obtained to track him to within a five-mile radius. You are a resourceful man, Mr Mentzer, and possess the necessary surveillance skills and equipment to track him down."

"Total fee payable is ten million dollars. Additional bonus is to be paid if I get the EMP to you in full working order."

"Agreed. We shall send you a packet of information on the hacker and the EMP. Additionally, you will receive access to our encrypted network to allow real-time mission updates and two-way communication. Failure is not an option, Mr Mentzer. The stakes are beyond high, and needless to say, we are not the only players searching for the virus or the device. Extraction is via a secure airfield outside London. You'll have safe passage back to a location of your choosing."

Kyle leaned forward, eyes narrowing. "And what guarantee do I have that your people won't try to double-cross me once I've handed over the virus?"

The lawyer's expression remained unchanged. "Our client values discretion and efficiency. You come exceedingly well-recommended, Mr Mentzer. We have no interest in crossing someone of your reputation."

"All right," Kyle said finally. "Send me the details. I'll get it done."

The lawyer gave a curt nod. "Good. You'll receive the first payment within the hour. We expect results, Mr Mentzer."

The call ended, the screen going blank. Kyle sat back, the wheels of his mind turning. This was no ordinary contract. It was a high-stakes game with other lethal operatives in play, all vying for the same target. The fee was incredible, perhaps enough for him to never work again. Kyle allowed himself a wry grin. Who was he kidding? He worked for the love of the chase, for the thrill of combat. He already had enough money to live out the rest of his life in the mountains in luxury.

He closed the laptop and stood up, his silhouette a stark contrast against the wash of Alps sunlight streaming in through the window. The thrill of the hunt surged through him. England awaited. He had a virus to recover, a hacker to eliminate, an EMP to steal, and ten million dollars to collect. The game was on.

CHAPTER THREE

"Did you get the biscuits she likes?" asked Kim Kane. She leaned forward from her seat in the back of Craven's car and stared at him through the rear-view mirror.

"I got custard creams from the English shop," Craven replied, smiling at Jack Kane's ten-year-old daughter. "I also got Jaffa Cakes, proper tea, and Battenberg cake."

"It's going to be fun, Uncle Frank. We can play Patience, watch movies, make cakes. I can't wait for her to come home"! Kim clapped her hands and glanced at her brother Danny, who shook his head as though her excitement were tiresome. Craven had called into the small English shop in Seville to pick up all the English treats his wife Barb loved best, and he and Kim had decorated their Spanish house in anticipation of Barb's return home from the hospital.

"Auntie Barb is going to need lots of rest," Kane said, turning in the front passenger seat to look at his children. "It's the summer holidays, so you two are responsible for looking after her. Do you hear me, Danny?"

"It's Dan," his son said, taking an AirPod out of his left ear. "I heard you."

"And don't eat all the Battenberg."

Danny grinned and shrugged as if he couldn't agree to so

serious a commitment. Battenberg was their family favourite, an almond-flavoured cake in pink and yellow squares coated in marzipan. It was the children's dead mother Sally Kane's guilty pleasure, and one they continued to share. A small way to keep her memory alive. It was a specifically English treat, just like Jaffa Cakes, but there were enough British ex-pats in Seville to warrant a few shops specialising in peculiarly English products. Craven wanted everything to be just right for Barb when she came home. He had missed her more than usual this time.

Craven and Barb had moved to Seville after Kane's early retirement from the UK police force. The weather on the south west coast of the Iberian peninsula was much better than in England's damp and dreary north west, and Barb could get excellent care for her ongoing cancer treatment at the Hospital Universitario Virgen del Rocio. Everything had gone fine at first. The climate helped her chest and improved her quality of life, but recently Barb had deteriorated; a few pains here and there, fatigue, napping mid-morning and early evening. The doctors had brought her in for more testing and Craven hoped against hope that she was coming home with him today.

Seville's streets bustled with activity as Craven drove alongside historic buildings of intricate Moorish architecture. He and Barb had done a few tours of the chief attractions, like the Giralda Tower and Plaza de España, but he wasn't a history buff. Craven preferred a bottle of beer and an afternoon watching golf to traipsing around a musty old building. Orange trees lined the road and their sweet scent mingled with the smell of roasting coffee and fresh bread from the nearby cafés. It was a warm day and the car's air-conditioning blew a steady stream of blissfully cool air into Craven's face. A pop song came on the radio and Kim sang along. Craven's mind wandered, and he worried about Barb. For the third time that summer morning, he asked God, if there even was a God out there, to please let her be OK.

The warm sun cast a golden hue over the city beneath a brilliant blue sky, where a few puffs of cloud drifted lazily by. The road became wider as Craven approached the hospital, its surroundings more planned and functional and less like the organic meandering of inner city streets. He parked at the hospital and the four of them walked towards the entrance. Craven sucked in a mouthful of fresh air tinged with a hint of Mediterranean flowers and led Kane and the kids to Barb's ward.

They travelled up to the fourth floor, nervous excitement keeping them silent in the lift as they marched along the sterile white corridors through the X-ray department towards ward five. Craven knocked once and pushed the door open to Barb's room and found her sitting up in bed. She saw him and clapped a hand over her mouth; her face was pale and her eyes red-rimmed.

"Barb, are you OK, love?" Craven asked, gathering her up in his arms.

"Auntie Barb, what's wrong?" asked Kim. Kane held her hand and shook his head to quieten his daughter, whose face looked as frightened as Craven felt.

The door eased open and a willowy, slim man in green scrubs and a white overcoat stepped in, holding a thick chart. He wore wire-rimmed glasses over sombre eyes and a trimmed beard around his angular face. "Ah, Mr Craven," began the doctor, in English with a thick Spanish accent.

"What's going on, doctor?" Craven asked.

"I'm afraid we need to keep Mrs Craven in for more tests. There's a chance her tumour might have spread to other organs, and we need to run further checks. Mrs Craven will stay with us for another week, at least."

"But do you think...?"

"We do not know at this stage, Mr Craven. Try not to worry."

The doctor smiled a professional, emotionless smile and left the room.

"I'm all right, Kimmy," Barb said, and beckoned Kim towards her. Kim ran to Barb, and they held each other warmly. Craven glanced at Kane and they shared a look of concern. Danny took out his AirPods and joined Kim to give Barb a bear hug and it brought a lump to Craven's throat. He wasn't an emotional man, born and bred in a working-class town where men crying was seen as weakness unless they were watching The Champ or Field of Dreams. Craven was a big man, a head taller than most, broad-shouldered, big-bellied and bald.

The burner phone he kept in his shirt pocket vibrated, and Craven took it out. The green-lit face showed a long set of numbers, none of them a recognised international dialling code.

"It's the number," he murmured, glancing at Kane. The number was a line set up by Kane's tech expert and old SAS buddy Cameron, which bounced around a dozen encrypted web-based phone exchanges across the world. It was a secret number, one used by people who needed their help.

Kane shrugged as though to say he could either answer it or leave it to ring out. Barb's situation was too delicate, the news too worrying to think about anybody else's problems. But Barb was happy with the kids, and Craven welcomed even a brief distraction to take his mind off the worry, anything to distract from the bone-shivering fear of losing the woman he had loved since he was a teenager. Barb was his everything, his soulmate, his one great love.

"Hello?" he answered, with the phone to his ear.

"Craven?" came a strained voice. On the move, the noise of its breathing grating down the phone line. A familiar voice.

"Yes, Cameron, it's me. What's going on?"

"I'm in trouble, mate. Deep shit. Someone is trying to kill me. I need you guys. Is Jack there?"

CHAPTER FOUR

"Speak slowly," Kane said into the phone. Craven had handed it to him the minute Cameron mentioned needing help. Kane left Barbara's private hospital room and opened the door to the next room, which was dim and empty. Craven followed him and the two men stood close, so both could hear Cameron's voice.

"I'm in deep shit, Jack," Cameron said. The line sounded fuzzy, with heavy breathing and footsteps. "Are you in the UK?"

"No, but I can be there this afternoon. What's going on?"

"I don't have time to explain. They've found me, Jack. Fucking hell. I saw them on my security camera video trying to come through my front door. Men with guns."

"Where are you now?"

"I left through the back door and I'm going through Newcastle city centre."

"Good. Stay where it's busy, but keep your head down. Who's after you?"

"I'm not daft, Jack. I remember our training. Jesus Christ, there's so many people here." Kane and Cameron had served in the army together, first in the Parachute Regiment and then in the SAS. Cam was a communications expert, a technical genius who had always been more at home behind a keyboard than holding a gun. Cameron had become an effective sniper and the team's comms expert. A rocket-propelled grenade had blown up a jingly van in Afghanistan whilst Cam was in the passenger seat. The blast had torn off half of his face and badly burned his body. Kane had dragged him out of the furnace, and Cameron had spent a year in hospital as doctors tried their best to rebuild the ruins of his face.

"Stay calm, Cam. I know you that know what you're doing. Who's after you?" Cameron hated being around people. The wound to his face had left him with horrific facial burning and he wore a mask to hide his face and hid himself away behind computer screens. He avoided people, afraid of children pointing, of women recoiling from his disfigurement. Kane could imagine him running through Newcastle's Bigg Market, its medieval centre thronged with people on a Saturday lunchtime, all staring at the strange man in the bizarre white mask.

"Jack, I have the Prometheus Code, and everyone wants it. If they get their hands on it, everything is over. Chaos will reign and the world order as we know it will be finished. Everything will change forever."

"What the fuck is the Prometheus Code?" asked Craven.

"No time to explain now. Contact me on this number when you get here. I'll keep it open until this time tomorrow. I need you, Jack."

Cameron hung up the phone and Kane stared at the handset. His friend needed him; more than a friend, a brother-in-arms. Cameron had helped Kane when he needed him most two years ago when he was on the run with Danny and Kim. Images flashed through Kane's mind, bleak memories of searching for high-value targets in sweltering tunnels, of IEDs blowing those tunnels to pieces with most of Kane and Cameron's SAS team inside. Memories of crashed Chinook helicopters and burning debris searing Kane's chest. A life of blood, fire, bullets and death.

"What's going on?" asked Craven, running a hand down his face.

"Cameron needs us. I'll go today, you stay here. Barb needs you, Frank."

"What kind of danger is he in? You might need me."

"You're needed here. Besides, it's the summer holidays and you can take care of Danny and Kim for me. They could let Barb out any day. You stay, I'll go. I'll keep in touch."

Craven smiled sadly and nodded.

Kim sobbed when Kane broke the news. Small, shuddering shakes of her little shoulders. He knelt to hold her, and Kim buried her face in Kane's chest. Her tears soaked through his white shirt to wet his skin. Kane's heart lurched; the heat of guilt burned within his chest.

"Don't go, Daddy," Kim wailed, her voice tearing through him like a high-powered bullet.

"I have to go, Kimmy. Do you remember my friend Cameron?"

"The man in the mask?"

"Yes, that's him. Well, he needs my help. Just like we needed his help a few years back. So, I have to go away for a few days. You and Danny will stay with Uncle Frank until I get back."

"But Uncle Frank can't do my hair!"

Kane laughed. "You can teach him." He stood and held his hand to Danny. His son shook Kane's hand with a reluctant floppiness. "Look after your sister, Danny."

"It's Dan," he muttered.

"Just look after her. Help Frank around the house. I don't

want him cleaning up after you."

"Whatever. Bye."

Kane ignored his son's belligerence, kissed Barb on the forehead, and left the hospital. He had tried to bond with Danny, taking him to Spanish La Liga football matches, going fishing together. But nothing seemed to work. He remained sullen and distant, as he had been since his mother had died. Kane wanted to be friends with his son, to share the closeness he saw so often between other fathers and their sons. But it would not come. Kane's children spent most of the year at boarding school, coming home on the weekends and during the holidays, and Kane tried to be present as often as he could. They needed him, but Kane was no replacement for their mother. He was not a tactile man, nor an emotional one. Most of what Kim needed she got from Barbara Craven, in terms of cuddles on the couch and Disney movies. Kane did his best, but the more he tried to get close to them, the further he seemed to drift away.

Taxis waited in a rank beside the hospital and Kane jumped into a Nissan smelling of too much pine air-freshener. He took the taxi to his home on the outskirts of Seville and asked the driver to wait. Kane ran inside and grabbed the leather travel bag he always kept ready to go with a fake passport and matching credit cards inside, along with two suits, underwear, and toiletries. The taxi driver took him to Malaga airport where Kane bought a ticket for a flight to Manchester airport leaving that afternoon.

Barbara's cancer was back. It always came back, hated and unwanted, eating away at her like a monster. She was a kind and gentle woman, and as Kane sat on the commercial flight, he wondered why it always seemed like it was the good people who suffered, whilst the criminals, drug addicts, and bad people of the world seemed to live forever. It was a simple and false premise, he knew, but it still wasn't fair. Without her,

Craven would be lost, and the world would be a darker place. Kane was deeply sceptical when it came to God, but hoped luck at least would be on Barb's side. She deserved a break. His thoughts turned to Cameron and the Prometheus Code, whatever that was. What kind of situation had his old comrade landed himself in? Whatever it was, it sounded like trouble. That was when people needed Kane, when things got so bad that nobody else could help. He was the last resort, the dealer of justice and avenger for the desperate, and he had to get to Cameron before it was too late.

CHAPTER FIVE

Kyle Lavine had never been to Newcastle before. It was a dreary place of grey buildings and sad-faced people in too-tight clothing. He had been to most major cities in the UK, and had fulfilled contracts in London, Glasgow, and Belfast. As an American, the UK was a strange place of terrible food, grim weather, and small, bleak cities. Most Americans held a romanticised view of its rich history and cultural heritage. Many longed to visit Buckingham Palace, Stonehenge, and the Tower of London. Lavine, however, hated the gloom and rain, the bad teeth and strange accents.

He had flown into Liverpool airport on a jet provided by his client, and from there drove a black Mercedes CLG SUV north along the M6 motorway and then the A69 towards Newcastle. The Di Marzio family of the Neapolitan Camorra housed part of its European distribution arm in London. Kyle worked regularly for the Camorra, removing rivals, silencing prosecutors, punishing distribution partners in far-flung destinations. So, a Di Marzio contact had provided the car and the weapons resting in a black bag inside the trunk. They were familiar with his weapons of choice after so fruitful a partnership, and he had checked with satisfaction to find a Sig Sauer P365 with spare magazines, an AR15 with EOTech sights front and back, a custom forty-five-degree safety catch, and a CMC flat trigger. They had even added the single-point sling and tourniquet he favoured on the stock. The bag contained five flash-bang grenades, a bullet-proof combat vest, three chemical grenades, a suppressor attachment for the Sig, four burner cell phones, and a medical supply bag. Most of the equipment harked back to his days on the teams, nuances learned in the desert, clearing rooms in dust-filled towns and villages. In those days, he had taken out high-value targets for his government, risking his life for a fraction of what a web developer in Silicon Valley earned. Now, he worked for himself.

Coordinates provided by his client gave an approximate location for the hacker's location and Kyle would begin his hunt there. The information packet gave Kyle more information on the Prometheus Code, and on the hacker whose lap it had fallen into. The hackers named the virus after Prometheus, the Greek Titan and god of fire, who defied Zeus and the gods of Olympus and gave humanity the gift of fire in the form of technology, knowledge, and civilisation. As punishment for his crimes against Zeus, the gods chained Prometheus to a rock where an eagle ate his liver each day. The Titan's liver grew back each night, only for the eagle to eat it again and again for eternity. Whoever named the thing certainly had a grand opinion of its capability.

The information packet went into detail about the virus and its construct, most of which went over Kyle's head. He was a simple assassin, but he wasn't a complete technological philistine and understood the gist. He stopped at a service station near Carlisle, took a toilet break and bought a pasta salad and a coffee. Kyle ate in the car and read over the details again. The Prometheus Code was a masterpiece of digital malice, engineered specifically to cripple the storied European banking system. Developed in the shadows by a clandestine syndicate of rogue state-sponsored hackers and disillusioned tech prodigies, it was the ultimate cyber-weapon designed to exploit the very foundations of modern finance.

The hackers, who called themselves the Successors, built the virus using polymorphic code, an advanced type of malware that could alter its appearance with each infection, evading traditional anti-virus measures. Its developers wrote the virus' core using a blend of low-assembly language for precision control over system processes and high-level Python for rapid deployment across various platforms. The Successors engineered the virus to be modular, with distinct components for infiltration, data corruption, and system manipulation.

To prevent such a valuable and dangerous piece of tech from being stolen or trafficked across the web, they used an external device to transport the Prometheus Code. It was the ultimate weapon designed to bring down an entire crutch of Western civilisation without a shot being fired. Its infiltration phase began with the device connected to any IP address where it would issue meticulously-crafted phishing emails targeting key employees at major European banks such as Deutsche Bank, BNP Paribas, Santander, and HSBC. The emails contained seemingly benign attachments that, once opened, silently installed the virus onto the bank's network.

Upon installation, the virus lay dormant, using sophisticated toolkits to avoid detection while it mapped the network's structure. When activated by plugging the hard drive into one of the target banks' physical servers, the virus launched a coordinated assault, corrupting transaction records, manipulating account balances, and overriding security protocols. It employed a distributed denial-of-service attack as a diversion, overwhelming the bank's online services and drawing attention away from the more insidious data corruption happening within. Simultaneously, a worm component propagated the virus to interconnected financial institutions and payment systems across Europe, ensuring a cascading failure. Back-up servers and disaster recovery systems were also targeted, rendering them useless and deepening the chaos. Kyle read the section describing its deployment twice, stunned at the levels cyber-terrorism had reached. When he first joined the US Army, there had been no such thing.

Deployment was staggered, hitting multiple institutions simultaneously, ensuring maximum disruption across European markets. The chaos that would ensue would see stock prices plummet, currencies fluctuate wildly, and trust in the financial system evaporate. It would bring about a perfectly-executed digital apocalypse designed to bring Europe to its knees. Or, as Kyle preferred to think of it, a fucking shit-storm. There was no mention in the packet about the EMP device and its link, or the virus' dependency on it. All Kyle had was the location to steal it from, which was enough.

He drove into Newcastle and parked the Mercedes within the radius of his target's last known location. The information packet gave the target's name as Tokyo Ghoul, a hacker codename or avatar. Kyle didn't understand that world, but he respected a hacker's need for anonymity as much as he needed to move in the shadows himself. Unseen. Ruthless. Deadly. He left the car in a multi-storey parking lot beside a shopping centre and walked through the city. Kyle wore a tailored wool suit and pressed shirt, with the Sig in a comfortable shoulder holster.

Kyle thought of trying Dungeons and Dragons stores, computer games stores or comic book stores to ask around about Tokyo Ghoul. One thing Kyle knew about hackers was that no matter the lengths they went to in order to hide their locations, they loved to brag about their exploits. Tokyo Ghoul could be an eighteen-year-old kid living in his grandmother's basement, or a forty-year-old woman in an apartment covered in Cheetos dust. Either way, he would find him or her. Police sirens blared only a few streets away from Kyle's location, so he followed the sound and found British police officers wrapping a length of yellow tape across an alleyway and ushering nosy onlookers away from the dingy gap between two clothes stores.

Kyle wasn't the only one searching for the Prometheus Code, and he felt bile rise in his throat. Five million dollars rested on his being the one to find it. And he would find it.

A short, red-faced policewoman shouted at a rotten-toothed homeless man across the security tape. Kyle couldn't understand much of what the man said because the Newcastle accent was broad and sounded like gibberish to his American ear, but she was distracted enough that Kyle ducked under the tape. When she glanced at him, Kyle nodded at her as though he were supposed to be there. In his suit, clean-shaven with a nondescript short haircut and forgettable Caucasian face, he looked like a detective, lawyer, banker, insurance salesman or whatever he wanted to be. The policewoman frowned and ignored him.

Kyle reached an ajar steel door, guarded by a serious-looking police constable.

"Can I help you, sir?" asked the officer in his thick Newcastle accent.

"Are there any other officers inside?" Kyle asked with his best American smile full of confidence and bone-white teeth.

"No, who are you?"

Kyle drove the centre knuckle of his right fist into the policeman's throat and pushed him through the door. He collapsed to a floor covered in drab brown linoleum, clutching at his crushed windpipe. He'd live, but would need hospital care for the foreseeable. Kyle's hunch had been right. The place was a hacker's den. Anime posters on the walls, arcade machines along the walls of the open-plan space with a modern, metallic kitchen and a server stack blinking and humming in one corner. A high-powered laptop lay smashed on the floor, beside a handful of hard drives and open PC game boxes. Someone had got here first; perhaps shots fired or signs of an assault had alerted the police? Kyle quick-searched drawers and cupboards until he found an electricity bill addressed to a Cameron Jordan.

Got you.

CHAPTER SIX

Kane landed at Manchester airport and hired a car from the Enterprise desk with his matching passport and credit card in the name of Mark Walters, a former Liverpool FC midfielder. Kane was of average height and build, wore his brown hair in a non-distinct short haircut and had a normal, forgettable face. He was the grey man, able to blend in anywhere without being noticed.

He left the airport in a hired BMW 520, joining the M56 motorway, then the M6 and eventually the A69 towards the north east. It was 6pm, seven hours since he had spoken to Cameron, so Kane took the phone from his jacket pocket, connected it to the vehicle's Bluetooth phone system, and dialled the last number Cameron had called from.

"Jack?" said Cameron's voice over the car's communication system.

"I'm here, Cam," Kane replied. "I'll be in Newcastle in twenty-five minutes. Where are you?"

"Hiding out in an old warehouse in South Shields. I'll text the location to this number."

"Are people still searching for you?"

"Yes. They raided my place earlier, turned the place upside down. The police are there now."

"I'll be there as soon as I can. Do you have any weapons, Cam?"

"Not here. But I have a stash near Gateshead. We'll pick them up when you get here."

"Good." Cameron was a former sniper and being an SAS operator who dabbled in the dangerous world of hacking and cyber-crime, Kane had hoped his old friend would have access to some firepower. "What have you got?"

"There's a lock-up there with a motorbike, a Glock 43 and a Glock 19, a signal-blocking device, a communication bodypack with press-to-talk earpiece microphones, my old regiment survival tin, a tactical vest, and a Colt Canada C8 carbine rifle."

"Jesus Christ, Cam, where did you find that gear?" Getting firearms in the UK was an extremely difficult business. With guns being illegal, any in circulation were usually old pistols with limited ammunition used by gangs and criminals. Obtaining the firearms Cameron had amassed was relatively easy in the USA, but not in the UK or any European country.

"I've got contacts. I knew I'd have to tool-up when I came across the virus."

"You're going to have to fill me in when I get there. Whatever it is you've gotten into, it sounds serious."

"This is as serious as it gets, mate. Hurry."

Kane sped along the dual carriageway until he reached South Shields on the south shore of the River Tyne. It was summer in England, but summer in the UK bore no comparison to the weather Kane had left in Seville. There it was all sunglasses, orange trees and t-shirts. The windscreen wipers on Kane's hired BMW hadn't stopped shunking across the car's front window since leaving the airport. Rain fell in a thin drizzle, too lazy and depressing to even be a storm or a heavy downpour. It just drifted from a formless iron-grey sky in a constant mist to soak the land in a damp, relentless fog.

Cameron's pinned location led Kane to a small industrial estate nestled within close-knit suburban houses built in the 1970s. Winding cul-de-sacs and identical streets sprawled around each other, every house the same, with white wood fasciae and garden fences painted in oak-coloured stain. Ford Mondeos and white vans filled the driveways, and Kane turned right at a strip mall with a newsagent, a laundromat and an insurance brokerage. A crumbling industrial estate backed onto the shops, a dreary place of mouldy plastic ceilings and corrugated roofs, faded signs and rust-coloured brickwork. Half of the units appeared empty, with the rest occupied by car repairers, carpet warehouses, a plumbers' outlet store and a greasy spoon café.

Kane drove around the industrial estate twice, noting the mechanics with beer bellies and grimy blue overalls, the squint-eyed man and his wife unloading carpets from a red van and the woman reading a newspaper in a Volvo SUV. He parked around the corner from Cameron's location and called his phone.

"Cam, I'm outside," Kane said as Cameron answered the call. "I'm coming in."

"Thanks, Jack."

Kane hung up the phone and stepped out of the car. Stiff after the two-and-half-hour drive as well as the flight, Kane stretched his back and slipped on his jacket. He pretended to check his phone and watched the woman in the Volvo through the reflection in his car's driver's door window. She appeared focused on her copy of the Daily Telegraph, which was suspicious. People under the age of fifty simply didn't read newspapers any more. Anybody waiting for an appointment or to collect a family member from one of the industrial estate's units would busy themselves doom-scrolling through Facebook, Instagram or X on their smartphone. The woman was in her late twenties with crow-black hair tied back in a severe ponytail. She wore clear-framed glasses and sucked on a vaping device, releasing plumes of smoke through her slightly open car window.

He'd lied to Cameron to keep him calm, but Kane was sure the woman was watching, and if so, then she was likely part of a surveillance team. Or worse, a kill team. He wasn't sure how she'd found Cameron's location, or why she hadn't tried to apprehend him or take the virus, but she was certainly not a civilian. He had no choice but to get Cameron out of there, and he still wasn't sure of the severity of his old friend's situation. There had been shots fired at Cameron's house. The woman could be an undercover police detective or part of an MI5 team. Neither of those forces would want to kill Cameron. Apprehend him and the virus, yes, but a gunfight in broad daylight was unlikely.

Kane left the car and approached the abandoned warehouse. He slipped under the metallic door roller, which Cameron had left open at waist height, presumably to let some light into the building. An abandoned lathe dominated the room, surrounded by various other complicated-looking engineering machines. The place stank of oil and decay and had the ubiquitous topless model calendar hanging on a wall above a musty workbench.

"Cam?" Jack called.

"Here," Cameron replied, leaning through the open door of an office with a glass window smeared with grease and thick cobwebs.

Kane stepped inside the office to find Cameron sitting on an old leather chair rocking back and forth. He wore a white mask with one eye blacked, and a khaki-coloured hoodie pulled up to cover his hair.

"Does anybody else know you're here?"

"No. Just you."

"What's in the bag?" Kane gestured to a rucksack resting on a desk littered with old car tyre brochures and flip calendars from 2019.

"My laptop and a few other bits. And the virus."

"Are you going to tell me what it is?"

Cameron gave Kane an overview and he listened patiently. When Cameron had finished his breakdown of coding, financial networks, collapsing the inter-bank lending framework, Kane asked, "Who made it, and how did you get it?"

Cameron reached behind his mask to itch his face and sagged in his chair. "As you know, since leaving the regiment, I've dabbled in cyber stuff. I use the internet to hack code and provide solutions to people. Like you do, but I use my keyboard instead of a gun. My line of work involved, shall we say, a certain type of people. I mix in certain online groups where we share the latest code-breaking solutions and algorithms on the dark web. That's where I first found out about the Prometheus Code.

"Society as we know it, is fucked. Politicians are weak, weaker than they've ever been. The rich get richer and the middle classes and below are screwed. Cost of living is skyrocketing, people can't afford to live, immigration is out of control and far-right parties are getting votes and winning elections across Europe. They are winning because people who wouldn't normally vote are pushed to the ballot boxes by the corrupt and failing state of the world we are living in."

"I get it. You don't need to sell it to me."

"Anyway, I came across a group on the dark web who called themselves the Successors. They had a piece of code I needed to gain access to a stolen Android app in pre-production, so I joined their group to get the code. As I got deeper in with them, they introduced me to radical ideas and thoughts on how we could use our skills to change the world."

"Change it by bringing down the banking system?" Kane couldn't hide the surprise in his voice. Cameron had never been a radical type of guy. He was an ex-SAS operator, solid, stoic and dependable.

"Somebody has to do something before everything collapses. There's a chance to change things and put a new structure in place, one the people can control for themselves. If we can do away with the old legacy banking networks and elite families controlling politics and systems, there's a chance to reset. Use blockchain, crypto, and new ways of living to get rid of the fucking vampires who are bleeding the world dry."

"We?"

"I joined the Successors. The Prometheus Code was their brainchild. The group is composed of rogue state-sponsored hackers and disillusioned tech prodigies from around the world. It came from the digital underworld, uniting people like me. Experts who have grown tired of governmental oversight, corporate greed and systemic corruption. Our motivation was rooted in a shared ideology: to dismantle the oppressive structures enslaving society, starting with the financial system which upholds them.

"We pooled our knowledge and resources to create Prometheus. A sophisticated virus capable of infiltrating, corrupting, and collapsing financial institutions. Our goal was to expose the fragility and corruption of the banking system. Its downfall would lead to a global reckoning, financial power shifting to the people, and a more just and transparent financial order."

"So, you built it?"

"No, I didn't. I coded some of it. I mean…"

"Who built it, then?"

"Chen Li. His avatar name is Storm Shadow. A Chinese hacker who defected from his government's cyber-warfare unit after a moral crisis. He sort of led the Successors. He built it and sent it to me."

"What's that noise?" Kane cocked his head, trying to focus on the buzzing sound picked up on his peripheral hearing as Cameron was talking. The noise grew louder, like a large bee zipping about in the warehouse.

"Drone," Cameron hissed and dropped to the floor. "Get down. Could be a kill drone."

Kane dropped beside Cameron and a small device with four arms topped with spinning rotor blades hovered at the window, watching Kane and Cameron, beaming a video feed of them to Kane knew not where. He searched the office for a weapon before the drone either brought armed men down on their location, or killed them itself.

CHAPTER SEVEN

Craven checked his phone for the twentieth time in ten minutes, only to find the home screen blank. Again. No calls or messages. He got up from the kitchen stool and watched Kim skating on the back patio in her roller boots. Danny was in his bedroom playing on his PlayStation, just as he did every day when he wasn't in school. The swimming pool shimmered like a mirror behind where Kim played, and Craven wondered why the children never used it. But then he never used it either. He had at first, swimming every day, pretending he enjoyed it. Then he'd just stopped. They had all just got used to it; he supposed. The novelty wore off.

Barb was due to have more tests that afternoon and he had received no update on the results. Craven could have stayed at the hospital and waited to receive the results with Barb, but the kids were bored, so he'd brought them home and made them some sandwiches. Barb had persuaded him to go. His being there wouldn't change the outcome, and she doubted if this set of tests would tell her anything she didn't already know.

Barbara had looked tired, Craven thought. Her skin had become so thin that it was almost translucent, like tracing paper stretched over her bones. Her eyes, once so sharp and beautiful, now seemed to have a dull screen, the whites streaked with tiny veins. Craven stared about their Spanish home, all shiny surfaces and hard edges, and hoped the cancer hadn't spread again. She had suffered enough. Barb deserved a rest, a break from the fear, pain, and suffering.

Craven thought about calling the hospital, half-dialled the number and then hung up the phone. He paced the kitchen, put dirty plates and cutlery into the dishwasher. Craven checked the washing basket, but it was empty and there were no clothes in the washing-machine drum for him to dry. He thought about checking the oil and tyre pressure on the car, but decided against it. Instead, Craven flicked on the television and sprawled on the large L-shaped sofa in his living room. The TV sparked to life, and he scrolled through the Spanish channels, which he could not understand because he couldn't speak a word of Spanish even though he had lived in the country for almost two years. Craven stopped clicking the remote when he came to the BBC News, but then clicked off again when he realised it was a show about politics.

After scrolling through Netflix for twenty minutes and almost watching a documentary about rock climbing, Craven decided to give Kane a call and see how things were going with Cameron. He went to the bedroom and pulled a fully charged burner phone from his bedside chest of drawers. He dialled the number, but it rang out. Craven put the phone back in the drawer and paced back to the kitchen. He checked his mobile phone again, but still no call from the hospital.

Craven decided to make the children an early dinner, so he took mince and vegetables out of the fridge and pasta from the cupboard. He paused and slammed his fist down on the marble worktop. Why hadn't the doctor called? All Craven wanted was to help his wife and for her to be OK. If he could, he would take her cancer and suffer the pain on her behalf. He would gladly take the tumours and the chemo and go through it all just to see Barb smiling again. But there was nothing he could do. No way he could help. He was useless and helpless.

He checked the phone again. Still no call.

CHAPTER EIGHT

The drone lurched sideways, its nose tilting like it was a sentient being. It hovered and shifted again as though it could see through the grimy window. Every time it moved, its motor emitted a high-pitched whine. Kane stared at it in a daze, its graceful motions hypnotic.

"We have to take it out," Cameron said, still lying on the floor, face covered by his white mask. "It's probably sending a video feed to someone. Whoever it is knows we are here, and the video feed will send images of our faces. Well, your face. They can use trawling software to search the internet for any other images of your face and have you identified in minutes. Drones can also carry nerve gas or an explosive device."

"How?"

"Haven't you seen those videos of soldiers in the war in Ukraine taken out by drones?"

"No. But I don't like the sound of it. Send a video to who? I still don't know who it is you think is after you?"

"Think? You went to my place, right? You saw that someone had gone there to kill me?"

"I saw."

"So don't make out like I'm some sort of fucking nutcase. This virus is beyond valuable, and beyond dangerous. If there's a drone here, then they know we're here. We need to move."

Kane's phone rang inside his jacket pocket, but he ignored the call. The drone buzzed in slowly through the office door and made straight for Cameron's backpack. He leapt to his feet and grabbed the bag, just as the drone turned to hover in front of him like a plastic insect. Cameron swung his bag at the drone, and it lurched away from him. Kane had little experience of drones. They weren't in use during his time with MI6, but he had heard Cameron's warning loud and clear and didn't fancy taking a dose of lethal nerve gas.

Kane picked up the leather office chair and threw it at the drone. He grunted at the effort of lifting the heavy metal swivel base and kept moving forward as the chair crashed into the small flying object. The drone clattered to the stained carpet and Kane stamped on it twice with the heel of his shoe until the plastic shattered and its mechanical whine was no more. He dashed to the window and opened the off-white pleated blinds with his fingers. The woman in the car was still there, sitting in her car parked twenty-five metres from the abandoned factory.

"I saw someone suspicious on the way in. She could be a member of a team watching us. Is there a back way out of this place?"

"Yes, there's an emergency exit at the rear. You shouldn't have come in if you knew the place was being watched."

"I wasn't sure. Come on, let's go. If they are watching the front, let's assume they are also watching the back."

Kane followed Cameron out of the office and across the factory floor, through the dust and discarded machinery parts. Cameron reached the back door and yanked it open. Sunlight flooded in through the doorway and Kane squinted at the sudden change in light. They stepped outside and Cameron crouched beside the door, scanning the area behind the factory for signs of any enemies. Kane crouched beside him, just as the wall behind thudded with the shrill impact of a bullet upon the prefabricated wall.

"Suppressed gunfire!" Cameron barked, voice muffled by his mask. "Back inside!"

They scrambled through the door as another shot slammed into the wall, and another into the door. They sat leaning against the rear wall and Kane peered into the mask covering Cameron's face.

"How did they find you?"

"I don't know. Could be anything. They could have been tracking me for days before I knew they were on to me."

"Who are they, Cam?"

"Foreign governments; China, North Korea, the US? Our government? Another member of the Successors? It could be anyone or everyone."

"Footsteps," Kane whispered and placed a finger to his lips.

The door banged against its warped frame, opening and closing slightly in the breeze. Kane and Cameron had not closed it properly when they had burst inside, leaving it to creak as it shifted on its hinges. A shoe crunched on pebbles and concrete outside. Kane waited, peering at the doorway, the heat of fear spreading in his belly. The woman in the car could be alone, or part of a team. Kane had done a full circuit of the industrial estate and had seen no other suspicious-looking characters. He didn't have any weapons, and whoever it was meant business. They had shot to kill him, and if Kane hadn't ducked by pure chance, he would be a dead man. To kill Kane and Cameron and snatch the virus, their attacker must enter the building. That gave Kane an advantage. He tried to imagine how he would make the insertion if he were hunting prey, just as he had countless times working for Mjolnir, a splinter MI6 black ops force.

Before Kane had time to let that scenario play out in his head, the back door burst open with such force that it clattered back on its rusted hinges and hit the wall. Kane tensed, but nobody came in. It was a test to see if the way in was clear, or if Kane and Cameron waited to jump the killer as they entered. After thirty seconds, a figure darted in, holding a suppressed MP5 up to its face and scanned the room, moving swiftly and agilely on the balls of their feet. They crouched against the wall, gun passing slowly across the room. The laser-beam sight on the weapon shimmered through the dreariness like a scene from a science-fiction movie. Dust motes caught in the green beam as the shooter scanned the factory, sweeping across old machinery, the light bending over hard edges and rusty chains.

Kan waited until the beam passed towards the office, on the opposite side of where he crouched silently, only five paces from the shooter. Then he leapt at the figure, not waiting for the muzzle to train around on him or Cameron. Kane grabbed the gun just as it fired over his shoulder. He drove a knee into the attacker's groin but found only bone. Sleek black hair flew about an angular face, and he recognised the woman from the car. She was six inches shorter than him, with piercing blue eyes.

The woman used the force Kane exerted holding on to the gun to pitch him off balance. She tucked her hip into his and tried to throw him, but Kane saw it coming and spread his feet wide to brace himself, hooking his ankle inside her leg. Her forehead whipped forward in a savage headbutt, but Kane leaned away and pushed her backwards. She twisted and snarled with fury, raking her foot down Kane's shin and instep. Pain flared there, and he twisted the gun hard, trying to use his greater strength to tear it from her grip. The weapon came up and she let go of it with one hand and punched him hard in the solar plexus. Kane wheezed in agony, and then Cameron was there. He punched the woman hard in the side of her face. She stumbled, twisted her hip, and booted him hard in the groin. Cameron groaned and fell to his knees.

Kane swung her about him in a full circle and then tossed her over his hip. She flew, and hurtled through the office window, smashing the glass with a crash which echoed about the high metallic roof beams. Kane ran through the door and kicked her in the stomach as she tried to rise. He ripped the MP5 from her grip and she snarled at him, face cut to ribbons by broken glass, a look of malevolent hate in her blue eyes.

"Who sent you?" Kane asked, pointing the gun at her chest.

"Fuck you," she hissed in a southern English accent that was hard to place.

"Who do you work for?"

She laughed and spat a glob of blood onto the filthy old carpet. "Everyone's coming after you, after it."

"Who sent you?"

She screamed and dived at him, whipping a knife from the small of her back. She moved fast across the floor, like a rabid animal. Kane shot her once in the head, spattering blood behind her like a burst fruit. She collapsed, body twitching, and he shot her again. Cameron burst into the office, limping from the blow to his groin.

"Shit," he said, when he saw she was dead.

Kane bent and searched her, unsurprisingly finding nothing. "We have to get out of here before the rest of her team comes in. They aren't coming to ask questions, Cam. They want that virus badly, and won't hesitate to kill for it."

"We can't take the back way or the front door. They'll have shooters watching the exit."

Kane searched the dingy factory but saw no sign of a side

door or any other way out. He glanced up at the roof and noticed a small hatch in the corrugated ceiling. "Up there. We go out over the roof."

Kane and Cameron clambered up the office wall, using the window frame for purchase until they reached the office roof.

"Careful," Cameron warned, testing the surface with an outstretched foot. "It's only plasterboard. Put your weight on that and you'll go straight through."

They skirted the edges of the roof, following the line of supporting joists until they reached the western wall. The hatch butted up against the breeze-block wall and was little more than a rusted rectangle cut into the corrugated steel. It had a circular handle embedded on its surface, but was too high for Kane to reach from the office ceiling.

"Give me a leg up," Kane said. Cameron grumbled and got down on his haunches. He made a cup with his hands and Kane stepped into it. Kane jumped and Cameron hauled his foot upwards. Kane balanced himself on the roof with outstretched palms to steady himself. He grabbed the handle, stiff from years of rusting high in the cobwebs and the musty damp. Kane yanked on it, almost fell, and yanked again. The ring was rough in his grip, flakes of metal falling into his eyes.

"They're coming, Jack!" Cameron hissed as the factory's back door banged open again.

Kane wrenched hard, and the hatch squealed open, sending a rain of rotting leaves, bird shit and litter from the roof through the gap and onto Kane's head. He reached up the gap and hauled himself upwards, propelled by Cameron's hand around his foot. He lay flat on the corrugated metal and reached down for Cameron. A gun-sight laser flashed on the wall and Cameron jumped. He missed Kane's outstretched hand and fell back to the ceiling joist. He jumped again and missed again. A suppressed gunshot spat and rattled against the wall.

"Hurry, Cam, or you're a dead man! Throw the bag to me."

Cameron tossed the rucksack containing the virus up to Kane. He caught it and placed it on the roof next to him. Cameron crouched like a coiled spring and then jumped. Two more bullets ricocheted off the roof around Cameron as Kane caught his hand. Kane grunted, palm sweaty, and hauled his friend through the gap. Cameron's body weight burned his shoulder, and Kane gnashed his teeth as he pulled Cameron through the gap. They collapsed together on the steel ridges, staring up at the sky as they caught their breath, and then ran.

They streaked across undulating rooftops, keeping low and unseen from the enemies who had shot at them. They would expect the fugitives to run for the far end of the line of industrial units, so half across Kane doubled back. He and Cameron sprinted back towards the disused workshop. Kane stopped just before it and climbed down a plastic drainpipe, and Cameron followed. They hurried around the factory and reached Kane's BMW. Kane opened the doors and looked up to see two men in jeans and polo shirts holding pistols pointed right at them.

Kane and Cameron jumped into the BMW and Kane pushed the start button. The engine roared into life and Kane sped away as gunfire thunked into the road and wall around his speeding car.

CHAPTER NINE

Kyle Lavine checked into a Travelodge as night fell. It was a run-of-the-mill British hotel, a simple room with all a travelling business executive or labourer needed to keep him or her comfortable before work the next day. Kyle unpacked his light bag, stretched into a twenty-five-minute yoga workout, and took a shower. He towel-dried his hair, sat at the functional desk and opened his laptop.

The laptop took a minute to boot up and run through its encryption protocol. Whilst he waited, Kyle opened a bottle of red wine bought at an off-licence close to the hotel and poured a half glass into the hotel room's plastic cup, which he found next to the instant coffee and tea kettle. Kyle took a sip of the wine, and longed for his home in the Alps where kept a fine wine cellar, stocked with hand-picked bottles sourced across France and Spain. This one was bitter and felt like sandpaper going down his throat, but it would do.

The laptop came to life, and Kyle searched for everything he could find on Cameron Jordan, which he now knew to be the real name of Tokyo Ghoul. Kyle sniggered at the absurd hacker avatar, taken from a manga anime character. He fished out the damaged laptop and other leads taken from Cameron Jordan's hacker lair and laid them out on the bed.

Once he had pulled together a picture of Cameron Jordan,

ex-SAS sniper and comms expert discharged after a horrific rocket-propelled grenade-related injury, he dug into Tokyo Ghoul. Kyle couldn't find much on the regular internet, but on the dark web, he found dozens of chatrooms with details and discussions on his exploits and links to various posts made by a group known as the Successors.

Kyle took the damaged laptop and connected it to his own machine, letting the programmes he had spent hundreds of thousands of dollars to buy do their thing. He had a loose grip on technology, but it was not his area of expertise. So, he had connections build programmes for him. Ways to search for identities across global law enforcement databases, vehicle registration tracking across every continent, access to military personnel files. Everything he needed to work as a globally active assassin.

Kyle scanned through records of Cameron's military service, much of it special forces missions with ruthlessly redacted passages. He built up a picture of known friends and associates, even stumbling across the rabbit hole of a man named Jack Kane, a friend of Cameron's from his regiment days, and by the looks of it, also an MI6 agent of some sort. Kyle made a list of addresses, contacts, places to look and hunt down his prey. He set up alerts on the UK police records database in case Cameron or any of his circle of contacts flagged at traffic stops, or engaged in any suspicious activity.

Cameron already had a missing person's file open and a file for the gunshots fired at his address. His address was linked to a report of an assault on a police officer guarding the home in the shooting's immediate aftermath. Kyle's own work.

He took another sip of wine and allowed himself to reminisce about his own days in the military. Fond memories, mostly. He had loved Delta; the missions, the weapons. Kyle had excelled in the desert, across multiple theatres of war, but he had never been good with other people. The teams wanted their operators to work together, to be a unit, to bond and to become like brothers. But Kyle had always been a lone wolf. So, when the operations dried up, eclipsed by greater oversight after Afghanistan, Kyle had called it a day.

Plenty of private military groups opened their doors for a decorated veteran and former Delta operator. But much of the work was mundane: protection, bodyguarding, training over and again with guys who loved to carry weapons but had very little actual combat experience. Then an old contact offered Kyle a job. Kill a subversive politician in central Africa. Kyle had jumped at the chance, and the money. Working alone suited him, flying into Africa, tracking his target until he had a detailed daily routine. Watching. Waiting. Then the kill itself and his extraction. That thrill had surpassed even his experiences as a Delta operator; the satisfaction of perfection and success.

Kyle sat back in the cheap hotel armchair. He had cast his net and now all he had to do was wait for the prey.

CHAPTER TEN

Kane wanted to leave Newcastle and travel to another large city like Leeds or Sheffield, but Cameron had refused. He hated public places, as was to be expected of a man who wore a mask to hide his face from the world. Gunfire at the industrial estate and shots fired at Cameron's home shook Newcastle like an upended wasp's nest. Sirens blared across the city in a constant wail. Radio news stations were alive with panic and bulletins describing closed roads, police checkpoints, and horror at the rare explosion of extreme violence.

Knife crime and gang violence occurred as regularly in Newcastle as in other British cities, but gunfire was rare. Mainly because firearms were so difficult to get in the UK, and an escalation of violence involving guns prompted a significant police response with the deployment of armed officers and specialist tactical units. CCTV captured at the industrial estate and surrounding areas would provide of the herringbone baker boy hat he had donned before alighting from the train. hours of footage for police investigators to trawl through, seeking images of those responsible, and it was only a matter of time before the faces of those responsible circulated on news outlets, unless MI5 suppressed the news. Especially if they were involved.

Cameron led Kane to his lock-up in Gateshead, a town further along the River Tyne. The journey took thirty minutes, and Kane and Cameron sat in silence. Kane kept his eyes on the road, the adrenaline leaking out of his body, alertness from the escape at the disused factory giving way to an avalanche of worry and overthinking. Kane's head spun with thoughts of who was chasing Cameron. Criminals, terrorists, agencies, or governments. All clearly deadly serious about obtaining the virus, given the extreme force they were prepared to use.

Thoughts of Danny and Kim mingled with worry about Barb and Craven. It was the worst time for Kane to be involved in something so serious. He needed to be in Seville, but he couldn't let Cameron down. Their bond was as close as family. They had been oppos together in the regiment. Friends and warriors dodging bullets and fighting for their lives.

Cameron pointed when Kane was to turn right or left through a warren of back streets lined with red-bricked terraced houses mixed with more modern buildings. They passed the Sage Gateshead, a curved glass and steel concert hall, and the Baltic Centre for Contemporary Art, a former flour mill converted to a centre for the arts. They turned away from the riverside and Kane glimpsed the Gateshead Millenium Bridge lit by downlights to accentuate its stunning architecture.

Every time Kane made a turn, the car's indicator clicked loudly, cutting through the silence between Kane and Cameron like a ticking clock. The silence became heavy and oppressive, and Kane was relieved when they eventually reached the lock-up. It was one of twenty small garages behind a paint factory, two lines of single-storey old-fashioned car-type brick garages with moon-grey sheet-metal doors. Cameron got out of the car and used a key to open the lock-up. He pulled the door handle towards him, and the door lifted to fold into the roof, rattling on its rollers just like a 1980s suburban garage.

Kane parked the car outside the lock-up and joined Cameron

as he flicked a light switch and a ceiling striplight flickered to life.

"Close the door," Cameron instructed, and Kane heaved the heavy roller down until its rattling bottom clattered against the cement floor.

"This must have taken a bit of time to put together, Cam," Kane mused as he stared around the lock-up. It was more like a hideout than a garage. Instead of rusting shelves with ageing cans of paint and old engine oil, racks of polished weapons hung on walls with ammunition magazines. A computer server hummed in one corner, complete with cooler and neatly-woven rows of red and yellow cables. In the opposite corner, a low bed and bedroll lay beside a work desk and a small plug-in heater. A gleaming motorbike rested near the garage door with a helmet hanging from its handlebars. A waist-high white fridge sat beneath the desk, and a free-standing clothes rail hung with spare jeans, t-shirts, underwear and boots.

Cameron shrugged. "If we learned anything in the regiment, it was to prepare and plan. Right?" Cameron took the laptop from his bag and placed it gently on the desk, plugging a cable into the back of the small but powerful machine. "Secure server. We can search and interact online here without being traced."

"Good. We can lie low here overnight and try to figure out exactly who is after you, Cameron. Whoever it is, they aren't messing about."

"I'm going to reach out to the Successors and see what's going on."

"Can we trust them?"

"I don't know. But we all designed the Prometheus Code together. If anyone can give us some information about what's going on, it's them." Cameron's fingers thrummed on his laptop keyboard with expert speed, the click-clack of keys loud in the small space.

"People are shooting at us, Cam. It's time you gave me more information on the Successors."

"Message sent. Let's see what comes back. There isn't much to tell. We are hackers. We don't tell each other much about our personal lives. Hackers aren't exactly the type who post selfies on fucking Instagram."

"Do you know any of them?"

"I already told you about Storm Shadow. His real name is Chen Li. There's also Viper and Ghost."

"Grown-up names?"

"Viper is Vladimir Grigoryev, former Russian cyber-intelligence officer turned online mercenary. Sick of his government interfering in foreign politics, he joined the Successors. Ghost is Rachel Vines. An American tech prodigy who once worked for a big Silicon Valley firm. I reckon she was CIA at some point, but she's never admitted that. She turned whistleblower about the misuse of data, then disappeared underground."

"You've all created this white-collar weapon, and any of you could have betrayed the rest. Imagine how much governments, terrorists, and organised crime syndicates would pay for its power?"

"Ghost just replied to my message. She's in the UK and wants to meet."

CHAPTER ELEVEN

"Does she live in the UK?" asked Kane.

"I don't know where she lives," Cameron replied after a pause.

"Alarm bells are ringing, Cam. You and your online mates build a super-virus capable of bringing down the world order as we know it. You end up with it in your possession, and an American member of your group is here in Britain at the same time that an elite kill team tries to take us out?"

"Maybe she can help?"

"Maybe she is the one trying to sell the bloody thing to the British Government, the CIA, the Russians, North Korea, Iran, Al-Qaeda, or God knows who."

"We can't stay in this lock-up forever, Jack. We've got to figure out what to do with the virus before somebody actually captures and uses it."

"Destroy it. Plug into your laptop there and wipe the virus out."

"It doesn't work like that. It's not that simple."

"It's held on an external drive, right? Give it to me and I'll smash it to bits. Problem solved."

"No, Jack. The hard drive is wireless, it's connected to the dark web via satellite internet. The virus code is held in a sort of cyber-escrow file. If someone destroys the external device, the cyber-escrow will unlock and deploy the virus. So, you can't just destroy it."

"So why doesn't whoever wants it just access it from the escrow file?"

"Only Storm Shadow and me can access it. And we must do it both at the same time to use the escrow file. One of us alone is not enough."

"This just gets better and better. Can you use your wizardry to un-code it on the hard drive?"

"Un-code?"

"You know what I mean. Can you hack the code and dismantle its capability on the hard drive?"

"It's worth a try, I suppose. But trying it would be incredibly complicated."

"But easier than running from machine-gun fire?"

"Yes." Cameron pushed his fingers behind his mask and kneaded the socket of his missing eye, shoulders slumped, and head bowed. "I never wanted to actually use the Prometheus Code."

"Why did you create it if you aren't willing to put it into action?"

"I thought we'd use it as a bargaining chip, a way to force through genuine change."

"Don't give me that, Cameron. I know you better. Why did you build it?"

"For change, for a better world."

"That's bullshit. We fought all over the globe to make a better world and look where that got us. We both live on the run, scarred for life, souls ruined by what we've seen and done. You had it sorted in Newcastle, plenty of money, doing what you loved. So why do this? You've become a terrorist, Cam. Exactly the type of person we spent most of our lives fighting."

"Don't call me that, and stop shouting. I'm trying to help people, not hurt them."

Kane paused and paced the lock-up, taking a minute to calm himself down before he said something he'd regret. "Let's meet this Ghost then and see what she's got to say. But we do it our way. Carefully."

"I don't want to hurt her, Jack. No violence."

"No violence? We were almost killed today!"

"It wasn't her. I know it."

"What do you know? You bash away at your keyboard and create a thing that could destroy Western Europe and now there are consequences. We must face up to that. This needs to end."

"Do you think it's been easy for me? What was I left with after the war? A fucked-up head and a ruined face. That's what. People can't look at me, children scream and point when they see my face. Do you think I want to wear a mask every day? This is what the army and the government left me with. Fuck all. Ghost gave me hope. We chat every day online. She knows more about me than anyone alive, and me about her. She wouldn't hurt me. Trust me."

Jack stared at his friend's white mask and the glassy eye behind it. The RPG explosion had ripped half his face off and left Cameron's body a mass of burned flesh and his mind a horror of tortured dreams. Jack understood loneliness and the need for a hand to hold in the darkness. His wife Sally was dead, his son despised him, and Kim needed him to be both mother and father. Jess Moore was the only woman Kane had been close to since Sally's death, and she had needed time alone after her ordeal as a prisoner in a Russian military camp. Kane had left her in the end. Jess needed time to heal and get back to normal life, and the one thing he could not provide was normality.

"All right. Let's meet her."

CHAPTER TWELVE

Kyle Lavine woke from an early evening nap to find his laptop lighting up like a Christmas tree. Notifications pinged, alerts flashing up at the screen's bottom right corner. He sat up and took a quick drink of water, stood and stretched his back, quads and hamstrings, and sat down at the hotel room desk.

His bespoke hacking tool bypassed the usual biometric verification requirements and dynamic firewalls. Kyle logged into the ultra-secure UK police database, which housed real-time data from law enforcement agencies across the UK. His screen flickered to life, showing the logo for POLARIS, Police Operational and Logistics Advanced Retrieval and Intelligence System. The interface opened up, and Kyle scrolled through a web of interconnected data points and live video feeds.

Reports of shots fired at an old factory in Newcastle. No bodies found but images of a man in a mask and another man running from the scene. Cameron Jordan. Tokyo Ghoul. The preliminary police report told of bullet holes in factory walls, broken office windows and traces of blood. All that violence but no bodies recovered reeked of an intelligence cover-up. This was getting serious. If MI5, or MI6, or another foreign secret service were involved, things were about to get frisky. Kyle stretched his fingers to crack his knuckles.

Kyle hammered his keyboard, fingers flitting across black

keys, navigating through the system, pulling up reports and alerts. He checked through layers of database-trawling programmes. Facial recognition identification flags popped up for the man with Cameron. Jack Kane, former soldier. Kyle attempted to access Kane's file, but the system restricted his access. Interesting. Kane was most likely one of Cameron's old army buddies come to lend a hand. To help get him out of the death trap Cameron had landed himself in. It might cause a problem, but one Kyle could easily eliminate. Two targets were easier to track; they left a bigger footprint. Now, he had two faces to follow, two identities to trace.

Information from POLARIS led Kyle to other networks, where he could access known associates, criminal records, addresses and historic vehicle ownership. Kyle poured a glass of red wine and sifted through CCTV footage of the incident, but he found that much of it was already blacked out. Accessed and deleted by whatever agency had removed the bodies from the scene. But not all of it. Jack Kane's face was clearly visible from a carpet showroom camera across the road. Grainy footage from a nearby petrol station showed a BMW with a masked man in the passenger seat. Kyle sipped his wine and grinned. He zoomed in to catch the vehicle registration and then cross-referenced it against roadside cameras on POLARIS. Timestamps, locations, logs, a precise route of the BMW fleeing the scene towards Gateshead.

Each click brought Kyle closer, the data leading him to his target like a wolf stalking a lamb. With meticulous focus, he followed the car through traffic light cameras, past a pizzeria. Right turn, and then left alongside a bingo hall. The BMW stopped beside a row of small garages and Kyle jumped out of his desk chair. The chase was on.

CHAPTER THIRTEEN

The evening sun was a red-burnished smear on the horizon, casting the River Tees in a golden hue. Kane and Cameron were south of Newcastle and Gateshead, on the banks of the Tees close to Middlesbrough, west of where the river's tidal estuary emptied into the North Sea. The meeting place was an old, disused boathouse, its peeling paint and worn wooden planks blending in with the reeds and thickets on the riverbank. It sat at the edge of the river and away from the prying eyes of the bustling city. It was the perfect place for a safe meeting, but a strange one for people who spent their lives in front of a keyboard.

Kane had slept surprisingly well on a bedroll on the lock-up's cold cement floor. After a day of dodging bullets and running from an enemy he couldn't yet see, Kane had fallen into an exhausted, dreamless sleep. He had bought them both a takeaway breakfast from a small greasy spoon café, and the bacon and egg rolls had kept both Kane and Cameron with full bellies. They spent the day searching for meet locations, Cameron exchanging messages with Ghost as she travelled north on a train from London.

Cameron had picked the boathouse, using Google Earth to search for a safe place to meet, somewhere accessible by both road and train. Ghost could walk to the location from a small railway station in fifteen minutes, and she had not objected to the isolated riverside location. In Kane's experience, this type of clandestine meeting usually took place in the heart of a busy city. It kept both parties safe, sure that the other wouldn't kill or harm them with so many witnesses present. Cities provided many escape routes: via public transport, inside buildings, cars, motorbikes and crowds to become lost in. An abandoned boathouse was risky, with too many places for a sniper to hide in trees, briars, bushes and hills. The same locations worked for anybody wishing to eavesdrop on their conversation using a listening device from up to nine hundred feet away. But Kane wasn't the one at risk here. It was Ghost and Cameron, and they both seemed fine with it.

Kane remained hidden. Ghost agreed to meet Cameron, and Kane showing up would spook her, perhaps force her to run or cancel the meeting. Kane waited in the lee of an upturned rowing boat, its splintered hull full of holes but with enough cover to keep him hidden from sight. Kane and Cameron both wore communication gear taken from Cameron's lock-up. Small body packs attached to their belts, with earpieces discreetly hidden from view. Just in case Ghost couldn't be trusted, and the place was already rigged with devices or dangers, Kane had checked the boathouse before the meeting, but found that the place was clear. It smelled of damp wood and the faint brine wafting from the river. The air inside was cool, tinged with the scent of decaying leaves blown in through the long-ago broken windows.

Kane adjusted his earpiece, ensuring his connection with Cameron was clear across the distance between boat and boathouse. "I'm in position," he said.

"Copy that," Cameron responded, voice clear through Kane's earpiece. "Feed is live and clear. Just like old times."

Cameron had been the comms expert in their SAS team, responsible for maintaining lines of communication with other teams and between operators. The words "copy that" from Cameron's mouth sounded just as they had fifteen years ago.

Ghost arrived a few minutes later. She came cautiously, stopping every ten steps to look around, waiting, listening for anybody on her trail, or waiting to ambush her. She was a slight figure dressed in a navy hoodie and jeans. Cameron stepped out of the boathouse and waved to her. She slowly raised a pale hand in greeting, lowered her head and walked in short, nervous steps towards him.

"I don't like this, Tokyo," she whispered, west coast American accent, voice just about audible in Kane's ear.

Kane peered through the jagged holes in the boat's timbers, but Cameron and Ghost were hidden inside the boathouse, so he scanned the surrounding area instead, conscious that this could still be a trap, half-expecting a team to come stalking through the trees with MP5s and black stealth fatigues.

"If anybody is listening to us, or knows we are together..." she continued. "This thing we built is like a monster. Uncontrollable and dangerous."

"Nobody knows we are here. You're safe. I've taken every precaution. It's good to finally meet you face to face."

Feet shuffled on the wooden floor, the sound loud in Kane's ear.

"All clear out here," Kane said for Cameron's benefit.

"It's nice to see you, too. You're taller than I expected."

"Have you heard from Storm Shadow?"

"No. Why did he send it to you?"

"I don't know. I haven't heard from him either. I wish we'd never built the damned thing."

"Same. We got in so deep, carried away with a dream of how we could change things. I never thought it could actually be..."

"...real?"

"Yeah. But it is. I can't believe what's happening."

"Do you live in the UK?"

"Yeah. I move around a lot. I have to."

"Did you look into Storm Shadow's or Viper's data?"

"I did. That's why I'm scared. Jesus Christ, but this thing is so fucked up. I've made copies of what I found on this USB drive. The agencies after the virus – they're not just rogue states or criminal organisations. It's worse. It's a coalition of secret service agencies from North Korea, Iran, Al-Qaeda, and China. They call themselves the Alliance. They want the Prometheus Code and will do anything to get it."

"Tell me everything."

"It's all in Storm Shadow's servers. He was in contact with them, trying to sell it to them. First separately, and they jumped at it, eager for a chance to bring down the West. Then they came at him together, pooling their resources to get their hands on the virus. He wanted a billion dollars for it. Each member of the Alliance has their own agenda, but they are united in this pursuit. They've already started sending agents into Europe, seeking the EMP, waiting for a lead to surface on the virus' location. They know Storm Shadow sent it somewhere, to someone."

"Have they come after you?"

"Not yet. But I'll never go back to my London apartment. It's time to move on again. I just want to get out of this mess."

"We must destroy it, Ghost. We must unlock the Prometheus Code and corrupt it before it falls into the hands of those who would use it for evil. So many people would suffer if the financial world collapsed in Europe. We knew it would, but we planned to replace the old world immediately with the world of blockchain and cryptocurrency. We wanted to build something. But they want to destroy the West and leave it in ashes. I need your help. Help me take the code apart. I know the pieces I coded, and you know yours. Between us, we must find a back door, a way to compromise its code."

"I dunno. It's too dangerous. I just want to forget about it all."

"We built it. We have a responsibility to destroy it."

A deep sigh, audible even through Kane's earpiece. "I'll try. But we work remote. Exchange information securely. We need to move fast. Before they close in on us. They will find us. They have resources beyond our imagination, ruthless determination and technology we haven't even seen yet."

The sound of a car engine in the distance caused Kane to sit up straight. Peering over the edge of the upturned boat, he spotted a set of headlights turning a corner two hundred yards away. "Tell her it's time to go. She can't go back on the train. We'll take her to safety, and she can go from there."

Cameron relayed the instructions to Ghost. She babbled a protest, surprised to hear Cameron wasn't alone.

"Stay close," Cameron said, guiding Ghost towards the boathouse door. "We'll get you out of here safely. Together we'll fix this."

The river continued to lap gently, water slopping against the riverbank. Cameron led Ghost towards the car and Kane followed. Every step measured and deliberate, his hand resting on the Glock holstered in his waistband, just in case the headlights were enemies come to kill. The stakes were higher than ever, governments desperate and in pursuit of Cameron and his diabolical virus. It was a dangerous path, but if anybody could destroy the Prometheus Code, it was the hackers who'd built it. With the right moves, if Kane could use his training and experience, they might just stay one step ahead of the enemies closing in around them.

CHAPTER FOURTEEN

Ghost sat silently in the BMW's back seat all the way back to Cameron's lock-up. Occasionally she would raise her head slightly, and hazel eyes would glance at Kane through the rear-view mirror, face obscured by her deep hood. They reached the line of garages and Kane did two loops around the block, checking for any suspicious vehicles, twitching curtains or suspicious characters hanging around on street corners. The area seemed clear, and Kane parked the car.

Inside the lock-up, Cameron clicked on the kettle and set up his laptop as it came to the boil. Ghost sidled in past Kane, skirting around him as though getting too close to him would burn her. He left her alone, not trying to instigate a conversation or even make eye contact with her. She opened her laptop next to Cameron's and tapped away at her keyboard, white characters flashing on the black screen.

Kane watched the two hackers work on their laptops, experts in a field beyond his understanding. Towards the end of his career in an MI6 splinter group, the world had already begun to alter. Battlegrounds shifted from competing field agents, assassinations, assets, and surveillance to the new war online. Agents with computer skills became more valuable to governments than highly-trained field agents. Hackers and cyber experts could manipulate elections and destroy governments through the power of social media without leaving their bedrooms. They could erase an entire existence from their desk before finishing a cup of coffee. The world was certainly changing, but no matter how skilled the keyboard warrior became, there would always be a need for a man with a gun. Someone to call upon when things became too desperate when the only solution was death or vengeance. Kane had been such a man in his life, and that blood still ran through his veins. Just as it did with those who hunted him.

"Can they find us here?" Ghost asked, her voice so quiet it came as a whisper.

"I've done all I can to keep the place safe," Cameron replied. "Secure, untraceable server. The place is owned and registered to a trust, not in my name. We should be safe here for a while. Tea or coffee?"

"I'm an American, remember? Coffee, please. Black."

"I should ditch the car," said Kane. "We've used it since Newcastle."

"Are you going to tell me who he is?" Ghost jutted her chin in Kane's direction.

"Jack is an old army friend. I trust him like a brother and you can, too. He knows all about Prometheus and the Successors. He's here to help."

"You told him everything?"

"I had to. They tried to kill me, Ghost. They'll come for you too. Maybe they already got to Storm Shadow, and we've heard nothing from Viper. We could be the last."

"I can't believe this," Ghost buried her head in her hands and began rocking back and forth. "Everything is out there. What sort of lives can we live now that the world knows what we've done?"

"It was always going to get out," said Kane, growing tired of the melancholy. "What did you think was going to happen when you created something so destructive? Someone always talks, especially if there's an opportunity to become rich. Chen Li took that opportunity and now Pandora's box is well and truly open. You can't put the virus back in. The only way to fix this now is to destroy it. Even then, you are both in danger. The Alliance seeking it now knows the construction methodology is in your heads. They'll hunt you relentlessly to recreate Prometheus. Your only chance at any sort of future life is to destroy it, let it be known the thing is gone, and you both need to disappear. New identities, remote destinations, no more hacking. A quiet, anonymous life. I'm sorry for calling it out, but there it is."

"Jesus, Jack. Go easy," murmured Cameron. Ghost began to sob, and Cameron rested an awkward hand upon her shoulder.

"I'll get rid of the car."

Kane rolled up the garage door and stepped out into the chill night. The Successors had been naïve to create Prometheus. Kane imagined them bashing their keyboards in secret, thrilled to push their skills to the test, each of them a loner, a nerd finding comradeship and kindred spirits in their online group. Their ideology had fired their passions: change, a new world, a better world for the poor and disenfranchised. He wondered if any of them truly believed it, or if they had gone along with the charade just to keep their friendship alive, to fuel the only thing which bound them together. Once they completed the virus, it was too late. Like Frankenstein's monster coming alive on the creator's table, too strong and unpredictable, impossible to control. A creation of science and technology which once born cannot be unborn.

Kane unlocked the BMW and sat in the driver's seat. They had to destroy Prometheus, and then disappear. Or the alliance of powerful, ruthless government agencies would capture them and farm their minds like slaves.

CHAPTER FIFTEEN

Craven put the phone down and stared at the handset in his trembling hand. A hollow, sick feeling churned in his stomach and his mouth hung open like a cave. Barb had sounded different on the call. Quiet. Afraid.

"Uncle Frank?" piped Kim's voice from the next room.

"Yes, love?" Craven replied, doing his best to mask the fear in his voice.

"I'm hungry."

Kane's daughter, like her brother Danny, was always hungry. It was nine o'clock in the evening and Craven had made them pasta Bolognese for dinner barely two hours ago.

"What would you like?" he asked. A task to distract him from thoughts of Barbara was welcome. He had visited the hospital earlier that day and waited as she went through yet more tests to assess the severity of her cancer, and if it had spread to any other organs. It would be another twenty-four hours before the results, and the Spanish doctors wanted to keep Barb in the hospital, just to keep an eye on her. All Barb wanted was to come home and relax with the children, and it had broken Craven's heart to leave her glassy-eyed in her hospital bed.

"Can I have egg and toast soldiers please, Uncle Frank?"

"Of course. Ask your brother if he wants some, too."

Craven went to the fridge and took out an egg and then a loaf of Bimbo bread from the cupboard. Even Kim's snack choice reminded him of Barb. Egg and toast soldiers was one of her favourites, a simple meal of a soft-boiled egg and two rounds of toast, buttered and cut into thin strips, or soldiers, to dip into the egg.

"He says he isn't hungry, Uncle Frank." Kim strolled into the kitchen and flicked a peace sign at Craven, which was her latest quirk. He smiled, wondering what he would do if he didn't have Kane's children staying with him. Probably waiting and sleeping at the hospital worried sick. "But he's not hungry because he ate a ham sandwich when you were on the phone."

Craven filled a pan with cold water and set it on the hob to boil. "Wash your hands and get yourself a drink."

"Was it Auntie Barbara on the phone?"

"Yes, she was calling to say goodnight. She told me to tell you she loves you."

"When is she coming home?"

"Soon, hopefully. Now, wash your hands."

The children were sensitive to Barbara's condition, not just because she doted on them and they loved her like a grandma, but because their mother had died three years ago. Kane did his best to be a good father, but he was often away, working, running, shooting, swanning around in his fancy suits, helping people in need. Kane and Craven had made enough money to keep both families secure for years to come, mainly by taking money from the enemies they defeated. Just like Robin Hood, as Kim had generously put it once. Danny and Kim attended a local boarding school close to Seville, and Barbara usually picked them up on Friday evenings whenever Kane was away and dropped them off again on Monday mornings. Kane wanted to be a better father, and Craven knew him as well as anybody could know a man like Kane, but he just wasn't built for fatherhood. Danny resented his father for his absences, and Kim was too young to understand.

The phone rang its ironically jaunty tone and Craven picked it up as he dropped the slices of bread into the toaster. It was a private number, and Craven frowned. Usually, that meant it was THE number. The number Cameron set up to bounce around dozens of VOIP exchanges before terminating on Craven's phone.

"Hello?" he said. Kane was already away on a job, and in serious trouble by the sound of their last conversation, and Craven hated turning down people who called the number because they were generally in real danger.

"Frank Craven?" said a gruff voice in a heavy Welsh accent. Craven was taken aback that the caller knew his name.

"Who's asking?" he replied.

"My name is Mr Jones and I'm calling from British intelligence."

"OK," Craven said, voice drawling as he waved Kim away. She was silently mouthing a question, asking him if it was Auntie Barbara on the phone.

"I need to speak to you and Jack Kane urgently. Are you Frank Craven?"

"How did you get this number and what do you want?"

"Kane's colleagues in MI6, former SAS servicemen with whom you both performed a particular task last year, gave it to me. Kane has got himself in deep this time. He's on the run with a chap named Cameron Jordan, and they are both in trouble beyond their wildest fears. They need to come in quickly, before the world falls in around them."

CHAPTER SIXTEEN

Kane left the BMW outside a busy fish and chips shop and walked the five streets back to Cameron's lock-up. Craven had called during the short drive with news that MI5 wanted Kane and Cameron to turn themselves in for their own protection. To those who knew no better, that seemed like a good idea. After being a fugitive from his own government, Kane was currently back in the intelligence services' good books after playing his part in a raid on a Russian private military base. But that was MI6, the international arm of British intelligence. MI5 had contacted Craven, the UK domestic intelligence service. Different agencies, different agents, different motivations.

He turned around a sharp corner and into a narrow street flanked by terraced houses with small wooden gates and no driveways. Cars parked bumper to bumper along the faded grey tarmac. Orange traffic cones filled any gaps to keep spaces free for their habitual users to return from whatever trips had taken them away from working-class suburbia. Kane had memorised the contact number that the MI5 agent had left with Craven. He dialled the first two digits, thought better of it, and cancelled the call.

In Kane's experience, government agencies were about as trustworthy as a hungry dog left alone with a T-bone steak. But Craven was right. This thing had grown legs and was beyond Kane's and Cameron's ability to handle. An alliance of foreign secret services agencies arrayed against him was too much, even for a man of Kane's skills. He decided to call the MI5 contact, but only after checking with Cameron first. Kane could not decide his friend's fate for him.

A black Transit van sped down the street, tyres screeching on the road as it turned a bend. Kane stopped in his tracks. There was something odd about the van. Blacked-out windows, travelling so fast this late in the evening and down such a narrow street where only one vehicle could drive through the opposing lines of parked cars. Kane set off jogging towards the lock-up and turned right just in time to see the van screech to a halt. Two men in overcoats and suits jumped out and set off running as the van turned into another street of the warren-like housing estate.

Someone had found them. Kane didn't know who. Could be assassins, could be the Alliance, could be British Government or CIA agents. It didn't matter. Men in suits jumping from a blacked-out van could only mean one thing, and Kane wasn't about to wait and find out. He sprinted along the street, veering as a dog's jaws snapped at him, barking from behind wrought-iron gates. He jumped over a scooter left lying on the pavement and entered the row of lock-ups. The van's brake lights glowed red at the end of the line of garages and two more men leapt from its side doors. Three more stood outside Cameron's lock-up. Men in long overcoats, shiny shoes and sombre suits, men come to take the Prometheus Code and destroy anybody who got in their way. Kane was about to get in their way, and he slowed his run to an ambivalent stroll, hands in pockets as though he had not a care in the world.

"Find somewhere else to walk," called one of the overcoated men, a big man with a Manchester accent. "This road's closed."

Kane ignored him and continued walking, adding a spring to his step for extra effect.

"Look, mate," the big man repeated, holding his hand out to

Kane as if to halt him in his tracks. "Roads closed. Fuck off and find another way home."

Kane closed the gap between them in five long strides, and another man, short with a trimmed beard and bald head, fished in his jacket pocket and pulled out a wallet complete with ID.

"We are from MI5, sir. This road is dangerous. Please find another way home."

"This one's my lock-up," Kane said, gesturing to Cameron's metal door.

"What's your name?" asked the big man.

"Cameron Jordan."

All three sprang to life, forming a circle around Kane and shouting at him to raise his hands and kneel.

CHAPTER SEVENTEEN

"I haven't done anything," Kane yelped. "What do you want with me?"

"You're coming with us, mate. On your knees. Now. Hands above your head."

Kane took a step back, putting on his best frightened face. "Are you arresting me?"

"You know why we're here. On your knees."

The big man snarled and took a step towards Kane with two black cable-ties in one hand. Considering MI5 had contacted Craven offering help, these men didn't seem very helpful. The aura of violence pulsed from them, the stink of threat palpable. They hadn't come peacefully; they came to take the Prometheus Code by force. Mr Jones had only called Craven fifteen minutes ago. The men facing Kane could be rogue agents, or men masquerading as MI5, but he doubted it. The agents must have been en route in the van at the same time Jones spoke to Craven on the phone. Untrustworthy bastards. They wanted the code just as much as the Alliance. Perhaps more. If the Alliance or the Successors deployed the Prometheus Code, it was beyond national security. It was an existential crisis for the British state and for London's historical and pivotal financial services sector.

Kane bent on one knee as though he was about to kneel and submit, and as the big man sneered and took a step forward, Kane exploded into action. He flexed out his leading leg, all his weight behind the blow, and the heel of his shoe connected with the big man's knee. The joint crunched like rotten wood and the big man howled in pain. Kane brought the heel of his hand around in an uppercut, slamming it into the MI5 man's jaw where neck met ear. He dropped like a sack of potatoes and Kane was already moving as the two remaining agents surged at him with ferocious force.

A punch sailed over Kane's head as he ducked, and he blocked a savage front kick with his forearm.

"Target has attacked us!" the bald man shouted into a microphone Kane could not see but knew hid in the agent's lapel or nestled inside of his ear. "Back-up required! Repeat, back-up required!"

Kane caught another kick and swept the standing leg from under the third agent, punching him in the throat as his back connected with the pavement. The bald man jumped on Kane, driving him to the cold stone. Kane grunted as his shoulder banged against the concrete, and he rolled just as the bald man scrambled on top of him, thighs squeezing, powerful hands searching for a jiu-jitsu hold that would grip Kane fast until more agents arrived. The lock-up door clattered as it rose from the ground, opening slowly to reveal Cameron's porcelain white mask and black-painted eye peering through the crack.

"Shit," said Cameron, and hauled the door fully open.

Kane lifted his hips and drove his arm beneath the bald man's left arm. He pushed his attacker's body away from him and then let him fall, head-butting the bald man full in the face. Gristle and nose mashed against Kane's forehead and his enemy tried to twist away, but Kane kept him close, driving his knee into the man's groin and butting him in the eye socket.

The bald man grunted, wrenching his entire body away from Kane, desperate to get away from the brutal onslaught. Kane let him roll away and then jumped to his feet, and stamped down hard on the bald man's wrist, shattering the tiny bones in his wrist. The bald man cried out and crawled away, cradling his ruined joint.

"Get Ghost out of there, quickly," Kane rasped. "There's more coming."

Cameron's mask nodded in understanding, and he disappeared inside the lock-up. Four more agents came pounding towards Kane from either side of the garage roadway, two from the north and two from the south. Kane drew his Glock and raised the weapon above his head, firing two shots into the night sky. The gunfire exploded like thunder, followed by screams from nearby houses. Kane knew most people had never heard gunfire before. It was always far louder than they expected it to be, like exploding close-range fireworks. Lights turned on, and curtains and blinds shifted as folk ran to look out of their windows and doors to see what could have caused such a loud noise.

The approaching agents all held guns, and they quickly holstered their weapons as too many witnesses watched their approach. Cameron ran out of the lock-up with Ghost holding his hand, wild eyes staring at Kane in terror.

"Find a car and steal it, Cam," Kane instructed. "I'll hold them off until you get away. I'll call your burner when I'm out of here."

"There's a bike inside, Jack. Don't get caught," Cameron said. He ran past Kane and clambered up the side of the opposite lock-up, turned and pulled Ghost up behind him. Cameron was a former SAS operator, and Kane knew his friend could steal a car from the next street over.

Kane took off his overcoat and let it fall to the pavement.

He rolled his shoulders and charged at the two agents approaching from the north. One of them whipped out a telescopic baton and Kane jumped at that man, slamming into him at full tilt, knocking him to the ground. As he landed, Kane lashed out and tripped the second man. The first agent grabbed Kane's hair, yanked his head back, and smashed his baton into Kane's throat. Pain shot through Kane's neck, and he choked, airway constricted by the impact. He rolled away, dodging another baton strike just as it cracked on the pavement beside his head. The second man, thin with a lean face, booted Kane in the stomach and Kane retched.

Instinctively, Kane curled into a ball as blows rained down on his back and legs.

"Get his arms," bellowed one agent, approaching from the south. "Get the cuffs on him."

Kane roared in anger, the heat of combat burning his chest, fury flooding his limbs with strength. The battle calm came over him, and despite finding himself amidst a brutal beating, Kane smiled inside. This was what he lived for. The sheer thrill of balancing upon the gossamer-thin line between life and death, of defeating an enemy who came to kill him. The joy of combat, the thrill of victory. It was a secret love, a thing never given voice to, a guilty pleasure nobody beyond his world could ever understand.

He let the rage overcome him, embracing it, becoming one with it. If he remained curled up, he would die or they would take him prisoner, and he would never see the light of day again. So, Kane surged upwards, unfolding himself from the foetal position like a lion leaping upon its prey. He drove his fist into one attacker's solar plexus and jabbed the knuckles of his left hand into another attacker's throat. A punch scuffed Kane's ear, and another drove into his kidneys as he bobbed and weaved between them. One attacker fell to his knees and Kane took a long step forward so that his knee cracked into the man's skull. A kick flashed past his face and Kane threw that man over his hip, following the throw by falling upon his attacker, all of his weight behind the elbow thudding into the fallen man's face, knocking him unconscious.

"Send everyone!" one of the remaining agents shouted. "All of them! Everyone!" He spat a gobbet of blood and raised his fists, so Kane kicked him hard in the groin, dodged a punch from another agent, and circled around the man. The agent who had shouted crumpled, clutching his groin in unspeakable pain. The fist came again, and Kane caught the arm, twisting it savagely before butting his hip into the man's thigh and dislocating the arm with a sickening crunch.

Kane left them there, groaning and writhing beneath the streetlights. Eyes peered at him through the neighbouring houses, but Kane ignored them. A siren wailed in the distance and car tyres screeched. Kane swore to himself. The van would return at any moment with more agents, and he had to run. He ducked into the lock-up and walked Cameron's motorbike into the doorway. Kane grabbed a helmet and a duffel bag from a shelf and threw as many of Cameron's guns, gadgets, grenades, and ammunitions into the bag as he could before tossing it over his shoulder.

The helmet slipped over Kane's head, and he started the bike's engine. It was a black Yamaha MT-07, sleek and low. Kane twisted the ignition key and the engine roared in a deep, throaty growl. The engine's purr vibrated through his hands, the bike humming beneath him, ready to unleash its power. He edged out of the lock-up, just in time to see the black Transit van come hurtling along the lane towards him. With a flick of his wrist, Kane twisted his hand around the accelerator and sped out of the lock-up. The back tyre flew out behind him, and Kane brought it around with his foot on the floor to keep the bike balanced. The 689cc engine shot Kane and the bike forwards and he leaned into the first bend. The van roared behind him, so close he feared it would smash into the bike and send him sprawling across the concrete.

Kane gunned the bike through the narrow, winding streets with the van hot on his tail. He leant into the bends and the bike responded with fluid agility. Houses blurred past, their windows reflecting his flashing silhouette. The rhythmic pulse of the engine accompanied his frantic heartbeat, pushing the bike to its limit on the turns, gradually pulling away from the chasing van. He turned onto a slip road and then merged onto a dual carriageway. Kane leant forward and let the bike power into the top speed, leaving the van in his wake.

As streetlights whizzed beside him, Kane hoped Cameron and Ghost had escaped. Now MI5 was on their tail, with all of the power of the British intelligence service behind them, their chances of getting out of this mess were reduced to a tiny fraction. Kane and Cameron had to evade not only an alliance of foreign agencies but now also their own government. Kane let the bike race at top speed, weaving between cars heading west, away from danger, head spinning with desperation.

CHAPTER EIGHTEEN

Kyle Lavine worked out in his hotel room. Stripped to the waist, he moved through a series of burpees, press-ups, and sit-ups. Sweat sheened his body, and his delts, biceps, quads and abdominal muscles burned with fatigue. When he was done, Kyle grabbed a bottle of chilled water from the hotel room desk and gulped it down. He sat down at the desk, upon which his Sig Sauer handgun lay deconstructed on a crisp white bathroom towel. Kyle stared at the shiny parts of his P226, his trusted companion, the weapon which had saved his life more than once, and which had earned Kyle his fortune. It was his tool, his livelihood, his weapon of choice.

The distinct scent of gun oil punched through stale hotel room air, mingling with the faint smell of metal and solvent. Kyle picked up the frame, the pistol's backbone, and inserted the trigger assembly with practised precision. The faint click of metal against metal echoed softly, like a symphony to Kyle's expert ear. Next, he slid the barrel into the slide, the cold steel smooth and reassuring in his hands, the soft, metallic scrape like a prelude to the weapon's lethal potential.

He carefully aligned the recoil spring and guide rod, snapping them into place with a muted, satisfying snap. Fingers moving deftly, he mounted the slide on the frame, each motion fluid from years of experience. The final click as the slide locked into place was sharp and definitive.

Kyle picked up a magazine which he had loaded earlier with 9mm rounds and checked it over, the weight balanced perfectly in his grip. The entire process took less than five minutes, his efficiency honed by countless repetitions in countless dire, desperate situations. He chambered a round with a smooth pull of the slide, the familiarly reassuring sound of readiness comforting. Kyle checked the sights one last time, the black finish of the Sig gleaming with deadly purpose. He took a deep breath, body prepared, weapon perfect and ready to complete his mission.

He showered, dried himself and dressed, taking his time. His expensive clothes fitted perfectly, the edge of his trousers and shirt ironed to a crisp finish. Kyle opened his laptop and for the third time watched Jack Kane fight six highly-trained MI5 agents in grainy CCTV footage captured from a camera above two rows of lock-up garages. Kane fought well using a mix of jiu-jitsu, boxing, and Krav Maga. His movements made efficient through years of actual combat rather than endless drills on the practice mat. Kane used maximum, unrelenting force.

The MI5 men were slow compared to Kane, even though many of them were bigger and stronger, and probably fitter. What Kane lacked in size and strength, he made up for in sheer brutality. Kyle appreciated that. He considered himself more of a leopard than a charging bear, or so he liked to think. Kane was the same, the ideal grey man, exactly what special forces and intelligence recruiters looked for. He was neither tall nor short, stocky nor thin. He was unremarkable to look at, an average face and short hair, forgettable, almost impossible to recall in a crowd. Much like Kyle himself. A shiver shook Kyle Lavine's shoulders, excitement at the prospect of engaging Kane in battle. An equal, perhaps. A man to test Kyle's skills, a worthy opponent.

Kyle spent an hour flicking through video footage, watching

Kane abandon the BMW beside a popular food takeaway. Kane had raced away from the fight at the lock-up on a motorbike and Kyle tracked the bike using the POLARIS tracking tool. His prey was on the run. Kane and Cameron Jordan would make desperate decisions in their bid to escape, in their fight for survival. Kyle's patience paid off, like a hunter waiting beneath a canopy of brush in the deep forest, poised for a deer to step cautiously within his sights. Kyle had watched, learned about his targets, waiting for their situation to deteriorate. Forcing them into poor decisions. It was time to strike.

Kyle snapped his laptop closed and quickly packed his bag. He checked his weapons and pulled on a zip-top sweater over his khaki shirt. He was ready.

CHAPTER NINETEEN

Kane spent an hour riding the Yamaha motorbike through random dual carriageways and winding country roads until he was sure no one had followed him. He pulled over at an A-road layby where the road curled around a steep hillside thick with pine trees. He removed the helmet and ran his fingers through his hair and stretched his body, sore from the kicks and punches to his head, arms, and back. The pine leaves smelled fresh, and Kane sat on a wooden picnic bench heavy with green lichen and knife-carved graffiti.

He took the burner phone from his jacket pocket to call Cameron but paused with it in his hand. His hands stung from riding the bike without gloves, and the muscle fatigue on his forearms suddenly reminded him of Afghanistan. Kane stared out into the pine trees, the darkened shade between the heavy boughs lulling him into a daze. He flexed his hands and remembered how his arms had ached the day a rocket-propelled grenade explosion burned the flesh from Cameron's face and body. Kane had dragged him to safety that day, and he could almost feel the weight of Cameron's limp body and how his arms had throbbed from the strain of lugging that weight through hot sand, blood, and debris.

The dusk of the pine forest shifted suddenly in Kane's reverie. His surroundings changed shape to become the jagged peaks of the Afghan mountains looming against the backdrop of a blazing midday sun. The hot drop of searing gold in the sky cast long, sharp shadows across the rugged, harsh terrain. The air about him was thick with the scent of dust and sparse vegetation, mixing with the acrid stink of diesel fuel. A distant rattle of gunfire occasionally broke the silence, a constant reminder of the perilous environment. Kane's mind took him back to Afghanistan, to a place of pain and suffering.

Kane and his SAS team were on patrol, three days into a mission to gather intelligence on insurgent movements in the area. The team wore standard desert camo uniforms and marched equipped with body armour, helmets, and L85A1 rifles slung across their chests. Each man wore his beard long to better blend in with and earn the respect of local fighters and warlords. Kane shifted his pack's shoulder straps slightly to relieve the pressure. Their gear was heavy, loaded with spare magazines, food, water, grenades, their survival tins, and other useful survival items.

A convoy of three vehicles moved cautiously along a narrow mountain pass, engines humming, gears grinding. A jingly van led the way, a common local vehicle adorned with colourful trinkets and jangling chains. Aziz, their local contact and guide, drove the jingly van with Cameron in the passenger seat, Afghan music blaring from the van's radio. Kane travelled in the second vehicle, an armoured Land Rover, his eyes scanning the horizon for any signs of ambush. Each of them had experienced attacks from insurgents dressed as civilians, heard stories of children or women carrying explosive devices beneath their clothing. The war was a nerve-shattering battle of attrition, dealing with friendly locals, and an enemy who looked and dressed exactly the same as the friendlies but who hated British and American soldiers with the utmost intensity.

Without warning, a whistling sound pierced the air. Kane's instincts kicked in just as the RPG slammed into the jingly van. The explosion was deafening, a violent eruption of fire and shrapnel that sent a shockwave through the convoy. The jingly van disintegrated in a cloud of smoke and flames, debris raining down like deadly confetti.

"Contact front!" Kane screamed into his comms device, adrenaline surging through his veins. He leapt from the Land Rover, ignoring the chaos and smoke around him, his focus solely on the wreckage. Aziz was gone, but amidst the twisted metal, he saw movement. Cameron. The distinctive sound of AK-47 gunfire rattled about the convoy, and the rest of Kane's SAS team returned fire, voices shouting and organising through the communications devices on Kane's helmet and armour.

Kane's eyes watered from the oppressive reek of burning rubber and charred metal. He ran towards the burning van, the heat like a furnace searing his skin. Cameron's screams cut through the noise, a harrowing sound that spurred Kane onwards. He kept low, running around smoking pieces of metal and wood, gunfire hammering into the road and vehicles around him. He found Cameron pinned beneath a crumpled door, his face and body burned to a mess of red and black flesh, his uniform scorched and smoking.

"I'm here, Cam! Hold on!" Kane bellowed, his voice barely audible over the crackling fire and secondary explosions. He dropped to his knees, hands shaking as he gripped the hot metal. Kane roared, summoning every ounce of strength. He pried the door open, the heat blistering his palms even through his gloves.

One of Cameron's eyes was gone, nothing but a blue-black smear around a cavernous hole. The remaining eye was wide with fear and pain, his terrified gaze flitting across Kane's face in desperation. His breaths came ragged and wheezing. "Jack... it hurts... hurts so bad," he gasped, his voice a fragile whisper.

"I know, mate, I know," Kane replied, voice breaking. He carefully pulled Cameron from the wreckage, taking care not to rip the burned flesh from his bones or make any damaged limbs worse. Bullets whizzed by, voices screaming in his ear, but Kane had to focus on saving his friend. Kane hoisted Cameron over his shoulder in a fireman's carry, every step a battle against the weight and the uneven ground crunching beneath his boots. "We've got to get out of here or we are all dead men," he muttered, more to himself than to Cameron.

The team provided covering fire, rifles booming as they laid down suppressing fire on the ridgeline where the RPG had come from. Kane moved with desperate urgency, his heart pounding in his chest. The landscape blurred, the harsh beauty of the mountains a stark contrast to the savage violence unfolding in the valley.

Kane reached the Land Rover and gently lay Cameron in the backseat. "Medic! Get the medic, now!" Kane screamed, his voice hoarse from the smoke. Blood and soot stained his hands and uniform, his face streaked with sweat and dirt. The medic, a young corporal named Charvis, rushed over, medical kit at the ready. He quickly assessed Cameron's burns and administered morphine to ease his pain.

"He's stable for now," said Charvis. "But if we don't get him to a field hospital ASAP, he's done for."

Kane nodded, his mind racing. He jumped into the driver's seat, determination etched on his face. "Hang in there, Cam. We're getting you out of here."

As the Land Rover sped away from the ambush, Kane's thoughts were a whirlwind. Although the mission was compromised, all that mattered to him was saving his comrade and warrior-brother's life. The road ahead was perilous with debris and could crawl with enemies, but Kane's resolve was unshakeable. Men who have fought together forge a bond in the crucible of combat. The bond was stronger than fear, and he would stop at nothing to ensure Cameron's survival.

The journey to the field hospital was a blur of sharp turns and rough terrain. Each bump jarred Cameron's frail, destroyed body, each second a race against time. The once majestic mountains now seemed menacing, their shadows a reminder of the danger lurking in every valley, in every village.

Finally, after driving for what could have been hours, the makeshift field hospital came into view. A cluster of tents and vehicles bustling with activity. Kane screeched the Land Rover to a halt and burst from the vehicle, shouting and waving for help. Medics swarmed the vehicle, carefully lifting Cameron clear and rushing inside the white tents. Kane stood and watched. Hands still shaking, eyes fixed on the medics working to save his friend's life. The reality of the situation sunk in, the weight of the day's events pressing down on him like a monstrous boulder. But Cameron was alive, and that was all that mattered.

Kane snapped out of his daze and found himself back in the layby. He shook his head to clear the memory and dialled Cameron's number.

"Jack?" said Cameron's voice as he answered the call.

"Yeah, Cam, it's me. Did you and Ghost get out of there OK?"

"I was worried about you, Jack. Thank fuck you made it out. We're fine. I ran through a house and down a couple of streets. All the focus seemed to be on you. I boosted an old Vauxhall Astra, and we made it out of town. We've just been waiting for your call."

"Listen, Cam. We can only trust each other. It's just us now. I know a place we can lie low for a night or two, an old MI6 safe house in the mountains. It's been abandoned for years. No home comforts, but it will do. I'll text the location to you now and meet you there."

Kane hung up the phone and pulled his helmet back on.

MI5 had tried to kill him, and he had yet to encounter the Alliance. But they were coming. Everybody wanted the virus, and all Kane wanted was to get Cameron and himself out of this situation alive. He started up the Yamaha and headed towards the Pennine mountains, head spinning with what might happen next and how to protect his friend.

CHAPTER TWENTY

Kyle Lavine drove an Audi A5 away from Britain's north east coast and into the Pennine mountains, the spine which runs down northern England like the back of a sleeping dragon. The Pennines run from the Anglo-Scots border in the north down to Derbyshire and Staffordshire in the Midlands. Kyle entered the Snake Pass, driving carefully along the winding road, which was as treacherous as it was scenic. It reminded Kyle of the American states of Montana or Nebraska, but somehow older, denser, less meandering. The road twisted and turned, a serpentine ribbon of concrete and tarmac cutting through the dramatic landscape.

Lofty, snow-capped peaks rose on either side of him, shrouded in the gloaming but visible beneath a full moon glowing in the sky like a torch. Rocky cliff faces dotted with hardy brush and rambling, ancient trees fell away into steep valleys. Night fog clung to higher elevations, blanketing the mountains in an eerie, almost mythical veil. Kyle could imagine old English knights riding these trails on their horses, swords in hand, as they hunted enemies in the mountain passes. The air was crisp, and Kyle opened the Audi's driver's window a crack and sucked in the crisp air, the scent of damp and wet pine filling the car. Kyle's eyes darted between the road and his laptop, which he had propped open on the passenger seat. On its screen, the POLARIS system tracked a Yamaha motorbike along the A57 road.

Sharp bends and sudden inclines commanded Kyle's full attention. He navigated each curve with the same precision with which he performed all tasks. Occasional sheep grazed close to the roadside, their woolly shapes like ghosts in the moonlit darkness. As Kyle descended into deep valleys, he passed through small hamlets, their quaint and narrow lanes a stark contrast to the busy, noisy and modern streets of New York, Boston, Los Angeles, and Philadelphia. The road dipped and climbed, each turn revealing sweeping vistas of moorland, crags, and distant forests. His target was close now, and the thrill of the chase pumped through Kyle's veins like a drug.

The blip on his laptop screen stopped, tracked by satellite imagery now that it had moved beyond the reach of city CCTV coverage and into the countryside. Kyle slowed the Audi, turning left off a meandering stretch of the Snake Pass and onto a country road covered by a blanket of decaying leaf mulch. This must be where Jack Kane and Cameron Jordan planned to hide out as they deployed or sold the Prometheus Code. They thought they were safe out here, far away from the MI5 team at the lock-up. That perceived safety was Kyle's ally. He pulled the car in tight to a grass verge and stepped out. He opened the trunk and took out a set of BNVD night vision goggles and pushed them over his head. The world turned green, and Kyle checked his Sig and fitted the suppressor. He took a combat knife from a small case, clipped its sheath to his belt, and popped a spare ammunition magazine in his pocket.

Kyle moved through the undergrowth, his shoes crunching on rotted leaves and fallen twigs. He moved quickly but carefully, slightly crouched like a predator. He left the path and moved into the forest, shifting around ash and elm trees, the world cast in a green-black hue by his goggles. An old house came into sight through the dense leaves and straggling branches. Its red-tiled roof and mould-stained walls spoke of abandonment, but a light flickered as a blot of white through Kyle's goggles. A fire, or small lamp perhaps. A sign of life? Or of the Prometheus Code and the men Kyle must take it from?

CHAPTER TWENTY-ONE

Kane parked the Yamaha beside a dirty Vauxhall Astra in a driveway heavy with scree, broken rocks, and fallen branches. A light flickered inside the building before him, and he breathed a sigh of relief because Cameron and Ghost were safe.

The safe house stood forlorn against the stark backdrop of the Pennine mountains, a relic of past operations long forgotten, missions Kane pushed to the back of his mind. Kane had stayed at the safe house ten years ago to rest and recover from wounds taken on a clandestine mission in Africa. He had performed many dangerous missions whilst part of the Mjolnir black ops division of MI6. Missions which, at the time, he was sure were in the interests of national security. Now couldn't be sure what their objectives were. He had taken lives and had blindly followed orders like a good soldier. The safe house, previously part of Mjolnir's debrief programme, had been abandoned for at least six years. Kane, Cameron, and Ghost now sought refuge in its isolation, using it to hide from their enemies.

Thick moss covered the cracked and mottled stone walls of the weathered and worn building. Ivy crept up the gable end, intertwining with the flaking paint of wooden window shutters. Several roof tiles were missing or broken, leaving gaps where rain and wind found their way inside. The front door creaked ominously, hanging slightly ajar, and Kane pushed it open and stepped into a hallway of broken tiles and pools of dark rainwater. The air was fusty inside, heavy with the odour of decay. An entrance hall led into a once-cosy living room, now filled with the detritus of abandonment. Thick layers of dust covered a sofa and dining table, both of which were coated in white sheets yellowed by age. A stone fireplace covered one wall, cold and unused for years, with a pile of old, dried-out firewood still stacked beside it.

To the left of the living room, the kitchen was in a similar state of disrepair, but Cameron and Ghost huddled around a lit stove as its flames cast dancing shadows upon the walls. Cameron jumped up and embraced Kane, and Kane held him tight. No words exchanged, two brothers relieved to be reunited and safe. The kitchen cabinets hung askew, contents long since stolen by time and wildlife. A film of grime covered the countertops, along with the remains of rodent activity. The rust stove stood as a monument to the meals once prepared there, its metal surface corroded and stained. Broken dishes and glass littered the floor, and Ghost stared up at Kane from beneath the shadow of her hoodie.

Kane swept the house just to be sure they were safe to spend the night. Upstairs, the bedrooms were echoes of their former selves. The first room's bed was a skeletal frame, its mattress sagging and torn with springs poking through the faded fabric. Mildew stained the wallpaper, and a broken window allowed the cool Pennine breeze to rustle tattered curtains. The second bedroom wasn't much better. A wardrobe lay fallen on its side, its doors hanging open, revealing nothing but dismal emptiness. He cleared the rooms and moved downstairs.

Outside, the gardens had become a wilderness. Once neatly trimmed, overgrown hedges spilled onto pathways and obscured the stone steps which wound around the garden leading to the front door. Wildflowers and weeds intermingled to create a chaotic tapestry of green, dotted with bursts of colour. Lofty, ancient trees of oak and beech stood like silent sentinels around the house, their branches swaying gently in the cool night breeze.

Kane sucked in the night air. This was only a respite, a break in the pursuit, a chance to seek the resolution he must find to destroy the Prometheus Code. The sense of age and ruin about the place was palpable, every creak and whisper of the old house a reminder of its long-forgotten purpose. Just like him, a relic from a distant age, a life that should be left in the past to rot and be forgotten.

He wandered to a thick oak trunk and gathered twigs and branches fallen in the mulch, trying to find dry ones to use in the stove for warmth. The place would do. It was safe. Or so Kane hoped.

CHAPTER TWENTY-TWO

Kyle Lavine stepped through the crack of an open front door. It creaked on rusting hinges, ajar just enough for him to sneak through without pushing the door further open, without making a noise that might alert his targets. He paused in the corridor, Sig pistol raised before his night vision goggles, scanning the stairs and entrance hall ahead of him for any signs of movement. All was still. He stalked along the broken tiled floor, careful not to step on any stiff leaves. Kyle pushed his back against the wall and scanned the living room. Seeing no sign of life, he entered the room and scanned it with his weapon until he was sure it was clear.

He exited the living room, each step a controlled movement with his weapon poised and ready to fire. A voice spoke in the kitchen, soft and hushed. A woman's voice. Kyle crept around the kitchen entrance and levelled his Sig at two figures sitting on dining chairs before a lit stove. Once wore a strange white mask, Cameron Jordan, and the other wore a baggy hoodie pulled up over her head. Kyle paused, his mind calculating his next course of action. Kill Cameron and he might never find the virus. Cameron could have the hard drive with him, or he may have hidden it somewhere secure. Kill the woman and he might frighten Cameron enough to cut through unnecessary questioning. In Kyle's experience, there was nothing like witnessing a skull being blown apart by gunfire to loosen a target's tongue.

Kyle readied himself and placed his finger on the curved trigger. He applied pressure, calm, ready to kill, poised to complete his mission with one squeeze of his weapon. In that split second, the back door heaved open, snapping Kyle from his focus. A man in a suit carrying an armful of wood sidled in.

"Cam, I brought wood for the..." the man began and then saw Kyle standing in the kitchen entrance wearing night vision goggles with a pistol in his hand. It could only be Jack Kane.

Kyle cursed to himself, indecision causing him to delay for a fraction of a second. Should he shoot the woman, Cameron, or Kane? In the game of death, to pause was to die. Kyle pointed the gun at Kane and fired, but just as his finger pulled the trigger, Kane tossed his armful of wood across the kitchen and Kyle's gun hand twitched in involuntary reflex. The shot went wide, slamming into the wall a foot to Kane's left.

Branches and twigs clattered against Kyle's outstretched arm and gun, and he batted them away. As he did so, Kane charged across the kitchen and leapt at him. Kyle fired again, but the shot missed, too high this time, and Kane thudded into him. Kyle fell backwards under the impact, his back smashed against the floor tiles, driving the air out of him in a great whoosh. Reflex curled him into a ball. Kane fell on top of him and punched Kyle hard in the jaw. Kyle's stomach and torso screamed with lack of air and his head spun from the punch. Panic made blood rush in Kyle's ears. Death was close, and the instinct to survive kicked in. Kyle tucked his elbow into his ribs, brought his gun close and fired it, hoping to shoot Kane at close range in the body, but again, the shot missed.

Another figure loomed from the kitchen, a man in a white mask. He ripped the gun from Kyle's fingers and booted him hard in the face. Kyle had read both men's files, and they were both former SAS operators, every bit the equal of Kyle's own Delta experience. If he didn't react quickly, Kyle was a dead man, and that realisation imbued his body with strength, the desperate strength of the dying, a fleeting, freakish strength to give a man one last chance to save his life. Kyle's head cleared, though the left side stung with pain. He pounced like a cornered animal. In one fluid motion, he flew at his enemies and whipped the combat knife from its sheath at the small of his back.

Kyle cannoned into Kane, driving him into the wall with a loud thud. He slashed his knife blade across Kane's chest and, as he jerked away from the blow, Kyle brought his arm around and stabbed Kane in the back. Not a deep blow, just an inch of steel tearing into Kane's flesh. Any more, and the blade could stick in muscle or tendon, so Kyle kept moving. Hot blood spattered his hand, wet and thick between his fingers.

"Stop!" Cameron Jordan bellowed from behind his mask, holding Kyle's Sig and bringing the weapon around to point at Kyle's chest. Kyle darted one way and lunged the other. Cameron naturally focused on the blood-stained knife hand, and Kyle attacked the masked man's blind side. He chopped the flat of his hand into Cameron's skull just above the blacked-out eye of his mask and Cameron staggered. The gun wavered and Kyle ducked beneath its muzzle and ripped Cameron's mask from his face with his left hand. Cameron fell to the floor tiles, clutching to hide his horrifically scarred face. It was a red, puckered, twisted mass of scar tissue. Cameron had no nose, just a hole in his face surrounded by scar tissue. His dead eye was cavernous and empty, and he looked like something from a nightmarish horror movie.

Kyle bolted for the back door. Better to live to strike again than to die here in a decrepit, mould-stinking house. He reached out for the door handle and the boom of a gun tore through the kitchen. Kyle staggered as a bullet tore into his side, knocking him to his knees with its terrible force. Pain flared there, like a horse had hoofed him. It wasn't the first time he had taken a bullet, but it was the first time he had fled from a target. Kyle bunched the muscles in his legs and surged forward, barging through the door and sprinting into the darkness, crashing into the undergrowth as he ran for his life.

CHAPTER TWENTY-THREE

"Jesus, Cam," Kane hissed through clenched teeth.

"I haven't done this for years," Cameron replied, holding up hands soaked in Kane's blood, a sewing needle and thread between his fingers. "I'm doing my best."

The bottom quarter of Cameron's mask had broken off when the assassin ripped it from his face and tossed it to the ground. He wore the mask, but his red, puckered fire-damaged skin showed through the broken section. Cameron dove for his mask the moment the killer disappeared through the back door, but not before Ghost glimpsed his face. She had gasped and Cameron cowered as he fitted the mask to his face. Even now, he kept his left side facing away and could not make eye contact with her.

Kane's survival tin lay open on the kitchen table. He carried the tin everywhere and had done since his days in the SAS. It held a knife with a serrated blade which could be used for cutting and also as a striker to start a fire, a wire saw with keyrings at each end, a flint and striker, waterproof matches, alcohol wipes, a tampon for starting fires or wound dressing, a button-sized compass, fishing line and hooks, a condom for carrying water, and a sewing kit for clothes and medical emergencies. The tin's contents were scattered across the dusty tabletop. An alcohol wipe soaked in blood, used to clean his knife wound, lay crumpled next to a cup of steaming tea.

Ghost winced and retched as Cameron passed the needle through the lips of Kane's chest wound. She tore her eyes away from the grizzly field medical procedure and worked on her laptop. She and Cameron had a way of using satellite connectivity to connect to the internet, so she continued the work of figuring out how to disable the Prometheus Code.

"They found us quickly. He wasn't MI5. Must have been an assassin sent by the Alliance."

"Too quickly. Keep still, Jack." Cameron leaned closer to the wound and made the last pass of the needle through Kane's skin. He tied off the thread and then moved around to Kane's back to start work on the stab wound.

"Is it deep?"

"Deep enough. You're a lucky bastard."

"We all are. He was about to take you out before I came in. We need to be more careful. The vehicles outside have been compromised. I winged him with the Glock, but he'll be back. And if the Alliance can find us, so can MI5 and anybody else who wants the virus."

"Things are worse than we thought," said Ghost, turning from her laptop. For the first time since Kane had met her, she took her hood down. She had elfin features and short hair dyed pure white.

"How they can be any worse? Everybody wants to kill us. We created a virus that might destroy Western civilisation as we know it, and we have nowhere to run!" said Cameron. He placed a hand on Kane's back to steady himself and began to sew the stab wound together.

Kane ground his teeth, fists bunched. The pain turned to

numbness and sweat pumped from his brow as Cameron put him back together after the fight with the assassin. "What happens now, Ghost?"

"I was working on the virus' code but couldn't figure out how to deconstruct the walls we created to protect anyone from disabling it. So, I went back into our old Successors' forum to see if there was anything in our chat that might help, from back when we were working on the code. I accessed Storm Shadow's emails and his hard drive, and it was him who tried to sell the Prometheus Code. It was Storm Shadow who alerted the Alliance to its existence and set off this entire chain of madness."

"Storm Shadow is Chen Li, right?" asked Kane, still trying to get to grips with the nicknames, or avatars, as hackers called them.

"It was Chen Li who persuaded us to build the Prometheus Code. He was so passionate about the need to change the world order. We were trying to make a change for good, to help re-balance wealth and help the impoverished and starving."

"I know all that," Kane snapped, anger in his voice. Whatever their original intentions, the Successors had created a weapon. "What have you found out?"

"So when I trawled Storm Shadow's messages, I came across an encrypted communication channel. He had meticulously planned the sale of the Prometheus Code. Storm Shadow had initiated contact, reaching out to an alliance of foreign governments like North Korea, Iran, Al-Qaeda, and China. The anti-NATO, if you like. Storm Shadow made the initial contact through a dark web forum frequented by state-sponsored hackers and intelligence operatives. Each party maintained their cover by using anonymised aliases and handled the negotiations with the utmost secrecy."

"This just keeps getting better." Kane turned his head to

Cameron. "What were you thinking?"

"I didn't know he was talking to the fucking anti-NATO, did I?"

Kane turned back to Ghost. "Carry on."

"Shadow's primary contact within the Alliance was a figure who refers to himself as Hydra. From what I can see from their various exchanges, Hydra is part of a high-ranking North Korean cyber-warfare unit. Hydra and Storm Shadow took their communications off the dark web and used secure, encrypted emails and a specialised messaging app that self-destructed messages once read. Luckily for us, Shadow kept copies of those messages in his personal records. He agreed to sell the Prometheus Code, and the price was fifty million dollars, to be transferred upon exchange via a complex web of cryptocurrency transactions designed to evade detection by inter-nation financial watchdogs.

"As you know, Cam, we agreed to store the virus itself on an unassuming external hard drive. We thought that was the best way to protect it. We aren't stupid, despite what you might think, Kane. A mundane piece of tech would avoid suspicion, and I honestly thought we would just shelve it. It was a task I enjoyed completing, and even though we all bought into Storm Shadow's ideology, I could never hurt anyone."

"Do the messages say how he planned to give the virus to Hydra? No virus, no cash."

"They planned to exchange the device at a covert meeting at a neutral location, a derelict warehouse on the edge of Amsterdam. The plan was foolproof, but as you know better than me, the world is full of untrustworthy bastards and things took an unexpected turn. The Alliance obviously wanted the Prometheus Code to do harm against the West, and equally obviously wanted to secure it without paying fifty million dollars to a hacker nerd with no experience of international espionage. Storm Shadow feared their betrayal and put a contingency plan in place. He sent the hard drive to you, Cameron, and I can tell from his data and search history that he knew you were a former SAS special forces soldier. Perhaps he thought you might fare better against the Alliance than he."

"But if he was going to Amsterdam to get his money, why send the virus to Cameron?"

"I can't find anything about that in his records. Perhaps he planned to fly to the UK first and pick it up? Who knows?"

"Did they come for him? Is Storm Shadow still alive?"

"He's vanished. Could be dead, or simply disappeared."

"At least we know it was Chen Li who went rogue. What about your other Successor friend? I can't remember his jolly pirate name."

"Viper?"

"That's it. Where is he, or she?"

"Gone quiet. Probably shitting himself," said Cameron. "Did Shadow tell Hydra about the EMP?"

"Not that I can see," replied Ghost. "He mentioned the need to reset electronic systems once the virus is deployed, explaining that the reboot of every banking system would trigger their deletion. The virus itself only corrupts systems through the interbank lending networks. The code then kicks in after reboot and wipes everything. All financial records, debt, bank accounts, gone."

"I don't understand," Kane gritted out, the last word elongated and high-pitched as Cameron tied off his last stitch and tugged at the stab wound.

"We built the virus so that it needs an EMP device to take out London's power momentarily. The banking system would never come back to life. Prometheus needs the reboot to kill it, and then our plan was to replace that system with transparent crypto, making everyone equal, destroying the establishment and making room for a new world order."

"I know what your crazy aim was, but tell me more about the EMP?"

Ghost fixed Kane with an angry stare, looked up him and down as though he were a piece of dogshit. "You know what an EMP is, right?"

"Yes, you've explained that before. And I know why you needed to kill London's power. But an EMP of that magnitude doesn't exist, and you lot might be brilliant hackers, but that's pure science, physics, invention, actual new technology."

"A company has developed an electromagnetic pulse device powerful enough to cripple London's entire infrastructure. Ironically, they are based in London's tech district. Zenith Technologies. A cutting-edge tech company, at the forefront of cyber-security and defence technology."

"You sound like you work for their sales team."

"I got that off their website. They must have links to the British military, or are shit-scared of an attack. I checked out their headquarters, and it's a fucking fortress. Ultra-modern security. Reflective glass encases the entire building, with biometric scanners and armed guards stationed at every entry point. Surveillance systems mounted on every corner, advanced AI-driven security system-controlled access to research and development and other sensitive areas. Their prized possession is their revolutionary EMP device, and they house it in a subterranean lab protected by reinforced steel doors and a network of sensors designed to detect any unauthorised access."

"How did you guys plan to get your hands on the EMP?"

"We were going to steal it." She said the words so matter-of-factly that Kane sniggered, despite his wounds. She glanced at Cameron for support.

"Our plan didn't really get beyond the development of Prometheus, and that we would somehow steal the EMP. We had rough ideas about how to do it, but never really got into the detail."

"It's safe to assume, then, that the Alliance will also want the EMP. Once they figure out that they need it to make Prometheus viable," said Kane. "Have you figured out how to destroy the virus yet?"

"No," answered Ghost, crossing her arms defiantly. "We built it so it couldn't be destroyed. We already told you about the escrow file preventing its destruction. Each of us worked on their own part of the code so that no one Successor had the power to understand the entire construct. It takes time to unpick."

"But can you unpick it?"

"We hope so," said Cameron.

"Let's get some rest for a few hours and move on. This place is compromised, and we need to find new vehicles. Our friend with the knife will be back to finish what he started."

"I don't think I could sleep in this place anyway," said Ghost. "Wait, what's that noise?"

Kane stood up, cocking his head as if the movement would increase his capacity to hear.

"Shit," hissed Cameron, hearing the sound at the same time as Kane. The distinctive whump-whump of a helicopter. "Chopper."

"They've come to kill us," said Kane. "Get your kit together and follow me. Cameron, arm yourself. It's go time."

CHAPTER TWENTY-FOUR

Kane pulled on his shirt and tucked the Glock into his trousers. As Cameron and Ghost closed their laptops and quickly gathered their tech equipment together, Kane grabbed the duffel bag he had taken from Cameron's lock-up. Inside was a Glock 43 and a Glock 19, a signal-blocking device, a communication bodypack with press-to-talk earpiece microphones, one flashbang grenade, a tactical vest, and a Colt Canada C8 carbine rifle, plus spare ammunition magazines.

"Put this on," he instructed, tossing the body armour vest to Ghost. She caught it and Cameron helped her fit it properly. "Are we ready?"

"Ready as we'll ever be," Cameron replied.

"Take the rifle, Cam, and a Glock." Kane handed Cameron the Colt Canada C8 and the Glock 43. Cameron checked the rifle and Kane tossed him a magazine and a spare. Cameron loaded the ammunition with a series of clicks and tucked the Glock into the back of his trousers.

Kane threw the bag over his shoulder and looked out of the broken window. The chopper thrummed in the darkness, but Kane couldn't see it from the window, which meant it was still far out in the forest or beyond one of the Pennine peaks, or it was coming from the front end of the abandoned house.

"Out of the back door. Let's go," he ordered. Kane had thirteen rounds in the Glock and a spare magazine in his pocket. Holding the pistol in his right hand and doing his best to ignore the tearing, throbbing pain from his knife wounds, he burst through the back door and out into the overgrown garden. Cameron took the rear and Ghost ran in between them, body armour on and head down.

Kane led the trio through the overgrown grass and weeds around the house's west side. They were deep in the Pennine mountains, so trekking through the brush wasn't a viable means of escape. Kane and Cameron could survive out there, utilising their old training to hike through the barren highlands and forest-covered valleys until they reached civilisation, but not Ghost. She would struggle and that would slow them down. MI5 would have teams out searching for them, teams with just as much training as Cameron and Kane, and with better equipment. They needed a vehicle to get away. The Yamaha wouldn't do, and so it had to be the old Vauxhall Astra Cameron had parked at the building's front.

They huddled together, skirting the house's wall around a side entrance. Kane booted a rusting barbeque grill out of the way and stepped over a coiled green hosepipe. The helicopter's hypnotic sound became a roar as its rotor blades blew leaves from the trees around them like a gale-force wind. Kane paused at the edge of the house, and a chopper came from the night sky like a dragon. It swooped over the treeline, sending the plants and trees into turmoil. Four go-fast ropes tumbled from its open side door and thumped on the front garden grass. The low, rhythmic thumping of the rotor blades became deafening as the Dauphin matte-black helicopter hovered before the house.

"Move, move!" Kane bawled above the din. At any moment,

armed soldiers would come sliding down those ropes armed and ready to kill. Kane had done it himself countless times, and he knew the drill. Once they hit the ground, they would unleash the uncompromising power of military force and Kane didn't want to be on the end of their MP5 automatic weapon fire with only a Glock in his hand. It was easy to picture the squad inside the Dauphin. They would be in black tactical gear, each operator equipped with state-of-the-art weaponry, suppressed HK416 assault rifles or MP5s, Glock 19 sidearms, and combat knives sheathed at their sides. They would have lightweight body armour, communication earpieces, and modular lightweight-load carry-equipment vests packed with extra magazines, grenades, and breaching tools. Night vision goggles would be securely strapped to their helmets.

Kane set off at a dead run, sprinting between the ropes, keeping low as the wind from the chopper buffeted him like a hurricane. Figures loomed above, surging from the helicopter beneath the night sky. The Astra was ten paces away and Kane covered the distance rapidly as soldiers began to make their descent down the ropes. Three paces from the vehicle, he turned and knelt, pointing the Glock at the ropes.

"Get the car moving," he yelled to Ghost as she ran alongside him. "We'll hold them off."

She stared at him for a moment, terror drawing her features downwards, her mouth open. Then Ghost understood, and she bolted for the driver's door. Two men reached the bottom of the ropes and turned to face Kane. They wore night vision goggles and black fatigues so that he couldn't tell if they were British Army, an MI5 hit team, or a private military force. It didn't matter. They hadn't come to ask politely for the Prometheus Code. This was a kill squad. A short burst rattled from a suppressed MP5 and Kane fired two shots in response but missed his target.

"Fuck these pricks," Cameron growled and blasted a burst of automatic fire from the Colt Canada C8. The two enemy soldiers fell, bullets smacking into the armour plates on their chests. Cameron turned his rifle upwards and shot at the chopper, bullets sparking as they peppered its undercarriage. The chopper shook; four more soldiers made the slide from its open door, and then it veered away. The helicopter banked to the left, dipped its nose and soared away above the trees; its pilot desperate to get away from Cameron's gunfire.

"Give me the Colt, you get in," Kane roared above the din.

Cameron handed him the rifle and jumped in beside Ghost. The ignition started up and Ghost brought the Astra alongside Kane. He fired a burst at the four soldiers and they rolled away as they hit the ground, coming up and firing their own weapons. The soil and grass around Kane exploded as bullets ripped through the turf and two rounds clanged against the car's bodywork.

"Come on, Jack!" Cameron bawled and the rear side door flew open. Kane backed towards the Astra and fired another burst. He turned and leapt into the vehicle and Ghost gunned the accelerator. The Astra roared into life, tyres screeching as it turned in the driveway. She switched the headlights on just as the enemy fired on the car. The window beside Kane exploded into thousands of glittering fragments and another bullet thumped into the door. As the car turned, the headlight beams shone on the four attackers, and they ducked their heads violently as they tore at their night vision goggles. The bright light would make the view from the goggles completely green, rendering them unable to see where the next gunshot came from.

Ghost used the momentary break from withering gunfire to force the Astra in a wide turn, tyres cutting through the long grass and throwing up clods of earth as she locked the steering wheel. The car turned, its back end slewing in the soil, and then raced up the driveway and out into the night. Gunfire crackled behind them, and Kane leaned out of the window to return fire. Ghost screamed as the car reached the end of the driveway and turned out of the gate because two more enemy soldiers leapt from the gate, waiting there to block any attempt at escape. They opened fire and battered the Astra with a hail of bullets.

The windscreen shattered, and Ghost screamed again.

"Keep your foot down!" Cameron thundered and opened fire with his Glock, shooting through the broken windscreen.

Adrenaline pulsed around Kane's body, and he fired a burst from the Colt. One soldier at the gate fell away with a bullet in his thigh. Blood misted the air and the sound of gunfire boomed inside the Astra, roaring in Kane's ears. Ghost sped away, gunning the Astra along the country road. Wind rushed in through the broken windows and the sound of gunfire receded behind them.

Kane turned and peered out of the rear window, but could see nothing in the darkness. They had escaped for now, but every hour their situation worsened, the lengths to which their enemies were prepared to go to becoming increasingly brutal. He sat back against the back seat and winced, holding his hand to the aching knife wound in his chest. Kane's back throbbed, and even though Cameron had cleaned and stitched the stab wound, Kane could still feel the cold steel inside his flesh ripping and tearing at his body.

A rumbling in his pocket distracted him. Kane carefully set the rifle down on the seat next to him. Cameron guided Ghost as she sped along the dark mountain road. Kane took the phone out of his pocket and answered the call.

"Hello?" he said.

"Jack?" replied Craven's gruff voice.

"It's me, Frank. There's a lot of background noise here." The car was like a wind tunnel with air whooshing through its smashed windscreen and door windows.

"Barbara's gone, Jack."

"What?"

"It's Barb. She's dead."

CHAPTER TWENTY-FIVE

Craven sat in Barbara's favourite chair, squeezing the arms with his powerful hands as though he could find some sense of her touch in the fabric where she had spent many afternoons reading, knitting, talking and laughing in the Spanish early morning sun. Light shone in through the wide, foldable patio windows and warmed Craven's face. He closed his eyes, fighting back a lump in his throat.

She was gone. The love of his life, his best friend, lover, the woman he had shared his life with. It had been a long night at the hospital, harrowing and hollowing. Danny and Kim were still asleep in their bedrooms, having only gone to bed in the early hours. Craven had not slept. Memories haunted him, regrets, fleeting images of happy times, and sad ones, too. He wished he had worked less when they were young and spent more time with her. Craven had worked hard as a young policeman, rising to detective, enjoying the life. In those days, it was common to work long shifts and then head to the pub for six or seven pints before returning home to collapse into bed. Now, he couldn't even remember the names of the men he had drank with, with whom he had wasted so much time. It had seemed so important then, to stay out with men he'd known for a fleeting moment in his life, whilst Barbara waited home alone.

Not completely alone though, for she held her grief close like a lover. She had lost babies during pregnancy, dreams of motherhood cruelly turning to ashes in her womb. An unfulfilled desire which hung about Barbara's neck like a millstone. If anybody deserved children, it was her. What a mother Barbara would have made. Instead, she lived a lonely life. She had plenty of friends, but the longing for a child was a cavernous hole. Craven had wanted it too, perhaps not as fiercely as Barbara, but he had shared her longing. Which, he supposed, was why they both doted on Kane's children.

Barbara passed away peacefully in her sleep. Craven had been out food shopping with the children when the call came. A Spanish doctor asking Craven to get to the Seville hospital urgently because Barbara's condition had suddenly deteriorated whilst they awaited yet more test results. He had left the shopping cart mid-aisle and raced to the hospital to find Barbara drowsy but smiling. Craven had held her hand, her touch warm, eyes afraid. The lump in his throat returned, and Craven couldn't bite it back. For the first time he could remember, he wept. His broad shoulders shuddered, and fat tears rolled down his rugged cheeks.

He had thought she would live forever, that the cancer would go and they would enjoy many years of retirement, talking, walking, watching their favourite television shows. Just being. But now she was gone. Lying cold on a slab somewhere, waiting for the bureaucracy work to complete so Craven could bring her home to England. Craven had ex-pat health insurance. His contact at the insurance company said it would take five to seven days to return Barbara's body to the UK. Then it would be a funeral close to where they had grown up in the north west.

There was danger in returning to the UK after all that had happened with him and Jack Kane in recent years, but Craven didn't care. He couldn't bury his great love in Spain. She had to rest close to her own long-dead mother and father, in the place where she was born, where they had lived so long together. Not always happily, for there had been many arguments, many moments when their marriage had creaked and groaned under the weight of years, disappointment at work and the allure of the pub. But in their later years, Craven had appreciated Barb more and more, and now she was gone.

For a fleeting moment, staring out at the Spanish sun, Craven wondered if it would be better if he went to join Barb, wherever she was now. Of anyone he had ever met, Barb would surely have gone on to a better place, if such a place existed. What was the point of carrying on if she wasn't around to share life with? His existence seemed pointless. He could live for another ten, perhaps twenty years alone, pining for his dead wife, his soul mate. Craven wondered what life had left for him. Would he end up alone and dribbling in an old person's home with nobody to come and visit him? Eating apple sauce and watching re-runs of Last of the Summer Wine?

The problem was simple. Craven was alive, and Barb wasn't. That was it. Their life together was over. He cuffed the tears from his face with his shirt sleeve. They would fly her body back to England for a funeral in a week's time. He didn't care about the risks. There was no reason to fear death any more. He would welcome it, in fact. Craven could never take his own life. For one, he knew that if it turned out that Barb was watching over him, she would have been furious with him for not picking up the pieces and living his life to the full. But if he died at the hands of his enemies, of the men who at that very moment hunted Jack across England, Craven thought - perhaps that wouldn't be so bad.

He groaned and pushed himself up from the chair. He went to his safe and fished out the passports Kane had left for him and the kids, not their own passports, of course. Craven would travel as Bob Paisley and the kids as Kim and Daniel Paisley. He'd get a flight into Manchester or Liverpool airport today and make the funeral arrangements. Then, he would join Kane's fight, put himself in harm's way, see what happened.

At least Kane still needed him. Jack had been desperately upset when Craven had broken the news of Barbara's death, but he was in deep shit and an extra pair of hands would help. That might even help Craven take his mind off his bereavement. Maybe. Kim didn't really understand what had happened to her Auntie Barbara, and Danny took the news badly, withdrawing deeper into himself, sullen and terse. Kim knew that Auntie Barbara was gone, just like her mother had gone. Craven thought her mother's loss might help the girl get to grips with Barbara's death, but she had asked when her Auntie Barbara would be back, and Craven didn't have the heart to go through it all with her again.

Time to go back to England. Arrange a funeral. Get into the bullets and mayhem with Jack Kane.

CHAPTER TWENTY-SIX

Kyle Lavine shuddered with pain and shivered with hate. He stared at himself in the hotel room mirror, his pale skin slathered in dark blood like he had bathed in it. The gunshot had ripped through his side like an arrow-tipped jackhammer, and he'd thought he must die as he fled the crumbling shithole of a house in Jerkwater, England. But he was a former Delta soldier, and he was Kyle Lavine. He was not an easy man to kill.

The run to the parked BMW occurred in a pain-induced daze. Kyle had reached the car without fully knowing how he had got there. The first aid kit in the boot contained a gauze, heavy wound-compression bandage, so Kyle had pressed the dressing against his wound and wrapped it tight with a bandage. That patch-up job had been enough to allow him to drive away from the Snake Pass and find a 24-hour pharmacy using his phone's map app. A sad-faced Asian man had sold him pincers, bandages, nylon sutures, antiseptic liquid and painkillers.

Kyle ground his teeth and picked up the pincers from the once white, but now blood-crimson sink. He curled his thumb and forefinger around the scissor-like implement and dug the tip into his wound. Kyle moaned and shook his head at the impossible pain. He dug around in the flesh above his hip, just as he had three times already since checking into the motorway services hotel. He had to get the remnants of the bullet out or the wound would become infected and rot him from the inside out. Kyle didn't have the luxury of checking into a UK hospital accident and emergency department to avail of the famous National Health Service and its free healthcare. Any report of a bullet wound meant a police report, and Kyle didn't need any sort of entanglement with the authorities.

His reflection in the mirror was grim. Sweat matted his light blonde hair against his forehead and his eyes burned with red-rimmed intensity. He removed the pincers and tossed them into the sink. He looked again at what he had bought, scattering the supplies with his blood-crusted fingers. Small tweezers, antiseptic wipes, a sewing needle, medical tape and a small bottle of rubbing alcohol. Kyle's hands shook, and he clenched his fists. He didn't have time to let pain or fear compromise his mission.

The bullet's entry point was a ragged hole oozing gelatinous blood. He soaked a white hand towel in the rubbing alcohol and pressed it to the wound, biting down on his belt to muffle his screams. It was excruciating, a white-hot flare threatening to overwhelm him. Kyle grabbed the tweezers, metal tips gleaming beneath the bathroom light. He probed the wound again, breathing hitching with each movement. Kyle thought he would pass out, and then the tweezers found two small bullet fragments. He pulled them free of his body, and though the fragments were tiny as they clattered into the porcelain sink, it felt like he had dragged an iron girder through his body.

Kyle poured more rubbing alcohol on a clean cloth and disinfected the wound, vision blurring as involuntary tears of pain rolled down his face. The wound was as clean and as safe as it could be. But it was still an open angry gash that needed to be closed. Kyle took a swig of whiskey from a bottle in his bag to still his hands. He settled himself and threaded the needle with nylon sutures, using his teeth to help knot the thread.

He positioned himself in front of the mirror, needle poised above the wound. Taking a deep breath, Kyle pushed the needle through his skin, the biting pain making him gasp. He worked methodically, each stitch a triumph over the agony. It was a slow and torturous process, his fingers slick with blood, making the needle slippery and difficult to control. Each time he pulled a thread tight, he whispered the name of Jack Kane. Kyle's body was drenched in sweat and his face turned ashen by the time he tied off the last stitch.

He covered the wound with gauze pads and secured them with medical tape. He took a moment to check the wound. The stitches were crude but functional and would keep it closed for now. Infection was a risk, but he was in a risky line of work. When he got back to the USA, he would check into a private healthcare facility, into a private room, rest and recover. That would come after Kane and Cameron were dead and the Prometheus Code was in the hands of his client. Kyle washed his hands and rinsed out the blood-stained sink and wall tiles, the smell of iron and antiseptic cloying in the air.

Exhausted, Kyle staggered to the bed and collapsed onto the mattress. He knew he needed rest to let his body recover, at least a few hours to regain some strength for the fight to come. The painkillers he'd taken earlier began to kick in and dull the pain, allowing him to slip into a fitful sleep.

Hours later, Kyle awoke with the sun streaming in through the hotel blinds, his side throbbing but the pain now manageable. He sat up gingerly, testing his mobility. The wound and the surrounding muscles were stiff and sore, each movement a reminder of the injury. But he could move, not enough to perform any yoga or any of his customary exercises, but he could force himself onwards. Kyle stood and inspected the bandage in the mirror and checked for any fresh bleeding.

He gathered his gear, carefully placing his weapons and

remaining medical supplies into a bag. He couldn't afford to waste a day resting in the hotel. Kyle had a job to do, and despite the pain and exhaustion, his resolve was unshaken. He had a mission to complete, and a bullet wound would not stop him. He'd been shot before, stabbed, blown up, and gassed. Kyle was a warrior. He forced himself to walk without a limp as he strode to his car, ready to resume the hunt.

CHAPTER TWENTY-SEVEN

"Where the fuck did you find this place?" asked Craven, staring at the loft-like apartment's high ceilings, steel factory lights hanging from long cords, exposed brick walls, and varnished ceiling timbers. Someone had gone to considerable trouble to make the place look old and rugged to match modern tastes, someone with too much money and too much time on their hands.

"Airbnb," Cameron replied. Kane's old army buddy wore the same white mask as usual, only now it was grimy and discoloured, with the bottom portion missing to reveal the scorched skin beneath.

"Is that supposed to mean something to me, lad?"

"It's an app used to rent properties for short periods of time," said Kane, busy making sandwiches on the white granite kitchen worktop. "Did anyone figure out the Wi-Fi yet?"

Kane had collected Craven and the kids from Manchester airport in a rented Volvo XC60 jeep and brought them to the apartment in Liverpool city centre. It had been a strange reunion in the airport's arrival lounge. Kim had whooped to her daddy in joyous greeting and ran into his arms. Kane had lifted her and held her close with a rare smile on his face. Danny had moped over with his head down and AirPods in and had reluctantly embraced his father when Jack pulled him close.

"Frank, I'm so sorry," Kane had said, and shook Craven's hand.

Everybody was sorry, but it didn't make any difference. Barbara was still dead. They had driven along the M62 motorway from Manchester to Liverpool in an awkward silence. Kane trying to make small talk with Danny about gaming, his son responding with monosyllabic one-word answers. Kim was full of chatter about the flight, the plane and its food, how she was looking forward to returning to her school in Seville to see her new friends. Craven had kept silent, staring out of the car window at the signs bearing the names of familiar towns. Warrington, Widnes, St Helens, Macclesfield, Runcorn. Places he and Barbara had visited, had friends in, lived in. Old memories of a life behind him.

Cameron and the woman Kane and Cameron insisted Craven call Ghost, even when he asked what her proper name was, had been waiting in the apartment pounding away at their laptops, talking a tech language Craven would never understand. The apartment was twice the size of Craven's Spanish home, a two-storey loft with spacious pine wood floors, leather sofas, and a monstrous television and a music system you could control from your phone, apparently.

"Who is Ghost, again?" Craven asked, walking up to stand closer to Kane in the kitchen area so they could talk quietly.

Kane took another slice of bread from the plastic-wrapped loaf and laid it down on a breadboard emblazoned with the target symbol synonymous with British mod culture. He nodded towards Cameron and Ghost, heads huddled together at the far end of the dining table.

"She's a hacker friend of Cameron's. She's with us for now,

whilst we try to sort this mess out for Cameron."

"Sounds like a right fucking mess, though." Craven took a custard cream biscuit from a pack lying on the worktop and dipped it into his coffee. "They made the virus. Now every dangerous bastard in the world wants it. Will kill for it. How are we going to get out of this one?"

"Destroy it."

"Great, chuck the bloody thing out of the window then, or throw it in the River Mersey and let's have done with it."

"It's not that simple, Frank. Trust me. They need to crack its code. To do that, they need time. We have to buy them that time."

"I'm sorry for bringing the kids into this shit-storm." Craven was sorry, but he had no choice. He didn't want to put Danny and Kim in harm's way, but he had to be in the UK when Barb's body finally arrived for the funeral.

"Forget about that, Frank. What choice did you have? What's happening with Barbara's funeral?"

Craven cleared his throat and drained the coffee left in his mug. "I have to wait for an official date for her repatriation. Once I have the date, I can arrange the funeral."

"Let me know if you need some help with the arrangements."

"What are you going to do, stop your mission to save the world from financial implosion, potential onset of anarchy and the collapse of every pillar of civilisation to arrange some fucking flowers for a funeral in Wigan?"

"You have been listening, then?"

"I'm not as daft as I look, am I? Actually, don't answer that. What can I do to help?"

"Danny?" Kane called over to the sitting area. Danny peered

around the black leather sofa with a frustrated look on his face. “Come and bring these sandwiches over for you and your sister.”

Danny took an age to peel himself off the sofa with the longest huff Craven had ever heard a human being emit. He walked slowly towards his father, shoulders slumped and head lolling like a prisoner going to death row. He took the two plates without saying a word. Craven opened his mouth to tell the boy to use his manners but thought better of coming between father and son. Danny was a polite boy, and there had been no problems with his manners in Spain. But now that Danny was in his father’s presence, good manners and polite behaviour seemed to have gone out of the window.

“If you want to help,” said Kane, “you can help me figure out what to do next.”

“Let’s get on with it, then.”

“We have enemies on all sides. MI5 tried to double-cross us, an assassin tried to kill us, and a kill team came in a Dauphin helicopter to take us out. I’m not sure exactly how many enemies we have at this point, but they aren’t going away. We need to buy Cameron and Ghost time to figure out how to destroy the Prometheus Code.”

“What are the options?”

“That’s what we need to figure out.”

“What about a diversion? A distraction to draw them out? Make them chase us whilst the boffins over there work their magic.”

“We could do that, Frank. But things will get heavy. Are you sure you’re up to it?”

“Up to it? You cheeky bastard. I was nicking gangsters when you were in short pants eating fucking Wham bars and flying saucers from a 10p mix.”

"I don't mean it that way. Barb's only just passed. Maybe you need some time out to process it all. To grieve. I know, Frank. I remember what it was like when Sally passed. I never took that time."

"What I need is to keep busy. Keep my mind occupied, and if we can find a couple of bad guys to take out the pain on, more's the better."

"Fair enough. There is something we can do, something to keep the dogs on our tail. The Prometheus Code only works in conjunction with an EMP. There is only one EMP in the world big enough to do the job, and it's in London."

"Sounds complicated. What's this EMP thingamabob got to do with us?"

"You and I are going to travel to London and steal it."

"Steal it?"

"Anybody who wants the Prometheus Code must also obtain the EMP. So, they'll be watching it, perhaps seeking to steal it themselves. So we go to London, make sure our enemies know we're there, and steal it ourselves whilst Cameron and Ghost work on the virus code."

"Where is the EMP?"

"In a high-tech, ultra-secure tech lab in London with state-of-the-art surveillance. Strictly guarded by private security."

"Sounds like a piece of piss, then. All we have to do is break into a top-secret, maximum-security building, steal something which is presumably fucking huge, evade top-quality security guards, and get out of there before our heavily-armed enemies shoot us full of bullets."

"Exactly. Without getting killed."

"When do we leave?"

CHAPTER TWENTY-EIGHT

Kyle Lavine leaned against the door of his hotel room fifty miles outside the Snake Pass on the outskirts of Warrington, a town nestled between Liverpool and Manchester. The air was stale inside the room, with its walls of faded wallpaper, carpet old and stained. It was a weathered businessman's stay-over type of hotel. Cheap rooms used by companies on a budget with breakfast included. He shifted his weight and winced, the pain from his wound a constant reminder of his failure at the abandoned house.

Kyle had wanted to continue and try to pick up Kane and Cameron Jordan's trail, but his wound forced him to check into another hotel. The injury needed a fresh bandage, and he needed to rest. It was hard to concentrate on the task at hand with his gear unclean, tossed quickly into a bag. It nagged at him. His weapons needed cleaning, his clothes needed to be ironed and folded. He also needed to exercise, though his wound made that unlikely.

His phone buzzed in his pocket, the encrypted device signalling an incoming call. Kyle sighed. Only one client had its number. He knew who it would be. Kyle lifted the phone to his ear and answered the call. A distorted voice crackled through the speaker; the sound layered with digital static designed to obscure the caller's identity.

"Mr Mentzer," said his client's lawyer, using Kyle's alias. "Our mutual client required an update. The matter has become urgent. I have looped our client, codename Hydra, into this call."

"Very well," said Kyle. He straightened, forcing himself to focus. "The Prometheus Code slipped through my fingers. The target was more prepared and able than expected. I am tracking them now."

There was a pause, filled with ominous silence. "This is unacceptable," said a metallic-sounding, almost robotic voice, the frustration palpable even through the electronic distortion. "The Alliance is losing patience. We trusted you with this mission because of your reputation. So far, you have only delivered excuses."

Kyle tensed his jaw, his eyes narrowing. "I don't make excuses. I am relaying facts. Cameron Jordan is a former SAS soldier, working with a former MI6 assassin. This is not like stealing intel from a fat corporate CEO's laptop. This is war. I'm closing in on the target. They won't get far."

The voice on the other end of the phone was cold and unyielding. "You've already allowed MI5 to get too close. They obviously know about the virus now. If they recover it, everything we have planned will be at risk. Worse, if one of our enemies captures the Prometheus Code and turns its powers on Alliance countries, the consequences will be catastrophic."

A bead of sweat trickled down Kyle's temple. "I'm aware of the stakes and I never fail. I'll retrieve the virus."

Another voice, this one deeper and with a distinct accent, interrupted. "Do not underestimate the urgency of this situation, Mr Mentzer. We've invested too much to let this slip away now. You have forty-eight hours to recover the virus. Fail, and the Alliance will have to take more... drastic measures." Kyle recognised the voice from a previous contract. It was Jafari, an Iranian operative known for his ruthlessness.

Kyle knew what that meant. The Alliance wouldn't hesitate to eliminate him if they thought he was compromising the mission. Jafari himself might be the man to do it. "Understood. I'll have the Prometheus Code in my hand within forty-eight hours."

Hydra's voice returned, menacing, rattling and coded like a robot. "Remember. We are always watching. Do not disappoint us again."

The line went dead, leaving Kyle alone in the sour silence of his hotel room. He pocketed the phone, his mind racing. The pressure was mounting, and now the clock was ticking. He had to find Kane and Cameron Jordan, retrieve the Prometheus Code and deliver it to the Alliance before MI5 or another power could intervene. Failure was not an option; his own life could depend on it.

Kyle stripped off his shirt and examined his wound. He carefully peeled off the blood-stained gauze and applied a fresh dressing. He laid his weapons out on a clean towel on the room's desk, took every gun apart, cleaned the parts and reassembled them. Kyle took his clothes from his bag and plugged in the hotel room's small iron. Kyle ironed his shirts and underwear and used the trouser press to press his trousers. The process of cleaning, organising and restoring things to proper order cleansed him. Refocused him. He was in control again, the master of his own kingdom. Then he lay down on the bed and closed his eyes, alarm set for an hour's time. A little rest to recharge his wounded batteries, and then back to the hunt.

CHAPTER TWENTY-NINE

Kane stood over Cameron and Ghost's shoulders, his arms crossed and a frown creasing his face. Craven turned to him with a vacant look on his broad face, like a child at school being taught algebra for the first time. Cameron and Ghost flicked through images on their laptops, images of a secure facility in central London, demonstrating how impossible it was to break in and steal the EMP device.

"Just so we're clear," surmised Craven, stuffing his hands in his pockets, "you're basically saying we're fucked?"

"No," Ghost retorted, swinging around to him with a glint in her eye. "We are saying it's going to be difficult to get in there and steal it. That's all."

"Extremely difficult," added Cameron.

Kane glanced to the Airbnb's bedroom, where Danny and Kim watched YouTube videos on their iPads, headphones on and oblivious to the conversation. He had spent the night before watching a movie with them in the room, talking about Barbara's death, and the death of their mother. Danny had said little, but Kim appreciated the closeness and the chance to remember Barbara. Kim had cuddled into him, and Kane had held her tight. They both needed that closeness, and despite the roar of danger and the Prometheus Code spinning around his head, it was a much-needed moment of calm within the maelstrom.

Danny was distant, not wanting to talk much, and certainly not wanting to be held. Kane feared he was growing apart from his teenage son, if they had ever been close at all. He was past the age now when a father and son are as close as best friends, between the ages of nine and twelve, when all a son wants is for a father to play football with him, to take him to a game and watch him play. Kane was lucky, he thought, to have had some of those years with Danny whilst he was in the witness protection programme. Some good years, but not enough.

He remembered mornings when a ten-year-old Danny would get up in the morning and stumble into the kitchen bleary-eyed and warm from bed. He would fall into Kane's arms for a huge cuddle, and then Kane would make his breakfast. Sally was alive then and Kane had been out of the service. They were simpler times, happier times. But then a lightning bolt of guilt stabbed through him, because Kane remembered that through those years of hiding, working a factory job, living an idyllic family life, all he had yearned for was his old job. The action called to him: the thrill of combat, the exhilaration of a gun battle, the euphoria of defeating an enemy. He hated himself for it.

"I can see all of your pretty pictures and building schematics," said Craven. "But how are we actually going to break and steal the bloody thing?"

They had agreed to steal the EMP device from its inventors' top-secret lab in London. Kane and Craven would draw attention away from Cameron and Ghost whilst they worked on cracking the Prometheus Code and disabling the device. Without the EMP, an enemy could never deploy it, and all they needed now was a plan on how to pull it off.

"What we are showing you are the blueprints and security schematics of Zenith Technologies, a high-security data centre and laboratory in central London," Cameron informed them, his voice serious, all business.

"I can see that. But can you explain to me how we are supposed to get in and bloody steal it?" Craven replied. Craven had thrown himself into the work, spending hours catching up on recent events and doing his best to understand what the Prometheus Code was and how Cameron and Ghost were involved. There was no talk of Barbara now, and no time for Craven to fall deeper into his grief, which the old detective welcomed. A distraction was as good as a cure.

"OK," Ghost exhaled. She ran her thin fingers through her short white hair and moved aside so Craven could lean in closer to peer at her computer screen. "Zenith Technologies is one of the most secure facilities in the country. Which is bad luck for us. But this isn't my first rodeo, so I spent most of last night pulling their systems apart. They've got multiple layers of security, each one more formidable than the last. But Cameron and I have worked up a plan for how we'll get through each one. And when I say we, I mean you two."

Kane gave her a nod to proceed. Ghost had opened up a little now that they were in the safety of a warm apartment with lots of coffee and no bullets flying past her head. Recent events had left her shaken; her former world of perceived safety sat behind a computer screen shattered by a storm of violence. She worked with her hood down, eyes bright and clever, piercings in her ears jingling as she turned her head.

She tapped at the backlit keys on her laptop and brought the device closer to Kane and Craven, displaying a video of a tall, modern-looking building. "First," she continued, "the immediate perimeter is guarded by a high-security fence patrolled by guards armed with tasers, pepper spray, and batons. The guard rotation changes every four hours, and we've pinpointed a fifteen-minute window when there's a blind spot in the patrol pattern. During that window, we'll cut the power to a small section of the fence by hacking into their server. Once the fence is down, you will slip through and make your way to the rear service entrance."

"Where they take deliveries? A staff entrance?" asked Craven.

"Exactly," Cameron confirmed, the laptop's glow reflecting on his mask. "The service entrance is guarded by a biometric scanner and a keypad requiring a unique passcode. We'll need to clone the fingerprints of one of their senior staff members. Ghost and me think that Dr Harris, the head of research, is our best bet. We've watched his movements back on old CCTV footage and he's a bit of a coffee fiend. Every morning, he goes to a nearby café. You will lift his prints from his coffee cup, and we'll create a perfect replica using a latex mould."

"Good," said Cameron. "Where do we get the latex?"

"There's an art and hobby shop in the Albert Dock shopping arcade close to this apartment. They sell sets for making dinosaurs and Disney princesses, that sort of thing. One of those will do."

"Dad?" called Kim from the bed.

"Yes, Kim?"

"Are you talking about Disney princesses?"

"We are as it happens. Uncle Frank says Ariel is his favourite."

"Really, Uncle Frank? Mine is Moana."

"Don't listen to your dad, love. His head's full of marmalade where his brain should be."

Kim laughed and put her headphones back on.

"For the passcode," Cameron continued, "I've intercepted their internal communications. The code changes daily, but we've managed to decrypt the algorithm they use."

"We?" questioned Ghost with an arched eyebrow.

"All right, you decrypted the algorithm. We'll have the current code on the day of the operation."

Kane leaned in to get a better look at the schematics. "And once we're inside?"

Ghost's eyes sparkled with excitement, and she exchanged a look with Cameron, a smile playing at the corners of her mouth. "Inside is where the real challenge begins. The interior is monitored by a network of cameras and motion sensors. You'll need to stay in the blind spots and use a signal jammer to disrupt the cameras intermittently. Jam them too long and the system triggers an alert. You should have a window of ten seconds to move each time we jam the system."

Craven grimaced. "Sounds tight."

"It is," Cameron admitted. "This isn't like breaking into some backwater office to steal papers from a safe. We are talking state-of-the-art security here. One wrong move and you guys are finished. You'll have security guards swarming all over you like a rash."

"Thanks for the reassurance."

"Do we have a signal jammer for the cameras?" asked Kane.

"You snatched one with my gear from the lock-up. I thought you'd only go for the guns, but you actually grabbed some useful kit. The jammer we have is for Wi-Fi and phone signals, but I've reprogrammed it to knock out any camera within twenty feet, but it's only effective for ten seconds," Cameron replied.

"Jesus, you two have been busy," Craven marvelled. "It's

making me tired just listening to you."

"It's your turn next, Frank. Let's just hope we can crack this code before they find us."

"Can you do it?"

"We are getting closer, but it's like trying to navigate a labyrinth with a surprise around every corner. But back to the plan. After the network of cameras, it's the security checkpoints. Each one requires a keycard for access. We'll need to get the cards from three specific managers: the head of security, the operations manager and Dr Harris. Once you have the cards, we can clone them using a high-frequency skimmer. We'll use these clones to bypass the checkpoints."

"We can lift Dr Harris' card whilst we get his fingerprint at the coffee shop. But what about the other two?" Kane queried.

"I've dug up some background info on both of them. The day before you go in, get hold of the cards and run them through the scanner app, which I'll put on your phone. I'll generate the clone, and you'll use that via your phone to gain access."

"We need to do this ASAP. Frank and I will travel down to London today and try to lift the cards tonight and tomorrow. So, we'll pull this operation off on the day after tomorrow."

"That gives us forty-eight hours to work through the Prometheus Code. What about Danny and Kim?"

"They'll have to stay with you, Cam. I can't bring them with me to London."

"I'm not your babysitter," snapped Ghost. "I don't have time to be nanny daycare. Look after your own kids."

"Hang on a second," Craven interjected, raising his voice. "He saved your life. You might have got away with a bad attitude so far in your life, but don't think a crew cut and a few piercings cut any ice with us. You'll do whatever we tell you to. You built this fucking thing, and we are the bastards who are trying to fix it. If you don't like it, piss off and try your luck out there on your own."

"Maybe I will. Seems like you need me more than I need you."

"Really? All right then. But before you toddle off into the big wide world, have a think about what you'll do next time a chopper full of highly-trained special forces soldiers drop on your fucking house. Or when a ruthless assassin shoves a gun in your face at the local Starbucks?"

Ghost glanced at Kane and cast her eyes back to the laptop, cheeks flushed red. Kane doubted anyone had spoken to her like that before, but perhaps the hard lesson would do her good.

"It's no problem, Jack," said Cameron. "The kids will be safe here with us."

"Thanks. Once we are past the checkpoints, what's next?"

"Then you're at the last layer of security. The biometric vault door. It requires a retinal scan and a voice recognition passphrase."

"You mean we need someone's eye and their voice to get through it?" asked Craven.

"Technically speaking, yes. Ghost found Dr Harris' retinal data stored in the facility's back-up database. We hacked it and created a contact lens that mimics his retina pattern. It's one of Ghost's spare lenses and we only have one. So don't lose it. I've synthesised his voice using samples from intercepted calls stored on their voice-over IP telephone system. I'll send them to your phone."

Kane stood back, impressed but concerned. "You've both done a good job. What are the risks?"

Cameron stood, fixing first Kane and then Craven with his good eye peering through the hole in his mask. "If any of these measures fail, the facility will go into total lockdown. Alarms will blare, doors will seal, and armed response teams will be deployed. You'll have only three minutes to get out if that happens."

Kane nodded, the scenarios of what his capture would mean for Danny and Kim playing out in his head. "And the EMP device? Where is it exactly?"

Ghost pointed to a square on the blueprints glowing on her laptop screen. "Sub-basement level three. Secured in a blast-proof vault. Once you are in, I'll need five minutes to bypass the digital clock using a customised algorithm. After that, it's a matter of retrieving the device and making your way out the same way you came in."

Craven rubbed his fingers across the crag of his jawline. "Sounds like a fucking nightmare."

Kane clapped him on the back. "We've no choice, Frank. It's this, or we might as well hand the Prometheus Code over to the enemy. We'll be in and out before they even know we were there. Cam, do you have any details on the EMP itself? What does it look like, and how are we going to get it out?" Kane was suddenly worried that the EMP might be a huge device, as big as a tank and twice as heavy. It could come in multiple sections with layers of complexity in its construction, making it impossible to extract from the lab.

Cameron's fingers danced over his keyboard until a schematic of the EMP device appeared, rotating 360 degrees. "They've made it compact, but powerful. It's designed to be a weapon, after all. That's Zenith's payday. Sell the EMP to the British or US government for billions. They haven't spent years developing it for the good of their health. Everything gone, electricity, all power, systems, everything. It's roughly the size of a small suitcase, about eighteen inches long, twelve inches wide, and six inches deep. It weighs around thirty pounds. Portable enough for you to carry, but packed with enough power to knock out the electrical infrastructure of central

London."

"How do we get it out?"

Cameron pulled the building schematic up on his screen. "Once you have the device, you'll take the service lift up to the ground floor. That lift is only accessible from the lower levels. From there, you'll move through a maintenance corridor that leads to an emergency exit. I'll disable the external alarms on that door so it won't trigger when you leave."

"What about the guards on the way out?"

Ghost smiled, recovered from her earlier embarrassment. "We'll use a diversion. I've hacked into the alarm system. Once you are ready to move, I'll trigger a fire alarm on the opposite side of the building. The supposed fire will preoccupy the guards, giving you a clear path to the exit."

Kane nodded, the plan playing out clearly in his mind. Just like the old days. "All right then. We grab the EMP and get out during the chaos. Sounds simple enough."

"Exactly," Cameron replied. "But we have to be quick and make no mistakes. Timing is everything in this operation. Miss the camera timings or mess up the cards or biometrics and it's game over."

Kane and Craven exchanged a lingering look. The weight of their mission hung heavy in the air. They were about to undertake a daring heist, to make a noise that would distract their enemies from Cameron and Ghost's location and secure the EMP. It was a high-stakes gamble, which, if it went wrong and their enemies secured both the EMP and the Prometheus Code, could change the balance of world power forever. Failure was not an option. The fate of countless lives depended on their success.

CHAPTER THIRTY

Kane kissed Kim goodbye, and she cried as he pulled away from the tight hug locked around his waist. He swallowed the lump in his throat, bent down and told her he loved her. Ghost took Kim's hand and led her to the apartment's kitchen. After her reality check from Craven, Ghost had come around to the idea of looking after Danny and Kim with a little more grace. She and Cameron let Danny watch their efforts to crack the Prometheus Code, and he had taken an interest in how they worked. Ghost had even run out to the local Asda and returned with two shopping bags full of supplies and a promise to Kim that they would bake together. Kim cuffed away her tears and followed Ghost to the kitchen.

"Look after your sister, son," Kane murmured, squeezing Danny's shoulder.

"When will you be back?" he demanded, looking at his father through hooded eyes.

"Two days' time. Just make sure Kim's all right. Watch a couple of movies with her, play some games together. You know how much she looks up to you."

"I heard you all talking, about how dangerous this thing is that you have to do. What if you don't come back?"

"I will come back, son. Don't worry."

Danny blew out his cheeks and shook his head. "How can you be so flippant? You might not come back, Dad. Not that you are ever around, anyway. But what happens to me and Kim if you get caught? Where do we go? What do we do? Uncle Frank is going with you. If you both get caught, we have nobody."

"Cameron will take care of you until I get back."

"A man who wears a fucking mask and can't be around people. Are you serious?"

"Don't use that language around me, Danny. Just do what I ask and look after your sister."

"Whatever, Jack. You go off and save the world. But who's going to save your own family? One day, you might actually put us first for a change."

"Danny, wait…" Danny pulled away and stormed off to his room, leaving Kane hollow.

"Ready?" asked Craven, opening the front door, coat on, ready to go.

Kane followed him out of the apartment and down to the open-air car park beside the wide River Mersey. Craven had loaded all the equipment and weapons in the boot, and Kane sat in the passenger seat of the Mercedes E-Class Craven had hired using his Bob Paisley ID. Bob Paisley was arguably Liverpool Football Club's greatest manager and one of Kane's favourite IDs that he had used since leaving witness protection.

They drove the four hours from Liverpool to London, going through the details of the operation on the way, and Kane didn't mention Barbara's passing. Whenever they had talked of it since Craven had returned to the UK, the old detective just brushed it off. Kane respected his need to not talk about it, and it would be another four or five days before they repatriated her body for the funeral, so Kane thought it best to let the grief wait until then.

Later that afternoon, Kane stood opposite the Beanhive, a quaint coffee shop in the heart of central London. He adjusted his sunglasses, scanning the area. He wore a clean navy Hugo Boss suit, white shirt and black loafers. The sound of Craven loudly munching a blueberry muffin and slurping on an Americano through his earpiece was so loud that Kane almost took the device out of his ear.

"Are you eating loudly enough in there, Frank?" Kane said, the microphone tucked behind his jacket lapel and picking up the audio. "I don't think the king can hear your jaws chomping in Buckingham Palace."

"I was going to get one for you, but you can fuck off now," Craven replied, mouth full of muffin so that the words came out as a mumble. "Keep the chatter to a minimum. People think I'm talking to myself."

Dr Harris of Zenith Technologies visited the Beanhive every morning and mid-afternoon for his coffee fix. As Kane glanced along the pavement busy with people in suits and smart office clothes, heads buried in their phones or talking whilst wearing AirPods, he spotted Dr Harris striding amongst the crowd, his long hair flowing in the breeze and his Avengers t-shirt tight about his portly stomach, Zenith keycard bouncing on a lanyard around his neck.

"He's coming."

"I'm ready."

Kane waited for a gap in traffic and jogged across the road, following Dr Harris into the coffee shop. Harris took a seat next to the counter and ordered his mid-afternoon Americano. He pulled out his phone and scrolled down the screen whilst he waited for his order. A barista with long sable-coloured hair waved to him, and Dr Harris returned the gesture, an awkward smile splitting his round face. Kane ordered a cup of tea and took a seat by the window, across the shop from Harris and Craven, who sat on the next table over.

A waitress with red hair and blue eyes brought the coffee in its oversized cup to Dr Harris' table. He thanked her and then took the cup to the shop's self-service station where he loaded it with two sugars and a touch of cinnamon. Harris returned to his seat and directed his attention back to his phone. Kane sipped his tea and waited patiently as Harris enjoyed his afternoon break.

"He's nearly finished," Kane said for Craven's benefit as Harris lifted the cup high to drink the dregs at the bottom.

"I'm on my way." Craven stood and placed his cup and muffin wrapper on a wooden tray. He carried it to the counter and laid it down, dug into his pocket for a handful of change, and counted it out slowly to leave a tip with his tray.

Harris got up and carried his cup towards the counter, where Craven was still counting out his change. Kane moved, speeding up, taking four long strides to get between a businesswoman in a pencil skirt and Dr Harris. Kane sidled in behind Harris and the businesswoman tutted loudly.

Craven placed his change upon the tray and turned just as Dr Harris placed his cup on the counter. Craven bumped into Harris, his considerable frame knocking the narrow-shouldered doctor backwards.

"Oh, sorry about that, mate," said Craven, smiling apologetically and grabbing the doctor's arm to lead him gently away from the counter.

"It's no problem, really," said Harris, stuttering over the words.

Kane swiftly grabbed Harris' cup, placing his own down and scooping up Harris' in one swift motion. He turned and sidestepped the businesswoman and strode out of the coffee shop, heart quickening with the buzz of success. He left the café and paused outside, where Craven waited impatiently.

Kane handed him the cup and took the phone from his jacket pocket. He had snapped a picture of Harris' Zenith passcard on its lanyard during the commotion. Kane opened the app Cameron had installed and held the camera image over the cup. The camera screen changed to a fluorescent colour and suddenly a dozen of Harris' fingerprints showed up as clear as day. A blue tick pinged on the phone and Kane tucked the phone back into his jacket.

"Got it," he said. Craven nodded and left the cup on the Beanhive's windowsill. They had the biometric fingerprints. Next: the keycards.

CHAPTER THIRTY-ONE

The first keycard holder was Richard Obafemi, head of security for Zenith Technologies. Cameron and Ghost had created an information packet on his habits and behaviours. It never failed to astonish Kane how they could take apart a person's life using their cyber skills and the information available on the web.

"It's frightening what these boffins can do nowadays," Craven observed as he and Kane pored over the details of Obafemi's life. "Nothing's private any more."

"Which is why we go to such lengths to hide our life in Seville," Kane replied. Cameron and Ghost's first entry point into Obafemi's life was through his bank account. That, Ghost had said, was the easiest way to build up a pattern of his life. Through his regular spending, they could see where he shopped for food and on what day of the week, what subscriptions he had, if he had children and paid crèche or school fees, if he was married and if his wife bought products associated with women using a joint account, if he owned a car and paid insurance, if he went to football matches and paid for a season ticket. A person's bank account laid open their life like a trail of breadcrumbs, giving Kane the opportunity to zero in on the best way to copy Obafemi's Zenith Technologies keycard.

Cameron and Ghost accessed Obafemi's computer using his Zenith email address obtained from the company's mainframe. They sent Obafemi a phishing email promising free entry into a competition to win free tickets to the next Rugby World Cup. Two weeks ago, Obafemi had used his debit card to pay for two tickets and some food at Harlequins Rugby Stadium in London, leading Ghost to the conclusion that his love for rugby was the simplest way to unlock the head of security's life. Obafemi had clicked the link embedded within the email, and now his life was laid open to Ghost and Cameron's genius.

Richard Obafemi was a husband and father of two children. His children played football at a local club in Ealing to which Obafemi made monthly membership payments, and they both had EA Sports games memberships. He or his wife shopped weekly on a Sunday at Tesco, had Netflix and Disney Plus subscriptions and two car loans. Obafemi was a member of First-Class Fitness, a health club close to the Zenith Technologies office in central London. His bank account showed monthly payment memberships, and that every Tuesday and Thursday evening he bought an energy drink from the gym shop. His emails held a copy of his gym entry card.

Kane and Craven caught the London Underground Jubilee Line from the Beanhive coffee shop towards Canary Wharf in London's financial district on the Isle of Dogs. It was early on Tuesday evening, and Richard Obafemi was due to make his regular trip to the gym. They waited outside a gigantic building with grand concrete steps across the road from First-Class Fitness and waited for Obafemi to arrive.

"There he is," observed Craven, jutting his chin towards a heavy-set black man striding purposefully towards the gym's entrance. He wore forest-green chinos and a white shirt rolled up to the elbows and carried a sports-type rucksack on his back. The keycard hung around his neck on a blue lanyard with the Zenith Technology name and logo in white against the deep blue.

"We've only one entry card," said Kane as they walked the short journey from the tube stop to the gym. "I'll go in, but I need you to distract the person behind the reception desk."

"Why? You have the card. You can just go straight in."

"These places take a picture of their members when they join the club. Whenever a member scans in, that picture pops up on the computer behind the reception desk. If the face doesn't match the person at the gate, they aren't getting in. They do it to stop members sharing their cards with friends and family, and I don't exactly look like Richard Obafemi, do I?"

"No. He's handsome and muscular."

Kane laughed, happy to see Craven cracking jokes again. "Just distract the desk worker when I scan the card."

"Don't worry, I'll take care of it."

Kane strolled into the gym, and Craven followed ten paces behind. First-Class Fitness was a two-storey building with large planes of glass giving passers-by a look at the fit people inside pounding on the treadmills, whizzing the pedals of exercise bikes, and lifting weights. Kane had worked out to a high level when he was in the SAS. His fitness regime had focused mainly on running, swimming, hiking with a heavy Bergen on his back, and lifting weights. Some lads in the regiment took the weightlifting to a different level, packing on muscle and bulking up to give themselves an advantage over the enemy in hand-to-hand combat. Kane never seemed to put much weight on through weight training, so he had focused on fitness and martial arts training. He had always preferred jiu-jitsu, karate, boxing and Judo to pumping iron.

As an agent of Mjolnir, the MI6 splinter group, Kane had given up weight training completely. His goal then was to blend in, to be the grey man, average, unremarkable. So he had run a lot, kept up his martial arts training, and spent a serious amount of time on the gun range. After the operation in Russia last year, Kane had promised himself that he would start running again after being caught out with a severe lack of fitness. He had remained true to his word and now ran five kilometres three times a week when time allowed.

Kane pushed open the heavy glass doors and entered the gym. Dance music pumped from speakers, bass thumping to motivate the white-collar workers to work off their frustrations through running to achieve their daily step count. Kane took out his phone and called up the copy of Richard Obafemi's membership e-card.

"Excuse me," said Frank Craven in his loudest northern voice, striding up to the front desk with a smile splitting his open face.

"How can I help you?" inquired the young man behind the desk. He was tanned, wore his hair short and perfectly manicured, and his huge biceps bulged beneath a First-Class Fitness polo t-shirt.

"I'm looking to join the gym, but I'm warning you, lad, I haven't lifted weights in a long time. What facilities have you got in there?"

Kane waited until the desk worker stood up to talk to Craven and then pressed his phone's screen lightly to the silver waist-high tower next to the metallic turnstiles. The tower beeped, and Kane pushed open the turnstile and waltzed through.

"I can probably bench press about one hundred and twenty kilograms," Craven said to the worker, and Kane chuckled to himself.

Kane quickened his pace and entered the male changing rooms through a swing door. Richard Obafemi had stepped before a set of lockers and placed his bag on a wooden bench. He sat down and took off his tan shoes. Kane walked past him to the next bench and took a white, fluffy towel from a rack beside the lockers. He slowly took off his jacket and waited as Obafemi changed into a t-shirt and shorts. After changing, Obafemi folded his clothes and placed them carefully in locker number 67. He then took off his lanyard and tucked it into the front pocket of his bag. He stretched his arms twice and then left the changing rooms, heading towards the gym area.

The locker room was empty, and Kane quickly took a hairpin from his pocket. He slid it into locker number 67's lock and deftly picked the basic locking mechanism. It clicked open and Kane took the lanyard and keycard from Obafemi's bag. He took a clear picture of the card with his phone, placed the lanyard back in the bag, and closed the locker.

Just as the locker slammed shut, the changing room door swung open and two young men in tight trousers and even tighter t-shirts bustled in laughing and joking. Kane slipped through the door after them and out of the turnstile exit to hear Craven talking at full volume to the desk worker.

"So, I said to my trainer, this is a bit light, mate. Add another plate on each side," Craven said. "But he checked the rack and said there are no more. That's the kind of weight I was shifting back in the day." Craven saw Kane from the corner of his eyes and turned away from the desk. "Anyway, I don't think this is the place for me, lad."

He followed Kane out of the gym and into the early evening bustle of Canary Wharf. Mission accomplished. Next: the operations manager.

CHAPTER THIRTY-TWO

The second keycard Kane required to get through the Zenith Technologies keycard checkpoint belonged to the operations manager, Natalie Jennings. She proved a tougher nut for Cameron and Ghost to crack. They had her Zenith email address from the hacked company database, but Jennings soundly ignored any of the phishing emails Cameron and Ghost came up with. They limited their attempts to two emails, as sending more than that in one day would raise suspicions. Cameron had tried an offer for a £500 Selfridges shopping voucher, and Ghost had tried a competition for a free iPhone, but neither had worked.

The hackers needed Natalie Jennings to click the link inside the email to activate their Trojan horse virus to establish a "man in the browser" attack and sniff her network for banking online logins and access codes. Eventually, Ghost had cloned a Zenith Technology email account and generated a quick and dirty staff survey with a same-day deadline. Natalie Jennings had completed the survey on her Tuesday lunch break and Ghost and Cameron were in. Natalie's life differed completely from Richard Obafemi's. Where he was all two point four children, Tesco, football and gym workouts, Natalie was a single woman who socialised. She went out most nights of the week, was also a gym member but rarely worked out, paid rent for an apartment somewhere close to Canary Wharf, and spent most of her salary on clothes and booze.

"I fucking hate wine bars," Craven opined, staring at the yuppie-looking bar across the road.

"There isn't much you don't hate, Frank. We won't be in there long."

"Let me guess. I create a distraction so you can get the card?"

"Not this time. You can enjoy a glass of wine whilst I get a scan of her card."

"Are you sure she's in there?"

"According to Cameron, she comes here every Tuesday with her team from Zenith for a weekly drink. Team building, I think they call it in the corporate world."

"Getting pissed is what we used to call it on the force."

"From what Cam and Ghost could extract from Natalie Jennings' bank statement, she normally heads into this place after work at five and stays until nine or ten. It's seven thirty now, so she should be well on her way."

"Two and a half hours of drinking wine? She'll be dancing on the tables."

"Let's see."

"Aren't we supposed to be drawing our enemies away from Cam and Ghost to get the focus away from Liverpool?"

"We have been doing that from the moment we arrived in London. This city has the most CCTV cameras per square kilometre outside of Asia. There are four hundred cameras per square kilometre. Which is a lot. Even New York only has twenty-five per square kilometre. So, our handsome faces are here for all to see. After the fight at the house on the

Snake Pass, and at Cameron's lock-up, MI5 will have facial recognition software searching the country for any sign of my face. They could come at us at any moment. And if MI5 is watching, then we can assume the assassin I shot at the safe house and whoever he works for is as well. Things are about to heat up, Frank. So be on your guard."

"Fair enough. Let's get this bloody card thingy, then."

Kane and Craven crossed the road and entered La Cave Wine Bar. The outside was all wood planes and crawling ivy, and inside the place smelled of pine and stale wine. People in smart suits and dresses sat at tables lit by small lamps or stood by the bar talking and laughing over tasteful music playing over the wine bar's sound system.

Kane checked the picture of Natalie Jennings on his phone and searched the crowd. From the pictures Ghost had copied from Jennings's Facebook and Instagram, she was a short woman with chestnut hair, a thick mask of make-up plastered onto a long, open face. He spotted her amongst a mixed group of women and men, half a dozen of them standing around two tall tables heavy with empty and half-full wine gasses. Their laughter and loud voices filled the wine bar, and three of them vaped from small metallic tubes and the billowing, sweet-smelling smoke from their mouths gathered around the ceiling lights like a thin, artificial fog.

"That's her," Kane breathed. Craven turned from frowning at a group of men in trousers without socks sipping at cocktails, to frown at Natalie Jennings' group.

"This place makes me sick. What's happened to the old-fashioned pub? Don't people just go for a fucking pint any more? I bet you can't get a packet of bacon fries in here. There isn't a gambling machine, and I'll bet you a pound to a bucket of shit that there's no darts board. Who the fuck comes in places like this?"

"These people do. Wait here. This won't take long."

Kane sidled through the busy wine bar until he reached the long oak bar. He tried to order two pints of beer, then stout, then IPAs, but the bar only served wine, whiskey or cocktails. A waiter in a shirt, bowtie and braces, with a scraggly beard and his hair gathered in a topknot, stared at Kane as though he were a simpleton. He ordered two whiskey and ginger ales and waited for the drinks. The barman brought them and Kane paid him with a tap of his credit card in the name of Mark Walters.

Carrying a heavy glass of whiskey in each hand, Kane turned and made his way back to Craven, taking a path through Natalie Jennings' group. Some moved out of his way, and he had to swerve around others. When he reached Natalie, Kane turned his back to smile and dodge around the women she was busy talking to, and backed into Natalie, knocking her handbag to the ground. She wasn't wearing her Zenith Technologies lanyard around her neck, and nor were her co-workers, and it was a safe bet that the keycard was somewhere in her Yves Saint Laurent handbag. The bag fell to the floor, and Kane dropped one of his whiskeys. The glass smashed, and the group shrieked.

"Oh, I'm so sorry!" Kane exclaimed, wincing and placing his remaining whiskey on the table. He bent to gather her bag and her spilled-out belongings. "I'll get it. Watch out for the broken glass."

"No problem at all," Natalie said with a smile. To say she was tipsy was generous. She tottered away on pale pink heels.

During the commotion of the smashed glass and the dropped handbag, two of Natalie's friends went to find someone to sweep up the glass and Kane scrabbled on his haunches to gather Natalie's bits and pieces. As he did so, he slipped his phone from his jacket pocket and picked up her keycard. He quickly took three pictures of it. The app beeped to confirm a successful scan and Kane stuffed the lanyard and keycard into her bag, along with a fallen lipstick, a small packet of tissues, and a set of car keys. Kane stood and handed her bag back. "Here you go."

"Thank you," she said, slightly embarrassed by the spill.

Kane left her, crossed the room and handed Craven the glass of whiskey.

"You're a sneaky bastard, Jack Kane," Craven said with a wink. He sniffed the whiskey and turned his mouth downwards as though it smelled like a donkey's arse, and then downed the lot in three gulps. "We've got everything we need."

"Now, let's get ready to infiltrate Zenith Technologies," Kane replied as they left the wine bar.

They had the fingerprints, the keycards and the passcodes. The pieces were falling into place. Kane scanned his eyes left and right across the pavement and road, and then across the entranceways to Canary Wharf's colossal office buildings. He paused, face lifted, making sure the dozens of CCTV cameras on each building and lamppost had ample opportunity to get a clear picture of his face. They would come soon. The agencies competing to get the uniquely dangerous Prometheus Code. London was so well-monitored that they could track him as he travelled across the entire city. It was only a matter of time. But at least their watchers, snipers, assassins, analysts, and special agents weren't paying attention to Liverpool, where Cameron and Ghost used all of their considerable skill to unlock the cyber labyrinth they had created. Danny and Kim were safe, as long as Kane could keep the focus on London and away from Liverpool. He couldn't break codes or hack databases, but he could cause enough trouble to keep all eyes on him.

Kane and Craven marched towards the London Underground tube station, preparing themselves. The real challenge lay ahead: breaking into one of the most secure facilities in the country and stealing the EMP device. They had to be flawless. One mistake, one slip-up, was all it would take. His experience in the SAS and the Mjolnir agency told Kane that operations rarely went as planned; what made them work was the operator or agent's ability to alter and shift with those changes, to adapt and think quickly and use his mind and sheer force of will to get the job done.

To fail could mean their lives, or worse, catastrophic consequences for Europe and the world.

CHAPTER THIRTY-THREE

As the train clanked into London Waterloo Station, Kyle Lavine stood by the carriage door, gripping his black sports kit bag tightly. The bag was inconspicuous. In his business suit and overcoat, Lavine looked like a businessman travelling to London for work. Which he was, but instead of sales, operations, accounts or marketing, Kyle Lavine came to kill. Instead of a laptop and notebook, his bag contained an array of deadly tools and weapons. Stowed safely inside was equipment provided to him upon arrival in the UK by the Di Marzio crime family. The Sig Sauer P364 with spare magazines, the AR15 rifle with EOTech sights and customised safety catch and trigger, five flashbang grenades, a bulletproof combat vest, three chemical grenades, a suppressor attachment for the Sig, three burner phones, and a medical supply bag.

The train came to a screeching stop at platform 13, and the doors hissed open. A man with a foldable bicycle alighted first, and then Kyle stepped out into the throng of passengers, blending seamlessly with the crowd. The voice of his client, the Hydra organisation, and Jafari, the ruthless assassin, played over and over in his head. He had already lost fifteen hours searching for Kane and Cameron Jordan and travelling to London. Jordan remained lost, but Kane's face had lit up Kyle's facial recognition search programme like a pinball machine. Kane pinged CCTV cameras across London, not even trying to hide himself from view. Which meant he was either stupid or up to something.

Waterloo Station was an undulating maze of steel and glass, bustling with activity even at this late hour. The air was thick with the scent of freshly brewed coffee and tea from nearby kiosks, mingling with the faint tang of industrial cleaner. The cavernous platforms and walkways beyond rang with a cacophony of clip-clop footsteps, snippets of conversations yelled into earphones and mobile handsets, and the occasional announcement crackling over the PA system.

As Kyle wove through the busy station, edging around people to avoid them brushing against his still throbbing bullet wound, he couldn't help but notice the subtle difference between the UK and his native America. British commuters moved with a reserved politeness, their conversations muted, holding doors open for one another, apologetically smiling if they crossed one another's path. American train stations were louder, more chaotic, with people often rushing and talking aggressively. The architecture in the UK was more historic, blending rusting iron and cracked marble old-world charm with modern functionality, unlike the typically plastic and concrete utilitarian designs back home.

Kyle moved purposefully through a sea of commuters, his wolf-like eyes scanning the surroundings. Hydra and Jafari could already be here, waiting for him to slip up, poised to eliminate Jack Kane, Cameron Jordan, and Kyle Lavine. He navigated past the busy concourse, where digital departure boards flickered with information and travellers hurriedly checked their schedules. The high, vaulted station ceiling loomed overhead, its architecture a blend of historic and modern.

He kept his head bowed to avoid the multitude of

CCTV cameras; face partially obscured by the brim of the herringbone baker boy hat he had donned before alighting from the train. The assassin's every movement was calculated, his presence unremarkable amid the busy station and its distracted throng of tired commuters. He passed a cluster of tourists gawking at a gigantic clock suspended from the ceiling, taking awkward-looking selfies of themselves pouting beneath the attraction. Kyle skirted them and stepped around a group of teenagers laughing loudly beside a sandwich stand.

Kyle's path took him toward the station's main exit. The weight of his mission bore down upon him, making his neck and shoulders tight. When he found a hotel, he would try some yoga stretching. He should be able to manage a few poses despite his injury. That would take away the tenseness from his muscles. He emerged on York Road. The street was alive with the pulse of the city, illuminated by the soft glow of streetlights and bright signs of nearby businesses. The stink of exhaust fumes blended with the aroma of street food wafting from a nearby food truck, creating a distinctive urban scent.

York Road was a bustling thoroughfare, lined with a mix of old and new buildings. Of the old British Empire, and the new, diminished United Kingdom. The brutalist architecture of the South Bank Centre loomed to one side, its concrete façade a stark contrast to the more modern structures nearby. Stereotypical London double-decker buses rumbled by, and taxis honked their horns impatiently as they navigated the stop-start traffic.

Kyle moved with the flow of pedestrians, blending in, mind focused on the task ahead. Kane was somewhere in the city, and his last known location according to the POLARIS system was Canary Wharf. One of Kane's known accomplices, Frank Craven, a former police detective, was with him. But no sign of Cameron Jordan. An updated information packet had arrived in Kyle's inbox with details of an EMP device, which his employers wanted as badly as they wanted the Prometheus Code. Zenith Technologies had developed the portable and powerful EMP device, and Kyle was sure it was no coincidence that Zenith's headquarters sat on Canary Wharf.

Kane was somewhere in London at that very moment, likely hunkered down and preparing for the next phase of his operation. Whatever Kane and Jordan had planned, Kyle was here to disrupt it, to take the virus and the EMP and send them to their graves. This operation had proved to be a test, both physical and mental, and Kyle took a deep breath to stop himself from becoming triggered by thoughts of his wound and of his previous failure. To be triggered was to become angered, and angry men made poor decisions. Kyle's hand brushed against the bulk of the sports bag, a satisfying reminder of the tools at his disposal.

He turned onto a side street, slipping into the shadows. The narrow alley was quieter, the road and bustle of the city fading to a distant hum. Kyle paused for a moment. He pulled out his phone and checked the encrypted message from Hydra. The intelligence was precise: Kane had been spotted two hours ago close to Canary Wharf underground station.

Kyle adjusted the strap of his bag and continued down the alley, emerging into Lower Marsh. A line of eclectic shops and cafés lined the street, their fronts darkened as the businesses had closed for the night. People from multiple, almost unidentifiable ethnicities wandered about, talking, smoking, vaping, walking their dogs, living their lives. They lived in the normal world, the world of nine to five, of TV shows, movies and pop music. Kyle, Kane and Jordan lived in another world, the world behind the shadows. There was a price to be paid for bucking the rules of their world, and Kyle Lavine was about to lay down justice and fulfil his contract. Once it was done, he would take a break. The payment was substantial, millions of dollars to add to his already vast sums lodged in offshore investments, Caribbean banks and property interests across the globe. He would take time to recover from his wound, to enjoy the fruits of his labour.

He was close, and Kyle Lavine could almost smell his quarry. This time there could be no mistakes. He moved with the agile confidence of a predator closing in on his prey, every step bringing him closer to his target. The thrill of the hunt pulsed through Kyle's veins, sharpening his senses. Kyle Lavine was a professional, and London would bear witness to his lethal precision.

CHAPTER THIRTY-FOUR

Craven and Kane approached Zenith Technologies under the cover of darkness. The towering sleek building at the heart of Canary Wharf was a stark contrast to the quiet, moonlit streets of central London. Craven wore navy chinos, tan loafers and a checked shirt which he and Kane had purchased from a high street store earlier that afternoon. Apparently, it was the type of clothing workers in the tech industry wore to work. They were comfortable, and Craven hadn't grumbled much. It could have been worse, he supposed. Craven hadn't worn a suit since he'd left the force and would have to wear one again in three days' time when Barb's body returned to England.

Reflections of the city's lights reflected in the smoked-glass façade of Zenith's modern fortress of high-technology. Every aspect of the building screamed impenetrability, but tonight he and Kane would prove otherwise. Two guards in grey and black uniforms sat inside a wooden guard hut roofed with corrugated steel. Both overweight, their eyes flicked from their phones to the security screens, which illuminated their faces with electronic light. Craven couldn't see fully inside the hut, but based on Ghost's intel report, he expected both men carried tasers, batons, and pepper spray.

Craven had made a few calls that day, between the various tasks he and Kane had undertaken to gain access to Zenith Technologies. Calls to undertakers, to the Labour Club where he and Barb used to live. The undertakers wanted to meet him, to sell him a ridiculously overpriced coffin and make the necessary arrangements. Craven didn't want to meet them, didn't want to talk about it at all. He just wanted it done. Barb was dead and no amount of talking could bring her back. The Labour Club would let him use their bar for drinks and sandwiches after the funeral when old colleagues and relatives he barely knew would shake his hand and offer empty condolences. The thought of it gave Craven heartburn.

They reached the perimeter fence, a high-tech barrier humming with electrical energy set back from the principal thoroughfare, with warning signs posted at regular intervals. Craven followed Kane around the fence, turning left to follow it towards the rear of the tall building.

"Almost time for the guards to change," Kane said over his shoulder. "As soon as I get the word from Cam, we go in."

Craven said nothing. He remembered the plan well enough. The guards were due to change, leaving Craven and Kane with a fifteen-minute window to get through the fence and into the rear entrance before the fresh guards took their place and began their shifts. They leant against the adjacent building, staring through streetlight-illuminated darkness at the wire fence. The quiet was Craven's enemy. His mind wandered, memories of Barb flooding his brain. Her laughing as a young woman. Then slightly older, crying after her first miscarriage. Her tousled hair first thing in the morning, her tired face lying in a Spanish hospital bed.

"Ready?" asked Kane, and Craven closed his eyes for a moment, thankful to be distracted again. To be taken away from his pain.

“The fence is down,” Cameron spoke through Craven and Kane’s earpieces. “Repeat. Fence is down.”

“Copy,” Kane replied.

They rushed to the fence just as it fizzled and powered down, leaving a narrow window for them to slip through. Kane pulled a small set of clippers from a backpack slung across his back and quickly clipped a waist-sized hole in the fence. They worked in the darkness between buildings. There was nothing here but the sheer, smooth concrete wall towering above them. Kane inched through the hole and beckoned Craven through. He dropped to his knees and crawled through the space, the jagged ends of cut fencing wires catching on his shirt collar, and he cursed under his breath. Another wire scratched the back of his head and he ducked lower, easing himself through the gap. Then he was through. Inside the perimeter, within the grounds of Zenith Technologies, about to risk his life to steal a device he neither understood nor wanted to understand. The danger was enough, the distraction welcome.

CHAPTER THIRTY-FIVE

Kane moved swiftly across the meticulously landscaped grounds. Craven followed, their soft shoes soundless on the concrete, the shadows hiding them from view as Kane skirted the CCTV cameras fitted high on the building's walls. Cameras which peered at the fence and sent a feed to the security guards in their gatehouse. The well-manicured lawns and strategically placed shrubs provided minimal cover, but the cameras didn't focus on the inside of the wall. So Kane and Craven darted from shadow to shadow, reaching the rear service entrance just as the two-man guard patrol passed by on their regular rounds.

Kane paused, crouched behind a raised flowerbed heavy with evergreen shrubs and conifers. The guards strolled towards the rear entrance, turned, and carried on towards the front of the building. Kane rose and beckoned to Craven to follow him. The service entrance was guarded by a biometric scanner and a keypad. Kane ran to the faintly glowing keypad beside a heavy iron-grey door. He removed his backpack and carefully removed the latex fingerprint mould. Craven had purchased a modelling kit at an art and hobby shop before leaving Liverpool, and together they had made the mould using the print lifted from Dr Harris' coffee cup. The mould was a perfect replica of Dr Harris' fingerprint. Kane slipped it over his finger and pressed his thumb to the scanner. He pressed his thumb to the scanner, and the device whirred softly before pinging and turning green.

Craven laughed delightedly. “I can’t believe that worked.”

“Now for the code. Cameron?”

“I have it. We decrypted the Zenith security algorithm and have today’s access code. The code is 4882.”

“Copy,” said Kane. Craven typed the code into the keypad and the door clicked as its locking mechanism shifted and swung slightly ajar.

“Come on,” Kane urged Craven, and pulled the door fully open using the cold metal handle.

Inside, the atmosphere changed instantly. Exterior gardens and modern design gave way to a sterile, high-security environment. The walls had a stark white colour, with metallic accents that reflected the harsh fluorescent lighting. The floors were polished concrete, their surfaces gleaming under the bright, artificial lights. Kane and Craven’s footsteps echoed ominously in the silent corridors.

They had studied the interior schematics that afternoon over cups of tea and coffee. A picture of winding corridors, laboratories, design and research workshops, offices and meeting rooms lay in Kane’s mind like a map. This wasn’t his first time entering an unknown building to perform a clandestine operation, and he understood that learning the layout intimately was the key to a successful insertion, and, more importantly, to getting out of there alive and undiscovered.

They moved cautiously, hurrying along the corridors, winding their way towards the next challenge: a network of cameras and motion sensors. Kane paused and knelt, taking the backpack again and rummaging inside. He pulled free the palm-size signal- jammer Cameron had programmed at the apartment in Liverpool. It was a Wi-Fi jammer re-coded to emit a low-frequency interference to disrupt the camera feeds temporarily to give them ten seconds to move through each section without triggering the alarm.

A pure white, rectangular box housed each of the wall cameras mounted on the long corridor ahead, with discreet wiring disappearing into the wall behind. A green LED light flashed below each camera, and Kane pressed the button on the jamming device and waited.

"The light's still green," Craven frowned.

"I can see that. Cam?"

"It's worked. Trust me. The camera's operational diode will still show green because the camera believes it's working correctly. We are blocking the signal it emits to the Zenith mainframe with image data. Go. You only have ten seconds."

"Fuck it," said Craven, and set off beneath the first camera's line of vision.

Kane's shoulders tensed. But nothing happened. No alarm, no shouting, no security guards' boots thundering down the corridor towards them. Kane followed, reached the second camera and hit the jammer again. They proceeded in that way and passed beneath half a dozen cameras until they reached the end of the long corridor. Kane turned right towards their next obstacle and froze. A security guard in his now familiar grey and black uniform leaned against the wall, scrolling through his mobile phone.

"I thought these corridors were supposed to be clear?" said Craven, touching his earpiece and glancing at Kane.

"He must be hiding down here, taking an unscheduled break," Kane replied.

"Is it a guard?" Cameron asked through their earpieces.

"Yeah. I'll have to take him out."

"Jesus, Jack. Don't kill him."

Kane strode down the corridor with the confident stride of a man who was supposed to be there. The guard heard Kane's footsteps and glanced up from his phone. He was an overweight man, slightly taller than Kane, with a thin moustache and dark-ringed eyes.

"Is it this way to lab seven?" Kane asked with his broadest smile.

"No mate, back that way and turn left," the guard replied. Just as he turned his eyes back to his phone, Kane drove the flat of his hand into the security guard's throat. The phone clattered to the gleaming floor tiles. As the man clutched at his windpipe and struggled for air, Kane punched him hard in the liver. He fell, curled into a ball, and Kane quickly gathered him into a rear naked choke, squeezing until the guard went limp.

"Is he dead?" asked Craven, leaning to peer down the corridor for any sign of the other guards approaching.

"No. Unconscious. Help me get him into that room."

Craven pulled open a narrow door cut into the sleek corridor and marked only by a white plaque embossed with a series of numbers. Inside were metallic racks full of cleaning products, bottles of chemicals, cloths, mops and brooms. They took an arm each and dragged the guard inside. Kane took his baton and taser and placed them inside his bag.

They left the room, and Kane dusted himself down, tucking his shirt back into his trousers. He hadn't expected to meet the guard there, but he quickly dealt with the problem without alerting the rest of Zenith's security team. So far, so good.

Kane and Craven approached the checkpoints, and Kane paused, grabbing Craven's arm.

"Wait a minute," he warned.

"What is it?"

"It's the checkpoints next. Let's just make sure we have the keycard order right. If we use the wrong card at a checkpoint, we are screwed."

"Shall I run through it again?" said Cameron's voice over the comms.

"Go ahead, Cam."

"All right then. First of all, it's the operations department. To enter that zone, you need Natalie Jennings' card. Once through, you can proceed to the south wall and travel down a floor in the lift. Once you exit the lift, the next checkpoint is for the security department. There you'll need Richard Obafemi's card. Stay on the south wall and head down to the next floor. That's the research and development department where you can only enter with Dr Harris' keycard."

"Then it's on down to the subterranean level and the EMP lab," Kane finished.

"Exactly. And the biometric security checkpoint. There, you'll need the contact lens programmed with Dr Harris' retina data and the voice recording I've lifted from the Zenith mainframe and left on your phone."

Kane set off with Craven in tow. It was night-time, and the corridors were deserted, the only sound the soft patter of their rubber-soled shoes on the sterile floor. They reached the first keycard door and Kane unlocked his smartphone and pulled up the replica of Natalie Jennings' keycard. He held the phone screen against the black glass pad and waited. The door unlocked with a soft beep. They marched through the operations department and its open-plan space with stand-up meeting whiteboards, sofas, strange-looking chairs and clear glass meeting rooms.

At the south wall, they took the lift down one floor to the security department. The door slid open to present the next security door. Kane brought up Richard Obafemi's keycard on his phone and pressed it to the clear glass beside the heavy door facing him. Again, the door beeped and clicked open. Kane and Craven stepped inside and walked through tight corridors surrounded by the security guards' locker rooms, a break room with microwave, sink, chairs and tables. Two guards sat inside on their break and didn't bat an eyelid as the two men strolled past the break room window.

Kane followed the south wall and took the lift down to the next level, emerging into a labyrinthine array of offices and labs. Frosted glass lined the walls, giving a ghostly translucence to the empty rooms beyond. The lighting was dimmer, subdued, casting long shadows across the floor.

"Last one," Craven remarked as the final barrier met them at the end of a short corridor. The biometric door vault door that protected the EMP device. The door was massive, made of reinforced steel with a sleek digital interface. Kane took the small thumb-sized case from his backpack and carefully dabbed the tip of his finger into the contact lens. He lifted to his eye, forcing his eyelid open to place the lens upon his eyeball. But he had never worn contact lenses before, and his eye fought back, lids flickering closed. He paused before the precious lens slipped off his finger. If he lost the lens, the entire operation was over.

"I can't get the lens in," he gritted out.

"I thought you were supposed to be the tough guy?" Craven said. "Give it here." Craven held out his finger and Kane carefully pressed the lens onto his fingertip. Craven tilted his head back and placed the finger on his eye. He blinked and then grinned at Kane. "Piece of piss."

Craven leant forward, allowing the scanner to read the

fabricated pattern on Ghost's spare contact lens. A thin wave of green laser passed over Craven's eye and beeped its acceptance without incident. Kane took his phone again and located the voice-recorded file in his notes. He pressed a button beside the retinal scanner with a small image of a face emitting waves from its open mouth.

"Speak now," prompted an artificial voice from the security system.

Kane pressed play on his phone and played the pre-recorded sample of seamlessly spliced words in Dr Harris' voice into the speaker. The vault door responded, mechanisms clicking and whirring as it unlocked. The door swung open, revealing the EMP device nestled inside.

The EMP was compact, roughly the size of a small carry-on suitcase. Its metallic casing gave off a faint blue glow. Kane rubbed his hands together and carefully lifted it from its glass shelf, taking the considerable weight of its compact but dense components. He turned to Craven and smiled, and the old detective clapped him on the shoulder.

Craven carried the EMP in a hard plastic box they had found next to the device's glass shelving. The two men retraced their steps, navigating through the corridors with a heightened sense of caution. They followed Ghost's plan, leaving the research and development section towards the service lift, accessible only from that floor travelling upwards.

Just as Kane was about to hit the button to call for the lift, an alarm sounded. It rang long and loud, undulating, echoing around the night-empty corridors in an unearthly wail.

"What the fuck is that?" shouted Craven over the din.

"Fire alarm," Kane replied. "Cam, what's going on?"

"I'm inside the system now, trying to turn it off," Cameron said. "But there's a problem, Jack. You aren't alone in there.

You’ve got company.”

CHAPTER THIRTY-SIX

Kyle Lavine was tired of losing, exhausted with waiting, searching satellite images, seeking his time to strike. The call from Hydra and Jafari had jangled him. Nobody spoke to Kyle Lavine that way. If he wanted to take shit for a living, he would have stayed in the US Army. His old Delta Force unit was elite and its operations were strictly classified and rarely made public. Every soldier he'd served with, or trained with during his years at Fort Liberty, North Carolina, was exceptional. Brave men, intelligent, physically outstanding warriors prepared to fight and die for their country.

They had recruited Kyle from the US Army Rangers, and the first four years of his life as a Delta operator were the best years of his life. They trained Kyle extensively in weapons, explosives, hand-to-hand combat, and driving and piloting many military-grade vehicles. He was an expert in counter-terrorism, hostage rescue protocols and insertion into urban, jungle, ice, forest and many forms of combat theatres. He vividly remembered special reconnaissance missions in the desert and in the jungles of central Africa.

Kyle had left school as soon as possible. Sports were his thing; football, baseball, athletics. He'd excelled at them all, picking up awards for football sacks in his sophomore year, and five rushing touchdowns. The academic side came harder, needed more focus. Kyle's father walked out on his waitress mother when only child Kyle was a baby. His mother had struggled to raise him, using alcohol and abusive boyfriends as a crutch to ease her pain. After a childhood of second-hand clothes, empty food cupboards and sneakers with holes in the bottom, Kyle had run to the army like a needy child into their father's arms.

He loved everything about the army, apart from the command structure. Orders came from the Joint Special Operations Command, often from officers without genuine field experience. When an entitled West Point blue-blood colonel took over, it was the final straw for Kyle. Tales of friends working private security and making fortunes in the UAE lured him to the Middle East, and Kyle had made a fortune. Once he struck out on his own and became an assassin, his wealth expanded beyond his wildest dreams. He was a wealthy man, and he often wondered what the boy's version of himself would think if he could see Kyle's home in the Alps. He had enough wealth now to retire, to enjoy the fruits of his labour. But the pull of combat was everything. What would he do, read and walk his dog all day?

Kyle took the tube to Canary Wharf, nestled amongst commuters blissfully unaware of the small arsenal in the bag at his feet. Jafari and Hydra were coming, he was sure of it. After this job, he would take a break, enjoy the vast sum he was about to receive in payment. But he had waited too long to strike, hoping for the perfect shot, the ideal chance to kill Jordan and Kane to avoid UK police attention, to retrieve the virus and fly out for a couple of months of rest and recuperation. Hydra had forced his hand, and it was time to choose violence.

That time was now, and time was running out. The time for stealth was over. So, he strode into the Zenith Technologies building with full force, unleashing his wrath without temper. Wearing his black Dior suit and a crisp white shirt, he marched up to the guard hut and shot the two security guards twice in the face with his suppressed Sig Sauer P365. The shots shunked and hissed as they left his weapon and slapped into the unsuspecting guards' skulls like the sound of a cleaver chopping meat. Their bodies jerked and blood and skull fragments splattered the guard hut window in a spray of crimson.

He snatched an access card from a dead guard's belt and marched through the hut and inside the perimeter fence. Kyle strode towards the main entrance and tapped the access card against the revolving door entry keypad. It beeped, and he pushed his way through the heavy doors. Another security guard stood up from the front desk with a surprised look on his face, and Kyle snarled as he fired three bullets into the man's chest without breaking stride.

Keeping the gun in his right hand, Kyle leapt over the security desk. The pain of his healing bullet wound stretched against its stitches stoked his controlled fury, reminding him why he was there and the job he had to do. Kyle smashed the red fire alarm button and pulled down on the lever. The entrance atrium suddenly thundered with a wailing fire alarm, lights flashing, the quiet, sleeping office coming to life. It was a warning. Kyle Lavine was here. Jack Kane was in the building somewhere, here to steal the EMP device, and Kyle was the hammer to his scalpel.

CHAPTER THIRTY-SEVEN

"He's killed the guards in the atrium," Cameron stated through the communications device. "I'm watching the cameras, and it looks like the same guy from the safe house."

"Shit," said Craven. "We'd better move. Security will be all over this place like flies on shit now the fire alarm's going off."

"Our out is blown," said Kane. "We can't use the service lift now. We've no way of knowing what's waiting for us when the doors open. Could be the killer waiting for us, or a dozen Zenith security guards."

Kane paused, trying to think. The fire alarm blared, loud and undulating. If the alarm didn't shut off soon, the fire brigade and the police would receive a notification from the Zenith network, and then the place would be even harder to get away from. The assassin had taken things to a different level. Once the police or fire service saw the security guards' bodies, they would call for armed response. The place would go into lockdown, surrounded by the police force's Specialist Firearms Command. The alarm suddenly switched off, leaving a ringing sound in Kane's ears and he and Craven stood in the cold, clinical corridor holding the EMP case.

"Got it," Cameron announced. "I'm watching the killer on

the cameras; he's moving down the levels. Looks like a serious operator. Be careful. Guards are sweeping every floor. You've got incoming. I'll look for another way out."

"Roger that," Kane replied.

There was no time to wait for Cameron and Ghost to analyse the building schematics and work up a new plan. Kane spotted a fire extinguisher to the right of the lift doors. Beside it was a floor plan with details of where staff should muster in the event of a fire.

"Look, here." He ripped the floor plan off the wall and proffered it to Craven, pointing to a greyed-out area west of the lift. "This looks like a maintenance hatch in the sub-basement. They must use it for cables and air-conditioning pipes. Cameron, can we get out that way?"

"I see it, Jack," came Ghost's voice. "Get to the hatch. It leads to an old utility tunnel. If you reach it, you have a small space to crawl through and bypass the guards. There's no way the killer can get in there unless he follows you in."

"Let's go," Kane ordered. He and Craven ran west along the corridor, turning left and right, following the floor plan.

"Hold up," Craven wheezed. His face glowed beetroot red and his chest heaved from the exertion. "I can't run like you, Jack."

"It's all right Frank, come on." Kane slowed to a fast walk, and Craven kept pace.

They turned another corner and came face to face with three burly security guards. The three men stopped dead, staring at Kane and Craven with mouths gaping open.

"Who are you?" demanded the guard on the left, a tall man with a lantern jaw. "What are you doing down here at his hour?" His eyes dropped to the EMP, and his hand reached for his small black taser.

"Wait," said Kane, raising his hands to keep the guards calm.

But it was too late. Kane surged forward as the lantern-jawed guard pulled his taser free of his belt. Kane grabbed his wrist and twisted it backwards, kicking out at his right knee at the same time. The man dropped to his knees and Kane smashed his head into the white walls with an audible crack.

Craven sprang into action, his shovel-sized hands punching the middle guard hard in the face.

"Stop!" screamed the second guard, his voice pitched with panic. He grabbed Craven by the shirt, and the two men wrestled together, twisting and turning like dancers. Kane pulled the telescopic baton from the lantern-jawed guard's belt and flicked it out to its full length. He cracked the extended baton over the punched guard's skull, knocking him out cold. Craven and the guard spat and grunted, each man pushing at the other, but neither skilled nor experienced enough to take the other down or strike a definitive blow.

"Let go of him, Frank," Kane said. Craven gave the guard one last heave and released his grip on the guard's uniform. He fell backwards against the wall and Kane cracked the baton across the guard's knees. He fell, moaning in pain, and Kane grabbed his hair and clattered the guard's head off the wall to knock him out.

They set off again, reaching the maintenance hatch around the next turn. It was little more than a waist-high patch of discoloured metal riveted to the wall. Kane used the baton to pry it open, and it took half a dozen tugs before the hatch popped open, ripping plaster and paint from the wall. Kane peered inside the dark, narrow tunnel. The inside was musty, filled with the rotting stink of damp concrete and rust.

"Don't suppose you brought a torch?" asked Craven.

Kane shook his head. He had his SAS survival tin and could light a fire with the matches and tampon, but that was designed to start a fire and would burn out in seconds. Kane thought about running back to the fallen guards to check their belts for a torch, but there was no time.

"We'll have to crawl in the dark, Frank."

CHAPTER THIRTY-EIGHT

Kane pushed the EMP case in first and crawled in behind it. Grit and tiny pieces of debris crunched beneath Kane's knees as he shifted into the darkness. Craven moaned, grumbling wordlessly behind him as the two men shuffled into the darkness. Every ten seconds Kane pushed the EMP case further ahead and then followed it, feeling with his hands to follow the cables and piping strapped to either side of the hatch.

Kane's eyes became accustomed to the dark, but it was pitch black. The only light came from the open hatch behind them, and Kane could barely make out the shapes of the walls around him and the surrounding cables.

"This fucking hole is getting smaller," growled Craven. The old detective's breath came in wheezy gasps. Kane felt the pressure, too. It was fear kicking in, playing tricks on the mind. Kane closed his eyes and fought against his encroaching memories, struggling to banish the nightmare he knew was coming for him. The horror of crawling through dark tunnels beneath a desert stronghold. He could almost hear the explosion of the IED which had killed Smithy and Carl, Kane's oppos in his SAS regiment. Kane had taken out a high-value target deep behind enemy lines, but the mission became compromised. Fire and shrieks ripped through those foul tunnels in a welter of screaming and death, and only Kane and one other squad member had survived. He could smell the burned flesh and acrid stink of explosives as he wriggled through the maintenance tunnel. Fear would kill his mind. So Kane counted as he moved, counting each shift of his knee, each time he placed his palms on the rough surface beneath him. His mind told him to curl up and wait for somebody to come and get him out, that there was no way out and that he was leading himself and Craven to their deaths. But Kane gritted his teeth and carried on. He overcame his fear and mastered the weakness of his mind.

The tunnel seemed to stretch on endlessly, but eventually, Kane saw shafts of light ahead. He pushed on, shoving the case in front of him until he reached a plastic grate fitted to the centre of the wall. Kane peered through the gate, the light hurting his eyes at first, but then, as the brightness turned into shapes, Kane turned to Craven.

"We've made it. There's a stairwell here," he panted.

Kane turned so that his back lay against the tunnel wall opposite the grate. He bunched his legs and thrust out with both feet. The grate crunched and ground against its screws as it ripped from the wall and clattered onto the floor beyond. Kane slithered out and sucked in a huge breath, as though he had emerged from a deep-sea dive. He scrambled to his feet and helped Craven clamber through the grate. They nodded at each other and made for the stairs.

"Cameron?" Kane said.

"I'm here, Jack," came the reply through his earpiece.

"We've come out at a stairwell. Possibly the emergency stairs supporting the service lift."

"I see it. Keep going up the stairs. Two flights. You will come to an emergency exit, which will lead you out into the staff car park."

Kane and Craven took the stairs two at a time, Craven blowing hard but determined not to fall behind again. Double emergency doors closed with a central barrier waited at the top of the second flight, and Kane kicked them open. Overhead lights illuminated a small car park, empty but for half a dozen vehicles parked in various spaces. During the day, the car park would be full, each spot reserved for senior Zenith executives. Now it contained only the Toyotas, Hyundais, and Fords of the night shift security team.

"Thank Christ we've made it," said Craven, stumbling out into the night air. Just as Kane was about to follow him, a door burst open along the corridor and a man stepped into the artificial light. He was a tall man with a bag slung over one shoulder and a suppressed pistol in his right hand. The tall man's eyes widened, and a mirthless smile played at the corner of his mouth. It was the assassin from the Snake Pass. Ruthless and deadly. The gun came up and just as Kane leapt through the exit, a gunshot spat from the weapon and crashed into the wall behind him. Another shot rang and punched into the emergency doors. Kane's stomach turned over, and heat kindled in his chest. The familiar beginning of fear and the heightened sense of combat.

"Bastard's shooting at us!" snarled Craven.

Kane grabbed his arm and dragged his friend behind a Hyundai Tucson SUV. They crouched behind the black vehicle and Kane dug into his bag, fingers closing around the familiar feel of the Glock's grip. He pulled the gun free, already certain the magazine was ready, and a round waited in the chamber. He stood and fired as the assassin dashed through the emergency exit doors. The gunfire boomed across the car park, but the shot missed. The assassin ducked and rolled. Kane fired again, but the bullet slapped into a raised timber flowerbed.

Kane ducked behind the Hyundai and searched again in his

bag and found the flashbang grenade. Kane pulled the pin and tossed it towards the flowerbed where the assassin waited to kill them as they moved from behind the car. The grenade exploded in a flash of bright light and an extraordinarily loud explosion.

"Quickly, Frank," Kane hissed. He threw the bag over his shoulder and burst into a flat run, Glock in his right hand. Police sirens blared in the night sky, flashing blue lights lighting up the high-rise office buildings looming above Canary Wharf like glass giants. Kane had been on the end of flashbang grenades himself. It would take minutes for the assassin to recover from the assault on his senses, giving Kane and Craven just enough time to make their escape.

They reached the car park entrance and vaulted over the barrier and past the security guard hiding in his guard hut. As they hurtled past, the guard peered at them with terrified eyes, trying to process the outburst of gunfire and grenade explosion in his normally boring and mundane night shift.

Kane and Craven ran across the street and into an alley running between two immense office buildings. But just as Kane was about to emerge from the alley, a police car turned the corner. Its headlights sweeping the street as it turned, siren blaring, lights on the roof flashing blue. Kane paused, and Craven crouched beside him. The brick beside Kane's head exploded, spattering his face with sharp stone fragments. He turned to glimpse the assassin entering the alley and cursed under his breath.

"Get down!" Kane shouted, pulling Craven into a nearby doorway. They pressed themselves flat against the wall, holding their breath as the police car slowed, the officer peering through his window into the alley. Kane and Craven exchanged a nervous glance, faces smeared with grime from their crawl through the maintenance tunnel and beaded with sweat from the escape. The police car sped up and blared its sirens again.

Kane risked a peek around the doorway, and another suppressed gunshot whipped against the wall. Kane ducked back behind the wall and readied his Glock.

"When I say go, take the case and make a run for it."

"What about you?"

"I have to deal with this before we can get away. I'll be right behind you."

Craven pursed his lips, read the stern look on Kane's face, and nodded reluctantly. Kane knelt and fired three shots around the doorframe.

"Now."

Craven burst from the doorway and pelted up the alley in the same direction as the police car. Kane fired another two shots and then ran. But he ran the opposite way to Craven. He ran towards the assassin. Kane kept firing, shooting in the direction the silenced shots had come from. A figure came from the shadows and fired a round, and Kane turned and dived onto the damp alley floor and rolled. He fired another blind shot and then saw him. The assassin came snarling from the shadows with a Sig pistol held in both hands, pointed at Kane's chest.

"Where's the EMP?" demanded the blonde man in a mid-western American accent.

Kane stood slowly, his Glock aimed at the assassin's head. "Gone. Is that what you came for?"

"That and you. Looks like I only get you."

"Who sent you?"

"Bad people, Jack. Dangerous people. Tell me where the EMP is."

"An American working for the enemy? You must have served. Delta maybe? SEAL? How would your old buddies feel if they knew you'd turned traitor?"

The American laughed. "Half of them turned to private security after the war on terror turned out to be a bullshit war. What do you know about it, anyway? Just tell me where the EMP is."

"What do you think will happen if Iran, Russia, or North Korea get hold of this thing? Do you think it will only hurt Europeans? The US economy will collapse. Think about your people. It will be worse than the last recession, incomparably worse. Everybody's 401k plans, savings, pensions, all worth nothing. The only currency worth anything will be crypto. Do your grandparents have their retirement funds in crypto?"

"Stop talking. Tell me where it is before I take your head off. Or, I can find your kids. Daniel and Kimberly, isn't it?"

Kane wasn't surprised to hear that the assassin was aware of his name. He'd probably seen Kane's file, his military record, perhaps more. But hearing Danny and Kim's names on the killer's lips sent a pang of fear shivering across Kane's shoulders. "We could kill each other now. Or settle this the old way. Man to man."

The American sniggered. "You Brits make me laugh. All bark and no bite. I'll kill you whatever way you want, pal."

The moment the American lowered his weapon, Kane charged at him. They came together like great stags, chests colliding, arms scrambling for holds. Kane hooked his heel around his opponent's leg and tried a hip throw, but the assassin saw it coming and braced himself, pivoting around to crash the butt of his Sig against Kane's head. Kane stumbled and raised his Glock and fired the weapon close to the American's ear. He reeled away as the gunshot boomed around the narrow alley. He kicked Kane away from him, and Kane grabbed his gun hand with his left, just as the American grabbed his right wrist. They struggled there, two killers, each trying to drive the other backwards. The American's pale blue eyes blazed with hate and determination; his square jaw set firm. Muscle corded his arms, and he drove Kane backwards and downwards, eyebrows rising slightly in anticipation of his triumph.

Kane let go, leaving a vacuum where his force had been. His foe stumbled forwards against the sudden lack of opposition and Kane head-butted him hard in the face. The American's cheekbone crashed into Kane's forehead, bone giving way with a muffled crunch. Kane grabbed his enemy's balls in his left hand and twisted savagely. The American contorted in pain, a strange mewing emitting from the tight slit of his mouth. Kane let him drop to his knees and drove his knee into the man's face, dropping him onto his back.

Police sirens blared and engines roared along the streets of Canary Wharf. The gunshot was like a beacon, attracting police cars like moths to a flame. Kane pointed his gun at his rival, his pure animal brutality urging him to fire and kill the bastard where he cowered in the filth. But to fire again was to bring the police right to him, to be captured, arrested, taken away from Danny and Kim forever. He bent to take the Sig, but the American swivelled on the ground and kicked it away, the gun skittering away down the alley into the path of blue flashing lights.

"If you come for me again," Kane said, peering again into those ice-blue eyes. "I'll kill you."

He left the American sprawled in the alley and sprinted after Frank Craven. They had the EMP; they had diverted attention away from Cameron and Ghost. Kane hoped it was enough. That during the downtime, the hackers had found a way to disable the Prometheus Code. Otherwise, he had brought together both the EMP and the virus, a lethal combination which could destroy Western civilisation as the world knew it. If any of the agencies in pursuit of the virus got both it and the EMP, there was nothing stopping them from destroying London and Europe's banking systems. Kane ran through the streets of London, finding Craven striding along Westferry Circus.

"Is he dead?" asked Craven as Kane came alongside him.

"No. More's the pity. The police came. We need to find a vehicle and get out of here. There has to be a way to end this thing. We can't run forever."

CHAPTER THIRTY-NINE

Craven and Kane came across a black Audi A8 parked in a guest parking bay to the side of a gigantic office block.

"This will do," Craven decided, and watched as Kane reached into his bag and pulled out a palm-sized electronic device. "What's that?"

"Signal-jammer and key-fob replicator," Kane replied. He approached the car and tapped the buttons on the device. Moments later, the car's locks disengaged with the satisfying clunk-click of a modern vehicle unlocking.

"I'll drive." Craven slipped into the driver's seat as Kane sat on the passenger side. Kane quickly connected the device to the car's onboard computer, bypassing the ignition system. The engine screeched to life and Craven eased it out of the parking bay. He drove away slowly, making a turn to enter the tangled streets of Canary Wharf. The night sky shifted with fast-moving clouds rolling like a shadowed sea, their undersides illuminated by thousands of lights shining up from London's nightscape. Kane put his gun back into his bag of tricks and pushed the EMP case beneath his legs. It had been a close-run escape. Craven thought he might have a heart attack in the maintenance tunnel, or that one of the assassin's bullets would take him as he ran for his life. Would that have been so bad, Craven wondered? Perhaps he should have delayed, run that bit slower, fought less hard, allowed death to come for him so he could join Barb in whatever afterlife awaited him.

Craven drove calmly past two police jeeps screaming in the opposite direction. He drove onto the A1261 and then onto the A13, heading out of central London.

"Back to Liverpool?" he asked. The whole idea of coming to get the EMP was to take heat away from Cameron and Ghost, so returning there made little sense.

"Yeah," said Kane slowly, with a frown.

"Shouldn't we just ask Cameron to pack up and meet us somewhere else, somewhere safe?"

"I don't think there is anywhere safe for us any more, Frank. Not until this thing is over. If Cameron leaves the apartment in Liverpool, he has to find transport to wherever we meet him. Once he's on the road, he's easier to catch. It's too dangerous."

"So, what then?"

"We go back to Liverpool. That bastard back there threatened Danny and Kim. By name, Frank. Cam has to have found a way to disable the Prometheus Code by now. If not, I'll take it so far away nobody will ever find it. I can't risk anyone coming after my children."

Craven swallowed at the distaste of that. He loved Danny and Kim like they were his own, and Kane was right. Nothing was worth risking their lives for. Cameron was a former SAS soldier, but that was a long time ago, and Craven was certain that the masked man couldn't protect the kids as well as their father.

He needed to cover the 220 miles to Liverpool swiftly and discreetly. The last thing they needed was to lead their enemies all the way to the apartment at the Albert Dock. It was night, and the roads were quiet, so Craven opted to take the M25 ring road to skirt the city and then join the M1 northbound. He punched Liverpool into the car's navigation system, and it showed an approximate travel time of four hours, but with stops to take a leak or take on coffee, plus whatever measures Kane came up with to evade surveillance, it would take longer.

As they sped along the M1, Kane called Cameron using their comms equipment and followed his instructions to reconfigure the jamming device, turning it into a GPS jammer that would scramble the Audi's exact location as they drove, confusing the sophisticated network of CCTV and satellite imagery their enemies could access in their attempt to track their progress.

"Stay under the speed limit," Kane warned. "We don't want any unwanted attention." He fished around in the bag again and pulled out a compact box, no bigger than a deck of cards with a series of small LED lights along one edge.

"Where do you get these things from? What the fuck is that, an ice-cream maker?"

"It's an IR blaster. An infrared blaster. I swiped it with the rest of this kit from Cameron's lock-up. The lights emit a field of infrared light invisible to the naked eye. They can blind most camera sensors, making the car licence plate unreadable to most cameras."

Craven nodded, pretending he understood what Kane was talking about. Their first stop was at a service station near Milton Keynes. Craven pulled into the petrol station and fuelled up the car, and Kane paid with his credit card in the name of Mark Walters. Inside the station, Kane tossed away their comms devices in case they were compromised. He bought two new burner phones and two baseball caps. Craven pulled on his cap and both men kept their heads low, ensuring that the CCTV only captured fleeting, obscured images of their faces. They bought large coffees and continued on the journey north.

"Do you know who he is?" Craven asked, darkness lying heavy over the motorway as the Audi cruised in the middle lane whilst trucks and lorries crawled along the inside, with bleary-eyed drivers carrying cargo from across Europe to deliver to different locations across the UK.

"American. Most likely former Delta or Navy SEAL, now working private contracts. Highly-trained. Skilled," Kane replied, staring ahead at the brightly-lit road.

"Like you, then."

"Like me," Kane agreed. "The Alliance must have contracted him to recover the Prometheus Code and the EMP, and to take us out if we get in his way."

"Is he alone?"

"Could be. But he's missed us twice now. His employers will look at other solutions. Especially now they know we have the EMP. We have both parts of the puzzle in our hands, the EMP and the virus, so we suddenly become even more attractive to our enemies."

"Aye, well. Let's destroy both of the bloody things and have done with it."

"That's the idea, Frank."

They merged onto the M6 motorway as a pallid yellow sun crept over the horizon to wash the sky with a pale orange glow. Craven kept the Audi within the speed limit, avoiding the temptation to gun the accelerator and speed north whilst the roads were quiet. Craven pulled in again an hour later at services close to Birmingham. Kane used his card to buy some clothes from a small store beside a jaded-looking café, and both men changed into jackets, snicker work trousers with side pockets on the leg and black t-shirts, so that they looked like a couple of electricians on the road.

Kane took over driving after Birmingham, and Craven

closed his eyes for an hour's sleep. He longed for a dreamless sleep, one empty of ghosts. The drive gave Craven a chance to think, and thought was his enemy now. Images of Barb lying on a cold slab in Seville waiting to be repatriated forced their way into his mind, no matter how hard he tried to repress or replace them by pondering their mission. He'd left her alone when they had spent a lifetime together. Alone and cold whilst he ran about the UK like an overweight, bald, budget secret agent.

Craven opened one eye and turned to Kane. "Do you think I should have stayed in Seville with Barb? Until she's home?"

"No, Frank," Kane replied, turning quickly to meet his eye before returning to the road.

"But her friends there aren't family. They won't be with her. Now that she's gone."

"They wouldn't let you in there, anyway. She's in the mortuary. You'd just be in the house alone with your grief."

Craven closed his eyes. "She never liked being alone."

"Barbara's gone, Frank. I don't mean to be harsh about it, but all that's left of her is a corpse. Her soul isn't inside it any more. It was her soul you loved, not what's left in that mortuary."

"Do you believe in heaven?"

"Frank, it's seven o'clock in the morning and we haven't slept all night. Are you sure you want to have this conversation now?"

"It's a simple fucking question."

Kane chewed his bottom lip for a moment. He paused before replying. "The things I've seen, and the things I've seen people do, make it hard for me to believe in God. What God could allow such cruelty and pain in the world? If you were God, wouldn't you just make the world a peaceful place where everybody was kind to each other, and folk lived in peace? Why create a world with suicide bombers, children killed by snipers, concentration camps, genocide, cancer?

"But if there isn't heaven, then where's Sally? I can feel her sometimes, watching me. We weren't close at the end. We'd broken up. When I was a Mjolnir agent, she wanted me to quit. I was always away, always off on an operation I couldn't tell her much about. She wanted me home to help with the kids and spend more time with her. Then, when I entered the witness protection programme, she had to give up her career and assume a new identity. I was there all the time. She hated it. All she wanted was her old life back. But I miss her, Frank. The way she was when we were young. The way she looked after she'd given birth to the kids. She was kind and funny. The better part of me. If she isn't in a good place now, watching over Danny and Kim, then what's the point of it all? If we just die and lie rotting in the cold earth when our lives end, we might as well give up. Do you believe?"

"Like you said. We have to believe. The bastards who want Cameron's virus and the EMP want us all to suffer. They want to plunge Europe into chaos, and they don't give a shit about the desolation it will cause. The poverty, the hunger, the war. They just see a chance at victory. There can't be a heaven for those pricks."

"I don't think it's that simple, Frank. Try to get some sleep."

They made one more stop close to Manchester, at a quiet roadside café. Craven had slept for an hour, but he felt worse when he awoke. Neck stiff, gritty and squinting. He and Kane ate a fried breakfast beside road workers and truck drivers, drinking tea and coffee from white mugs. Kane watched the road for any sign of following vehicles, but the coast was clear.

Craven drove the last part of the journey, taking the M62 motorway towards Liverpool. They drove along the River Mersey, edging past the Liver Bird buildings in morning commuter traffic before reaching the Albert Dock as a cold sea rain drifted in from the estuary.

"Daddy!" Kim squealed as Craven and Kane opened the apartment door. She sprinted across the wooden floors and leapt into Kane's arms, kissing his face and hugging him tightly.

"What about your poor old Uncle Frank?" Craven asked, putting on a pretend hurt face.

"I love you too, Uncle Frank," she added, and flashed him a smile that melted his heart.

Danny was still in bed, but Cameron and Ghost greeted them warmly, and then both reverently examined the EMP device.

"Well?" asked Craven as Kane clicked the kettle on to make some coffee. "Did you work out how to kill the virus?"

"We're almost there," Cameron said, voice slightly muffled by his mask. "We have unlocked most of the firewalls and the sections we coded ourselves. We're close, Frank. Danny has been helping us. He's showing a real interest in coding and computers. He can already use a lot of the functionality on my laptop."

"Thanks for looking after him, Cam. It's good to see him find something he can get his teeth into. We need to work even harder on breaking the Prometheus Code down. It needs to happen quickly," Kane said. "Our enemies will find us before long, and they won't stop until we're dead and they have both devices."

Craven, Kane and Cameron sat around the breakfast table whilst Kim ate a plate of scrambled egg on toast. Kane briefed Cameron on the operation to steal the EMP and Cameron provided more details on his efforts to unpick the Prometheus Code. Craven took a sip of his coffee, and he heard the front door click open. He saw Ghost in the doorway and almost dropped his mug.

"What are you doing?" asked Cameron, standing slowly.

"Sit down, Cam," she said, speaking slowly in her American drawl. Ghost carried a bag over her shoulder and the EMP case in her hand. The bag contained the Prometheus Code hard drive. In her right hand, she had a gun pointed at the breakfast table. "I'm sorry."

"Put the gun down," said Kane, and slowly slid from his chair to stand in front of Kim, protecting her from Ghost's line of fire.

"I can't. It's so much money. If you try to follow me, I'll shoot you. I've rigged an explosive device in Danny's bedroom, which I can detonate remotely. Anybody follows me and this entire apartment turns to fire and ash."

"An explosive device?" Cameron said, bewildered. "What are you talking about? In Danny's room?"

"It's rigged and ready to blow, Cam. Don't test me on this. I'm sorry, but it has to be this way."

Craven took a step closer to her, but Kane caught his eye and shook his head slowly to warn him against doing anything rash. Ghost had betrayed them, and it was a gut punch.

"They've promised you the world," Kane said, keeping his voice calm despite his son lying asleep next to a bomb. It never failed to astonish Craven how Kane could control his emotions like that. Danny wasn't Craven's son, but his head was swimming with anger, fear, and shock. "But what do you think will happen to you once you hand the Prometheus Code and the EMP over to the Alliance?"

"I won't care," she said defiantly, shifting her grip on the EMP case. "I'll have fifty million dollars in the bank. Freedom. Nobody will ever find me."

"You'll never live to see that money, Ghost. They'll take what they want and kill you."

"I'm not that stupid, pal. I've taken precautions. I know more about this world than you do. Than they do. I can disappear in a web of encryption, never to be seen again."

"But what about the reasons why we built Prometheus?" asked Cameron. "We didn't build it to sell to an alliance of powers who want to wage war on the West, to crush our civilisation and wield power over us, to grind us into the ground. We built it to change the system, to even out wealth, to empower the weak and poor."

"Jesus, Cam. Are you really that naïve? Storm Shadow tried to sell it first. He realised the opportunity in the virus, the value of it. He blinked first. And now I'm going to take the money and run. Before someone else does. Don't tell me it hasn't crossed your mind."

"Never. We have to destroy it. It's the only way. Put the gun down."

"Everybody shut the fuck up!" Ghost shrieked, the gun wavering in her hand. She glanced at Kim and licked her parched lips. "Any move and I'll shoot you. Follow me and the bomb goes off."

"Ghost, wait!" Cameron begged, holding out his hand to her. "We can figure this out. Don't do this. Please."

"I'm sorry." She slipped out of the door with the Prometheus Code and the EMP, everything their enemies needed to destroy Western civilisation.

CHAPTER FORTY

The door slammed closed on its hinges and Kane burst to his feet.

"Take Kim and get out of here," he said to Craven and Cameron. "Wait for me in the shopping arcade."

"But, Jack…" Craven began.

"Just do it, Frank. I've got to find this bomb and disable it. Get Kim out!"

Kim started to cry and reached out for Kane, but Craven picked her up and ran for the door. Cameron froze where he stood, eyes fixed on Danny's bedroom door.

"Cam, go," Kane growled through gritted teeth.

"You can't do this on your own, Jack, I'm the one with the knowledge of explosives, not you. Remember how many IEDs and makeshift devices I dismantled during the war?" Cameron spoke with steely determination, his eyes still riveted on the bedroom door. Kane opened his mouth to object, but understood in that moment that his friend was right, He needed him.

Kane walked as calmly as possible to Danny's bedroom and Cameron followed, quickly grabbing his laptop bag. As they crossed the open-plan flooring, Kane fought against his racing heart rate and the panic threatening to flood his senses and cloud his judgement. There was a bomb in his son's bedroom. Ghost could trigger the device at any moment and kill Kane's son with the flick of a switch. Kane knew little about her, but he doubted Ghost was a killer, and hoped she could not kill an innocent teenage boy. But what about the people she worked for? What if the American assassin waited for her outside the building? He would trigger the bomb and not lose a minute's sleep over it.

Kane opened the door to Danny's room, darkened by closed blackout blinds. Danny lay on his side, arm hanging out of the duvet, snoring quietly. Peacefully, blissfully unaware of the life-threatening danger hidden in his room. Quickly, Kane searched the room, his mind racing through the possibilities, whilst Cameron padded in slowly behind him. The room had a compact-sized desk fixed to the rear wall, and beside Danny's iPad was a digital clock. It was a standard-sized, square device with large analogue numbers on a black screen housed in a white plastic case. The set-up was crude but effective. Two thin wires ran from the device to a small bundle of C-4 hidden beneath the desk. Where Ghost had got C-4 was a problem for another day, but her new masters were anything if not resourceful, and ravenously hungry for the Prometheus Code.

A tiny red light blinked at the bottom right-hand corner of the clock, the digital device's link to the active remote trigger. Ghost had betrayed them. She had devised a plan that exposed Kane's deepest vulnerabilities. She had stolen the deadly virus and the EMP. Rigging the bedroom was cruel and personal. Ghost's ability to rig the bomb indicated she was trained, possibly former CIA, as Cameron had previously told him he suspected. It didn't matter. She could have been a rogue implant within the Successors all along. Working for herself, or for an intelligence agency. This was the new world, where the power to wage behind-the-scenes intelligence wars rested with those who could control the world from behind a keyboard. The game had changed. The players were now people like Ghost and Cameron, using their understanding of code and cyber-crime to manipulate the world to their will.

Kane crept beside Danny's sleeping form whilst Cameron hung back. He could wake his son and usher him out of the apartment. But Danny would panic seeing both Kane and Cameron there together. He wouldn't understand, and in the time it would take Kane to explain, Ghost could trigger the device and kill them all. Kane's old training kicked in as he examined the device. Other than the explosives, Ghost could have easily acquired the components for the device: a basic digital clock, a bundle of wires, and then the C-4. The sophistication lay in the triggering mechanism – a repurposed smartphone linked to the device and taped to the back of the clock. The phone screen displayed a simple app Ghost had likely coded herself. She could detonate the bomb with a single tap of the linked phone in her possession.

Kane knew they had limited time. They had to defuse the thing before Danny woke up, or Ghost activated the trigger. Kane glanced at Cameron whose hands moved with practised precision as he now stepped forward and examined the clock. Carefully setting it down, Cameron picked up his burner phone and accessed the apartment's Wi-Fi network. Kane knelt beside him and carefully lifted the wires to examine the device's construction. It was far beyond his basic knowledge. The trigger ran through the digital network, and Kane worried that if they tried to remove the wires from the C-4, the whole thing would blow. He cuffed sweat from his brow and stared up at Cameron in askance.

"It's triggered by an encrypted signal through the Wi-Fi network," his friend whispered. "I'll try and get into it and disable the trigger so I can remove the C-4." Cameron took the laptop bag from his shoulder and slipped out his laptop. He crouched and opened the machine on his knees, gently tapping away at the keyboard to work his magic. It felt like an eternity to Kane before Cameron whispered again. "OK, I'm in. She's operating the trigger through the apartment Wi-Fi. I'm disrupting the link between Ghost's device and the bomb. I'm creating a quick and dirty networking jamming script, using my laptop to flood the area with irrelevant signals."

Sweat trickled down Kane's brow, hoping that Cameron's solution would work. Suddenly, the red dot blinking on the clock face stopped, signifying that it was no longer linked to the remote trigger and Kane gripped his friend by the shoulder, silently celebrating the small victory that might just save his son's life.

"It worked, Cam. You're a genius." Kane hissed after a sigh of relief. With the immediate threat neutralised, Kane turned his attention to the bomb itself.

"I don't have the steady hands I once did," Cameron said, his masked face staring down at his shaking, scarred hands. "You do it, and I'll guide you."

Kane closed his eyes and tried to remember his training, the weeks he'd spent going through basic bomb construction. Kane had disarmed bombs in the field before, but mostly older, more basic versions used to rig doors with explosives or remove devices from beneath vehicles. Nothing in this modern, digital era. That was Cameron's field, and as Kane carefully picked up the device, Cameron nodded and pointed to show him what to do.

"We need to disable the timer," Cameron spoke in a low, steady voice. "Look there. You can trace the wires from the digital clock to the C-4. Ghost has likely rigged it to detonate if tampered with, so we need to sever the correct wire." Cameron paused and swallowed heavily. When he spoke again, Kane noticed a quiver in his voice. "Any wrong move could trigger the explosion."

Kane exhaled and calmed his breathing, wiping his sweaty

hands on his trousers. Cameron pointed again. "That's the primary wire. That connects the clock to the detonator. That's the one we need. You got it, Jack?" Kane nodded at his friend, and then slowly knelt and then lay on his back, looking up at the small brick-shaped block of explosives. He clamped his jaws tightly and pulled the wire free of the C-4. No explosion. Kane exhaled a sigh of relief. Before he could wake Danny and get out of the apartment, they also had to remove the detonator.

Cameron gestured, violently shaking his head whenever Kane touched the wrong part of the bomb's inner workings. It was delicate work, requiring steady hands. Following Cameron's guidance, Kane carefully unscrewed the casing and gingerly removed the detonator cap. He gently pulled it away and slid from under the table. The bomb was completely neutralised, and Danny was safe. For now. Kane and Cameron exchanged a long look of relief, Cameron's single eye burning with emotion. He gestured towards himself and then the door, indicating that he would leave before Kane woke Danny, and Kane nodded in understanding. After he watched Cameron leave, Kane turned to watch his son sleep, seeing Danny as a baby in his soft eyelashes and the curve of his cheeks. For a moment, he wondered what he would do if he lost his son. It was unthinkable. Unbearable. The Alliance had to be stopped. They had threatened Kane's family and come within a hair's breadth of killing his son.

Kane gently shook Danny's shoulder, and he rolled over, grumbling. He opened one eye, saw his father and tutted.

"What is it, Dad?"

"It's time to wake up, Danny. We must leave."

"It's Dan, not Danny," he muttered, blearily.

Kane lingered, leaning into his son to embrace him. But Danny turned away into his duvet. How could he have brought his children into harm's way again? But what choice did he have? This was their life. As Danny rose slowly and gathered his things, Kane gave up hope of drawing his son close. The moment had passed and if Kane forced him into a hug, Danny would be suspicious. Kane grabbed his own gear and ushered Danny towards the door. They had to track down Ghost. The betrayal burned deep, and Kane had not expected it. But his focus was unwavering. They had come for his family, and Kane would stop at nothing to prevent the disaster Ghost would enable the Alliance to unleash. Kane would make them pay for threatening his family. It was time to fight back.

CHAPTER FORTY-ONE

Kyle Lavine had killed three security guards and two police officers to escape from Canary Wharf. He left London on a National Rail train heading north, again, with the city screaming behind him with sirens and high-alert police protocols. Gun violence was rare in the UK, unlike Kyle's home country, where single shootings were barely worthy of making an evening news bulletin. He hadn't wanted to kill the officers, but they had cornered him in an alley across from where he'd fought Jack Kane and there was no way out. So he had shot them both. Kyle couldn't allow them to arrest him, nor become embroiled in hand-to-hand combat with two men. He knew they were honest men just trying to make a living, providing a service to the people. But he didn't care.

Movies, books, and media convinced people that soldiers were wracked with PTSD and remorse for the men they had killed in action. But that wasn't Kyle Lavine's experience. He knew men who suffered PTSD because of explosions, witnessing friends slaughtered, or coming close to death themselves. He understood that and probably had a touch of it himself from all he'd experienced during his time as a Delta operator. But killing was different. Man was an animal built to kill. It was in human DNA. Kyle was sure of it. Humans had killed each other since the dawn of time. First, for grazing rights, access to river water to obtain precious metals or wealth from a rival group or village. Then for women, land, power, wealth. Killing was as natural to man as it was to a shark or a lion. Kyle felt for the police officers' families. He understood their grief. But they knew the risks when they took the job, and so did a soldier. It was the way of things. Kill or be killed, and Kyle Lavine was a killer.

Fleeing Canary Wharf on foot had taken longer, but was safer than trying to make his getaway in a vehicle. It had been night, with few vehicles on the road and the police were vigilant. Kyle had moved in the shadows, through alleyways, skirting behind buildings, blending in with the dark until he'd crossed from the Isle of Dogs and back to central London. The train ran from London Euston Station direct to Liverpool Lime Street station in approximately two and a half hours, and the first train departed at 5.30am, which suited Kyle. The train was musty and small but with comfortable seats in blocks of four on either side of a table. For the first part of his journey, a student sat in the seat across from him playing too loud music in earphones, but it was a small price to pay. The student left the train after an hour, leaving Kyle alone.

The train gave Kyle a chance to sleep after a night spent hunting. It also allowed him to travel without worrying about cameras or surveillance. The blanket of London CCTV certainly captured his face. As he sat on the train sipping bad coffee, Met police analysts investigating the shootings would pull his face from the night footage and send his image to every force in Britain, and to every news and media outlet. Time was running out. He had to deal with Kane and Jordan before the net closed in around him. The UK police force did not differ from the US police; they hated a cop killer.

The alert had come through to Kyle's phone shortly after leaving London. A notification from Hydra to inform him that both the EMP and the Prometheus Code were in Liverpool. A grainy video message informed him that Jafari was already in the UK, and that an agent of theirs had got the devices from Jack Kane and Cameron Jordan. Kyle's mission objectives had changed; the devices were secure now, so instead of an operation to recover high-value digital tech, he was now tasked with a much simpler objective. Kill Cameron Jordan and Jack Kane.

Kyle hated being told what to do. He was nobody's lackey. If he'd have wanted to be ordered around, he would have stayed in the army. Kyle stared out of the train window at the dreary English town flashing past him. Redbrick buildings and tiled roofs, grey concrete buildings, all smacking of the 1980s. It was old and stale, like the UK itself. Kyle had half his fee already resting in his Antiguan account, and it would be the easiest thing in the world for him to catch a plane out of this shithole and return to his lodge in the Alps. Fuck Hydra and Jack Kane.

If only it was that simple. Kyle Lavine cared nothing for Hydra and their misguided objectives. Jafari was a well-known and ruthless assassin. A terrorist responsible for various high-profile bombings and assassinations across the world. Kyle wanted nothing to do with him. He didn't even want to breathe the same air as an Islamist fanatic. He had spent years hunting those bastards in the desert, and that war would never be over. The reason Kyle went north was professional pride. Kane had got the better of him twice. They had been face to face, had even exchanged words. Kyle wasn't used to losing, and he couldn't get the stink of defeat out of his nose. The humiliation of it. It lived inside his head, distracting him, annoying, and suffocating.

He would kill Jack Kane. Not for money and certainly not for Hydra, but because he wanted to. The flashbang grenade was so basic, a tactic special forces operators learned in the first weeks of training. Simple, yet effective. Kyle hadn't expected it.

Allowing himself to be deceived by his location, perhaps even underestimating his opponent. That wouldn't happen again.

A message from Jafari remained unopen on Kyle's encrypted phone. He wouldn't read it, had no interest in allowing himself to be triggered by a terrorist ordering him about like a dog. Perhaps he should kill Jafari once he'd dealt with Kane. Do the world a favour. Either way, the fight was coming. Coming soon. Kyle's temper was already blown. He'd run riot at Zenith Technologies, not even attempting an insertion by stealth. Now it was outright war. Kill Kane and get out of the UK as quickly as possible.

CHAPTER FORTY-TWO

Kane watched Craven push Kim on a swing in an urban playground three miles from the Albert Dock apartment. She laughed as the old detective tickled her belly every time the swing came close to him. Then she would swing away as Craven made monster faces, only to tickle her again as the swing returned above the poured rubber playground floor. It was good to see her laugh. Kane couldn't remember the last time he had made her giggle like that. Danny leant against the playground fence watching YouTube videos on his phone, as far away from Kane as he could be without actually leaving the playground.

"Can you find Ghost?" Kane asked over his shoulder.

"I'll find her," Cameron replied, sitting on a park bench hammering away at his keyboard again.

"How?"

"I put a tracker on the hard drive as a contingency plan. So that we could find the hard drive if it got away from us. If the other side took it."

"Won't she suspect that?"

"Maybe. Who knows what goes on in that head of hers? I had no idea, Jack. I was wrong to trust her."

"Tell me about Ghost again. She tried to kill my son. She understands explosives and isn't afraid to use them. I want to understand her. Check her records and whatever you can access and try to find out who she has betrayed us to. My first guess is that the millions of dollars Chen Li, or Storm Shadow as you call him, planned to sell the virus for got into her head like a worm. What was it, fifty million dollars? That'd turn anyone's head. She had his emails and therefore everything she needed to pick up with the Alliance, or whoever else he was dealing with, and take up his original arrangement."

"This is the profile I've built up on Ghost. We already know her real name is Rachel Vines. She was born and grew up in Palo Alto, California. In the heart of Silicon Valley. Her parents were both computer engineers, and she showed an interest in coding at an early age. Her parents entered her into various coding competitions, which she usually won, and they nurtured her talent. Palo Alto was the perfect backdrop for her early forays into programming and hacking. It's not like growing up in Grimsby or the Orkneys and having a dabble in basic scratch coding. Palo Alto is the home of tech culture, with cutting-edge access to the companies and schools at the forefront of programming and hacking. But by the time she was in high school, Ghost was already creating advanced software and had graduated from winning local comps to national coding competitions.

"Her school records show that she was a standout student, consistently achieving top grades and earning many accolades in maths and computer sciences. Her exceptional SAT scores and a sackful of recommendations from tech industry leaders paved her way to MIT, where she majored in Computer Science and Engineering. She excelled at MIT, graduating summa cum laude. Which to army grunts like you and me means she passed with the highest distinctions. She maintained a perfect GPA and her senior thesis on quantum encryption caught the attention of industry giants and also governmental agencies.

"Her time at MIT changed her. Ghost was far away from the idyllic life of Palo Alto and the cocoon her parents had created for her. She joined various hacking enclaves, learned about sociology to understand politics, and took an interest in world affairs. She cut her hair, started to dress in hoodies and baggy jeans, frequented socialist and subversive society meetings. I found her government records, and they recruited her into a covert CIA programme aimed at identifying and nurturing top talent. The recruitment was subtle, starting with an innocuous campus meeting with a careers advisor who gradually revealed the opportunity. They spun the agency to make her believe she could help change the world. She came to understand that future wars won't be fought on battlefields with tanks and machine-guns, but with keyboards, servers, viruses, and code. Attracted by a chance to make a real difference in the world and to use her skills for national security, Ghost agreed to join the CIA.

"After graduation, she took a job working for a leading Silicon Valley company. Whilst there, she stumbled upon unethical practices involving data privacy breaches and manipulation of algorithms for financial gain. Her CIA handlers did not want to break the crimes and show their presence in the tech community. Ghost decided to blow the roof off it anyway and blew the whistle. It resulted in a massive scandal that rocked the tech world. She went underground to avoid retaliation, and then her expertise became invaluable to the CIA. Her insights exposed the agency to the inner workings of social media mega-firms and start-ups. It looks like she was still part of the CIA when she joined the Successors."

"And you worked on the virus believing she was no longer with the agency?"

"It sounds stupid now, knowing what we know. But yeah. I thought she was as done with that world as I was with the

British military. We kind of bonded over it, our former lives, and the change we were fighting for. I'm sorry, Jack. I didn't mean for you and your family to be put in danger. You saved my life."

"And you helped me save Danny's life," Kane said. "Let's figure out where she might have gone. Let me see her file."

Cameron handed Kane his laptop, and Kane clicked through the various screens. Her dossier was extensive. Cameron had quickly pulled together details of her academic achievements, her CIA recruitment process, and her subsequent work. The file contained high-resolution images of her life at MIT, commendations from professors, and encrypted communications between Ghost and her CIA handlers. Cameron's file painted a comprehensive picture of her journey, but little about the woman herself. Though he had been in her company for the last few days, Kane had no idea about her personality, other than that she was quiet, sullen and withdrawn. Ghost looked and acted like a stereotypical hacker, straight out of a Hollywood movie. She had the short white hair, no make-up, hooded eyes and baggy clothing. She seemed to be driven, like Cameron and the rest of the Successors, by a desire to change the world, but part of Kane doubted that. If a hacker wanted to change the world for good, why not steal money from big corporations and banks and deposit the money in charity accounts as an anonymous donation? Why not move to a Third World country and help dig wells or build housing?

"Why did you really join the Successors, Cam?" Kane asked.

"I told you, we have the same aims, the same goals."

"I don't mean that. I mean, when you are online, and you join these groups. Why do you do it?"

Cameron sighed and stared at his hands. He reached up and took his mask off, letting Kane see the true extent of his fire-ravaged face.

"Look at me, Jack. I can't go out in public. I can't meet a mate for a beer or join a local martial arts gym. I can't do anything. The war left me a monster. I'm alone. Do you know what that feels like? Day after day with nothing but my computer and nobody to talk to but similar people online. People who don't have friends beyond cyber chat rooms. You remember how I was, but I'm not that man any more. The war and the army fucked me over, Jack. When I joined the Successors, I had friends again. We'd chat all day. Work on the complex code for Prometheus, solve problems. It was like being in the regiment again. Like when we were brothers."

Cameron's face bore the indelible marks of his horrific RPG encounter. The left side of his face was twisted and discoloured, a grim tapestry of burn scars. His skin, once smooth, was a landscape of deep grooves and ridges, the result of extensive grafts and reconstructive surgeries. Cameron's left eye was gone, nothing but a cavernous black hole surrounded by puckered skin stretched like pink paper over his skull. His lips were uneven, pulled tight by scar tissue, leaving his face and expressions a grim shadow of their former selves. Kane remembered Cameron as he was; young, handsome, athletic and funny.

His body told a tale of the violence Cameron had endured. Patches of scar tissue covered his chest and arms. Some areas made smoother by skin grafts, others rougher where the burns were deepest. The skin varied in colour from pale, almost white, to angry red, and the texture was uneven and rough like desert hills. His scars extended down his left side, a painful reminder of the flames that had licked at his flesh. The healing process must have been agonising, each breath a battle against searing pain. Kane remembered visiting Cameron during his recovery and physical therapy. It was a brutal process, pushing Cameron to stretch and move despite the agony. Cameron had wept that day. He'd asked Kane why he hadn't left him in the truck to die and Kane remembered the pain of seeing his friend and warrior-brother in such agony.

"So, you found comrades in the Successors. Friends. You were part of something again. It was the same for Ghost. The girl in these files is a loner. Her parents raised her alone, sitting in her room coding instead of playing with her friends. No soccer, swimming, or hanging around in her friends' bedrooms for Rachel Vines. It was all computers and coding competitions. Her photos from MIT aren't of drunken nights, boyfriends, or movie nights. They are of her winning awards or class pictures. She found the same thing as you did. Ghost wasn't in the Successors to save the world; she was there for friendship. To find other voices out there in the ether, other lonely people whose only dream is for a hand to hold in the dark. Someone to share their loneliness, other lost souls to talk to and share a common goal."

"All right, Jack. So what if that's all it was? I know we created something dangerous, but for a while it made me feel like a human again. My days had purpose. I had a reason to live. Is that so bad?"

"No. But you could have coded a new database for libraries or a method of tracking whale ocean patterns. Anything but a virus aimed at bringing down the Western economy."

"Maybe we were led in that direction? Storm Shadow suggested it and we rose to the challenge."

"Now Ghost's sold it to the highest bidder."

Kane handed Cameron the laptop, and Cameron brought up a screen with lists of messages. "Seems to me she's sold it to the Alliance. There's a message here from someone named Jafari, who says he'll meet her in the UK for the exchange."

"Good. That's where we'll strike. Use your tracker, Cam, and find out where she is. When she arranges the meeting, we'll be waiting."

"Daddy?" Kim yelled, and Kane smiled as she waved at him from the playground. "Look at me!" Craven had twisted the swing ropes around into a coil with Kim at the centre. He let it go, and the swing spun around as the ropes unravelled and Kim squealed with glee.

Then, in the midst of Kim's joy, three white vans and a black Range Rover hurtled around a corner and came to a screeching stop beside the playground. Kane stared as van doors slid open and men in black tactical clothing, armed with MP5s and wearing balaclavas leapt out.

CHAPTER FORTY-THREE

Four armed men burst from each van, each one clad in black, clutching what looked to Craven like machine-guns. Two men in dark suits stepped out of the Range Rover onto the pavement, their gaze shifting from Kane to Craven.

"Go! Go! Go!" one man in black bawled. Each of their faces was hidden behind balaclavas like the men Craven had watched storm the Iranian embassy on television in 1980. Two of the men in black knelt and opened a large plastic case and a drone the size of a football buzzed into the sky above the playground.

"Frank!" Kane called to him across the playground. "Protect Kim!"

Craven bent and swept Kim into his arms, lifting her from the swing into a bear hug.

"What's happening, Uncle Frank?" she said, voice lifting in pitch as she became alarmed. The world seemed to slow on its axis, puffs of white cloud paused in the pastel blue sky, cars driving through Liverpool's back streets reduced their speed to a crawl between densely-packed terraced houses and ten men with guns advanced on the playground. They moved low, rifles held before them, hurrying with professional smoothness, and their presence could only mean death or capture.

"Don't worry, love," Craven whispered into Kim's ear. "I won't let them hurt you."

Craven rushed towards the plastic wire fence encircling the playground with Kim in his arms. He glanced over his shoulder at Kane, who was already moving. Cameron vaulted over the playground fence with his laptop under one arm like a rugby ball and fled towards the tangled network of early 19th century houses with their redbrick fronts, net curtains and wooden gates.

"Hold your fire," barked one man in black. "Two children present. Non-lethal force only."

The first thing Craven thought of when he heard the words non-lethal was a taser. They had introduced the electrocuting weapons during his final years on the force, and Craven had witnessed first-hand what fifteen hundred volts could do to a man. He set Kim down gently beside the fence and turned to face the onrushing soldiers, fists balled and anger surging.

"Danny, follow Cam," Kane yelled to his son. Danny sprinted across the playground, around where Kane rushed to hold off the armed men. He leapt over the fence in one jump and ran after Cameron, who disappeared between a row of houses.

"On your knees," growled the first armed man who approached Craven. He was a wiry man and stood a head shorter than Craven, his frame as narrow as Craven's was thick "We're MI5 and you are under arrest. Step away from the girl. On your knees, hands above your head."

If he gave her up, they would take Kim away. Kane was a wanted man, and as far as Craven knew, Kim had no other relatives to take her in. They would put her into care, into the system which Craven had seen produce so many criminals, so many innocent children broken and twisted into feral, vicious, damaged young people. There were some good care homes out there, but others were hell, and that could not be Kim's fate. Craven bunched his muscles. Kim sobbed in fear. Anybody could identify themselves as MI5, as police, army, or even the prime minister, but without identification, they could be anyone. With every man and his dog hunting the Prometheus Code, Craven's defensive instinct reared its head. The wiry man lowered his gun and pointed at Craven with a gloved hand. The rifle hung against the man's chest by a black strap, and he edged closer to Craven, pulling plastic cable-tie handcuffs from his belt.

Craven reached and grabbed the outstretched hand and pulled the man in black towards him. Craven punched him in the gut with his left hand and then kicked him into the second man in black's path. That second man in black snarled and pushed his winded colleague out of the way.

"Run, Kim!" Craven bellowed, but the little girl didn't move, so stricken was she with terror.

The second man reached out for Craven, and the old detective kicked him hard in the bollocks. He yelped and fell to his knees, and Craven punched him in the nose. Shouting filled the playground as violence exploded between the swings, slides and climbing frames where children usually played, but now military force descended with brutal power. Craven drove his shoulder into a third attacker, and that man wrapped his arms around Craven's waist. He tried to lift Craven from his feet, hoping to dump him on his back. Kim screamed and fury pulsed through Craven's body. He thought of Barb, of the unfairness of her death and his grief. If this was his time to die, so be it. He would do it protecting Kim, ready to join Barb wherever she was in spirit.

Craven howled like a wild beast. He drove his elbow into the man in black's head, and as the arms loosened around his waist Craven leant forward and using all the old-man strength in his huge frame, he picked up the assailant and dumped him headfirst onto the rubber floor. Another man hurtled at Craven, and he blocked a punch with his forearm, then pulled the man into a vicious headbutt. Craven tossed that attacker aside like an old rag and scooped Kim up into his arms.

Craven ran. Commotion screamed around him like a storm, men shouting orders and groaning in pain, Kim weeping. Craven lumbered back towards the fence and lowered Kim over the side. He placed one hand on the fence to leap after her, but hands grabbed at his back and belt. Craven growled like a trapped bear. He swung his brawny arms around the latest attacker. No finesse or martial arts skill, just wild anger and the urge to protect Kim at all costs. Craven flung him against the fence and grabbed his skull in powerful hands. Craven smashed the man's head against the fence and then reeled as two batons rained blows down on his shoulders and body.

The first man Craven had dropped surged to his feet, recovered from Craven's assault, and drove his elbow into Craven's stomach. The air whooshed out of him like a burst balloon. Craven dropped to his knees as more baton strikes hammered into his body. A blow thumped into the side of his head, blinding his vision. Volts of electricity shot through his body like fire and the world went dark.

CHAPTER FORTY-FOUR

My children. Kane's head swam with the overwhelming desire to protect Danny and Kim. A man in black combat gear shouted at Kane to surrender, barked to identify himself as MI5. That meant they were agents responsible for Britain's national security, their goal to protect the nation against threats from within. Kane couldn't trust them. They had attacked him already at the lock-up and again at the safe house on the Snake Pass. One man in black fired a taser and Kane darted to his left to avoid the twin prongs fired from the bright yellow, gun-shaped weapon. Kane rolled towards the man, kicked his attacker's knee out and drove his hip into a second attacker, throwing him to the spongy rubber playground floor and punching him in the throat.

Danny sprinted across the playground following Cameron. *Good. Keep moving, son.* Danny angled his run away from the MI5 operatives. He darted towards Kim as though to get to her before they did, but the men in black were already advancing and he could not get to her without risking them both being captured. A harrowing look twisted Danny's features as a cruel but necessary decision played on his youthful face. He veered away, making for the furthest point away from the MI5 men. He had done the right thing, the hard thing. Saved himself rather than both him and Kim risking capture.

"Danny, take this," Kane bellowed, and threw Danny the backpack containing his burner phones, the Glock, and the rest of his equipment. He couldn't risk being captured with the guns or losing them to his attackers. Danny caught the bag, glanced at Kane with large, frightened eyes, and then carried on at full tilt in the same direction as Cameron.

Craven stood before Kim, doing his best to keep their assailants at bay. Kane ran to his left to block an armed man who made to cut off Danny's escape. He crashed through a set of swings and Kane bundled into him, driving them both to the ground. He rolled with the black-clad enemy, the body armour and MP5 pressing hard into Kane's body, each man trying to rain down blows on the other. A second attacker struck Kane on the back with a baton and Kane grunted in pain. The baton came down again, but this time Kane rolled away so that the weapon crashed into his adversary, scrambling on the rubber flooring. Kane reached up and grabbed the wrist of the man with the baton and twisted it savagely. The man cried out and Kane dragged him two steps towards the swings, using the painfully sprained wrist to lead the armoured operator who stumbled after him. Kane wrapped the swing rope around the MI5 man's neck twice and yanked down hard. The man choked, gasped, and jerked his legs furiously.

Kim screamed and Kane turned to see Craven sprawled on the ground with coiled taser wires hanging from his body and a man in black carrying Kim towards one of the white vans.

"Kim, no!" Kane choked in horror. She was thirty feet away, and six men stood between Kane and the man bundling his daughter away. They were armed with MP5s, and could easily have eviscerated Kane, Cameron, and Craven with gunfire by now. That they had held back in fear of harming Kim, Danny or a passer-by gave their claims to be MI5 some credence. That reluctance to fire gave Kane a moment to act. He ran from the swing towards the six men between him and his daughter.

There was no enemy left behind him to pursue Danny or Cameron. Craven was down and out of action, and Kane couldn't let them take Kim.

The closest man in black set his feet and grabbed his taser, but by the time he had drawn the weapon, Kane was upon him. Kane lashed out with a front kick and pinned the enemy's forearm to his body armour, making it impossible for him to draw his weapon. Kane followed the kick-up by ducking and turning into the man's midriff. A second attacker swung at him with a telescopic baton which sliced through the air where Kane had been a fraction of a second earlier. Kane brought his right elbow up and over his torso and cracked it into the baton-wielding enemy's face. With his left hand, Kane grabbed the first black-clad man's trousers just above his combat boots and yanked the leg ferociously towards him so that the man flew from his feet. Kane picked up the baton and blocked a punch with his forearm just as another enemy charged him, driving Kane to the ground. Kane rolled, keeping his hips up, and stabbed down with the baton so that it jabbed into the enemy's groin. He made a high-pitched mewling noise and rolled away from Kane, who kicked him viciously in the face.

A van door slid open and the man carrying Kim bundled her into the vehicle, and rage surged inside Kane like quicksilver. MI5 or not, these men were kidnapping his daughter. Kane had served his country for years, had killed in the name of queen and country, but he was fighting for his daughter now. MI5 had brought the fight to him. They had attacked him, without talking and without warning. Kane ripped the MP5 from his attacker's chest and quickly unclipped the belt from around his waist. A heavy belt hung with spare ammunition magazines, a knife, three grenades and a taser. Six men lay groaning on the playground floor. The rest circled around Kane, tasers and batons held tight in their fists. Kane slung the belt over his shoulder, raised the MP5, and fired off a quick burst of three rounds in the air. The men in black paused and trained their weapons on Kane.

"Bring my daughter to me," Kane commanded and moved through the playground like a stalking lion. He trained his weapon on the two men in suits beside their Range Rover. The drone hovered above him, shifting every few seconds like a monstrous bee, sending images of the confrontation back to MI5 headquarters.

"All we want is the hard drive," said one of the suits in a Welsh accent, a stocky man with receding slicked-back hair. "Come in quietly, Kane, give us the Prometheus Code and your daughter will be safe. We know you didn't build the virus. All we want is to secure it and destroy it."

"And if I don't?"

"We'll have to take you by force. You are her and Danny's only living parent. They'll both go into care. Into the system, Jack. You know what that means, don't you?"

Kane shuddered at the thought. His little Kim in a care home. Not whilst he lived and breathed.

"Tell your men to get back, or I'll kill you where you stand."

"Put the gun down, Kane. It's over. You used to serve your country. Why turn traitor now?"

"You offered peace once before. You called my friend and offered a meeting and then sent a chopper and agents to kill us. Don't talk to me about traitors and betrayal."

"That was an unfortunate situation. I did not give that order, Jack. If I wanted you dead today, I could have put a sniper in any of these houses and taken you out before you knew we were even here. Think about that. You know it's true. I just want the hard drive. You have the EMP too. We aren't stupid. Hundreds of cameras picked your face up in London. You didn't even try to hide yourself. There's something else going on here, and I want to help you. Come in and we can sort this thing out."

Kane began to lower his gun, and then his instincts kicked in. Trust no one. Kane fired a shot and the Range Rover's rear window exploded in a hail of glass. The two suits ducked and covered their heads.

"Next one goes in your skull. Get them back."

"Get back!" the stocky, suited man called.

The armed man backtracked away from Kane, forming a protective ring around the vans.

"Bring Kim to me. Now."

"Not going to happen, Jack. You're firing your weapon in a residential area, putting innocent people's lives at risk. The Prometheus Code is a threat to Britain's national security, and you will hand it over to us. You'll be reunited with your daughter once we have the code. If you open fire again, we will shoot back."

Kane swore under his breath. He'd have to kill them all to get to Kim. It was impossible to engage so many enemies in a gunfight and live. He would have to find another way to free Kim. Kane's stomach lurched. MI5 had his daughter and there was nothing he could do about it. Not now anyway. But he would find a way. Craven was down, groaning and rolling on the playground floor, stunned by the taser volts shot into his body. Kane would have to leave Craven, too. There was no other way. If he turned himself in, MI5 would take him to a secure facility and put Kim into care. They would chase down Danny and Cameron and pick them up later today, or days from now. But a man who couldn't go out in public and a frightened teenager would be easy to find. As long as Kane was free, there was a chance he could find both Kim and Craven. If he was captured, he could do nothing. The Alliance had the Prometheus Code, and now the British Government had Kim and Craven. Kane's world was on fire, so he did the only he knew how to do well.

Kane fired another burst from his MP5, shooting out the tyres on the Range Rover and first van. Whilst the suits and the men in black shielded their heads and shrank away from the gunfire, Kane pulled a flashbang grenade from the belt over his shoulder and ripped the pin free with his teeth. Before the armed men could react, Kane tossed the grenade at them and ran. The grenade exploded with a bang that echoed around the housing estate like a thunderclap, followed by a flash of bright light.

"I'll find you, Frank,' he said, pausing beside Craven's stricken form. The big man opened his eyes a crack and nodded his understanding. "I'll find you and Kim. Trust me."

Kane left Craven and Kim and ran for his life.

CHAPTER FORTY-FIVE

"With all due respect, sir, I would have Kane and Jordan in custody right now had you not cut me out of the loop and sent a kill team into the Snake's Pass like something from Black Hawk Down. Let me do my job."

MI5 Agent Gareth Jones slammed the phone down and sat on a battered swivel chair in his sparse office. His jacket hung on the back of his closed door and he sipped at a cup of lukewarm instant coffee. The fluorescent light in the panelled ceiling flickered slightly, casting a harsh glow on the stack of files spread out across his desk. He knuckled at tired eyes and ran his hand over the stubble on his heavy jaw. Jones was a stocky man in his late forties with a square jaw and chestnut eyes that had seen more than their fair share of the UK's dark underbelly. He was forty-five years old, his once muscled rugby player frame now run to fat around his gut and chin, with a failed marriage and an eight-year-old son he rarely saw behind him. He glimpsed his reflection in the blacked-out monitor on his desk and smoothed down his thinning slicked-back hair, a testament to the stress and pressure of his job.

Jones worked between MI5 headquarters at Thames House in London, and other facilities across the UK, such as Walsingham House, where he was now. Security within the facility was tight. Guards patrolled the corridors regularly, their boots echoing off the hard surfaces. These guards, many of whom were former military personnel, had undergone advanced training and were equipped with body armour, tasers, and sidearms. They communicated via secure radios, ensuring coordination and rapid response to any incident. Strategically placed panic buttons throughout the facility allowed staff to call for immediate back-up if needed.

The facility's control room next door was a hub of activity. Here, operators monitored live feeds from the surveillance cameras, tracked the movement of guards and prisoners, and coordinated security efforts. A team of dedicated security professionals manned rows of monitors, keyboards, and communication equipment in the control room.

Despite its high-security measures, Walsingham House was designed to be discreet. It blended into its surroundings, looking like any other mundane government building from a distance. This anonymity was its greatest defence, allowing it to operate without drawing unwanted attention. Jones had travelled from London because a high-value prisoner, Frank Craven, awaited questioning and it fell to Jones to conduct the interview. Walsingham was a fortress of top security and secrecy where MI5 conducted their most sensitive interrogations, extracting crucial information before deciding the fate of their prisoners. The facility stood as a testament to the lengths the agency would go to protect national security, a place where secrets were uncovered and threats neutralised, often before the outside world even knew they existed.

Jones had grown up in a small fishing village in south Wales, the son of a former coal miner, who had been out of work and bitter for most of Jones' life. The one thing Jones' father had given him was a sense of duty and patriotism, as well as a desire to rise above the working class and get out of his small town where men drank, and women worked to support husbands who lamented for an industry and way of life gone forever with pit closures and nationalisation. After excelling in school, much to his parents' surprise, Williams attended the University of Cardiff where he studied criminology and played rugby. His academic prowess and natural leadership on the pitch caught the attention of MI5 recruiters, and he was offered a position shortly after graduation.

Jones had married his university sweetheart young, but in truth, he was more devoted to his career than to his relationship. She had her own career in HR, and they had been apart more than together. Whatever love they had in college waned into a mortgage and grudging partnership, then accidental parenthood. She had hated him then, forced to take maternity leave and then to place their child in childcare to return to her career, after a year where colleagues had taken their chance to leapfrog her on the greasy pole of corporate promotion. Jones loved his son but was happy to be free from the shackles of marriage, and his apathy at receiving divorce papers had not surprised him.

Over the years, Jones had risen steadily through the ranks of MI5, proving himself in various counterterrorism and intelligence operations. He could speak Urdu, Arabic and some Punjabi, and had found his niche seeking terrorist cells amongst Muslim communities across the UK. He had found and arrested dozens of rogue imams who twisted the words of the Koran to radicalise disenfranchised young men, youths who thought the world owed them more, men with no prospects, left behind by society, who found purpose and zeal in the words of fierce men who spoke of a holy war, martyrdom and the glory of radical Islamism. The men Jones captured were extradited if they were immigrants or placed in secure facilities if they were UK citizens. Jones had become deft at interrogation, both on-camera justifiable methods and off-camera brutal techniques to destroy a man's mind and reduce him to a compliant wreck. Now, as a senior officer, he handled some of the agency's most critical missions.

Despite his weariness and his impressive career, Jones' zeal to protect his country was far from jaded. He remained fiercely patriotic, driven by a deep-seated desire to protect his country from all threats. Jones had questioned extremists who hated Western culture with the utmost intensity. He knew better than most that people worked every day to destroy Western civilisation. They hated the West as if it was only yesterday when Richard the Lionheart had invaded the East and butchered countless Muslims before the gates of Jerusalem.

Jones put his coffee cup down and picked up the file detailing the virus. Despite all the hate he had seen, all the attempts he had thwarted to bomb, destroy, and incinerate his country and culture, the Prometheus Code had truly shaken him. The virus, engineered by the rogue group known as the Successors, had the potential to cripple the entire European financial system. It would destroy all data held by the major institutions on interbank lending, loans, mortgages, shares, investments, pensions, insurance and savings. If the financial systems failed, society failed. There would be anarchy, and the very fabric of civilisation would collapse. Jones' superiors were even more spooked than he was. This was no bomb threat at a train station or football match, which were acts of terror designed to kill and maim British subjects. This was a Doomsday scenario. The stakes were higher than they had ever been in Jones' career. His orders were explicit: recover the virus at all costs.

He took a deep breath and opened Frank Craven's police file. Craven had been a detective in Manchester's Serious and Organised Crime Squad before recently retiring. His record was run-of-the-mill. In his early days, he had dismantled criminal networks, mainly heroin and cocaine dealers, and had received commendations. But his later career seemed to have stagnated. Craven had been warned about his behaviour and language and had bounced around different squads and initiatives. Jones knew the type, saw them every day in the halls of MI5. Old men living on the back of former glories, doing the bare minimum to survive and get through each day. Men over the hump of their career with more than an eye on retirement, golf, gardening, travel, or whatever floated their boat. The file painted a picture of a dedicated, if somewhat unorthodox, officer who had once had a knack for getting results. But now Craven found himself entangled in a web of espionage and cyber-terrorism, a far cry from his days on the streets of Manchester.

Jones couldn't shake off a feeling of unease. He knew Craven was not the enemy, but he was a crucial link to finding the virus. When Craven encountered Jack Kane, it turned his life upside down. Kane's file sat like a breeze block on Jones' desk. A file thick with SAS missions and MI6 operations, most of the details redacted. Somehow, Kane had popped up in Warrington a few years ago and torn the place apart. Jones couldn't quite follow the dots between the different blacked-out references, but it seemed like someone had blown Kane's cover while he was in witness protection. He had been a wanted man for a while, but then last year MI6 had revoked that status and cleared his record of any outstanding arrest warrants and crimes linked to his name. Jones would have to follow up with MI6 and try to piece together the puzzle of Jack Kane. Work for another day.

Jones had Craven in custody, and Kane's daughter was with the juvenile division, being treated with kid gloves. Craven and Kane had possession of the Prometheus Code and Jones had to secure it for the British Government. Kane's known associate and former SAS soldier Cameron Jordan was a member of the Successors, which made him a threat to national security. Craven's interrogation had to be handled delicately. As he reviewed the file, Jones noted the details of Craven's last known activities and found a reference to his recently deceased wife, whose body was pending repatriation to the UK. Jones' superiors were clear. Orders passed to him verbally: use any means necessary to extract information from Craven. The Alliance of state and non-state actors vying for the Prometheus Code, including North Korea, Iran, Al-Qaeda, and China, posed an unprecedented threat. If the virus fell into their hands, the consequences would be catastrophic.

Jones closed the file and stood up, adjusting his shirt. He slipped on his too-tight suit jacket and shot his cuffs. He glanced at his reflection again, this time in the opaque windows of his office. His face showed lines of age and determination, while his eyes gleamed with resolve. Jones left his office and made his way to the interrogation room. Colleagues stared at him from open-plan office spaces, conversations dropping to hushed silence as his footsteps pounded the polished tile floors. His mind raced with possible outcomes. He knew he must tread carefully, balancing the need for information with the ethical boundaries of his profession. Even if those ethics could be stretched in so serious a case as this. The future of Britain depended on what happened in the next few hours. With a final deep breath, he placed his hand on the handle of the room where Frank Craven waited, ready to begin the interrogation that could change everything.

CHAPTER FORTY-SIX

Craven awoke with a jolt, the aftermath of the taser still coursing through his body like electric venom. He shivered, body damp with sweat, mind swimming with the impossible hole he found himself in. Craven's muscles twitched uncontrollably, bruises from the fight at the playground pulsating. His head pounded with a relentless, dull throb. The sharp taste of copper lingered in his mouth, a grim reminder of the voltage that had incapacitated him. He struggled to regain his bearings and realised that he was strapped to a stretcher. His memory came back in painful flashes. Images of himself being wheeled through the sterile, dimly-lit corridors of an MI5 facility. Kim. It came back to him: the playground, her capture, Jack's escape.

The journey to the facility had been a blur. After the taser sent him into an electrocuted fit, they had hustled him into an unmarked van. Rough hands had secured his wrists with plastic handcuffs, blindfolded, and driven to a clandestine airstrip. He remembered the van clattering over speed bumps, pressing him into the metallic sides of the vehicle as it sped around corners and flew along a flat motorway. Then fresh air as they bundled him up the steps of a small aircraft. No sign of Kim in these flashes of events, no sound of her voice. He hoped Kane, Danny and Cameron had got away, but he did not know if they were alive or dead. The engine roar of the plane hinted at a short, covert flight. When they finally removed the blindfold, Craven realised he was in a secure, hidden location. He tried to recall the length of the flight. He guessed he was somewhere in the Midlands, but couldn't be sure.

The building itself was nondescript. A low, grey structure with reinforced concrete walls and minimal windows. It was designed to blend into the natural surroundings, making it almost invisible from the air, and so far from major roads civilians would never stumble across it, or be found by those with a desire to hunt it. Security was tight. Craven had glimpsed high fences topped with razor wire, surveillance cameras covering every angle, and armed guards patrolling the perimeter and corridors. The interior was stark and functional, with narrow hallways leading to small, windowless rooms.

Craven sat up, clutching at his pounding head. He gnashed his jaw and forced his senses to sharpen. The room was chilly, lit by a single overhead bulb casting harsh shadows on the concrete walls. The air smelled of disinfectant and old sweat, the heady mixture filling his nose and making his stomach churn. His cell door cranked and creaked as its lock turned. Craven turned his head and fought against the straps holding him down against the stretcher, but the restraints across his elbows, knees, and stomach held him fast. Two men in combat trousers and bland polo-shirts stormed into the cell, faces stern, mouths curled into contemptuous snarls. They ripped open the straps with excessive force, hands rough as they yanked Craven upright and dumped him into a metal chair and tied his wrists to the armrests with plastic zip-ties.

A stocky man in a snug, expensive-looking suit and brilliantined hair entered the cell and waved the two men away with a jerk of his head. His fine clothing and demeanour exuded an air of authority. The door slammed closed and Craven swallowed, his dry throat like sandpaper, as he recognised the man from the playground attack. The man stared at Craven, piercing dark eyes boring deep into Craven's soul, as though he already knew his deepest secrets. The suited man carried a bulky orange file under his arm and set it down on a metal table between them and sat down, his movements deliberate and controlled.

"Mr Craven," the man began in a deep Welsh accent. "I am Mr Jones. We have some questions for you."

"We've spoken before. On the phone," Craven rasped, voice hoarse from thirst. "You fucked me over, sent men with guns and a fucking helicopter after us. Why do you think I would trust you or tell you anything? Have I got the word "dickhead" tattooed across my forehead?" Craven licked his leather-dry tongue around his mouth, trying to steady himself. He knew the game. Craven had interviewed scores of criminals down the years, had seen and tried every technique and subterfuge to get them to talk. It was clear from his eyes, the hard lines across his forehead, and the grey-black stubble on his chin that this Welshman would also know it all. A man of experience, an MI5 agent and master of psychological pressure.

"That was unfortunate. It wasn't my choice. Or my order."

"Don't piss up my back and tell me it's raining, taffy. Tell me what you want and fuck off."

Jones sat back in his chair and smiled mirthlessly. "Don't you think I've heard all of this false bravado before?" He picked up a pitcher of water and poured some of the luxurious liquid into a plastic cup. "Do you want a drink?"

Craven said nothing. Jones leant forward and held the cup to Craven's lips. He was so thirsty that he couldn't resist, so Craven leant forward and gulped down the cool water.

"If I wanted you dead, you would be so already. We have Kim Kane, but the rest of your merry band of cyber-terrorists and nutcases are on the run. I will not torture or threaten you,

Frank. But that is within my power, should I wish it. I could send the girl to the worst hellhole in Britain, pack her off to a young offenders' institution, put her in the bleakest care home in London, Birmingham, Glasgow, Liverpool or Belfast. How long would she last in one of those places? Or I could pull out your teeth and fingernails, gouge out one of your eyes, subject you to a nice bit of water-boarding. I could stop the Spanish authorities from flying your wife's body home later this week, or have her corpse thrown into the sea, or left in a rubbish dump for rats and insects to eat her eyes and lips."

"Fucking bastard!" Craven howled, bucking against his restraints. How dare this man threaten to do those things to Barbara? The thought of it made Craven retch and cough against the stinging bile in his throat.

"But I don't want to do any of those things, Frank. We could just stay calm and have a little chat. I don't want to hurt you. All I want is to protect this country."

"What do you want to know?" Frank asked, his voice even hoarser.

"Let's start with the virus." Jones leant forward and made a pyramid with his fingers. "We know a rogue faction calling themselves the Successors has developed it. We know your pal Cameron Jordan is one of them. The Prometheus Code has the potential to cripple the European financial system. We aren't daft, Frank. We have eyes and ears everywhere, looking out for this exact type of threat. What we don't know is who currently has it, and how it's going to be deployed."

Craven took a deep breath. He had nothing to hide. It wasn't his device, and he didn't want it. "I'll tell you what I know if you promise to return Kim to me once we are done here. I want to drive away with her in a car. That's all I ask."

"Tell me first. Then we'll see how valuable the information is."

"Listen to me, you pompous prick. That little girl is gentle and sweet. She doesn't have a nasty bone in her body. Not like you and me. The world hasn't got to her yet. She's good and kind and you are going to let her and me go. I want your word and I want it in writing. This fucking virus is nothing to me. I'll tell you everything. I don't give a shit about my life, but I won't let you hurt my Barbara's body, and I'll die before I let you ruin Kim's life."

"Fair enough. I'll do as you ask. Tell me what you know."

"In writing first."

Jones shook his head and screeched the metal legs of his chair as he pushed himself backwards. He left the cell then returned minutes later with a white piece of A4 paper scrawled with his agreement to Craven's demands. "Now. Go on."

"I don't have all the answers, but I can tell you what I know," Frank explained, detailing how the virus was engineered to exploit vulnerabilities in the financial networks, specifically targeting the infrastructure of major banks. "It's capable of wiping out data, causing massive financial losses and chaos. The EMP device is a separate but related threat, designed to take down electronic systems on a large scale. Together, they can bring an entire region to its knees. You need both for it to work. The virus to take out the systems, and the EMP to reboot it all without possibility of recovery."

Jones nodded, taking notes with a blue biro and a leatherbound A5 notebook. "And the secret agent? Your friend Jack Kane? What is his role in all this?"

Craven hesitated. He was prepared to spill the beans on everything related to the Prometheus Code, which was just a horror story that had to be stopped and prevented from being activated by those who would hurt the UK and its people. But he didn't want to talk about Kane or incriminate him. "He's trying to prevent the virus from being deployed, that's all. Cameron Jordan asked for our help, and that's how we got involved. Cameron isn't a bad guy either. The Successors developed the fucking virus like a pet project between geeks. They are people without friends, sat at home in the dark bashing away at their keyboards. They found solace in the challenge of coding the bloody thing, but most of them never expected it to actually become a reality. We had the virus and the EMP, but they're gone. One of the Successors betrayed us and plans to sell it to the Alliance, to a man named Jafari."

"Jesus Christ. Who betrayed you?"

"Her name was Ghost. I think her real name is Rachel Vines. I don't know why these fucking computer people give each other silly names."

"She and Cameron Jordan are the last of the Successors. We suspect Storm Shadow is dead, and the Alliance got to Viper two days ago. His tortured, mutilated body washed up on a beach in Turkey."

"Aye, well. I don't know anything about that."

"How much time do we have before she hands the virus and the EMP over to Jafari?"

"I don't know. Before you landed in a kids' playground with your goons in balaclavas with machine-guns and fucking tasers, we were about to figure that out."

"Can you find the device?"

"I can barely find my keys, never mind a hacker who can manipulate the internet to hide their location."

Jones smiled, agreeing with Craven's point. "Who's behind the Alliance? We have intelligence from MI6 pointing to a coalition of state and non-state actors; North Korea, Iran, Al-Qaeda, China. Can you confirm this?"

Craven sighed and grimaced at the ties chafing his wrists. "I haven't got a clue. You are talking to the wrong man. Do we really need these handcuffs? Do you think I'm going to fight my way out of this place?"

"You were aggressive when we arrested you."

"That's because your men had telescopic batons and tasers in the presence of a small girl. Machine-guns as well, for fuck's sake. Kane and Cameron have the information on the Alliance, not me. The countries you mentioned sound about right, though. The virus and the EMP would be valuable weapons for any country or group looking to attack the West. Cameron and Ghost were working to piece that puzzle together."

"Did you know Ghost was, perhaps, still is, CIA?"

Craven winced, worried he had given away crucial information that might hurt Kane and the mission. But Jones was clever. You didn't get to become a high-ranking MI5 officer by being stupid. There was no point backtracking now. "Yes. Ghost took the virus and the EMP."

"Did you know she was CIA?"

"I told you already. I don't know anything. I was late to this party. Just here to lend a hand whilst I wait for..."

"For your wife's funeral?"

"Don't talk about her. Look, I don't know how the virus works or how Ghost plans to get it to the Alliance. All I can tell you is what I have seen so far."

Jones leaned back, considering Craven's words. "All right. What's Kane's next move? Where is he now?"

"How should I know? As far as I know, you had arrested him just like me. But apparently Kane got away, which isn't much of a surprise. You'll never find him unless he wants to be found. Kane isn't like other men. He's highly-trained and brutally ruthless. He is smart. Smarter than you and anyone in your teams. If you want my advice, just leave him. Let Kane do his thing. He'll find the Prometheus Code. You should just wait until he does and then swoop in to take the Alliance down. The more you chase him, the harder you make it for him."

"You're not making this easy, Craven. You're not giving me much. We need that virus contained. If Kane is truly on our side, on the side of our country and its people, he needs to cooperate. Help me find Kane, and we can work together to stop this threat to our country's very existence."

"Who said Kane is on your side? MI5 tried to kill us. With a fucking helicopter."

"That was regrettable."

"That's the understatement of the year. If you want Kane to work with you, you need to get a message to him. Tell him honestly what's going on. If you didn't give the order for the attack at the Snake Pass, you need him to understand that. But what sort of a friend kidnaps a man's daughter? He'll never trust you whilst you have Kim. Return her to him, arrange the exchange, and talk to him there. He can help you. But would you help an organisation holding your daughter prisoner?"

The questioning continued for hours. Jones probed every detail, every connection. Craven tried to offer information where he could. Jones asked about Craven and Kane's relationship, what sort of work they did together, but Craven gave him little. Kane was a man in the wind, and in the few years they had known each other, he had grown into Craven's closest friend. The questioning wore Craven down, constant repetition and relentless twists and turns over every point. Craven fought to stay alert, knowing that revealing too much could endanger Kane and the mission. Craven had no sense of time inside the cell. The interrogation could have taken one hour or five. Eventually, Jones stood and signalled to the guards via the camera mounted on the wall.

"I haven't forgotten our deal. But you're going to stay here for a while, Mr Craven. Think about what we've discussed.

We'll talk again soon."

Jones left Craven in his small, sparsely furnished cell. The door closed with a heavy bang and Craven stared at the small metal toilet, the hard-looking pallet bed, and the bleak walls. He was alone with his thoughts, which was exactly where Craven didn't want to be. He stood and shuffled over to the pallet bed, intrusive thoughts already battering their way into his consciousness. Barbara alone in a Spanish mortuary, Kim crying, frightened, separated from her father and from Craven himself. The weight of the situation bore down on him. Craven had to protect Kane, Kim and Danny, and stop the impending disaster, all while navigating the treacherous waters of MI5's interrogation.

CHAPTER FORTY-SEVEN

Kyle Lavine's laptop lit up like a Las Vegas slot machine. Alerts pinged from a dozen security systems he was monitoring for any sightings or notifications related to Jack Kane. He used a combination of satellite imagery, real-time CCTV feeds, and the POLARIS system to pinpoint Kane's movements. All hell had descended on Kyle's target in the backstreets of Liverpool. He watched footage of three vans and a Range Rover swooping down on a children's playground, and of the ensuing fight. It had to be MI5. The British police didn't have that sort of operational capability, certainly not to strike using agents without identifying markings on their clothing. Kane had escaped, as had the boy and Cameron Jordan in his pathetic white mask. The old policeman and Kane's daughter were captured.

Kyle flipped from CCTV to satellite imagery and followed Kane through Liverpool's streets, using a North Korean satellite passing over the UK on its orbital path around the globe. No UK-owned satellites were in place to give a view of the UK's north west at that time, and MI5 would certainly have no access to the Korean images. Kyle allowed himself a smile as the three figures reunited in a ginnel lane running between two rows of terraced houses. He followed them to a derelict pub, where they stopped to rest and hide.

Kyle closed his laptop and stared out of his hotel window at Liverpool's historic docks and across to the city's modern skyscrapers. He had tracked his prey to Liverpool after the near miss at Zenith Technologies and was about to close his fist around the man who had eluded him, annoyingly and embarrassingly. Jafari and Hydra had sent messages to confirm that the Prometheus Code was in their pocket with a handover meeting scheduled in two days' time. A member of the Successors had sold out the others, which, with the sums of money involved, was inevitable. Kyle didn't care. The mission to take out Kane and Cameron Jordan was now about professional pride more than the vast sum he would receive once the job was done.

Liverpool was a small city compared to US standards, a historic city of only a half million people. What it lacked in size by American standards, the city made up for with its history. The Beatles were famously born and began their rock n' roll journey in the city and Kyle could see their Yellow Submarine Museum from his hotel window, backing onto the murky grey waters of the River Mersey. It was only a thirty-minute drive from Manchester, and the city suburb of Merseyside grew Liverpool's population to one and a half million people. Its size reminded Kyle of San Diego, but its history went all the way back to the times of the Vikings. The city's peak period had come during Britain's industrial revolution when its port and railway made Liverpool one of the most important cities in England. It was about to become the scene of Kyle Lavine's triumph over one of his most elusive targets.

He adjusted the volume on his earpiece, listening to police chatter and the emergency services for any sign of their pursuit of Kane and Jordan. Kane was clever and lethal; he had shown that at Zenith Technologies and the old country house. Kyle grimaced and gingerly felt the stitched bullet wound on his side to remind himself just how dangerous a target he hunted. Kane was only ten minutes away, and Kyle had to prepare.

Kyle moved through a sequence of yoga poses, ignoring the stitches stretching at his side. He stretched and held himself in the various forms, body sheeted with sweat and muscles sliding over one another as he primed his body for action. He took out the hotel iron and ironing board and pressed his trousers and shirt, took a quick shower and slipped on his clothes. Kyle laid his weapons out on the bed to go through one last check, and his mind drifted back to his days in Afghanistan with Delta Force. He closed his eyes and could almost feel the night-time chill and the sweltering daytime, the earthly smell of dry sands and the fresh smell of the mountains. He frowned as he recalled the monstrous shit-pit in Kandahar and other vivid memories of his time at war.

Kyle recalled one mission vividly. An assignment to eliminate a high-value target hidden in mountainous terrain. They chose Kyle for his exceptional marksmanship and his ability to operate alone. He had been a sniper and usually worked with a spotter, but that mission had been a lone wolf operation. Kyle breathed in deeply, and he was there again, perched on a rocky outcrop, holding the M110 semi-automatic sniper rifle. He had loved that rifle; he had taken it apart and cleaned it obsessively, so that he could almost do it with his eyes closed. It fired 7.62x51mm NATO rounds, had a modular rail system, and adjustable butt-plate. The telescopic, front-mounted sight was accurate, and Kyle had fired thousands of range rounds at various distances so it became an extension of his own vision and could fire accurately up to 800 yards.

He watched the target's compound through the scope, waiting for the perfect shot. Hours passed, but Kyle's patience remained unwavering. He scanned the high walls and outbuildings, scope drifting over a herd of bleating goats and four boys kicking a football beside a gun-mounted pick-up truck. A muezzin sounded the call to prayer, and Kyle watched him climb a tower to sing how great Allah was and then shifted the scope to watch as men came from the various single-storey buildings to make their prayer.

The target appeared, striding confidently beside two of his guards. Men in baggy trousers and khaki-coloured shirts with beards and hair gathered beneath their Pakol hats. They were Taliban fighters, and Kyle's high-value target was a bomb-maker and engineer of a recent attack on a US patrol where three Marines had lost their lives. Kane controlled his breathing and squeezed the trigger with cold precision. The shot echoed through the valley, and the target dropped six hundred and fifty yards away from Kyle's location. He rolled away and marched through scrub and scree across the valley towards his extraction point. A Black Hawk helicopter had whisked him away, the roar of rotors blending with the adrenaline pumping in his veins.

It had been a perfect kill and a perfect mission. Nobody to annoy him with prattling small talk, nobody telling him what to do, and a kill at the end. Kyle filed the memory away in his mind and slid the Sig P365 into a holster and clipped two spare magazines to his belt. He slid on a lightweight jacket to hide the weapon and hoped today would go just like that mission. Calm, ruthless, precise, and successful. He grabbed the AR15 with its EOTech sights, his bulletproof combat vest, suppressor attachment for the Sig and his medical bag.

Kyle left the hotel room wearing a cap low to hide his face, knowing that his face could be targeted after the deaths at Zenith Technologies. He had shaved his fair hair to a buzz cut to change his appearance, but the cap couldn't hurt. Kyle strode out into the cobbled streets of the Albert Dock and crossed a busy dual carriageway, marching towards the heart of the city. He reached the old buildings of the inner city, like something out of a film set during the turn of the 19th century, but where people wore tracksuits instead of cloth caps, and drove cars almost as valuable as the houses they lived in.

He entered an old warehouse two streets away from the abandoned pub and climbed up to the roof. Kyle laid down a towel taken from the hotel and lay down. He took out the AR15 and nestled it into his shoulder, the action familiar, the movement satisfying. He scanned the abandoned pub across the street around it for any sign of his quarry. It was quiet. A man with thick dreadlocks walked a large dog, and a woman dragged a small child across the road by its hand. Music blared from a car, and the hum of city life droned in Kyle's ears.

Kyle adjusted the sights and trained his weapon on the pub. Its faded, chipped sign said The Dog and Dart, a typically quaint name for an English pub, he thought. Weeds grew about the foundations, and graffiti covered the walls with tags Kyle couldn't read. Old wood pallets covered the long-ago smashed windows, and dark timbers covered the doors. One of those timbers had shifted aside, and Kyle's sights landed on a man wearing a white mask. He almost laughed with the thrill. It was Cameron Jordan. He panned the sights slightly and found Jack Kane. Kane's face was tense. The weight of his mission was heavy on his shoulders. Kyle noted the pub's layout, entry points, and all potential escape routes.

The gap in the boards only allowed Kyle a narrow field of vision, and Kane wouldn't stand still. He kept moving, in animated conversation with his teenage son. Kyle thought about changing position. A rooftop across the street might give him a better shot through a south-facing window. He had to get it right. He only had one shot. If he missed, Kane would disappear, forcing Kyle to hunt him all over again. Precision was key.

He waited, watching, anticipating, enjoying the power and control over Kane's life. Kane came into view again, and Kyle's finger hovered over the trigger. He took a deep breath, ready to fire, but the boy got in the way and the opportunity disappeared. Kyle took his eye away from the sights and rolled onto his back. Sniper kills were impersonal. It would get the job done, but Kyle would miss the look of terror in Kane's eyes as he realised he had met a better soldier, a fiercer killer, a more skilled opponent. He wanted that victory. He wanted Kane to die knowing he had been outfought and outsmarted. A closer kill, then. One where he could smell Kane's blood and restore his own warrior's pride.

CHAPTER FORTY-EIGHT

Kane pushed the timber board with his shoulder. It creaked against rusty nails and then snapped. Rotted wood gave way and Kane stumbled forward into the gloom of a long-abandoned pub. The Dog and Dart looked like it had been empty for a decade, water dripping from a collapsed roof into a dank puddle behind a bar sprayed with faded graffiti. A black and white cat leapt from a window ledge and disappeared into the dimness. The place reeked of piss and damp, and Kane peered out of a boarded-up window at the sky above.

"It stinks in here," spluttered Danny, lifting his hand to his nose as he staggered in behind his father.

"We just need somewhere to hide for an hour or two." Kane strode across the pub, stepping over fallen stools and broken tables to peer out of a north-facing window.

"I need to find a place to sit," said Cameron. He followed Danny in through the broken boards. "I have to get online and see where Ghost is going."

"What are we going to do about Kim and Uncle Frank?" Danny asked.

Kane continued to stare out of the gap in the window

boards, angling his head to get as full a range of sight as possible.

"Dad, are you listening to me? What are you doing?"

"What?" Kane replied, and then turned and walked towards his son. "Sorry. They had a drone at the playground, so I'm just checking they haven't sent more up to follow us. Drones these days carry thermal imaging, so they can see our heat signatures even inside a building like this."

"I said, what are we going to do about Kim and Uncle Frank?"

Kane grabbed him by the shoulders and nodded. He turned to Cameron. "Are you connected?"

Cameron sat on an old bench stripped of its cushions with his laptop on a table half-splintered and wobbling on fragile legs. "Yeah, I'm online. There's a Starlink satellite orbiting within range. I'm using that. Should be able to pick up my tracker on the hard drive soon."

"Don't ignore me, Dad!" Danny exploded.

Kane turned back to him. "I'm not ignoring you, Danny. We just have a few things to figure out."

"How many times have I told you? It's Dan. They took Kim. We don't know where she is, or if she's OK. Isn't that our priority now? Getting her back?"

"Absolutely, but we have to see where Ghost had taken the Prometheus Code…"

"Jesus, Dad! Put your own family first, for once in your life."

"You and Kim always come first."

"That's bullshit, and you know it. You toss me a bag of guns, grenades and God knows what, and send me running into the back streets of Liverpool. I didn't know where I was going or if those men with machine-guns were going to catch me. I was scared, Dad. It was lucky I came across Cameron. You haven't even asked me if I'm OK!"

Kane chewed his bottom lip. The truth stung him like a whip. All his life Kane had put his missions first and his family second. That was a bitter truth to face up to.

"Danny, it might seem I like I put work before you and Kim. But I'm not an insurance salesman or a mechanic. I can't just leave my work at five o'clock and come home to kick a ball with you. My work is serious. If I don't do the things I do, then people get hurt. That's just the way it is."

"So, you do think what you do is more important than us? Great. When have you ever kicked a ball with me, Dad? When have we ever played a PlayStation game together? You haven't even come to watch me play football or tennis."

"I will, son, I promise, but first we..."

"Don't say we have to retrieve the virus, Dad, or I swear to God I'm leaving right now."

"Calm down, Danny."

"Don't tell me to calm down!" Danny flung the back containing Kane's weapons into a dingy corner and walked away with his head in his hands. "It's Kim, Dad. She's probably terrified and alone. Think about her instead of your mission. Let somebody else fix it. Why does it have to be you? What would happen if you weren't here? Some other agents or soldiers would go after the virus."

Danny's words tore at Kane's heart like a jagged knife. Nothing hurts more than a truth a man knows but keeps buried within himself. A flaw, or hole in his duties as a father or husband. Visions flashed before Kane's eyes of pictures his wife Sally used to send him whilst he was away on Mjolnir business or with the Regiment. Images of a tiny Danny in his first football kit, or Kim at swimming lessons. All milestones and memories Kane had missed in the service of his country.

But the truth was deeper than duty and the excuse of national security. Kane did what he did because he loved it. He lived for the action, for the feeling combat gave him. For the unmatchable adrenaline rush of hand-to-hand combat, or a firefight and victory over an enemy who had tried to take his life. It was a desire and a love impossible to give voice to. Danny would never understand.

Kane loved his children, and he was all they had left, even though he knew he was a terrible father.

"We'll get Kim back before we go after the virus, Danny. I give you my word. I haven't been there for you; I know it and I'm sorry. I'm sorry your mother died and I'm sorry Auntie Barbara died. If I could change things, I would do it in a heartbeat."

"Just words! Always promises. We'll do this one day, or that sometime in the future. What about now, Dad?"

Kane hadn't forgotten about his daughter or Craven. They were in MI5 custody and were both British citizens. The reality was that Kim was better off with MI5 for now than she was with Kane. He was in the field, pursued by killers and government agents, so every moment was a hair's breadth away from grave danger. Kim was safe and secure in MI5 custody. She would be upset. Danny was right about that. But she wasn't in harm's way. They would feed her; Kim would have a warm bed and MI5 operators trained in childcare would make sure she was comfortable until they found a suitable care home for her. The obvious assessment of any family court in the country would determine that Kane was not a fit father. Kane wouldn't let them take his daughter into care, but for now, he actually thought it was better for her to remain with her captors. But there was no way to explain that to Danny. Kane could feel his son slipping away from him, could almost see the last tenuous strands of their relationship disintegrating in that crumbling pub.

"We go for Kim now. Before we go after the virus. She is in MI5 custody, so it won't be easy to free her. I'm talking about infiltrating a high-security detention facility and breaking out with a ten-year-old girl. Before we track down a cyber-terrorist and the Alliance, who will most likely send ruthlessly-trained killers to get the virus. We are deep in the shit here, son. It doesn't get any deeper or more serious. I'll get Kim, and you are going to help me. I just need to figure out where they are holding her."

"How do you do that?"

"I still have a few contacts in MI6 I can try. It won't be easy. The best solution is I can call in a few old favours and have Kim released, but that's unlikely. The worst solution is breaking her out."

Danny nodded and stopped pacing the room, relief sagging his shoulders.

"Wait!" exclaimed Cameron. "I've found Ghost. The signal's still active and I've locked onto her. She's heading west."

A movement flickered in the corner of Kane's eyesight. Something shifting in the shadows. Kane's neck prickled with warning, exactly like the feeling a person got when someone was watching them out of sight. A figure crouched beside the rotten timber Kane had moved to enter the pub. At first, Kane thought it was a dog, come to inspect the interlopers in its urban territory. Sunlight shifted through broken window boards, illuminating dust motes and changing shadows. A shaft of light broke through the gloom and illuminated the figure of a man and a rifle. Instinct kicked in and Kane threw himself towards Danny, tackling his son like a rugby player as a suppressed gunshot spat a bullet through the fetid, damp air. Kane hit the floor hard, making sure to land on his back, so Danny landed on top of him. Kane kept tight hold of his son and rolled away, teeth gnashing, desperate to drag Danny out of the shooter's line of sight before the assassin killed them both.

CHAPTER FORTY-NINE

"Stay down, Danny!" Kane thundered, and Danny stared at him, slack-mouthed.

Another shot fired the bar behind Kane's head, shivering its old oak timbers to send a spray of splinters over Kane and his son. Kane scrambled further behind the bar, dragging Danny with him, scrambling to get further beyond the attacker's line of sight. Kane let go of Danny, his heart pumping. They found themselves trapped inside the Dog and Dart with nowhere to run. The killer had the drop on them, and Kane frantically cast his eyes about the broken-down pub, searching for an escape route. The windows were all boarded up, heavy-duty nails and screws and thick boards applied by council workers, no doubt frustrated at repeating the task every time squatters or drug addicts pried them open in search of shelter. There would be a stairway somewhere behind the bar space, leading up to living quarters on the first-floor. Thoughts rushed through Kane's mind in fractions of a second, fears that the first-floor would be a rotten ruin unable to take the weight of a person and was anyway unlikely to lead to a more suitable means of escape.

Kane pushed Danny back with his arm and leaned forward. He tentatively peered around the bar just in time to see

Cameron close his laptop and stand up. His masked face turned towards Kane, single eye watery behind the white facade. Cameron's arms stretched out as though he welcomed an old friend, welcoming his fate, at peace with what must happen next.

A large calibre bullet tore into Cameron's face, smashing his mask and spraying blood and gore across the filthy, damp-ruined wall behind him. Cameron's destroyed head snapped backwards, and another bullet tore through his chest, sending Cameron sprawling into the debris of broken stools and tables.

"No!" Kane roared. One of his only friends was gone. A man whose life Kane had saved, a brother whom Kane had fought beside, killed beside, survived beside. A man he loved with a bond which only those who have experienced combat can ever understand.

"Dad, here!" said Danny. He pushed the backpack across the dust-covered floor.

Calm descended. The horrific grief of witnessing his friend slaughtered replaced with focus and the chance to kill an enemy. Kane ducked and dragged the bag towards him. The bag containing his weapons.

"It's over for you, Jack Kane," sneered a voice in an American accent. "There's no need for the boy to die. Show yourself and end it now, and I won't kill him."

Kane zipped open the bag and pulled out the handgun, the Glock 43 taken from Cameron's lock-up. His hand curled around the familiar mouldings on the grip and he lifted it from the bag. The compact pistol light in his hand, a weapon weighing just over a pound, its slim polymer frame snug in his palm and fingers. Kane quickly pulled the weapon into both hands, its matte-black finish as dark as the pub's interior, the American's words ringing in his head. He could offer a reply, try to lure the assassin into a conversation to buy more time.

But Kane couldn't bear to talk to the man who had just killed his friend. He wanted to kill him.

He removed the magazine and checked it. Seven 9mm rounds. More would have been better, but seven would have to do. He pushed the magazine into the grip until it locked, then pulled back the slide to release it. The weapon clacked as the round loaded. The weapon had no safety catch; it was designed for simplicity and speed. To kill quickly. Just what Kane required.

Kane exhaled and bunched his leg muscles. He surged above the bar and fired at the dark doorway. The semi-automatic gun gave a crisp recoil, a little more pronounced than a larger weapon, but Kane had fired the pistol before, and so adjusted for it. Kane ducked again and listened to see if his enemy groaned in pain or dropped dead or moved to fire his rifle. The stink of burnt gunpowder mixed with the damp, smoky metallic tang lingering in the air. He turned to Danny and nodded to reassure his son. Danny lay with his hands over his head.

"Fuck you then, Jack," the American called. "I'll kill you both."

Feet shifted on the grimy floor as the killer moved position. Kane dropped to his side, leaning on his shoulder, and pointed the Glock around the bottom of the bar. The killer ran on light feet, leaping over Cameron's corpse to secure a better vantage point. Kane fired again, the booming pop of gunfire loud in the empty pub. The bullet smashed into window boards behind the assassin, and he quickly dropped to his knees and brought his sniper rifle to bear. He fired two rapidly suppressed shots that slammed into the bar just as Kane tucked himself behind the thick oak.

"Move to the other end of the bar," Kane whispered to Danny. His son got on all fours, and he crawled to the other end of the bar. Kane waited with his back against old, broken fridges where once beer and soft bottles waited for thirsty customers. Kane was trapped. He checked the bag again, but he had used the grenades he had quickly grabbed from Cameron's lock-up in previous fights. There was nothing in there but spare magazines and his medical tin. He had five rounds left and couldn't afford to waste any more. The sound of feet shuffled, moving lightly in the dust and broken furniture. The killer was on the move again, armed with a powerful rifle and Kane did not know how many bullets the enemy had, or what other weapons he had at his disposal.

"When I fire, run for the door and get out," Kane whispered to Danny. Danny shook his head to say no, his face drained white with fear. The odds were stacked against them. A ruthless killer had come to end Kane's life, but if he could at least save Danny, he could die knowing his children were safe.

Kane readied himself, knowing that his next action could be his last. Cameron was dead and the Prometheus Code in the ether. Perhaps it was over, but there was no time to dwell. Danny made himself ready to flee and Kane flexed his hand around the Glock's grip. Kane surged upward and squeezed the trigger. He had no time even to train the weapon on his enemy's new location. He simply fired to draw the assassin's attention to give Danny time to make his escape. As he fired, Kane saw the killer crouched behind an upturned stool, five yards away from where Kane's bullet slapped into the pub wall.

Danny ran like a hare, keeping low and disappearing through the wooden board in the doorway. Kane moved his arm, bringing the gun around to aim at the killer. A man with a shaved head stared at him through the sights of a long sniper rifle. Kane tensed, ready for the rifle shot about to rip into his body and take his life. A window board creaked, and the assassin suddenly swung his rifle to the left. Kane followed the movement to where the black and white cat stared at them both just before it disappeared between a wooden pallet and the window frame. Kane took his opportunity; he pulled the trigger and shot the assassin in the shoulder as the American brought his rifle back around.

The assassin fell backwards under the impact, a cloud of his blood misting the air. Kane moved quickly, running from behind the bar. He leapt over a broken table and reached the wounded killer just as he rolled over in a desperate attempt to bring his rifle around to return fire. Kane kicked the rifle aside and trained the Glock on the assassin's face. The rifle went wide, but the killer wasn't finished. He ignored the gun pointed at his face, understanding that he was in a fight for his life. He tried to kick Kane's legs from under him, but Kane checked the kick with a raised foot. Kane shifted at the shoulders and shot the assassin in his right arm. The American spasmed in pain and then slowly turned his head, staring up at Kane with hate-filled eyes.

"Bastard," the assassin grunted through locked teeth.

"You killed my friend. A man I served with," Kane hissed. He stared at the American, at the conflicting emotions of fear, pain, and rage playing out in the shifting expressions on the stricken killer's face. Tar-like blood leaked from his wounds, pushing back dust and grime to make viscid puddles on the floor.

"We're the same. Both of us are killers. You're no better than me. That fucking cat saved your life. You don't have to kill me."

"Everybody says that before the end."

"You don't. I can just leave. You'll never see me again."

"I have no choice, and you know it."

"Not here, not like this." The assassin grimaced at his surroundings, at the blood and filth staining his fine clothes. The American licked his lips and pressed the tips of each finger to his thumb in an effort to calm himself.

“You’re a contract killer?”

“Yes.”

“Who are you working for?”

The assassin’s head moved from side to side, and he licked once again at dry lips. “Hydra. The Alliance.”

“Where is the meeting set for the exchange of the Prometheus Code?”

The assassin swallowed hard. Kane didn’t need to tell him he was losing too much blood from his wounds or threaten him with death. They shared the same trade, knew how these situations played out. The Glock pointed at the assassin’s face implied enough threat.

“How could you beat me? I had the drop on you. I was prepared.”

“Where is the meeting?”

“Close to London. They plan to take the virus and the EMP from your traitor and use it within twenty-four hours. A man named Jafari will be at the meeting, and he will set off the EMP and let the virus loose.”

“Then?”

“Then what? Chaos. A change in the world order. A shift in power to the east. The end of Western dominance.”

Kane glanced at the rifle and the assassin’s equipment. “Were you Delta or a SEAL?”

“Delta.”

“You would bring down your own country for money? Traitor.”

The American opened his mouth to object, and Kane shot him in the face. The bullet hammered through the assassin’s eye and into the brain beyond. Scarlet blood and fragments of skull splattered across the soiled floor.

Kane took the assassin's bag, his spare ammunition, and the sniper rifle. One threat removed. It was time to find Kim and Craven before time ran out.

CHAPTER FIFTY

Kane strode across the empty, abandoned pub towards the door, where Danny waited for him outside. Time was his enemy, but as he passed Cameron, he had to stop. Kane paused, staring down at Cameron's lifeless body. Was death a release from his pain? Kane wondered how alive Cameron had actually been since suffering his wounds in Afghanistan. Another life wasted in the service of his country. Blood pooled around Cameron's ruined skull, a stark contrast to the pallor of his skin. The sight of his friend, former SAS soldier and brilliant hacker, reduced to a cold, still corpse, made Kane sick with grief. Guilt cloyed in his chest because he must leave Cameron's body where it lay. Dishonoured and alone. Cameron had been more than a friend. He had helped keep Kane's son alive. He was a brother in arms, someone Kane had once saved from the jaws of death in Afghanistan's hellish mountains.

The memory of that harrowing day came flooding back with painful clarity. A routine patrol turned into a nightmare by a rocket-propelled grenade. Kane could hear again the deafening roar and the rending of metal. The heat was searing, like coming face to face with a blacksmith's furnace. Kane had dashed to the truck, turned into a twisted, burning wreck by the explosion. He had ignored the shrapnel and flames and pulled Cameron from the inferno even as bullets flew around him.

After the attack, they transported Cameron to a military hospital on the outskirts of Kabul. Kane had been permitted to visit Cameron on a quick break between operations. The military hospital was a vast, utilitarian structure. A former government building transformed into a field hospital with beige, crumbling walls and a stink of death, antiseptic, and sweat clinging to it along with the ghosts of dead war heroes. Guards and barbed wire surrounded it, and a high wall with machine-gun mounts made the building militarily secure. Inside, the hospital was a hive of activity. Medics and doctors rushed between patients on gurneys and beds. Rows of beds filled the wards, occupied by wounded soldiers with all manner of injuries. Some groaned in pain, others lay eerily still. Kane vividly remembered the fear of walking through that hospital, of a soldier's worst nightmare; the grievous wound that does not kill. The hospital reminded Kane, as it did all soldiers, that war brought risks beyond death. Kane had looked away from a man with a missing leg wrapped in bloody bandages, and another missing an arm below the elbow.

Kane had found Cameron in a special burns unit, a sterile room bathed in harsh florescent light, reserved for those who suffered from the all-too-common burn wounds inflicted during explosions. Bandages swathed Cameron's face, leaving only one eye visible, and that single eye flickered with pain and recognition when he saw his friend. Cameron's head moved slightly, and the eye winced. Kane had wanted to reach out to him then, to hold him somewhere where the fire hadn't scorched his flesh, but he stayed back, shuddering with grief at his friend's plight.

The doctors were doing all they could, applying ointment, changing dressings, and administering pain relief. Cameron's burns were beyond severe. The medical team had been optimistic about his chances of recovery. An SAS officer had visited Kane's team to report on their injured comrade's progress before Kane had left for Kabul. The officer had spoken of skin grafts and rehabilitation, and of a long and painful road to recovery. The horror of Cameron's injuries and the empty eye socket it left him with haunted Kane, and now he was gone.

Kane couldn't take his eyes off Cameron's dead body on the pub floor, the memories coming too thick for him to break away. He recalled the aftermath of Cameron's hospital treatment. His resilience had been remarkable. Despite the pain and scarring that would forever mark his body, he had fought through his recovery with a determination that had impressed everyone around him. Eventually, they sent Cameron back to the UK for further treatment and rehabilitation. They arranged the journey home with care. The army organised a medical flight to monitor and ensure his comfort, followed by transportation to a specialist hospital in Birmingham.

Back in the UK, the army had provided extensive support to help Cameron adjust to civilian life, including undergoing physiotherapy to regain mobility and receiving counselling to cope with the trauma. The army also tried to help him find a new purpose, encouraging his skills and interest in computers for use in a civilian capacity. That part of his journey had been where Cameron fell away from his rehab programme. The injuries to his face and body made him withdraw, his mental state beyond repair. He took to wearing a mask to hide himself from the world, retreating into his lonely home in Newcastle. A husk of his former self.

Standing over Cameron's body in the dirt and filth of the Dog and Dart, Kane felt a crushing sense of loss. Just as he had when Sally died, as Craven must have felt with Barbara's passing. Kane had saved Cameron once, but that had been a different Cameron. The old Cameron had died in an RPG attack in Afghanistan, leaving another man with the same name in his place. Memories of their shared experiences, the laughter, the dangers faced, the bond forged in the pressure-cooker environment of war, all came rushing back. The pain of losing a comrade was profound, a gnawing emptiness that left Kane in despair.

Kane knelt beside Cameron and closed his friend's eye with a gentle hand. The assassin's bullet had been swift and merciless, leaving no chance for survival. Anger welled up within him, a fierce burning rage at the sadness of it all, and at the men who had brought the assassin to Britain's shores. Cameron had left the battlefield behind, only to be struck down in a different kind of war. A secret war, and one which Kane had dragged Cameron into the day he had knocked on his door with Danny and Kim after Sally's death.

He thought about that time he had visited Cameron in the field hospital in Kabul, of the long hours between missions they had spent talking about their hopes and fears. Losing him now felt like losing a part of himself, a piece of his past that could never be reclaimed.

Kane stood, his resolve hardening. He would honour Cameron's memory by finishing what they had started, by ensuring that he would not allow the wrong hands to use the virus that Cameron had worked so hard to build and protect. The mission was now beyond the dangers to Western civilisation. It was personal. Cameron's death was a stark reminder of the stakes involved, a hammer-blow illustration of the dangers they faced. Kane realised he had to be stronger, smarter, and more relentless than ever before.

With a last look at his fallen friend, Kane turned away with the weight of grief and determination on his shoulders. He picked up Cameron's laptop and bag and left the Dog and Dart. The road ahead was fraught with peril, but he was ready to face it head-on. For Cameron, for his children, for their shared past and the future they had fought to protect.

CHAPTER FIFTY-ONE

Kane and Danny stopped to eat dinner in a 1950s-style diner in Liverpool city centre. Kane left Danny to read the menu whilst he took a burner phone outside to dial an old contact.

"Hello?" said a clipped, nondescript English accent.

"Stead? It's Jack Kane."

"Well, well. Jack. Still alive?"

"Still alive. I need some information."

There was a pause. The sounds of a busy city rumbled behind Kieran Stead, a man Kane had once known as Jameson and who probably also went by a dozen other names in his role as an MI6 agent. He could be in London, Cairo, Mexico City, Singapore, or any city across the world.

"I see. What makes you think I can help you, Jack?"

"The information I need is of a sensitive nature. I thought that after the operation in Krasnodar, you might help me."

"That was an operation to help you, as I recall. We helped you get a woman out of a Russian private military camp, Jack. Why should I help you again now?"

Stead was right. Partially. Calling him was a long shot, but Kane had few places left to turn. "We took out a threat to British and European security on that mission. Men died; Scooby died."

"That's right. We wiped your warrants and made you a free man in return."

"You did. But I need one more favour. It's not just for me, Stead. I'm caught up in the middle of something. Even more of a threat to our country than the threat we faced last time."

"Go on, I'm intrigued."

Stead stayed silent until Kane finished filling him in on the details of the Prometheus Code, the EMP, the Alliance, the American, Craven, Kim, Ghost, and Jafari.

"I am not in the country, Jack. I am aware of the Alliance, but not aware of the Prometheus Code. If what you say is true, which I have no reason to believe it is not, then you are in serious trouble and MI6 needs to be involved. You say MI5 has taken your daughter and associate into custody and that they are in pursuit of the virus. I'll verify all of that. But listen to me carefully. I know Jafari, and he is not a man to be trifled with." Stead's voice became low and measured, filled with the weight of countless years in the field.

"Jafari," Stead continued, "is a name that sends shivers down the spines of intelligence officers worldwide. He is the scourge of MI6, the CIA, Mossad, and a dozen other agencies. Nobody knows his real name, but we have pieced together a detailed dossier over the years. He first emerged as a formidable Taliban soldier in the early 2000s, known for his exceptional skills in guerrilla warfare and an almost supernatural ability to evade capture. His brutality in battle became legendary, earning him a fearsome reputation amongst both his enemies and his allies.

"Around 2010, something changed. Intelligence suggests Jafari became disillusioned with the Taliban's cause, perhaps seeing greater opportunity elsewhere. A boy who probably began life as the son of a goat herder, or mountain farmer, suddenly had a taste of power, a sniff of wealth, and that combined with religious zeal is a powerful motivator.

He vanished from the battlefield, only to reappear as a mercenary for hire. His transition from a Taliban fighter to an international assassin was swift and seamless. The man is a ghost, moving through the shadows, leaving a trail of bodies and chaos in his wake.

"Jafari's exploits have earned him a reputation that is both feared and respected in the underworld and the intelligence world. He has taken out high-profile targets across the globe, from corrupt politicians to powerful drug lords, all while avoiding capture. His methods are varied but always efficient; poison, long-range sniping, hand-to-hand combat. Jafari has no moral compass, no hesitation.

"I know all about Jafari, more's the pity. The bastard flashed up as the chief suspect for the assassination of a European diplomat in broad daylight, using a synthetic poison that is still untraceable. I worked that case, and the more I learned about Jafari, the more the layered onion of his exploits appeared. He single-handedly dismantled a South American cartel by eliminating its leadership in a single night. The list goes on. The man is a surgical instrument of death.

"The very fact he could enter the UK is a testament to his resourcefulness. He has a network that spans continents. Forged documents, bribed officials, covert entries, he uses them all. Jafari is wanted by multiple governments, including those in Europe and the Middle East. He has never stayed in one place long enough to be caught. His entry into the UK was likely facilitated by the Alliance. His very association with them shows he has made peace with Middle Eastern countries he has crossed in the past."

"Jafari is about to take possession of the Prometheus Code and the EMP. The Alliance has tasked him with setting it off in London twenty-four hours after he secures it."

"Jesus, Jack. I need to notify MI5 to scramble a team to intercept him."

"They can't intercept him, Stead. You know that. They'll send in a team, and unless they can get an SAS team scrambled quickly, they'll bungle the job. This is an operation beyond local forces. Anything but the SAS won't cut it. I can stop him. I'm in the UK right now, armed and ready."

"What is it you need from me?"

"I need my daughter, and Frank Craven back."

"You said they are in MI5 custody. I can't just order their release."

"You can find out where they are being held and give the location."

"So you can cause havoc and kill some good MI5 men to get them out?"

"Or find the person with enough clout to authorise their release."

Stead sighed. "For fuck's sake, Jack. How do you get into these situations? In fact, don't answer that. Leave it with me. I'll call you back on this number."

CHAPTER FIFTY-TWO

Danny drank his Oreo-flavoured milkshake, finishing it with a loud slurp as the thick chocolate liquid reached the bottom of the tall glass. Kane slid into the booth on the side of the table facing his son and sipped at his glass of Coke. Danny barely noticed Kane's return, so engrossed was he in Cameron's open laptop. Danny had cried when Kane met him outside the Dog and Dart, sobbed because Cameron was gone, and at the sheer terrifying horror of it all. He was a teenager, a schoolkid with more problems than most, and had more experience with death than any kid should suffer. A boy Danny's age should have few worries, and his head should have been full of football, girls, socialising with friends and his studies, not a fight for his life with a deadly assassin and the desperate hunt for the Prometheus Code.

Kane and Danny sat in a cosy booth at Fonzy's Diner, a quaint 1950s-style restaurant nestled in a quiet corner of Liverpool. The diner was a time capsule of mid-century Americana, a nostalgic escape from the present. It was a five-minute walk from the Yellow Submarine Beatles Museum, and pictures of the Fab Four adorned the walls, along with other singers more appropriate for the 50s, like Buddy Holly, the Everly Brothers, Little Richard and Chuck Berry. The red vinyl seats, slightly worn but impeccably clean, offered a comfortable place to relax and recover, even amidst the ticking clock mission to get Kim and Craven back, and to stop Jafari and the Alliance. Kane had wanted to find a car and head quickly south to await Stead's call and get closer to the Prometheus Code exchange meeting. But Danny had been through a lot, and the boy had to eat. An hour at Fonzy's Diner would do them both good.

Glass condiment bottles, a small vase with plastic flowers, and metallic napkin dispensers adorned the chrome-edged tables, adding to the retro charm. Kane glanced around at the walls decorated with black and white photos of other rock 'n' roll legends jumbled up with vintage advertisements and neon signs. A brightly-lit jukebox played Elvis Presley's Hound Dog, filling the air with a lively, upbeat tune. The aroma of sizzling burgers, crispy fries, and freshly brewed coffee wafted through the diner, mingling with the sweet scent of milkshakes being blended at the counter.

Fonzy's had a checkerboard tile floor, and the gleaming stainless-steel rims on the counters and stools reflected the ambient glow of neon lights. The waitresses, dressed in pastel uniforms complete with white aprons and paper hats, moved efficiently between tables, taking orders and delivering plates with friendly smiles.

"Kim would like it here," said Danny, without breaking his focus on the laptop.

She would, Kane thought. He checked his phone for the fourth time in four minutes, waiting for Stead to call him back with a solution to the Kim and Craven problem. Kane and Danny had both ordered classic diner fare: cheeseburgers with all the trimmings, fries, a side of onion rings for Danny, and the monstrous milkshake.

Danny took a bite of his burger, ketchup, and mustard smeared on his cheek. Kane smiled. The simple joy on his son's face was a stark contrast to the dangerous world he found himself plunged into. Kane wished he had found more time to do things like with Danny, the simple things. The things that mattered. The vibrant, nostalgic atmosphere of the diner provided a comforting backdrop, a reminder of simpler times and a brief break from their dire situation and the grief of Cameron's brutal death.

The sound of the sizzling grill, the clinking of cutlery, and the chatter of other diners created a lively, comfortable ambience. The waitresses glided between tables, refilling coffee cups and delivering plates with practised ease. One of them, a cheerful woman with a beehive hairstyle, stopped at their table to ask if they needed anything else.

"No thanks. Just the bill, please," Kane said. Their time was up, as pleasant as it had been. Kane glanced at the clock on the wall shaped like a classic car, its hands ticking away the minutes. The peaceful meal couldn't last forever.

"I've figured out how to use the tracker Cameron put on the Prometheus Code hard drive," Danny said with an excited smile. "See?" He turned the laptop so Kane could see the screen. A blue dot moved slowly across a map of the UK. "She initially headed west as though heading for Wales, but now she's diverted south."

"Good work, Danny. I mean, Dan," Kane corrected himself. "See what else you can find on there that might be useful. It's time to go. I should get a call about Kim and Uncle Frank soon. We need to be on the road."

Danny packed the laptop away and shoved it into Cameron's bag. As the jukebox switched to Buddy Holly's That'll Be the Day, Kane felt a pang of nostalgia for his old life, for the time he had spent in the witness protection programme. He had worked a factory job then, had come home each night to kiss Danny and Kim on the forehead and put them to bed. It was a simple, idyllic life, and that part of it remained in his head as a rose-tinted glimpse of what life could be. But both he and Sally had been unhappy in the programme. She'd longed for her old career and status, given up to go into hiding, and Kane missed the thrill of action. Kane sighed, aware of the bittersweet nature of these rare moments. Sharing a meal with his son, even amidst the pressure and danger of their situation. He vowed to cherish that time with Danny because it might be a while before they could enjoy such simple pleasures again.

CHAPTER FIFTY-THREE

Gareth Jones stared out of his office window at fields shifting like waves as a summer wind blew across the valley to move fields of wheat like a rolling sea. His office was one of the better ones at Walsingham Place. The MI5 secure facility outside Bishop's Stortford, forty miles and an hour's drive from London, was an imposing structure. A fortress of modern security measures masked by a façade of nondescript government utility. Situated in a secluded, deeply wooded area, it was surrounded by a high, barbed-wire fence and concealed by dense trees, which helped to keep it hidden from prying eyes. The facility was a squat, concrete building with small, solidly reinforced windows that gave little indication of the activities inside.

Jones hadn't been home for two days because he spent that time interviewing Frank Craven, ensuring proper care for Kim Kane, and working with the agency to figure out what to do with the prisoners and how to address the threat of the Prometheus Code. The call from MI6 came like finding a missing jigsaw piece. An agent named Stead laid out Jones' options, with the backing of the highest security clearance available. Jones was to scramble a team of special forces operators and agents ASAP to counter the threat of the Alliance, now confirmed a credible and serious threat to British national security.

The corridors outside Jones' office buzzed like a smashed beehive. Scrambling a team to counter so serious a threat was a complex exercise of liaising with the armed forces. Getting sign-off from senior executives in Thames House for budgets and officers took time and bodies. Stead confirmed much of what Frank Craven had outlined, and Jones now fully understood the threat his country faced. The headache, however, was what to do with Frank Craven and Kim Kane.

Stead and MI6 wanted Kane's help to stop the high-profile bad actor Jafari and whatever team, as yet unidentified or quantified, he had brought to the UK to crush Western civilisation. Jones had objected until MI6 shared an unredacted copy of Kane's military and MI6 file. Kane was a top-level black-ops agent and former SAS soldier. He was an assassin, spy, sniper, and special agent. The things Jones had read were beyond anything he had seen in his career. He hadn't believed shadow MI6 groups like Mjolnir existed, but they did. Kane had spent a life fighting in the shadows. Highly-trained, deadly and ruthless, he had eventually turned witness against his former masters in what turned out to be a bloodbath played out on the streets of England.

MI6 was no longer the international force it had once been. A shift to political correctness, increased oversight, and a greater focus on cyber-intelligence over old-fashioned fieldwork had seen their former army of supremely skilled field agents profoundly reduced. Stead had alluded to that during the conversation when Jones had asked why they could not simply allocate another MI6 agent to this operation. The answer was brutal. There was nobody available with Kane's experience. The few agents MI6 had with Kane's skills were either on other jobs in distant locations or were no longer active. It was Kane or nothing. Jones trusted his own people, but to fight a killer like Jafari, he needed a killer of his own. So it must be Kane.

Jones had a dilemma. Deny Stead's request to free Frank Craven and Kim Kane so they could return to Kane's side or release them. To keep them meant sending Craven to a remand centre pending charges, which Jones hadn't fully thought through or decided upon, and placing Kim Kane in the state's care. To release them was highly unorthodox, and to return a child to her father meant placing her in danger. Stead indicated that if Jones did not set Craven and Kim free, he could expect a visit from Kane, who would seek to take them by force. Which would make Kane an enemy of the British state instead of the man to save it from Jafari.

An attack on Walsingham Place was unheard of. At its entrance, a fortified gatehouse controlled access to the premises. Armed guards manned the post, and checked the credentials of anyone approaching the facility. Despite UK gun laws, and because of the nature of the prisoners held temporarily at Walsingham Place, the guards had advanced weaponry. They carried Heckler and Koch MP5 submachine-guns with Glock 17 pistols, ensuring they were prepared for any threat. Surveillance cameras with facial recognition software covered every angle of the perimeter, linked to a central security room where operators monitored feeds around the clock. In short, it was not a place a man could break into easily. Jones would have laughed off the threat had he not seen Jack Kane's file.

Jones glanced beyond the gatehouse to where a winding gravel road led to the main building. A thick, bulletproof glass door protected that entrance, which required multiple levels of clearance to open. Only authorised personnel could enter by using a combination of keycards, biometric scans, and security codes. Inside, the walls were painted a clinical white, and the floors covered in grey, non-slip tiles. It was impossible for Kane to break in and free his daughter and friend. But that didn't solve Jones' dilemma. He half-expected his phone to ring at any moment with an order from Thames House to release the prisoners and begin to liaise with Jack Kane and MI6 to intercept and stop Jafari.

Craven was being held in the facility's heart, inside a series of interrogation rooms and cells. The cells were tiny, windowless rooms with reinforced steel doors with soundproofing to prevent communication between prisoners. Each cell was equipped with a single cot, a toilet and a sink, providing only the most basic amenities. The guards could open thin viewing slits on the heavy, reinforced doors from the outside to check on the prisoners without opening the doors.

Jones indulged himself, imagining Kane attempting to infiltrate Walsingham and inevitably being captured before entering the building. If he could even steal an hour alone with Kane, Jones could prise a wealth of information from him. He imagined holding Kane in an interrogation room, a single table with two chairs bolted to the floor. A harsh space with recording and video equipment designed to be intimidating, with no personal touches, just bare, cold functionality.

The desk phone rang, and Jones stared at the blinking light. He reached out to pick up the handset and then paused. If his superior officers asked him to agree to MI6's request, he had no choice but to do it. But if he could keep himself involved, if he could lead the field team working with Kane to pursue Jafari and the Prometheus Code, it presented an opportunity. He didn't agree with it. Kim Kane was far safer in custody than in harm's way beside her father. It offered Jones a chance to leapfrog the Ruperts, his peers with private school backgrounds, with relatives and links to the upper echelons in London. They had a far greater chance of promotion than a working-class lad from Wales, but here was a chance.

"Jones," he said, raising the handset to his ear.

"You have my friend and my daughter," said a calm voice on the other end of the phone.

Jones froze. A shiver ran across his shoulders. The caller could only be one man. Jones clenched his teeth and shook his head, forcing himself to think. Invasive thoughts bounced around his head as he tried to think of the right thing to say. "Jack Kane," he said, and then cursed at himself silently for not fully thinking it through first. "How did you get this number?"

"Are you going to release my daughter and my friend, Mr Jones?"

"Turn yourself in, Kane. Make it easier for both of us. There are serious issues for me to deal with here, a threat to our country and our very way of life. The last thing we need is a vigilante running around fucking everything up. Even us talking here is taking up time when I could be executing a plan to recover and neutralise the Prometheus Code."

"So you are aware of the danger we face. Have you heard from MI6?"

"Mr Stead has made contact. Yes."

"I'm expecting a call back from him shortly."

"Stead relayed your ultimatum. We don't take kindly to threats. It sounds to me rather like terrorism."

"I just want my daughter and my friend back. Are you going to release them?"

Jones paused, sweat beading his brow. Whilst there was no way Jack Kane could hope to infiltrate Walsingham House, his file had made interesting reading. Kane was a dangerous man. Perhaps he had the skills required to pull it off? What if Jones denied the request and Kane killed multiple officers, men and women Jones worked with, talked about football and current affairs with? But there was a flip slide to that coin. What if Jones released the girl and the former detective, in a clear breach of security protocols, and his superiors came down on him like a tonne of bricks?

Jones' MI5-issue smartphone pinged, and his desktop simultaneously flashed with a notification. An email. Jones opened up his desktop and his secure email.

"I'm waiting, Mr Jones. Are you going to free them, or do I need to come and get them?"

The email was from top brass in Thames House, a forwarded email from Mr Stead of MI6. It told Jones to release the prisoners, form his team and work with Jack Kane to find and neutralise Jafari and his team. Jones braced himself against his desk. This was a complete breach of protocol, but he had neither the time nor the inclination to question his superiors.

"I'll release them, Kane. But you and I need to talk if we are to work together to avert this disaster."

"I work alone. Shall I meet you in front of Walsingham Place?"

"It might take time for me to get there and arrange the release."

"You're there already, Mr Jones. I'm looking at you in your first-floor office. You could do with a better-fitting suit, by the way."

CHAPTER FIFTY-FOUR

Frank Craven sat in the backseat of the black SUV, his hands cuffed in front of him with the now familiar plastic cable-tie-like cuffs. Kim Kane sat next to him, leaning in, head resting on her shoulder as she dozed. He squinted through the tinted windows, trying to work out where MI5 was taking him. The vehicle hummed quietly as it navigated the winding roads. The countryside whizzed past, lush green fields dotted with trees and the occasional farmhouse. It was early morning, and a light mist hung over the landscape, carrying the earthy smell of wet grass and distant rain.

The agents around him sat in silence, their eyes scanning the surroundings with practised vigilance, an air of anger in the curl of their lips and the hardness of their eyes. Craven had no idea how Kane had orchestrated his and Kim's release, but he thanked God that his time in detention was over. He knew it was Kane because Jones had let it slip during the release process at the MI5 holding facility. A bitter tone to his voice, advising Craven to thank his friend for bending the rule of law like a reed in the wind.

The agents inside the SUV wore plain black suits, not expensively well-tailored like the suits Kane favoured, more like high street-looking cuts. Craven noticed the bulges under their jackets, no doubt pistols, probably Glocks. That thought made Craven smile internally. He didn't know what sort of guns they were. He could only think of two manufacturers' names and hoped with a faint shake of his head that he wasn't beginning to think like Kane. The agents were all business, and their tense demeanour suggested the gravity of the situation.

As they approached the rendezvous point, Craven's heart rate quickened. The location was a desolate, abandoned industrial site, just off the A3, south of London. It had once been a bustling factory, but was now a skeleton of rusted metal and crumbling concrete. In stark contrast to the countryside, the air around the industrial estate was heavy with the smell of oil and decay mixed with the faint, acrid stink of old fires. Craven had two, maybe three, days before Barbara's body arrived in the UK for her funeral. His time in a bleak MI5 holding cell gave him too much time to dwell on his grief, but perhaps he'd needed it. Craven hadn't stood still since Barbara's death, hadn't fully processed her loss in his emotionally stunted former detective's brain. He had wept in the cell, had cried like a child at the prospect of a future without her in it. Perhaps he has needed that time. God, he missed her.

The SUV pulled to a stop next to a dilapidated warehouse. Craven could see patches of graffiti on the walls and broken windows, which gave the place a sinister look. The agents got out first, white earpieces in their ears, checking the area before one of them opened the door for him. Jones led the exchange detail himself. His stern face peered into the vehicle and he took a firm grip on Craven's arm as he escorted him out. Another agent reached in and gently woke Kim, helping her step out of the vehicle.

"Stay close," warned Jones, his voice low and controlled.

Craven glanced around, his eyes adjusting to the dim light filtering through the light fog. Another car approached, a sleek black Jaguar. It stopped a few yards away and two figures emerged. Jack Kane in a sharp Hugo Boss suit, and Danny Kane in jeans and a hoodie.

Jones nodded at Kane, who gave a curt nod in return. The protocol was clear. No sudden movements, no unnecessary chatter. The agents kept their hands close to their jackets, ready to draw their weapons if necessary. Kane walked forward, meeting them halfway between the cars.

"Frank," said Kane, his voice carrying a hint of relief. "Glad to see you're still in one piece."

"Daddy!" Kim called. She shook free of the agent behind her and ran to Kane with unbridled happiness. He swept her up into a crushing hug.

"What's going with your hair?" Kane laughed, examining the crude job Craven had done to tie it into what might loosely be called a ponytail.

"I did my best," Craven grumbled. "I don't know how you did it, Kane, but my arse was going numb lying on that concrete cell bed. So, my arse says thank you."

Jones crossed his arms over his chest.

"Jafari needs to be stopped," stated Kane, brushing Kim's hair away from his face.

"We have a deal," said Jones. "MI6 says we are going to work together. I've seen your file, your full file, Kane. So I know what you can do. I'm a straight shooter, and I say it how it is. I don't like it. Not one bit. You're lucky there aren't any other MI6 covert agents close by to take this on. But why they couldn't fly someone in to take over, I don't know. So, we've turned to you, an agent inactive for years, a man who grassed on his colleagues and then burst his own witness protection identity. You've tuned up some good MI5 agents over the last few weeks and cost us Christ only knows how much money chasing you around the country. If it was up to me, you'd be rotting in a cell right now. MI6 has gone mad, if you ask me. The top brass wants it this way and I follow orders, so I'm putting a support team together as we speak. We expect results quickly."

"Can you get SAS operators on your team?" Kane ignored Jones' barbs about his ability to get the job done. MI6 had changed. Budget cuts, the interference of political correctness and a shift to cyber-intelligence had reduced the number of active field agents beyond what Kane knew was required to combat the threats from foreign enemy powers. Kane was Britain's best bet to stop Jafari. Stead knew it. So did anyone from the old school of intelligence and clandestine operations.

"No. They are all deployed abroad. The one black ops unit on standby in the UK has had to attend to another matter off the coast of Dover."

"That's bad news. We need SAS precision on this job. I need to get my son and daughter to safety, and then we'll get to it."

The exchange was swift. Jones removed the cuffs, and Craven rubbed his wrists, feeling the blood flow back into his hands. The agents maintained their tight formation, eyes ever watchful, stances rigid.

As Craven moved towards Kane's car, he took in his surroundings one last time. The industrial wasteland, with its rusted machinery and overgrown weeds, was a fitting location for the clandestine handover. It was a place where honest men had once worked hard to build their businesses, to build a future for their families. Now, it was a rotting wreck of former glory. Much like England, Britain, and the former empire. It provided a place for exchanging secrets without prying eyes, where deals could be made in the shadows.

Kane opened the door to the Jaguar and placed Kim gently in the back seat. He walked around the car and opened the front passenger seat for Craven. "Get in, Frank," he said. "We've got work to do."

Craven nodded and slid into the car, his bruises from the fight at the playground still tender. He glanced at Jones and his agents, feeling a mix of anxiety and determination. As they drove away from the abandoned site, he couldn't shake the feeling that this was just the beginning of a much larger, more dangerous game. But for now, he was free, and he had to help Kane stop Jafari and prevent a catastrophe.

CHAPTER FIFTY-FIVE

Kane lifted Kim and carried her to the hotel bedroom. She had fallen asleep on his lap watching children's Netflix shows on her iPad. It was precious time Kane needed with his daughter. Just to sit and be together. To stroke her hair, tell her she was safe. To tell Kim he loved her. Craven had become so infuriated after the delay to their operation that he had to go for a walk to clear his head. Kane had turned his burner phone off after the third missed call from Gareth Jones of MI5. He just needed an hour with his daughter. Kane lay Kim on the hotel bed and covered her with a duvet. He kissed her forehead and closed the door.

He had checked into the hotel using his final remaining identity, Steven Heighway. A budget hotel close to Greenwich in London to use as a base before the operation to intercept Ghost and Jafari's meeting.

"Any luck, son?" Kane asked, moving into the bedroom area where Danny sat at a desk, peering into Cameron's laptop.

The dimly-lit room hummed with the low buzz of the laptop's internal fans and the click-clack of Danny's fingers across the keyboard.

"I think I have her," Danny said, without taking his eyes off the computer screen.

Kane peered over Danny's shoulder as his son's fingers moved deftly over the keyboard, and lines of code streamed across the screen as he triangulated the signal.

"Looks like you've taken to this like a duck to water."

"We did a tonne of coding at school last year, and I kind of followed it up myself at home. But Cameron showed me a lot over the last few weeks, and that really got me interested. It looks complicated, but what I'm doing here is only copying what he showed me."

"He was a good man." Kane placed a hand on his son's shoulder. There had been scant time to process Cameron's brutal death; that time would come once this operation was over, but Kane still wanted Danny to know that he understood the pain of losing a friend.

"Yeah, he was. I miss him." Danny glanced at Kane's hand, and in a rare show of emotion, he placed his own hand over Kane's. "There," he muttered, eyes narrowing as the screen displayed a pulsing red dot. The virus was on the move, currently held by the double-crossing Successors hacker, Ghost.

Kane leaned in and watched the red dot move along a map of London. His heart quickened, and he gripped Danny's shoulder tighter. "We can see where she is at street level?"

"Yeah, Dad. I've got a lock on her. She could be moving to the exchange point."

"Good work, Dan. I need to notify Jones and MI5. Any idea where she's headed?"

"Looks like Covent Garden. She's taking a long route, but she scoped out the Jubilee Market Hall earlier today and is now heading back in that direction. I checked out the market hall and it's going to be busy at this time of day, but it also has lower levels with limited access which might work."

Kane clapped his son on the back and turned on his burner phone. It pinged with voicemails and text messages, which Kane ignored as he dialled Jones' number.

"Where the fuck have you been?" Jones blared in his broad Welsh accent.

"Taking care of something more important," Kane replied.

"More important? Jesus Christ, I knew this was a mistake. Bloody MI6 cowboys."

"We've picked up Ghost's signal, and she's headed for Covent Garden, most likely to meet with Jafari. I'm in London and will be at the location in twenty minutes."

"Talk about last minute. I've been trying to contact you for the last hour, Kane. When I call, you fucking answer." Jones' voice shifted from strained to outright shouting and Kane had to move the phone away from his ear.

"We don't have time for a dick-measuring competition. I'll be wearing a communications set, earpiece, and microphone. Craven will send you the frequency so we can communicate."

"Don't do anything rash. This isn't the wild west, Afghanistan or some covert jungle mission. This is London. I'll scramble my team and meet you there as soon as possible. I'll patch into your comms, but stay in touch. Do nothing without my permission. Understand?"

"Roger," said Kane and hung up the phone.

Craven came through the door with two takeaway coffee-style cups in each hand. "Stirred yourself, have you?" he said, spotting Kane slipping on his suit jacket. "I've got myself a coffee and you a tea."

"It's on, Frank. Danny has picked up Ghost's signal and I'm off to Covent Garden to intercept the Prometheus Code and the EMP before she hands them over to Jafari."

"I see." He glanced at Danny and peered down the hall towards Kim's bedroom. "What about the kids?"

"I need you to stay here with them. Danny is using Cameron's laptop to track Ghost and I need you to run comms here to keep me updated and give me eyes on where she is heading."

"I can do that."

"The tracking technology only works on Cameron's laptop, so we can't hand over the tracking to MI5. I don't want to give them Cam's laptop until we have cleaned it down of any sensitive information. He could have records of our communications, including the false documents he prepared for us, passports, credit cards, aliases and potentially our location in Seville. So we run it all from here. Jones will come on heavy and demand to take over, but don't let him. Our lives are inside Cameron's secure servers, where we keep our money, everything."

"Got it."

Kane had the remaining weapons from Cameron's lock-up, plus those he had taken from the dead assassin at the Dog and Dart. The sniper rifle was too large to carry around the streets of London. He preferred to carry a Glock handgun, but he had three spare magazines for the assassin's Sig and a belt and holster to carry both weapons and ammunition. Kane put a folding combat knife into his pocket. He had three grenades, two flashbangs, and a smoke grenade. They were too bulky to carry without a bag, so he left those behind. Kane tucked the communications earpiece into his ear and then attached the body pack to his belt and tucked the throat microphone behind his shirt collar.

"Dan," he said, and smiled as his son looked up from the laptop. "Listen to Frank. I'm going to need updates on where Ghost is heading, and to access CCTV in Covent Garden. If you know how to do that, great, but if not, let Frank know and we can get the intel from MI5."

"OK, Dad," he replied. "And Dad? Be careful."

Kane winked at his son and made for the door, determined to stop Ghost from handing the Alliance everything they needed to crush Western civilisation.

CHAPTER FIFTY-SIX

Covent Garden was bustling with movement. A mix of tourists, street performers and locals going about their day. Kane jumped out of a taxi close to Covent Garden tube station and paid the driver in cash. Although it was summer, ominous clouds the colour of a bruise shifted overhead, hanging low over the city like an upside-down sea. It was a humid day, and the taxi had been stiflingly warm. The driver had refused to put the air- conditioning on, complaining that the cab, like most black cabs in London, was electric. If he ran the vehicle's air-conditioning all day, he would spend half of his shift fighting for the too few car charges dotted about the city. So Kane came from the taxi with beads of sweat on his forehead and beneath his shirt, and was glad of the high-street breeze to cool his skin.

The historic Jubilee Market Hall, with its iron arches and Victorian charm, made sense for the clandestine exchange. Kane made the brisk three-minute walk from the station to the market, steeling himself for what must be done.

"Has Ghost arrived yet, Frank?" Kane said to Craven through his comms device.

"She circled thc placc four times, and then drank a slow coffee around the corner," said Craven. "The tracker says she's on the move again now, though. She's entered the market and is walking slowly through it. She's nervous."

"So would you be if you were about to hand over the virus and EMP to the Alliance."

"True. Head for the market and we'll keep you posted."

"Have you been in touch with Jones?"

"Yeah. He's doing his fucking nut in. He wanted access to the tracking, but I told him to piss off. Jones didn't like that."

"I'd better talk to him before I go in. Over and out for now."

Kane reached behind him to the comms body pack attached to his belt and turned the frequency dial one click. "Jones, can you hear me?"

"I can hear you. I can see you now. We have you on CCTV," said Jones.

"Do you have Ghost?"

"Don't know what she looks like, do I, boyo? You won't share the tracker. Half the fucking people in London wear jeans and hoodies."

"How far away is your team?"

"En route. ETA twenty minutes."

"Keep in touch."

"Wait for my order before you do anything, Kane. Don't forget."

"Roger."

Kane reached Jubilee Market, weaving his way through a throng of strolling tourists in sunglasses clutching brightly-coloured London travel maps. The market, housed in a grand Victorian iron-and-glass structure, spoke of an older, charming London and tourists lapped it up. The lofty arched windows and intricate ironwork cast dappled light on the cobblestone floor. Stalls overflowed with vintage clothing, handmade jewellery, artisanal foods, and kooky antiques. As Kane made his way into the atrium, the air was thick with the mingling smells of freshly brewed coffee, sizzling street food, and fragrant flowers.

Vendors loudly parroted quirky sales pitches about their wares, rising above the murmur of haggling and chatting customers. A street performer played a jaunty tune on a guitar. Shoppers and tourists wove through the narrow aisles, their footsteps echoing against the stone. Kane sidestepped a child tugging on her mother's hand and pointing at the guitar player. People moved in and out of the boutique shops, old pubs with brightly painted signs, and cafés with outdoor seating adorned with climbing ivy and vibrant hanging baskets. Kane turned a corner, striding past Georgian redbrick buildings faced with ornate stonework.

"Kane?" came Craven's voice in Kane's earpiece.

"Where is she?" he replied.

"Moving down to the lower levels. The signal we have is basic. All we can tell is that she seems to be in the same place, maybe a lift. The signal is getting weaker as she moves below the building."

"Got it. I need to talk to Jones." Kane reached for his body pack again and switched the frequency. "Jones?"

"Here, Kane."

"Ghost is on her way down to the lower levels beneath the market. We can't track her that far down. I need to know what's down there. Can you get the blueprints or schematics of the building?"

"One step ahead of you. I'm looking at it now."

"How do I get down there?"

"There's a service lift just ahead of you on the left. Take that and go down to the bottom floor. Cleaners and workers in the shops and cafés use it. There are three main entrances to the lower levels, one through the back alleys outside the market, another via a stairwell in the centre of the market, and the service lift close to your location."

"OK, I'll make my way down."

"When my team arrives, we'll secure all three entrances, which are obviously also the only way out of the lower levels. We have no eyes on the lower levels. There are no cameras down there. You will be on your own. This is an observation-only mission for you, Kane. You find Ghost and watch her until my team arrives. Do not engage with her. If Jafari is there, do not engage him either. Our ETA is now eighteen minutes."

Kane reached the lift, its silver door tucked away in a gap between an ice-cream shop and an art gallery so that it was barely noticeable. A young woman with long black hair in cornrow braids loped towards the lift with a passcard in her hand. Kane hurried to catch up as her card beeped on the small keypad on the lift front. The lift slid open; she stepped inside, and Kane followed. He smiled at her, and she looked him up and down as though he were a piece of shit on her shoe. Kane ignored the insult. The lift jerked into motion and travelled down one level, where the woman stepped out into a level busy with similar workers, which Kane thought was likely where they took their coffee and lunch breaks.

The lift doors closed, and Kane pressed the B button for the basement. The lift travelled down quickly, its gears and mechanics grinding outside in the lift shaft. With a ping, the lift stopped, and the doors opened. Kane stepped out into the corridor of faded brick lit by overhead strip lights. The air grew cool and damp as he moved through the lower level, the dim light casting eerie shadows on the timeworn walls. Kane dropped his hand to the Sig and rested his fingers on the grip.

A shape moved to his left, and he spotted a figure moving slowly, back to the wall. The poor light showed only the person's outline, but Kane could make out the unmistakable cowl of a pulled-up hood. The figure carried what looked like a suitcase in each hand.

CHAPTER FIFTY-SEVEN

"I see her," Kane whispered into his earpiece, but no voice replied. Kane guessed he was too deep below ground for the comms to work. He was on his own. Ghost moved around a bend and Kane followed, moving quickly and silently. Kane reached the bend and pushed his back up against the wall. He slid closer to the edge and risked a peek around the corner.

Ghost stood with a case in each hand, and seven people stared back at her. Jafari's team, armed and alert. Their eyes darting around the narrow space, tension palpable. They wore combat gear with shemagh scarves pulled up over their mouths and noses.

"Do you have the money?" Ghost said, her American voice mouse-like in the dank space.

A tall man stepped forward with what looked like a business card in his hand.

"I transfer the funds to the requested accounts," he said in English with a heavy Pashto-Afghan accent. "Here is the authorisation code. You can check. We wait."

"I can check myself." She took a step backwards and set the cases down. Ghost rummaged in her jeans pocket and pulled out a phone. She swiped twice on the screen and then peered closer to it; her face illuminated by the device's soft glow. "The money's not there. What kind of crap are you trying to pull?"

"No crap." Jafari shrugged. "Did you bring devices?"

"What do you think these are, my luggage?"

Kane stood with his back against the damp wall. Ghost was nervous, using sarcasm to mask her fear. Kane slowly slid the Sig from its holster at his waist. He carried the weapon with one round already in the pipe and was ready to fire should he need it. It was too early to strike and too late to get to Ghost. Kane would have preferred to get to her before the meeting, to relieve her of the virus and the EMP before she met with Jafari and his crew. The exchange was underway, but Ghost was a young woman more comfortable behind the safety of her keyboard, and Jafari was an experienced spy, killer, soldier and mercenary. This was his business, his profession, and Ghost was in way over her head.

"We must check the things work. If they work, then we send money," said Jafari. Kane hadn't risked another peek around the corner. If Jafari's men saw him, it would be a bloodbath with Ghost caught in the middle. He hadn't got a clear view of Jafari or his team. Their scarves hid most of their faces.

There was a long pause before Ghost finally said. "Fine. Take them."

"Good."

Boots stepped on the cold floor and Kane presumed one of Jafari's team had taken the cases. Kane winced. Ghost had handed over the virus and the EMP and had lost control. The minute she entered Covent Garden with the devices, she had surrendered her hand. A more sensible approach would have been to leave the hard drive and the EMP in a secure location, perhaps a locker in a bus depot or safe deposit box in a bank. At the meeting, give Jafari the key once the money had been transferred and confirmed. Provide a safe exchange.

"OK, boss," said a woman's voice, in what Kane thought was a Chinese accent.

"The Prometheus Code and the EMP are verified," said Jafari.

"Now do I get my money?" asked Ghost. Kane could hear the vulnerability crack in her voice.

"No. Now you get what you deserve."

A bullet spat from a silenced weapon. Silent and deadly. A body collapsed to the ground and the loudest sound was the clatter of a brass bullet casing hitting the cold stones. Kane readied his weapon, bringing it up to his chest in two hands.

"Mashallah," said Jafari in Arabic, which Kane understood. God has willed it.

Jafari and the Alliance had the Prometheus Code and the EMP device. Kane could not let them leave with it. He set his jaw and burst from the behind the wall. Ghost was dead, a puddle of deep crimson blooming around her head from Jafari's death shot. Kane fired a round at Jafari's chest, and the tall man gasped and fell backwards. Kane fired three more rounds at the enemies gathered behind their leader. He kept moving as he pulled the trigger. The sound of the Sig exploded around the narrow corridors, and Jafari's team sprang into action.

Jafari rolled on the floor, Kane's bullet absorbed by his bulletproof body armour. He fired a suppressed pistol, and the bullet ricocheted off the concrete ceiling above Kane's head. He dived towards an electrical control box on the opposite wall and crouched behind it for cover. Kane raised his weapon above the box to fire again but cursed and shrank back as one of Jafari's team levelled an AK-47 assault rifle. The machine-gun fired, shredding the air with its deafening roar. Bullets slammed into the floor and wall and Kane waited. The AK-47 was a powerful weapon, and when fired, it caused the shooter's aim to lift with each shot. To re-aim the weapon, the shooter needed to take their finger off the trigger.

The firing stopped, and Kane lay flat on the floor and extended his gun hand. He fired into the smoke left by the AK-47 and the shooter howled in pain. Jafari was on his feet and his team was moving away from Kane's position. One of the enemy tried to reach the AK-47 shooter but gave up the attempt under Kane's fire. They had retreated farther into the gloomy corridor and gunshots came from the murk, forcing Kane to shrink backwards.

He curled up behind the electrical box as bullets whipped and sang about him, each moment giving Jafari and his team a greater chance to escape. The gunfire stopped and Kane rushed from behind the box. He fired two shots into the darkness and ran after the enemy, leaping over Ghost's corpse and darting past the writhing AK-47 shooter. A door banged in the distance and Kane sprinted towards it. He found a steel emergency door and kicked it open. Daylight flooded into the doorway, the brightness blinding Kane for a moment. He shielded his eyes and forced them open just in time to see a black van speeding away down a back alley.

Jafari had escaped through the alley exit at the rear of and below the markets. Kane bent over and pressed his hands onto his knees. A Range Rover came screaming down the alley from the opposite direction into which Jafari's car had disappeared. Four heavily-armed operators leapt out with MP5s at the ready.

"Black van gone that way. They have the virus and the EMP. If you move fast, you might catch them."

"Go, go, go!" commanded one operator, and the Range Rover sped away.

"What the fuck happened?" barked Jones in Kane's earpiece.

"Ghost's dead. The Alliance has the Prometheus Code and the EMP," Kane replied.

"I fucking knew it. You're a fucking liability, Kane."

"I clipped one of Jafari's men. Let's see what he has to say. It's not over yet."

CHAPTER FIFTY-EIGHT

Gareth Jones closed the door and wiped his hands on a cloth. It was harder to get blood off skin than water, some of it always remained. He frowned when he noticed spots of garnet-coloured blood had marked the rolled-up sleeves of his white shirt, and flecks of the captured terrorist's blood still spotted his forearms.

It had taken just fourteen minutes to break the prisoner. Jones had not led the work himself. MI5 had other agents for that job. This time, it was a woman Jones had never met. A middle-aged agent with green eyes, auburn hair and a voluptuous figure. A veteran of the war in the Middle East who had barked instructions at Jones to pass her such a tool or hold the subject's head still. Which Jones had done, struggling to keep the grimace of distaste from his face. Women were far better at interrogating and terrorising Islamic fundamentalist men than their male counterparts. The perceived humiliation was simply too much for such men to bear. The dishonour for men of a culture so extreme that a father would kill his own daughter for besmirching his honour by dating a boy without permission, or for not wearing her hijab in public. The threat of not achieving martyrdom was as persuasive to Islamic fundamentalist fighters as the knife she wielded against Imran al-Fahd's groin.

Jones marched up the corridor deep within Thames House into a room thronged with MI5 agents. Men and women in suits hunched over computers, talked on the phone, busy trying to avert the biggest threat Europe and Britain had faced in Jones' lifetime. Kane's face peered out at Jones from a conference call screen. Jones poured himself a cup of insipid coffee from a push-down canister and winced at its acrid taste. He needed the coffee to keep calm. Despite letting the Alliance get away with the Prometheus Code and the EMP, Kane had refused to cooperate with Jones' team. Instead, he had withdrawn to his hotel, which Jones' people frustratingly hadn't located yet. Kane had said he didn't feel safe inside Thames House. Which he wasn't, or at least would not be if Jones got his way.

"Is this thing on?" Jones asked his team, gesturing towards the screen.

"Yes, sir," said Banks. A thirty-something woman and an excellent agent. She was the daughter of Nigerian immigrants and the most capable of Jones' team.

"Kane, can you hear me?"

"Loud and clear. What did you learn?"

"Sharing intel now, are we? You have shared fuck all with us, Kane. Why should I tell you what we know?"

"Because you have no choice. I'm your best hope in stopping them from deploying the virus and the EMP. So let's cut the bullshit and get to it. They'll likely strike between three and five in the morning when London's streets are quiet. What did you learn from the prisoner?"

Jones balled his fist. Even the sound of Kane's voice annoyed him. His assumption that Jones would give up the intel was both grating and correct. Jones had little choice with his superiors breathing down his neck, and supportive of Kane's involvement. "Even though your operation to intercept the hacker Ghost was an unmitigated disaster resulting in the loss of her life, and the loss of the Prometheus Code and the EMP device, we managed to salvage something from the shitstorm.

"We have images of Jafari and his team leaving the markets. The prisoner gave us supporting intel. Jafari has a core team, and then a supporting crew of twelve soldiers. Jafari chose each member of his core team for their unique skills and unwavering loyalty to the Alliance. The team of six agents he has assembled is a deadly force, each bringing their own brand of danger and expertise. Imran had nothing to divulge on the twelve supporting soldiers, other than that they are mercenaries and veterans from various wars across the globe, recruited by Jafari as hired muscle."

"How many operations have you conducted which have gone to plan? We need to adapt, Jones. We need to move as the op changes and shifts around us. You'd better give the details of each one of Jafari's crew, so I know who I'm going up against."

Jones gestured to Banks, and six pictures replaced Kane's face on the screen.

"The first of Jafari's merry band of horrible bastards is Khalid al-Nasiri," Jones continued. "As you can see, he's uglier than a bulldog licking piss off a nettle. Banks, you can take over the briefing from here." Banks took Jones' place in front of the conference call screen, allowing Jones to stand back and take a moment's rest.

"Khalid appears to be the brains behind the operation," said Banks in her serious, no-nonsense voice. "A former senior intelligence officer from Iran known for his brilliance and cold-blooded efficiency. He has orchestrated several high-profile cyber-attacks and covert operations for the Iranian Revolutionary Guard. His background in cyber-warfare and espionage makes him indispensable. Gaunt with piercing eyes. His ability to anticipate the Alliance's enemy's moves and counter them with surgical precision makes him formidable.

"Next up is Kim Hyon-hui. A young woman in her late twenties, and a prodigy from North Korea. The state groomed her from a young age to become one of their top cyber operatives. With a degree in computer science from Kim Il-sung University and a history of working on state-sponsored hacking projects, she is important to Jafari, his key to understanding the virus and its component code. She is skilled in coding and decrypting, and her ability to penetrate secure systems is unparalleled. Her slight frame and quiet demeanour belies a sharp intellect and an even sharper resolve to serve her country's leader and regime.

"Rashid al-Zawahiri is Jafari's explosive expert. Rashid came up within the ranks of Al-Qaeda and is notorious for his expertise with different types of bombs. From the horror IEDs you would have seen and experienced in Afghanistan to larger, more destructive demolition charges. He has a burly physique; his body is covered in scars from bombs gone wrong, and two fingers are missing from his left hand. He has been with Jafari for fifteen years. They came up through the ranks together and Rashid is Jafari's go-to guy for his private mercenary operations.

"Zhen Liu is a former PLA Special Forces operative from China skilled in close-quarters combat and stealth operations. Standing at an average height with a muscular build, she is a dangerous woman. We know through our collaborations with the CIA that Zhen has carried out many assassinations for the Chinese Government before going out on her own. Her proficiency with both firearms and hand-to-hand combat makes her Jafari's enforcer.

"Farid Ibrahim is a suave, well-dressed Saudi national responsible for funding Jafari's team and ensuring the flow of money passes from the Alliance into Jafari's secure accounts. He has connections deep within the wealthy elite of the Middle

East and has access to vast sums of money and resources. Farid makes sure Jafari and his team have everything they need, from weapons and advanced technology to safe houses. Despite his polished exterior and business-like appearance, he is a master manipulator, capable of bending others to his will with financial clout and persuasive tactics. For a man who has never seen active combat, he is not afraid to get his gun off.

"Imran al-Fahd is your friend from beneath the Jubilee Market. You shot him through the shoulder and Jafari had no qualms about leaving him behind. He is a Syrian national with a background in smuggling and logistics. He's the one who made sure things ran smoothly for the Alliance team's insertion into the UK. He is renowned for orchestrating the transport of arms, equipment, and personnel across borders with remarkable efficiency. Imran's knowledge of covert routes and safe passages in and out of the UK was important to Jafari. I say was, because now Imran belongs to us. He is giving up all kinds of intel on the Alliance to our interrogator.

"Last of all is Jafari himself, and I believe you have received a briefing about his background?"

"I have, from your illustrious leader."

"Fuck you, Kane," Jones called. "Good work, Banks. Thank you." She smiled and shifted to the left to allow Jones to take his place in front of the camera.

"Did Imran al-Fahd give us a steer where Jafari plans to attack?"

"He did. Banks, bring up the details." Jones paused as Banks worked on a laptop to bring up detailed maps, blueprints and surveillance photos. "Can you see the visuals, Kane?"

"I can. Send them to my secure email address so I can check them in more detail."

"Will do," said Banks.

"As soon as you share the tracking signal on the virus' hard drive," Jones added.

"It's gone dead. Either Jafari's people have found the tracker on the hard drive, or they are out of range. Besides, I told you already," Kane replied, shaking his head. "I can't send it to you. Cameron was a tech genius. A wizard. The Gandalf of computers. I can't understand how he coded that tracker or got close to the encryption and complexity he built into his tracking software."

"Gandalf? Really? Just fucking share it."

"He made it ridiculously complex so that Ghost, who was also an expert hacker, wouldn't trace or detect it. If I could share it, I would. Just send me the schematics, Jones. I can find them anyway if I need to."

Jones sipped at his coffee, gurned at the foul taste, and placed it on the table as far away from him as possible. "Jafari's plan is audacious. He intends to implant the Prometheus Code at the heart of London's financial district and then set off the EMP in the same building to wipe out London's entire electrical power. We believe he has already deployed the virus' phishing element, in anticipation of phase two deployment where he must insert the virus' hard drive into a local server. When the grid recognises the outage and boots up again, our financial markets and systems are gone. The target for deploying the virus is Heron Tower in the heart of London city."

Jones paused as Banks brought up images of the immense structure. The screen moved around the giant skyscraper, like a helicopter camera travelling up its shining sides and then zooming out to show its scale within the city.

"Heron Tower, or 110 Bishopsgate to give it its proper name, is one of the most secure buildings in the city," Jones continued. "It houses several financial institutions and data centres. Its security measures are top-tier. Biometric scanners at every access point, 24/7 surveillance with thermal and motion sensors, and a dedicated security team with armed response units.

"Jafari's team will probably gain entry using a combination of social engineering and brute force. They have insiders who will provide them with authentic access cards and biometric data. For the final security layers, they plan to use a sophisticated cyber-attack to temporarily disable the internal systems."

"Once they reach a server room, they can plug the virus' hard drive straight in. Did Imran say how they plan to deploy the EMP?"

"From the rooftop. The location is strategic. It's central to the power grid and offers a high vantage point. Once the EMP goes off, it will create a citywide blackout. The chaos also provides Jafari and his team their window to escape. All our systems will go down with everything else in the city."

"What happens when the power comes back on?"

"When the power grid reboots, the Prometheus Code will have already infiltrated the European Financial networks. It will wipe out every piece of financial data, causing irreversible damage. Banks across Europe will lose transaction histories, account details, financial records. It will be like the end of the fucking world. Think about the average person or business today. Nobody carries actual cash, everything is digital. When the Prometheus Code is deployed, all of that disappears. People won't be able to buy food, fuel for their cars, governments unable to issue payments. Society as we know it will collapse."

The gravity of the situation hung heavy in the room and through the conference call screen.

"Presumably he plans to go in at night. Tonight," said Kane.

"Imran didn't know. But we are working on that basis. After

you confronted them beneath the market, Jafari knows we are onto him."

"I'll be ready. I'm going to need entry cards, or whatever else I need to access the building. Can you provide those? Or cut the power so I can enter the place without needing to find my way around its security measures?"

"Calm down, Kane. You aren't going in there like the Lone Ranger. I've put a team together from MI5 and other forces to support you. Even though it beggars belief that you are involved at all. These are some of our best operatives, each one with unique skills critical to this mission."

"Let me guess. You are going to talk me through the background on each one?"

"Yes. You are going to listen and work with them. That's how you get into Heron Tower. Is there anything else you need for the mission?"

"Yes. Guns. Plus ammunition, grenades, a comms jammer, night vision and thermals just in case, rope, and your assurance that you won't come after me when this is over."

CHAPTER FIFTY-NINE

Kane stretched his shoulders as he listened to Jones droning about his team and the mission. Now that Kane had the location and the details of Jafari's team, all he needed was MI5's help to override the building's security systems. He neither needed nor wanted MI5's team, but listened to the briefing to keep Jones happy. To Kane's left, Danny and Craven worked at pulling together as much information on the target building as possible. It was mid-afternoon and come nightfall, Kane knew he must pit himself against Jafari and his team.

A photograph of a gigantic, muscular man appeared on the conference call screen. "This is David "Tank" Miller, a former Royal Marine Commando," said Jones. "He's our heavy weapons and demolitions expert. He'll carry an array of weapons, including a HK416 assault rifle, grenades, and breaching charges. He'll handle any obstacles Jafari creates and provide firepower support."

Next, an image of a wiry sharp faced woman replaced Tank on the screen. "This is Sarah Jenkins. She is trained in covert operations, stealth, and bypassing systems. She can help you get past the tightest security without raising alarms."

A third image showed two men in tactical vests and army fatigues. Men with hard faces and steely eyes. "These men, Robert Turner and Jimmy Ojukwu, are experienced soldiers from the Parachute Regiment. As I am sure you can appreciate, they can provide support with defensive tactics, close-quarter combat and are handy fuckers in a gunfight. They'll also carry HK416s and Glock handguns. Don't engage the enemy without them or Tank by your side."

"We don't want to form a perimeter around Heron Tower until we are sure Jafari has begun his attack. Keep your agents back until we know Jafari is inside. I'll meet you a half mile away to collect my gear."

"My team will be there, and you can proceed together."

Kane nodded. "I suppose you have put together a plan of attack?"

"We have. You and the team will split into two groups, with one group securing the EMP site and disabling the device before it can be deployed. The other will focus on stopping the virus upload. So one makes for the EMP on the roof, the other searches for Jafari in the building itself."

"Needless to say, time is tight. Once Jafari is inside the building, we perhaps only have an hour to stop him."

"Exactly. Timing and coordination will be crucial. Any delay or misstep could mean disaster. Teamwork, Kane. Do I need to explain that concept to you?"

"I hear you, Jones. I'll see you and your team later."

Kane hung up the conference call and stood, turning to Craven.

"Well?" asked Craven. "Jones likes you about as much as a turd in a swimming pool."

"He just wants to convince himself and everyone around him he's in charge. In an organisation where most senior officers are middle- and upper-class, Jones has an unmistakeably Welsh accent he can't conceal. He's risen to his current rank on results and capability, not what school he went to or who his father plays golf with. Jones is competent enough. He doesn't like or trust MI6, just like MI6 don't like or trust MI5."

"It was the same on the force. The lads in the Met Police used to make my arse wink."

"I'll meet Jones and his team to get the gear I need. After that, I'll work alone. I need you and Danny to find whatever else you can on Cameron's laptop. I'll need to know when Jafari enters the building. Dan, have you figured how to access CCTV cameras using the London City feed?"

"I think so, Dad," said Danny. He turned the laptop so that Kane could see the screen. "I'm inside their mainframe. Cameron's software is fairly intuitive. He'd shown me the basics and I think I've got the hang of it. I just need to pinpoint the actual cameras facing Heron Tower."

"Good work, son."

Danny grinned, and Kane's heart swelled. Even though they faced an impossible task, this was the closest Kane had felt to his son for a long time. They had bonded over the mission, found common ground in what had to be done. Danny seemed to have found his calling and had taken to cyber work as though he was a seasoned professional.

"I've also looked at the work Cameron and Ghost were doing on the Prometheus Code," Danny continued. "They were close to figuring it out. Cameron detailed his progress in a video blog on his secure server. It's almost like a live stream of him explaining what he had done and how to put his and Ghost's work together. He was almost there, Dad. I think I can put their work together. Maybe. I'm not sure."

"If you can put their work together, what can we do with it?"

"Well, I think it will disable the Prometheus Code."

"Can it be done remotely?"

"I think so, Dad."

"You are making a big difference here, Dan. I'm proud of you, son. If the tracker comes back online, let me know."

It was a brief moment, fleeting, but one Kane treasured. For the first time since Sally's death, Kane felt close to his son, felt the bond between them strengthening. Kim slept soundly in the hotel bedroom, safe with Craven. Safe for now, at least.

"Frank?" Kane said. "We've talked about this before. But if the worst should happen, take care of Danny and Kim for me."

"Bloody hell. Do you have to ask me that every time you are about to face certain death? Of course I'll look after them. If you ask me again, you might get a kick in the balls next time I see you. And before you ask, yes, I remember how to access your offshore funds and the trusts set up for the kids. Go and stop Jafari and come back in one piece."

Kane and Craven shared a wry smile. Kane left them in the hotel, the weight of responsibility hanging heavily on his shoulders. The fate of Western civilisation depended upon the operation's success. If Kane failed, the future of Danny and Kim, as well as the lives of millions of people in Europe and the US, would be destroyed. Failure was not an option.

CHAPTER SIXTY

Kane met Jones and his team half a mile away from Heron Tower. The MI5 field control centre was three transit vans, four Range Rovers, and an entire street in central London cordoned off from the public with yellow police tape. The MI5 team took over the back of one van, checking weapons repeatedly, sharing combat stories, filling each other with bravado before the mission. Kane left them to it. He waited, leaning on the corner of a building drinking tea from a Styrofoam cup.

Jones was true to his word and provided Kane with the weapons and equipment he had asked for, along with black combat clothing and a bulletproof combat vest. Trousers, shirt, boots, even black camouflage paint to put on his face. He wore a communications earpiece and microphone set to receive comms from Danny and Craven, and Jones' team simultaneously.

Kane checked over the gear until he was happy with each piece of kit. The MP5A3 rifle was fitted with a suppressor and holographic sight. He made sure the weapon was safe and pulled back the charging handle, checking the chamber for any obstructions. Kane loaded a thirty-round magazine into the magwell with a satisfying click and pulled the charging handle back, letting it snap forward, chambering a round. He screwed the suppressor onto the barrel, its matte-black finish blending with the weapon.

The Glock 19 Gen 4 gun was modified with an extended magazine and a threaded barrel for a suppressor. Kane racked the slide back and checked the chamber before inserting a fifteen-round magazine. He racked the slide again to chamber a round, the action quiet but firm. The suppressor twisted onto the barrel, making the weapon longer but deadly quiet.

The MP5 hung close to his chest on a strap, and the Glock sat comfortably in a waist holster. Kane carried a black backpack containing the grenades he had requested and a set of MI5 night vision goggles. The goggles were also equipped with advanced thermal imaging. They weighed just under a pound, making them easy to handle and carry.

"The bastards are out there somewhere," said Jones, appearing at Kane's shoulder.

"They've probably been here all day. Hiding. Waiting."

"We've had agents sweeping the city all afternoon, especially this area. They found nothing."

"Jafari and his team are the best, hand-picked for their skills. We could look for a year and never find them. Thanks for the kit," Kane replied.

"Did you meet the team?"

"I met them."

"Use them, Kane. Don't go in there all gung-ho. We have one shot at this."

Kane checked his watch. It was almost three o'clock in the morning. "We'll get them, Jones. You might even get a promotion when it's all over."

Jones reared up, his face flushing with anger until he noticed the gleam in Kane's eye. He calmed quickly and chuckled under his breath. Kane peered across London's night sky at Heron Tower's sleek glass façade shimmering under the city lights. It stood out against the horizon, towering at 230 metres tall, illuminated by soft, blue-tinted lights that accentuated its modern architecture. The tower's spire pierced the night like a blade. Surrounding buildings like the Gherkin and the Cheesegrater added to the cityscape. A hub of business and finance, about to come under attack from enemies of Western culture.

The tower nestled in the heart of the City of London. At 3am the streets were eerily quiet. The usual hustle and bustle of the financial district replaced by a stillness broken only by the occasional hum of a distant car or the echo of unseen footsteps on the pavement. The air was cool, heavy with the faint scent of rain on concrete mixed with the lingering aroma of food from nearby late-night takeaways and restaurants.

A few taxis and delivery vans made their way across the empty streets, leaving the roads around the tower, including Bishopsgate, largely deserted. Streetlights and the ambient light from the vast towers lit the streets, so that darkness fell upon that part of London.

"Kane?" said Craven's voice in Kane's ear.

"What is it, Frank?"

"Danny's picked them up. Jafari and his team are entering the building from the rear. They're going in, Jack. With more guns than you could shake a shitty stick at."

Kane turned to Jones, who had a finger pressed to his ear. He glanced at Kane. It was time to stop Jafari and the Alliance with extreme prejudice.

CHAPTER SIXTY-ONE

Jones watched Kane and his team lope off into the night and returned to his command truck. He was beyond tired, in that gritty-eyed hyper-awake ether fuelled by coffee, fear, and adrenaline. This had to work. There was no other choice. MI5's commanders were on standby for any updates, tuned into the live feed from Jones' command truck systems. The Prime Minister had received a briefing, and the US President and his security command were on high alert. It didn't get more serious or more desperate than this.

The fabric of Western civilisation was at stake, but there was an opportunity on the knife edge of Kane's mission. Jones pulled open the van door and ducked inside, curling his lip with guilt at his own ambition. If Kane could stop Jafari, if he could prevent the Alliance from loosing the Prometheus Code upon the world, then MI5 command would hail Jones as a hero, the agent who had quarterbacked an operation which saved the world. He could pick his next promotion, his next operation, his new team. Everything he had dreamed of and worked for since leaving the Welsh valleys rested in the lap of a man he neither liked nor trusted. It was time to trust him, time to believe that Kane would get this done.

"Show me the feed of Jafari entering the building," Jones commanded.

"On screen now, sir," Banks replied without looking up from

her laptop.

Another agent handed Jones yet another cup of tepid coffee, which he took with a curt nod. Everyone inside the command truck was bleary-eyed, shirt collars open and sleeves rolled up. The stress in the room was palpable. The camera feed from a nearby alleyway flickered to life on a monitor screen. A dark van emerged from under the cover of a shadowy overhang and slid silently along the street. The rear doors opened, and five figures emerged, each moving with practised precision. Jafari led the team, his willowy, lean frame unmistakable. His darting eyes, visible even on the grainy footage, scanned their surroundings with an intensity that sent a chill down Jones' spine. Twelve operatives fanned out around the five, drifting from the night like wraiths with submachine-guns held before their faces as they shifted across the street.

Jafari and his team wore black tactical gear. Balaclavas obscured their faces, making identification impossible. Each carried a small, sleek backpack, likely containing their tools for infiltrating the tower and unleashing the Prometheus Code. They approached a side entrance to Heron Tower, an access point typically reserved for maintenance and cleaning crews.

"Can you zoom in?" Jones asked. Banks rolled her fingers over her laptop's touchpad and the footage expanded on the screen.

One of Jafari's team, a burly figure with a heavy-duty-looking laptop, connected the device to the electronic door lock. Within seconds, the door clicked open. They slipped inside and the door drifted shut behind them. Banks shifted the footage to a camera inside the building. Jafari's team moved rapidly but cautiously along the entrance corridor and into a lobby deserted save for a lone security guard stationed at the front desk. A wiry figure with a compact build approached the guard from behind with a silenced handgun in one hand. The muzzle flared three times, and the security guard slumped dead against the desk.

They proceeded to the lift bank. Jafari slipped an access card from his pocket and swiped it through the reader. A card he had either stolen, or his team had cloned. The lift doors opened, and the team filtered inside. Three of Jafari's support team remained in the lobby and the rest moved upwards.

A camera inside the lift picked up Jafari's team, as one of them bypassed the floor selection panel to access the control panel behind it. The tech-savvy member of the group worked quickly, re-routing the lift to a secure floor without triggering any alarms. They worked efficiently and effectively. Every MI5 agent inside the command truck stood glued to the footage, and Jones' concern grew with each passing second.

Jafari reached the secure floor and the camera footage switched again. The lift doors opened onto a corridor lined with reinforced doors and additional security measures. Jafari and his team donned night vision goggles and continued in the darkness, only the outlines visible via the security cameras. They encountered a biometric scanner at the entrance to the server room. Jones watched as Jafari produced a small handheld device and attached it to the scanner. The screen flashed green, and the heavy door unlocked. They were in.

"Kane, do you read me?" Jones said into a comms microphone.

"Loud and clear," Kane replied over speakers in the command truck.

"They've infiltrated the tower and are already on the secure floor."

"I'm in too."

Jafari's infiltration was almost flawless, other than the dead security guard. They had shown no hesitation in dispatching the innocent man. The fate of the West lay in Kane's hands now, but he was already inside the building, already racing to stop the enemy. The hunt was on.

CHAPTER SIXTY-TWO

Sarah Jenkins opened the door with a swipe of a pre-programmed access card and Kane slipped inside the same door through which Jafari and his team had entered moments earlier.

"One of you stay and guard this door," instructed Kane, rising from a crouch to slip through the open door. "I'll take point. The rest of you follow." He held the MP5 in his left hand, the weapon secured by a strap tied tight so that the weapon nestled against his combat vest but with enough give for him to level and fire the weapon when needed.

"I ain't staying nowhere," barked Tank. He was a head taller than Kane, and twice as thick across the shoulders with a spade of a beard and eyes hungry for combat. "Jenkins. You stay."

"Jenkins stays with me. Turner, you hold the door."

"Yes, sir," responded Turner. He took up a position inside the door, weapon ready and focused.

"Tank. You do as I say, or you go back to Jones and the command truck. Is that clear?"

"I don't take orders from you," sneered Tank. "You ain't no officer. Lead on, spy boy. Don't get in my way."

Tank was a problem Kane didn't have time to deal with. He set off down the corridor, trailed by Jenkins, Tank, and Ojukwu.

"There are three of Jafari's men in the lobby," said Craven in Kane's earpiece. Kane took the instruction but gave no response. He held up three fingers and pointed beyond the door which led to the lobby to let the MI5 team know what lay ahead.

Kane opened the door softly and slipped inside, keeping low. The lobby was poorly- lit by a fraction of its usual lighting. The place would switch to full brightness in the morning to welcome workers to their day, but now it was dim and still. Kane kept to the wall, moving slowly northwards, coming about a granite reception desk where the dead security guard had collapsed over a desk and keyboard. Three silver turnstiles barred the way in, and behind the security desk were visitor toilets and the lifts. Kane paused. An enemy operator patrolled the opposite wall with his weapon held in both hands. Kane searched the wide entranceway and spotted another enemy soldier making the same patrol along the western wall.

"I see the bastard," growled Tank. He levelled his weapon, and before Kane could stop him, the big Marine opened fire. His MP5 spat a burst of silenced rounds. Two shots slammed into the wall behind the first enemy, and the third hit a large reinforced glass window panel, shattering it with a loud crack.

"Shit," Kane cursed. He brought the MP5 to bear and peered down the holographic sight. The enemy operator fired a burst from his own weapon but Kane ignored the gunfire spattering around him. He aimed the laser sight at the enemy and squeezed the trigger. The Alliance soldier's head snapped back, splashing the cracked window with bright blood.

The second enemy soldier died as Ojukwu peppered him with a hail of bullets.

"Oh God," gulped Tank, curled into a ball at Kane's feet. "Fucking hell. I'm hit. I need a medic. Get me a medic!"

Kane knelt beside him. Tank was shot through the arm and thigh. None were life-threatening wounds, but viscous blood oozed through his combat clothing and formed a thick pool on Heron Tower's shiny floor tiles.

"Your fight is done," said Kane, without pity. "You can help us by shutting your mouth. Take the pain." Tank shook his head from side to side and let out a loud animalistic mewing sound. Kane gripped his face hard, forcing the Marine to look into his eyes. "Take the pain. Take it!"

Tank stared into Kane's soul, saw the ruthlessness there. Whether he feared Kane might finish what the enemy bullet had started, or realised what he must do for the operation, was impossible to tell. But Tank ground his teeth and nodded. He rocked from side to side clutching at his wounds, but remained silent. Kane took the grenades and breaching charges from Tank's pack.

More gunfire peeled out from behind the reception desk and Kane rolled to his left with his weapon levelled. He fired again, and the enemy ducked just in time to avoid the hail of bullets.

"Ojukwu is down," said Jenkins, voice high-pitched with horror. Kane glanced to his left, where Ojukwu lay sprawled on the floor tiles, his head blown apart above his ear by a bullet's exit wound.

"What the fuck is going in there, Kane?" said Jones' voice over the comms. "Half the team is dead, and you haven't even got through the fucking reception lobby yet."

Kane pulled the earpiece out and let it dangle against his combat vest. He shifted silently across the floor, changing the angle of sight towards his target. The enemy popped up behind the desk, but before Kane could fire, Jenkins shot the enemy in the shoulder, sending him spinning. Kane surged to his feet and ran, leaping over the turnstiles and reaching the enemy as he rolled to his feet, sagging on one side from his ruined shoulder. Kane shot him once in the face. No hesitation. No mercy.

CHAPTER SIXTY-THREE

"Jones wants to talk to you, sir," said Jenkins. She came to stand beside Kane, blue eyes darting from the dead enemies to the lift shafts. "He's quite animated over the comms."

"That was an excellent shot," Kane said, ignoring her comments about Jones. "Do we need to worry about these lifts?"

"What about Tank and Ojukwu? What about Turner?"

"Nothing we can do about Tank and Ojukwu now. Ops shift and change, problems occur, and we must overcome them. Turner needs to do what I asked him to do. Stay close to me. You look after the tech, and I'll deal with everything else."

"But Jones is insisting, sir, he says..."

"It doesn't matter what he says. It's you and me now. The lifts?"

Jenkins slipped off her backpack and pulled a small box with multi-coloured wires corded about a green screen. She pressed it against the lift control panel.

"Employees here need a swipe card to use the lift. This bypasses it. Jones says half of Jafari's team are on the twelfth floor, the rest are on the roof with the EMP."

"We go for the EMP first. Without that, they can't deploy the Prometheus Code."

Jenkins pressed her device against the lift keypad. It dinged, and the lift clanked into action behind its silvery metal doors.

"Let us out on the floor below the roof," said Kane. "We'll work our way up from there."

They entered the lift and Kane checked his rifle as the metal box hummed and cranked upwards, powering him towards his enemies. The door slid open, and Kane moved out with his weapon held before him. He swept the floor, lights above pinging on as their sensors recognised movement below. Kane turned and entered the stairwell. He moved cautiously up the stairs, following the protocols for sweeping stairs drilled into him during his time in the SAS. As the stairs bent around to the right, Kane crouched and covered the next level with his weapon whilst Jenkins climbed the turn and followed the same process until they reached the exit door leading to the roof.

Kane gently pushed the door with his left hand, but found it locked. Jenkins tried one device and then another, but the door would not open.

"They've locked it," she said. "Could have barred it from the other side or rigged it with explosives."

That made sense. These men were fighting for the Alliance, to achieve what their governments had fought a century for. The EMP was crucial to their mission. Kane expected to face at least six of Jafari's soldiers, and perhaps three of his core team. Every entry point would be secure, with weapons trained on every door to take down anybody who tried to stop them.

Kane fished in his backpack and withdrew the set of night vision goggles and one of Tank's breaching charges. He took the protective strip from the malleable, brick-sized block of C4 explosive. It came with a protective case and a remote detonator. Kane pressed the charge against the door, ensuring it was securely attached. He inserted the detonator, a small cylindrical device, into the charge and connected it to the remote trigger.

He beckoned Jenkins to follow and retreated twenty feet down the stairs. She stared at him, questions in her eyes, clearly wondering what the enemy would do when Kane blew the door open. The explosion would invite a barrage of gunfire it would be impossible to avoid.

"You stay and cover the door. No matter what happens. Wait here," said Kane, settling the night vision goggles with thermals on his forehead.

Before she could answer, Kane pressed the trigger. The explosion reverberated through the confined space. A sharp, deafening crack forced Kane to shield his face with his arm. The air filled with the acrid smell of burning metal and explosives. The door ripped from its hinges, falling, twisted and crumpled by the force of the blast. Smoke and debris scattered down the stairwell. A whoosh of cold air blew from the rooftop to swirl the smoke like a jet engine.

Gunfire crackled from the rooftop and bullets ripped into the stairwell wall opposite the door. Kane waited, jaw clenched. He pulled two grenades from his pack, a flashbang and a smoke grenade. The barrage of bullets hammered above Kane, and Jenkins shrank, curling up into a ball as the bullets tore through the air and shredded the wall, scattering cement and debris all around them. After what seemed like an age, the gunfire relented, and then stopped. The enemy was confused. They had expected whoever was responsible for the explosion to come charging through the door, but nothing came. Kane lowered his night vision goggles over his eyes. Pulling the pins with his teeth, he tossed two grenades through the door and sprinted into the smoke after them.

CHAPTER SIXTY-FOUR

The AN/PVS-31A night vision goggles with thermal overlay were lightweight and sturdy and the padded headgear fit snugly about Kane's skull. The goggles hummed softly as Kane powered them on, bathing his vision in an eerie green glow overlaid with the vivid red-orange contrasts of thermal imaging.

The smoke grenade canister hissed, spewing thick swirling clouds of grey smoke that obscured the rooftop area beyond the door, and the flashbang exploded with a deafening crack. A searing flash of light from the grenade hammered the senses of the enemy shooters, confusing and temporarily blinding them.

Kane dashed through the smoky doorway with the MP5 poised and ready to shoot. His heart thumped in his chest, expecting gunfire, running towards a heavily-armed and ruthless enemy, and he did not know if he faced three enemies or ten. His breath came in short, sharp gasps and the goggles' thermal overlay transformed the world around him. The smoke became a translucent veil, barely impeding his vision. Enemy bodies crouched with hands over their eyes, or poised with weapons pointing at the swirling smoke, gave off heat signatures in brilliant hues of red, orange, and yellow against the cooler blues and purples of the surrounding buildings.

The smoke concealed Kane's charge, and he loomed from it like a vengeful demon. He remained hidden, and the bodies of his enemies glowed like flames. The enemy stumbled in disarray, ghostly figures whose body heat radiated them in vivid, unmistakable clarity. Their movements were slow and frantic, and Kane was ready to kill. He paused in the smoke and fired controlled bursts from the MP5, each shot finding its mark with lethal accuracy. The enemy, illuminated in the thermal scope, fell one by one, their heat signatures fading from vibrant red to cooler hues as they collapsed.

Kane moved like a predator, legs bent, weapon held before him. After each burst of fire, he changed position and fired again. Four enemies fell in quick succession. They hollered instructions to each other, and gunshots crackled across Heron Tower's rooftop, seven hundred and fifty-five feet above the ground. Kane kept moving, sweeping the rooftop.

"Allahu Akbar!" bayed a man's voice. Kane turned towards the voice just in time to see the muzzle of a weapon flash. A bullet thumped into Kane's combat vest, and it was like being kicked by a horse. The impact flung Kane to the floor, and the air whooshed from his body, leaving him winded and clutching at the impact on his chest. The night vision goggles became cloying as he gasped for breath and Kane ripped them off his face. His body wanted to curl up into a ball, to find his wind and cradle his badly bruised chest, but to stay was to die.

The gunman fired again, and Kane rolled as bullets smashed into the ground around him. Panic surged inside him and he scrambled to get a hold on his rifle. He had let go of its grip as he fell, and the MP5 was twisted in its strap. Kane caught the grip but couldn't get the weapon around his body. The strap coiled beneath his body, and he could not train the weapon on his enemy. The figure came closer, and Kane recognised Khalid al-Nasiri, the former Iranian officer and intelligence agent.

He came at Kane through the gloom, weapon levelled, face contorted into a rictus of hate.

Battle calm descended on Kane, panic and fear smoothing like a wave crashing against a golden beach, changing into the soft sigh of the shore. The cool air high above London's skyline kissed his neck, amidst the sound of al-Nasiri rambling words of hate under his breath and the crunch of his boots on debris scattered across the rooftop. Other figures shifted in his peripheral vision, at least four more enemies beyond al-Nasiri. Kane released his grip on the trapped MP5 and drew the Glock from its holster. Al-Nasiri spotted the movement, and his narrowed eyes enlarged, teeth bared, weapon rising. Kane fired the Glock just as its barrel passed the holster's edge. Without aiming, he fired once into the toes of al-Nasiri's boot. He howled in pain, firing his weapon wildly with one hand. The rifle blazed too high, and Kane shot al-Nasiri again in the throat.

The Iranian toppled, clutching at the ragged, bloody flesh at his neck. He gurgled as his lifeblood pumped out between his fingers and Kane used al-Nasiri's body as a shield as the remaining rooftop enemies opened fire. Bullets tore into al-Nasiri's torso, and he jerked and shook under the impact. Kane lay his arm on top of al-Nasiri's body and fired the Glock. He dropped one enemy and winged another. Bullets cannoned around him, and Kane thought he must surely die.

A scream erupted like a banshee screeching in the darkness. Kane turned and Jenkins stood in the smoky doorway, screaming with terror and firing her MP5 at the remaining Alliance enemies. The remaining two enemies fell, and Kane breathed a sigh of relief. Jenkins ran to him, her face pale and drawn.

"Are you hurt?" she said, reaching her hand down to help Kane up.

"No," he replied. "I told you to stay."

"If I had, you'd be dead."

Which was true. Kane took her hand, and she pulled him to standing. "Let's find the EMP, quickly."

They set off across the rooftop, searching for the EMP device in its case.

"This is Rashid al-Zawahiri," Jenkins prodded a corpse with three fingers on one hand with her shoe. "Bomb-maker."

"That's ten of Jafari's crew gone. Three of his team left, and another three of his merc soldiers. Go carefully. They'll have comms. They'll know we're on the roof."

Jenkins nodded, and they split up to search the roof.

"Found it," Jenkins called from the south east corner.

Kane ran towards her, pushing his MP5 and its strap to his side, the Glock still in his hand. A small figure burst from the shadows, pistol hand extended and shot Jenkins twice in the chest. Jenkins grunted and flew backwards, hammering into a cement structure and slumping to the floor. Kane sped up, closing on the enemy figure in three long strides. The figure turned to him and just as Kane was about to pull the trigger; the enemy ducked lightning-fast and spun, kicking Kane's legs out from under him.

His back slammed hard into the floor, and before he could react, a boot crashed into Kane's hand, driving the Glock from his grip. Kane twisted and hooked his attacker's ankle away with his left hand. The figure fell and Kane grabbed its gun, yanking at the weapon. The attacker landed and agilely sprang to its feet, but in the movement, the gun came free and skittered across the floor. Kane surged to standing, and a front kick crashed into his shoulder. The enemy was a head shorter than Kane, a Chinese woman staring at him with focused malice. It was Zhen Liu, the Chinese special forces operator. Kane swung a punch, and she sidestepped, hammering her fist into Kane's gut.

Kane stumbled. A knee connected with his cheekbone, and an elbow thumped into the side of his head. Zhen Li was fast, too fast. Kane drove into her, wrapping his arms around her thighs, lifting, and dumping her headfirst into the tarmac-lined roof. Zhen Li moaned in stunned pain, and Kane punched her in the nose. She writhed and twisted, striking out with fists and elbows. Kane's nose and lips bled freely. He scrambled with the enemy, trying to land a blow, but Zhen Li was faster, more skilful. Kane groped at his waist and found the handle of his knife as another elbow smashed into his eye. Kane ripped his knife from its sheath and drove the point ten times in rapid succession into her thigh and midriff, his forearm pumping like a jackhammer. She screamed and tried desperately to get away from Kane's blade, but he leapt on her and drove the point up into the soft skin beneath her jaw, twisting the blade savagely. Blood pumped from the wound and soaked his hand and sleeve. Resistance ebbed away as her life seeped out in a flow of hot crimson and Kane rolled to his back, gasping with exhaustion.

He crawled to his knees, body aching from Zhen Liu's onslaught, face bloody and torn. He grabbed the EMP case and stumbled to where Jenkins lay on her side, trying to rip the body armour away from her chest.

"The vest absorbed the bullets," Kane said. "We have the EMP, but they'll come for it. Next is the virus. But they'll come at us with everything. Stay here if you need to recover."

"Fuck that," Jenkins said through clamped teeth. It was Kane's turn to help her to her feet. "Let's finish these bastards."

CHAPTER SIXTY-FIVE

Kane pressed his earpiece back into place and moved to the stairwell, carrying the EMP in one hand and his MP5 in the other.

"Craven? How's Danny doing? Any progress on putting together Cameron and Ghost's work to disarm the virus?" Kane said.

"Jack!" replied Craven's gravelly voice. "What's going on in there? We have no visibility inside the building. Jafari's team has knocked out all CCTV and blocked us from accessing Heron Tower's mainframe."

"I have the EMP. I'm going after Jafari now. Is Danny any closer to cracking the code?"

"To be honest, I have no idea. He seems fairly confident. He's nodding at me here, but he says he can't tell if it's going to take two minutes or two days. It's a complex puzzle, and he's doing his best."

"I'll keep comms on. Let me know the moment there's any progress."

Kane stepped into the stairwell with Jenkins at his shoulder. He picked his way through the debris left by the door explosion and headed back towards the secure floor where Jafari and his remaining team worked to install the Prometheus Code hard drive into the building's servers. Kane's body ached after the fight on the rooftop. His body wanted to limp, to stop for a moment and rest, but Kane focussed his mind and forced himself to continue. Jenkins followed, wheezing after the bullet strikes to her combat armour. They followed military protocol for descending stairs, one covered each turn with their rifle whilst the other descended and waited at the next turn to cover in return.

Jenkins descended the stairs, taking her turn as Kane covered her path. When she reached the bottom, she levelled her weapon and aimed down the next flight. The moment her rifle poked over the bannister, a hail of bullets exploded and peppered the surrounding wall. She shrank back and glanced up at Kane with a mix of fear and anger playing out on her face. Kane hurried down the stairs to join her.

"Did you see how many?" he asked, shouting to be heard above the relentless barrage of gunfire. Jenkins held up two fingers and pointed down the stairs. Kane took up position next to her. He quickly burst around the stairwell corner and opened fire. Peering down the sight, he saw two of Jafari's mercenaries positioned on either side of the section of stairs leading to the secure floor. They flinched away as his gunfire slammed into the surrounding walls and then emerged to return fire. It was a stalemate, no way through them other than a long gunfight with both sides protected by concrete walls. Kane took the pack from his back and searched inside, but all of Tank's grenades were gone. Kane threw the pack to one side and cursed under his breath.

No time for caution, no time for fear. Kane set his feet against the stairwell wall and flung himself into the downward stairs. He crashed against the far wall, keeping himself as low as possible, shortening the angle between him and the rightmost shooter. The enemy saw his chance, shifting slightly to take better aim and kill the man who had taken out half of his crew and came to kill the rest. Kane resisted the urge to fire wildly, the urge brought on by panic and anger. He held his breath and shot the enemy fighter three times in the leg. The Alliance mercenary cried out and fell forward, and Kane shot him once in the back and again at the top of his skull.

Without hesitation, Kane surged to his feet. He took two leaps down the stairs and threw himself down the remaining steps. The second shooter opened fire, but Kane was already in mid-air and the bullets cracked into the place he had been moments earlier. Kane landed heavily on his side and shot the enemy in the stomach. He doubled, dropping his weapon to clutch at the wound and Kane stood. The enemy dropped to his knees, blood pulsing through his fingers. He peered up at Kane and babbled under his breath. Tears streamed down his face and spittle flecked his beard as the man came face to face with death. Kane shot him once in the eye and once in the forehead. No mercy.

Kane and Jenkins reached the secure floor, marked by "Authorised Personnel Only" signs, and locked by a keycard scanner and biometric pad. Kane gestured to the scanner with his rifle, showing that Jenkins should work her magic and unlock the door. But she shrugged and pushed the door gently with the muzzle of her MP5. It moved lightly a few inches on its hinges, and only then did Kane notice a device fitted to the keypad by Jafari's team to override its lock and allow them entry.

"Kane, don't you ignore me, you bastard," growled Jones' voice in Kane's earpiece. "I heard you over the comms."

Kane moved five paces slowly away from the door. "What is it, Jones?"

"You have the EMP. Don't let Jafari take it from you. If you can, take him out."

"Roger that, Jones." Kane sighed, his mind too alert to listen to Jones grandstanding for the sake of any higher-ups listening in on the conversation.

"And Kane? Good luck. The entire country is depending on you. Come back to us alive."

Kane flicked his earpiece out and checked his MP5. He removed the magazine and clicked a fresh one into place.

"Here," he said, handing the EMP case to Jenkins. "Hold the door. Guard the EMP and keep your weapon trained on the entrance. If Jafari or any of his crew come out, kill them. If anything happens to me, take the EMP and get out. They can't unleash the Prometheus Code without it."

Jenkins took the case and placed it behind her. She knelt and readied her weapon to cover the entrance to the security floor. Kane moved to the door. He had two choices: enter softly, cautiously, in case Jafari's soldiers had weapons trained on the entrance or go in full force and surprise them. Only three of the enemy crew remained, including Jafari himself. They knew most of their team had perished, and that the sound of gunfire in the stairwell had subsided, so they would either believe their comrades had died in the exchange, or that Kane and Jenkins were dead.

"Kane!" Jenkins hissed. She pointed at her earpiece, so Kane pushed his own back into his ear.

"Kane, receiving," he said.

"Jesus, Jack," said Craven, voice high-pitched with exasperation. "Where the fuck have you been?" Kane refrained from giving the obvious sarcastic reply, choosing not to mention that he had been embroiled in a life-or-death gun battle with Alliance terrorists. "Danny's done it; he's figured it out."

"Calm down, Frank. Figured what out?"

"He's cracked the Prometheus Code."

Kane leant back against the wall, his head swimming. "What? How?"

"I don't understand it. I'll let him explain."

Kane's earpiece crackled as Craven passed the microphone to Dany. "Dad, it's me. I've done it."

"I don't understand, son. Explain."

"I followed the videos Cameron left on his secure server and got to where I understood his code and the code Ghost had worked on, but they wouldn't knit together. It was as though the work Ghost had done was missing a vital component, a piece of the Successors algorithm she either couldn't figure out or had left on purpose."

"Danny, I'm in a tight spot here. Is there a short version?"

"Sorry, Dad. Anyway, I couldn't figure it out. But then I checked back through the secure emails Cam had saved between the Successors and saw that Storm Shadow had put a back door into the thing. Cameron had mentioned that the hard drive could be accessed from an escrow back door in the cloud. Only he and Storm Shadow had access to it, and to trigger it needed them both to log in at the same time. Storm Shadow referred to it as the Styx, which I remembered from school is the name of the river in Greek mythology, which leads to Hades, the underworld, and Prometheus was a Greek, so it all kind of fit together. By taking the Styx, we keep the world as it is now, in the state Storm Shadow and the Successors hate so much. I found the code for the Styx in the files Ghost lifted from Storm Shadow's files, so I logged in via two different IP addresses using Storm Shadow's and Cameron's logins and deployed it using remote access, and it did the trick."

"So, have we neutralised the Prometheus Code?"

"Yes, Dad."

Kane threw his back and laughed with sheer joy.

"Unbelievable work. Well done, Dan. I'm proud of you, son." Kane glanced at Jenkins as she pumped the air with her fist and grinned.

"Thanks." Kane couldn't see Danny, but there was a genuine warmth in his voice, something that had been missing between them for a long time. "What now?"

"Sit tight. I'll be home soon."

Kane readied himself to end the mission, to take down Jafari and his crew by any means possible.

CHAPTER SIXTY-SIX

Voices barked beyond the security door. Jafari and his two remaining fighters argued, shouting at one another. A woman's voice screeched in Korean and a man replied in furious Arabic, neither understanding the other, and the confusion gave Kane the opportunity he needed. He kicked open the security door and strode inside to find rows of blinking server stacks with brightly coloured wires coiled neatly about metallic shelving. Kane checked one row, and then the next until he came across three men beside an open case.

Kim Hyon-hui, the diminutive North Korean hacker, stood with a gun pointed at the tall, muscular figure of Jafari, whilst Jafari's last living mercenary aimed his rifle at her head. Jafari's hands were up, palms facing outward, and his weapon lay at his feet. She howled with fury, gesticulating at an open case on the ground and at a server stack beside her. They had discovered that the Prometheus Code virus was compromised and that their mission had failed. Danny had done the impossible. The youth who only a week ago had been a sullen, aimless teenager, had become a man and saved the West from its darkest enemies.

Kane took the window of opportunity and fired his weapon. He aimed for Jafari's head, but at the last moment the Alliance mercenary shifted position and Kane's bullet tore through the side of his face like a monster's claw. It ripped away cheek and ear and splashed blood across Jafari's face. Kim Hyon-hui turned and gaped at Kane, and he shot her in the stomach below her body armour. Jafari ducked behind a server stack and Kane set off in pursuit. He ran along the corridor, leaving Kim Hyon-hui writhing in a slick puddle of her own blood. Jones might appreciate a prisoner to interrogate, Kane thought, and she would hold a wealth of information about North Korean cyber capabilities and online attack strategies.

He reached the end of the server stack and slowed, readying his MP5 to fire at Jafari as he turned. But Jafari burst from a crouched position and grabbed Kane's weapon. He tore it from the strap and cast it aside, driving his knee into Kane's stomach and forcing him backwards. Kane reached for his Glock, but Jafari came at him with a wickedly curved Karambit knife. The Karambit flashed at Kane's right hand and he drew it away from the Glock before the blade sliced his fingers off. It was a deadly curved blade designed for slashing and tearing and resembled a tiger's claw. A metal loop at its base, which hooked around his thumb, held the knife with its sleek ebony handle and razor-sharp hooked blade secure in Jafari's hand. Jafari attacked again, the blade flashing at Kane's face.

Kane slammed into the servers behind him and whipped his own combat knife from his belt. It drew faster than the Glock, and Kane slashed the blade at Jafari's throat. The enemy darted backwards, and his jet-black eyes shone with malice.

"Time to die, godless whore's son," Jafari snarled in English. His lip curled in contempt. He knew his bid to crush the West was over. But Jafari saw his chance at martyrdom, at everlasting glory, and he came at Kane with vicious savagery. The Karambit flashed like lightning, slicing faster than Kane could parry. Jafari's cruel blade carved a gash in Kane's forearm, another across his midriff, and then opened up his shoulder with a deep slash. Kane grunted at the pain and lunged with his own blade, but Jafari leapt nimbly away. Kane cut at him, but Jafari eluded the blow and dragged his knife across Kane's thigh.

Kane sagged. *He's cutting me to pieces. He has more skill.* Death was close, its breath on Kane's neck sending a shiver down his spine. He lashed out again, and Jafari swayed away as the knife passed by harmlessly. But Kane reached behind him and dragged a heavy chrome-coloured server from its housing and allowed his knife to swing wide, so that his left arm came about like a windmill and the server cannoned into Jafari, knocking him from his feet.

Kane snarled and kicked Jafari hard in the face with the heel of his boot. He dropped his own knife and the server and grabbed Jafari's knife hand. Kane yanked Jafari's thumb with all his strength, the crack and crunch of bone audible over the thrum of the surrounding servers. Jafari cried out in pain and Kane ripped the Karambit from his grasp, tearing the loop from his mangled thumb. He sliced the blade across Jafari's face, laying open his nose and lips like raw meat on a butcher's block. Jafari burst to his feet and ran like a hare, with one hand clutched to his ruined face. He fled towards a small office at the end of the security room, running from Kane's savagery and the pain of his terrible wound.

The Glock slid smoothly from the holster at Kane's hip and with a round already in the pipe; he shot Jafari in the back of his leg. Jafari fell and rose quickly, foot slipping in his own blood, and limped on. Kane strode after him. He grabbed the back of Jafari's hair and drove his head through the office window with full force. Glass shattered and Jafari slumped to the floor, face sheeted in blood, anger replaced by despair.

"I curse you to hell," said Kane. "To the fires of Jahannam, for the murder of innocents I condemn you. You are no martyr; paradise is denied you. Nobody on earth will remember your name."

Jafari opened his mouth to protest, but Kane cut his throat with one swift slice of the Karambit knife and left his enemy to die. It was over. The Prometheus Code was safe, and Jafari was dead. The pain of Kane's wounds tore at him, but he and Jenkins limped from the Heron Tower victorious, to where Jones and MI5 waited. All Kane wanted was to go to Danny and Kim. To hold them close and be a family.

"That was close, Kane," said Jones with a grin. He clapped Kane on the shoulder and then grimaced at the blood dripping from Kane's fingers, only some of it his own. "Back to Thames House. We have medics there who can treat you before a debrief."

"No thanks," said Kane. "My family is waiting for me. And we've got a funeral to go to."

CHAPTER SIXTY-SEVEN

In an office across Europe, deep in the Krasnodar hills, a dozen men in military fatigues gathered in a small office overlooking a valley which swept away east into the Black Sea. They listened as a woman finished her presentation, stern faces exchanging concerned glances. Men with scarred, lined faces. Veterans and commanders of the Valknut private military company.

"So Jafari failed," said General Yuri Balakin, his blue eyes set deep within the slab of his face. "This Jack Kane has caused us too many problems, I think."

"Yes, sir," said McGovern. Her presentation ended, and the large screen behind switched to the Valknut logo of a skull wearing a beret surrounded by a symbol of three interlocked triangles. "He is an MI6 assassin and the single biggest threat to our client's aims for the West."

"Contact Hydra," Balakin continued in his stern voice. "Tell our client that we will pursue this enemy of the Alliance. I want Jack Kane dead. I want his bones crushed to dust and his skull brought to me."

The men in the room nodded their agreement and left without further comment. Balakin was a Russian military veteran. He was a former lieutenant colonel and brigade commander of a Spetsnaz GRU unit, a decorated veteran of the first and second Chechen wars, and not a man to question lightly.

McGovern bit her tongue to keep the smile from her face. Kane was the reason she was stuck in Krasnodar Krai, away from her home, banished from England forever. He had ended her career with MI6 and was the father of all her misfortunes. Hate broiled inside her like a volcano. She might not have the power of MI6 behind her, but she was now a Valknut intelligence officer of the Valknut group and had the ear of the fearsome Yuri Balakin. Kane had thwarted an attempt on Europe's financial systems, and it was one victory too many for the former assassin and SAS soldier.

Balakin paused in the doorway and turned back to face McGovern. The heat of his gaze forced her to look at the floor rather than meet his icy stare. "Kane must die, and I want you to tell me how. Have a proposal on my desk by this time tomorrow. No excuses, no more failures."

McGovern nodded and, as Balakin left, she blew out a sigh of relief. McGovern clenched her fist. It was time for revenge, time for Jack Kane to suffer for what he had done to her. Jack Kane must die.

AUTHOR NEWSLETTER

Sign up to the Dan Stone author newsletter and receive a FREE novella of short stories featuring characters from the Jack Kane series.

The newsletter will keep you updated on new book releases and offers. No spam, just a monthly update on Dan Stone books.

Sign up to the newsletter at https://mailchi.mp/danstoneauthor/sgno14d1hi for your FREE ebook

Or visit the Dan Stone website at https: https://danstoneauthor.com

ABOUT THE AUTHOR

Dan Stone

Dan Stone is the pen name of award winning author Peter Gibbons.

Born and raised in Warrington in the North West of England, Peter/Dan wanted to be an author from the age of ten when he first began to write stories.

Since then, Peter/Dan has written many books, including the bestselling Viking Blood and Blade Saga, and the Saxon Warrior Series.

Peter now lives in Kildare, Ireland with his wife and three children.

ABOUT THE AUTHOR

Dan Stone

Dan Stone is the pen name of award winning author Peter Gibbons.

Born and raised in Warrington in the North West of England, Peter/Dan wanted to be an author from the age of ten when he first began to write stories.

Since then, Peter/Dan has written many books, including the bestselling Viking Blood and Blade Saga, and the Saxon Warrior Series.

Peter now lives in Kildare, Ireland with his wife and three children.

Printed in Great Britain
by Amazon

0a9ac4eb-e0c0-4a62-8a24-186a557bb4eaR01